The Luncheon Club

The Luncheon Club

Michael Pakenham

To order additional copies of this book, contact:
Xlibris Corporation
0-800-644-6988
www.xlibrispublishing.co.uk
Orders@xlibrispublishing.co.uk
300158

To my family with all my love

Also by Michael Pakenham

Fiction
The Bitter Web
The Judas Son
The Walnut Tree

Biography
The Polish Exile

Author's Note

My thanks go to Chris Sawyer for all the hard work put into editing the book and correcting my spelling. To Veronique Baxter of David Higham for her encouragment. To Jeannie for her valuable suggestions and tactful criticism. And to all those involved at Xlibris.

Belinda Musgrove took a deep breath and slowly pushed back the bedclothes. Her bed was a mess, testament to yet another restless night. As her feet touched the deep pile carpet, her head thumped with such ferocity that she thought it was about to explode. It was the cheap red wine she had drunk the night before; God knows how much of the stuff she had poured down her throat. She had, as usual, slept naked, and now she shivered as she shuffled painfully towards her en-suite bathroom. She stopped briefly to pull back the yellow curtains, revealing a large sash window and a view of a small but perfectly manicured garden. She felt a frisson of pleasure. The autumn sun was just creeping above the row of chestnut trees that almost hid Winchester prison from view, illuminating the flower borders and reminding her that they needed a little TLC. She knew the roses had signs of black spot and she made a mental note to spend the weekend doing some much needed garden maintenance. Eight years ago, when she'd bought the house, the garden had resembled a rubbish dump; she'd sweated many long hours turning it into what it was today.

With an air of excitement she continued her journey to the bathroom. She was on a high; her life was coming together. Hopefully, the last piece of the puzzle was about to fall into place. Happiness, emotion she had begun to feel would forever elude her, was just round the corner. There had been other moments, but they had all ended in disappointment. She was due a little luck. She turned on the bath taps, adjusted the heat and poured in a generous helping of rose bubble bath. Feeling slightly nauseous, she lowered herself into the warm, scented water.

She lay back, waiting for the nausea to subside, thinking of the last few weeks. At last, all the hours of loneliness that she'd endured might be coming to an end; it was an exciting prospect.

After a while her expression relaxed, the frown of pain disappeared and a light smile played around her mouth. She might have been tempted to stay at home and finish reading the Maeve Binchy novel she was enjoying, but this was to be the last lunch and Polly was coming with her. She was excited, alive and it felt great.

Chapter One

Winchester, England.

Polly Gordon adjusted her headband, her lithe, tanned body glistening under the lights. She was nearing a stirring victory and adrenaline was pumping through her body as never before. She liked to win. What was the point of playing a game unless you had the urge to beat your opponent? She wiped the sweat off her brow with her middle finger and gripped the little green ball with determination. If she won this point the game was hers, the match secured and the Laurel Ladies Squash team would be well on the way to promotion into the 1st division of the Hampshire league.

She lob-served, aiming for her opponent's backhand corner, then moved to the T, her eyes focused, her body taut. Her opponent's racquet hit the wall as she attempted to make contact with the ball, but to no avail; the ball landed perfectly, dead at her feet. The game was Polly's. She leapt into the air, arms held high, a smile of triumph flashing across her red face as she turned to smile at her team-mates in the gallery. Only then did she remember to hurry towards her opponent and shake her hand.

"Bad form," the disgruntled loser whispered.

That led to a rather edgy supper, with Polly being careful not to sit next to her sulking opponent. There were few smiles and a lot of sour faces. Polly sensed that the opposing team were somewhat surprised by their defeat.

"Haughty bitch that one," whispered Emily Roper one of Polly's team-mates, nodding in the direction of the opposing captain.

Polly smiled at Emily. "You can say that again. Wish they would leave."

Which they did half-an-hour later. "Now we can enjoy the fruits of our victory," said team captain Belinda, waving an arm at the barman as she settled comfortably onto a stool and rested her muscular arms on the bar top. "What's it to be girls?" she asked. "Wine all round?"

There were nods of thanks and the barman poured five glasses of white wine.

Polly smacked her lips. "Oh that's so good," she enthused, taking a sip of the cool liquid. "I can't believe I won tonight."

"You're positively glowing, and you played a fine game," complimented Belinda. "Count yourself as a regular member of this team from now on."

That was something Polly was not expecting. Although all the first team players were her friends, apart from Belinda who had always been rather aloof, Polly had never expected to get the call. It had just been a dream. She beamed at Belinda. "You really mean that?"

"I never say things I don't mean," Belinda stated, moving to sit beside Polly and fixing her with her striking green eyes. "You're good and you will get even better."

Compliments were thin on the ground in Polly's life and she knew that one from Belinda was rare. She felt one of Belinda's hands come to rest on her thigh. She blew out her cheeks. Belinda smiled. "I'm sorry I behaved so badly after I'd won," she managed to say a little breathlessly, edging away from Belinda.

"Oh don't give it another thought," said Belinda. "Their captain should have defused the situation instead of behaving like a cow. I've played against her several times. Beaten her all but once and always been greeted by a scowl, never a word of congratulations. I hate bad losers."

Polly smiled and glanced at her watch. A touch of panic stroked her nerve ends. "Gosh look at the time. I ought to be getting home."

"Come on Polly, have another one," encouraged Emily. "That husband of yours won't miss you."

Polly was torn. She wanted to stay, but her husband would only moan. "No I'd better not, thanks. I couldn't face Phil cursing at me most of the night."

"Well, I don't know what he's got to moan about," stated Emily. "Has he ever come home sober from the pub? I don't know how you put up with it."

"I ask myself that question all the time," Polly said with feeling, twirling her empty glass in her hand, and in no mood to defend her husband. "He's a right wanker," she continued, ripening to her subject. "Why I didn't see that a year ago before I married the slob I'll never know."

"It was your crusade as you called it," Clarissa Duncan, another member of the team reminded her.

"Oh yes, my crusade! How I ever thought I could change him beats me. Choosing a brain-dead man was a *very* bad decision. But I thought I was in love. No, don't give me that look, I really did. I thought I could save him from himself and mould him into a decent man. And he's good looking, you must admit that."

"Would be if he shaved, I suppose," said Emily.

Polly smiled and continued. "I didn't know what to do with my life. I was fed up with spending money, fed-up with the inane chatter of my friends. I couldn't get a job anywhere, except as a till-girl at a supermarket, and I bet I'd have made a mess of that as well; figures aren't my forte. I was just an idle, rich lay-about, bored out of my skull. Marrying Phil seemed an excellent idea at the time: new friends, new life. Well, it's sure been a new life, but as for friends . . . Jesus! Who would want Phil's drunken mates as friends? And it was putting two fingers up at my mother. She was horrified by my choice; she thought I was moving one step nearer the gutter. Dad was much more understanding."

Emily nodded. Phil was a definite arsehole, but she'd met Polly's mother and she was a number one bitch. She could see that Polly would have got little support from that quarter, and Polly had confided that as much as she loved her father, he was firmly under her mother's boot. Even so, marrying a loser like Phil, who had been a spectacularly incompetent barman at her parents' local pub, had not been the wisest choice.

"He's a waste of good oxygen," Emily added.

"I know," agreed Polly taking no offence.

"How can you change someone like that?" Emily asked.

"Good question. But I felt confident. I thought I could change his habits: get him to change his socks more than once a month; introduce him to soap; get him to have a hair cut and wear something else other than a filthy T-shirt and sliced-up jeans."

"You needn't have married him," suggested Sophie London, the last member of the team.

"When in love you make mistakes."

"Leave him," said Emily firmly.

Polly shrugged. "He bores me, and even the compliments have dried-up. He used to say nice things to me, like: you're so beautiful doll, so fucking clever. But once I'd bought a house near to his beloved pub in Easton and he reckoned he'd got his lazy feet under the table, all that changed. Now he says he resents my money. Can you beat that! Do you know, he had the cheek to tell me that he was fed up following me around like some dog watching me spend money? Christ, he's keen enough to spend it when I give him the chance! And another thing, he's turned out to be a couch potato, and I like to party. All he wants to do is either get pissed out of his skull with his mates or lay on our sofa, drinking Stella and watching crap on the television." She decided not to add that he was also becoming violent.

"Definitely time to leave him," said Belinda. "He's a bastard. I think you should have that second drink. If he's drunk he won't miss you."

Polly turned to face Belinda. "Why not?"

Belinda smiled at the barman. "Same again all round please."

"What are you going to do, Polly?" Belinda persisted. "You can't go on like this."

"I'm going to think about it," Polly replied. "I got myself into this mess and only I can get myself out of it." She picked up her glass, raised it towards Belinda and said, "That's enough about Phil, let's savour our win tonight."

"Sounds good to me," said Emily, relieved to get away from the subject of Phil. It was easy to see why Phil had been attracted to Polly. Her long, reddish hair, her winning smile, her long legs, her vibrant nature and wide brown eyes made an intoxicating cocktail. And then there was the pile of money unwisely given to her by her father when he'd sold his estate agency. What Polly had seen in Phil remained a mystery.

"Cheers to a good evening's work" said Belinda, reaching out to touch Polly's hand. "Are we all okay for Thursday?"

Polly blushed. "Yes, eh yes, I'm fine for Thursday, wouldn't miss it for the world." Evenings away from Phil were to be treasured. They gave her freedom, a sense of space, of being herself again and of belonging to something worthwhile.

"Well, I'm for home, said Emily. "Got to get the house in order before Jack comes home tomorrow."

The girls nodded, drained their glasses and picked up their bags. "Time for us all to go," said Sophie. "See you Thursday."

They walked together down the steps into the club car park and headed for their respective cars. Polly's was a low-slung black Porsche. Another thing Phil moans about, she thought. Too bloody flashy. Well up yours, Phil because I don't think you're going to be around for long. She slid behind the wheel with a sigh, throwing her racquet and bag onto the seat next to her. Being single again was quite an appealing thought, especially now that it seemed she might be a regular member of the squash team. She didn't want much out of life, just contentment and a bit of fun, something she now knew she'd never get from Phil. At twenty-four she wasn't ready to put on slippers at eight in the evening and sit watching some ridiculous programme on the box while Phil burped and farted over his beloved Stella. Feeling that she had reached a decision, she gunned the engine, smiled at the satisfying roar from the exhausts and pulled out of the parking space. Telling her mother was going to be humiliating. She would nod and point one of her well-manicured fingers at her and say, "You should have listened to me in the first place." Not one word of sympathy would come from that foul mouth. Hopefully, her dad would throw her one of his secret sympathetic smiles. She felt light-headed and it wasn't the wine.

Chapter Two

It was eleven-thirty by the time Emily Roper stepped into the small hallway of her two bed-roomed semi on the Romsey Road. She threw her squash bag and bunch of keys onto a table then headed for the kitchen and a drink of water. The room was comfortably warm, but a little airless, having been closed up all day, so she threw the window open. The sound of the neighbour's radio immediately invaded her space. She grimaced and hurriedly closed out the sound. She could do without the beat of heavy metal so late at night. She was finding it difficult to adjust to living in a town with the endless noise that seemed to beat at her brain most of the day. It had been her choice to live in Winchester where they were close to the railway station for Jack; it was convenient for her work as well, so there was not much point in making a fuss. She poured water into a large glass and dropped down onto a chair, resting her elbows on the kitchen table, which was piled with unwashed cups and old newspapers. She made a mental note to do some housekeeping before Jack came home tomorrow.

She dreamed of Jack Talbot every minute that he was away from her. They'd lived together now for three and a half years, and she loved him more each day.

"Don't be daft," Mary, her younger sister had said to her when Emily divulged this piece of information. "How can you love someone more each day?"

"Quite simple," Emily had replied. "Because it's Jack, and if you knew Jack like I do you would understand. I only have to look at him to go weak at the knees. He's just so perfect."

"Oh yuck," her sister replied. "I can't take all this treacle nonsense. It makes me want to puke."

But it was true. Jack had been the first man Emily had wanted to sleep with. She had resisted losing her virginity with some courage, determined not to surrender it in a one night stand, which would probably have been a messy affair on the back seat of someone's car. She'd ignored the jibes of "frigid bitch" from those who had tried, and failed, to get into her knickers, and the looks of disbelief from some of her more promiscuous friends. She knew her stance was not the norm, but she'd never regretted it for a moment. Jack had been struck speechless, amazed that someone as desirable as Emily had, at the age of nineteen, never slept with another man. It had proved to be the foundation of their relationship.

"I admire you," he'd said. "It can't have been easy."

She'd smiled into his blue eyes, and said, "You can say that again! I'm not saying I wasn't tempted. Old fashioned you might say, but I knew that's what I wanted to be when I finally fell in love."

She had fallen in love with this uncoordinated, laid-back bean stick the moment she'd set eyes on him, on her first morning of lectures at Edinburgh university. He'd taken a little longer—all of a week—to be smitten by the red-haired, five foot six bundle of energy that had exploded around him. Emily ran her index finger over the ridge of her glass remembering her appallingly sluttish behaviour as if it were yesterday. But Jack was to die for and she'd been unable to stop herself. It's lust she'd told herself, it will soon subside; five years on, their relationship just seemed to get better and better. She had often tried to analyse why they were so in love when many of their friends seemed to be going through terrible heart-rending love affairs. Was it that Jack now held down a good job with Wither's, a London solicitors, and stayed at his house in Cheyne Walk, Chelsea, four nights a week? Did absence really make the heart grow fonder? Or was it that they were the perfect fit and nothing could tear them apart? They had discussed marriage, and decided that they would think about it. Emily was beginning to think she might like to have a baby. Jack had not been quite so keen. Emily had not pressed the point; she was sure he'd come round eventually.

She drained her glass and stretched. It was time for bed. She'd get up early and flash round the house with the Hoover before going off to work, happy in the knowledge that when she got home, at about seven, that night, Jack would be back. By then he'd have been to the supermarket and have supper on the go. "Not home made," he'd say with a smile, "but the best I can do." Emily would eat anything, however much she disliked it. On the table by their bed would be a bunch of pink roses. Every Friday since he'd moved in, it had been the same, but never boring, because Emily worried that one day she'd come home and find the oven empty of *Tesco finest* and the roses absent. She gathered the dirty cups from the table and put them in the sink, then yawned and turned to go up the stairs.

Tomorrow she'd be walking up the stairs with Jack. As usual on a Friday night, it would be a very swift supper.

Across town, only a short walk from Romsey Road, was Chilbolton Avenue. It was a salubrious area and one hell of a lot more expensive. There was a certain snobbery attached to owning a house in the avenue. It meant you had almost certainly arrived at the top of the earning ladder. Most of the couples were middle-aged or retired, their children either at university or fled the nest. The majority were awesomely boring, the wives struggling to give the best cocktail parties, the most innovative Friday night dinners, the best barbecue on the smartest patio, while desperately trying to hide the wrinkles that grew more worrying every year. It was a constant battle to keep up appearances and grow old gracefully.

The men, on the whole, were overweight, inclined to drink too much and tired of their spouses.

The avenue was a tight knit community of middle class England. All prospective purchasers were vetted by an unofficial committee, every estate agent briefed. Inevitably temptation, in the form of an offer well over the asking price, sometimes won the day.

Sophie London was one of those who had punched a hole in this genteel bubble and slipped through the net, throwing the avenue into panic.

"We are, after all, a tolerant society," explained the eminent banker to his irate neighbour as he tried to justify why he had sold to a young, latte-coloured woman who planned to live there with her two black nieces.

"They won't fit in," was the muttered remark.

Sophie was twenty-seven when she drove up to the door of number seventeen. She was already a successful fashion designer; her bags sold worldwide and her shoes were in great demand. She had chosen Winchester because it was near her parents' old farm; only a year after their deaths, she wasn't quite ready to cut the umbilical cord completely.

A year on, the avenue was still in shock, not quite sure how to cope with this strikingly gorgeous girl. The twenty-first century still harboured its racists and quite a few resided in the avenue. To make matters worse, many of the women felt threatened by Sophie's svelte figure and undoubted beauty. They might have tired of their partners, but they were well aware that the sight of Sophie might get the testosterone pumping again in their husbands.

Her tyres crunched on the gravel drive and the security lights bathed her dark blue BMW coupe in their white glow. As was her habit on a Thursday night, Samantha, Sophie's black and white cat, was sitting rather judgementally by the front door. "Hi Samantha," Sophie called as she popped the door open, retrieved her squash kit and racket from the back seat, and extracted herself from behind the wheel. "Bad day again I suppose?" Samantha gave her a look of utter disgust and hunched her back. Her food bowl was empty and she was hungry. "Okay, okay, I get the message you stroppy girl," laughed Sophie. "If you weren't so spoilt you'd be out there catching mice instead of sitting here trying to make me feel sorry for you. Come on then." Sophie picked up Samantha and hugged her to her chest. For the time being the cat was her only companion in the large house.

"A house big enough for a large family," the estate agent had stressed with a supercilious smile, suspecting that Sophie would be the last person the avenue would want in their midst.

"Why on earth does a girl like that want to live in such a big house?" The avenue wondered. When someone was eventually brave enough to ask her, Sophie's reply was met with stunned shock. It was bad enough having her in their midst, but two teenage Jamaican girls was really beyond the pale. Property prices would plummet.

Clarissa Duncan was always the last of the team to leave the squash club. She enjoyed having one quiet drink on her own: gin and tonic, no ice no lemon. That was the way she liked it. She was the oldest of the team by four years, making her thirty-two, and she was the poorest, but that didn't trouble her. She enjoyed playing squash and was as at ease with her life, and with the other girls in the team. They were a mixed bunch, she thought, sipping her drink. Emily Roper was sweet, totally wrapped in her love affair with "*wonderful, to die for, Jack.*" As for the others, well, Sophie London was a very pleasant girl, but so focussed and successful that she was slightly intimidating, the very opposite of Polly who was definitely all at sea with life. Belinda, under her show of ultra efficiency, was kind hearted, but Clarissa sensed that their captain might be keeping a secret that could surprise one or two of her less observant team-mates. Given that she shared none of their ambitions, their rivalry, and certainly not their svelte-like figures, Clarissa was surprised by how well she fitted into the group.

She wondered how other people saw her. Did they laugh at her short, muscular legs, her large breasts that she refused to encase in a bra except when playing squash, her untidy appearance, her refusal to wear make up?

Or did they accept her as she was: a cranky veggie organic farmer? Actually, hardly a farmer; a smallholder was a better description.

On ten acres, five miles west of Winchester, Clarissa grew organic vegetables and fruit, which she sold at various farmers' markets. She kept about thirty chickens, depending on the cunning of the neighbouring foxes, but she had long abandoned keeping ducks. It was a battle she'd never win and it was against her moral code to shoot anything, even a thieving fox. That was why she never wore make up. Okay, she knew that an increasing number of brands used no animals in the formulation of their make up, but she was not prepared to take a risk. Anyway, she didn't want to plaster her face in slime. She was content with her appearance, even if it was a rather weather-beaten look for someone in her early thirties. Clarissa was a realist. She knew of several people who would have been long dead if it hadn't been for drugs that had been tested on animals. She accepted that until something better came along, certain animal experiments were an evil necessity. So, her life was a compromise, and she was content with that.

She drained her glass and smiled her thanks to the barman. It was time to go home to her partner, Ted, a man five years her senior, who suited her needs perfectly. He was a wow in bed, and Clarissa loved sex. They had not married.

"Can't be doing with all that mumbo-jumbo stuff in a church, and what's a piece of paper anyway," she'd told him when he'd been brave enough to broach the subject of marriage.

Ted was content to go along with her atheist views. He loved her exactly as she was. "I don't want a flat-chested model," he'd once told her, playfully squeezing a large breast. "I want something I can get hold of."

"Ted Harvey, you're irrepressible she'd retorted. "But I love it."

He also went along with her vegetarian beliefs, even though he didn't share them. In fact, there was nothing Ted liked more than sinking his teeth into a rare steak, or going out and shooting a rabbit for his dinner. "It's a bit of mystery to me why we get on so well," he often said to Clarissa.

"It's my charm and my looks," Clarissa joked.

But to Ted it was no joke. As he told a fellow stall holder on a bitterly cold trading day: "She's the best thing that has ever happened to me and I love her foibles. Makes her much more interesting you know."

"And where did you meet her?" the stall-holder asked.

Ted laughed. "At Winchester Farmers' Market, five years ago. She was struggling to sell her last three bags of potatoes and I was walking back to the car park, my head bent against the biting wind, cursing a man in a picture gallery who had refused to buy one of my paintings."

"Ah, you a painter then?"

"Let's put it this way, I like to call myself one. Anyway, we ended up having a drink in a pub and that was it. Immediate attraction, you might say, even though over our first pint she told me I needed a haircut and a good square meal. She was right on both counts, so I found myself following her home and that, you might say, was that.

She fed me baked beans with a poached egg on top and it was delicious. Soon we were yakking away like old friends. I told her my parents were dead, that I had no siblings and lived in a leaky old bungalow with my dog, Charlie, and some rats. When I plucked up enough courage to tell her that I tried to earn a crust by painting, she just smiled and said that all painters looked a mess."

This is exactly what Clarissa had told a close friend over coffee. "It's certainly not his good looks or his money. Like me, he's usually skint. He's heavily built, average height and three-quarters bald. He reminds me a bit of a bulldog I once had. What he lacks in good looks he makes up for in his attitude towards life. He is so wonderfully laid back. A week after meeting him, where do I find myself? In his bed, with the rats playing games above our heads. It was great, really fantastic, but I told him the next time it would be at my cottage without the rats as companions. Five years on, he and Charlie are still with me, surrounded by dust, a few sticks of furniture and, for most of the year, box upon box of vegetables and fruit. Ted's money from the sale of his bungalow has been invested, hopefully to ease the pain of our old age when we can no longer tend my small holding and Ted's hands are too arthritic to paint."

Clarissa's old Morris sat in solitary state in the club car park. She never bothered to lock it. Who on earth would want to steal something so battered, so muddy, so obviously a risk to life and limb? She tugged at a door, which reluctantly opened, and threw her racket and clothes onto a back seat that was as muddy as the outside. She sank onto the torn upholstery, wiped the windscreen with a dirty cloth, and crossed her fingers as she turned the ignition key. The old engine groaned but started. Luck was on her side tonight. It might even be an uneventful drive home.

Chapter Three

Clarissa was sitting in the passenger seat of Sophie's BMW. The team had just won their sixth match in a row. She felt good, relaxed at the idea of having supper with Sophie. It was something she had thought she would never do, but the invitation had been hard to refuse given that Ted would be back late from Bath where he was trying to sell his paintings and she had been at a farmers' market all day, and her fridge was starving. Sophie had picked her up to take her to the club so it had seemed churlish to refuse. Anyway, it would give her the chance to get to know Sophie better.

"Good win tonight," Sophie commented.

"All the better as we thought we'd lose."

"You played well."

"I think we all did," replied Clarissa.

"It certainly got Belinda excited," laughed Sophie. "What do you think about her idea of a lunch in Winchester for Emily's birthday?"

"I think it's good," said Clarissa a little hesitantly. "But I think The Hotel du Vin is way out of my league."

"Nonsense, we all should be there. And if it is more than you can afford, I'll help you out."

"That is something I would never accept, but thanks for the offer."

"Sorry Clarissa, I didn't mean to offend you."

"You haven't."

"Good."

"And it really would be fun to have a birthday lunch," added Clarissa.

"Actually, I think we ought to make it a monthly thing," said Sophie. "You know a little wine and a good gossip. I might float the idea when we all meet again."

"I'm not too sure I could afford that. I might have to sell my old Morris," Clarissa joked. "But seriously, it will put pressure on our budget and Ted gets quite tetchy if I overspend. £30 may not seem a lot to you, but to me it's another row of potatoes to plant and several extra pickings of runner beans."

Sophie allowed herself a smile in the dark. Clarissa really was so unlike anyone else she'd ever met, spending, if the stories could be believed, half the day shagging Ted and the rest rushing round a small dirty patch of land trying to eke out a living. Well the shagging might be okay, but working your arse off on a dirty piece of ground seemed a very joyless way of trying to make a living. She kept her opinion to herself. Besides, they were home. "Here we are," she said swinging the BMW into the drive.

Clarissa gazed out at the large red-bricked house, lit-up by security lights. It must have cost Sophie a bomb, but then if you were a highly paid designer no doubt there was no need to worry where the next penny was coming from. As she eased herself out of the car, she reflected that she was breaking one of her rules: never become too friendly with anyone who was in a different earning bracket than herself. At some point it could become embarrassing; if you couldn't stand the heat, get out of the kitchen pronto, but it was too late to turn back.

"That was lovely," Clarissa said some time later, pushing herself into the luxurious embrace of a sofa. "Best vegetarian meal I've had for years." She took another sip of what she knew was a very good white wine, certainly one she would never waste her hard earned cash on, and sighed. "You have certainly done well for yourself, Sophie. But what I'd like to ask . . . No, that would be impertinent."

Sophie shook her head. "Rubbish. Ask away."

"Are you sure?"

Sophie sat back in her chair. "Absolutely."

Emboldened by the wine, Clarissa took a deep breath and jumped right in. "All this—the pictures, the furniture, the carpets and the china, affluence all around us and yet no boy friend. Don't you ever want to share it with someone? Are you too busy, like so many young ambitious people today? Look at you, so different to me. You're elegant, beautiful, most men would say stunning, yet you've told me you haven't had a boy friend for several years. If I had all this, I would want to share it more than anything. Or else what is the point?"

Sophie twirled her glass between her long fingers and smiled. A slightly sad smile Clarissa thought. "I'm not a born loner, I would like a partner if I could find the right one, but I'm a bit choosey," laughed Sophie. "I will be sharing the house, not with my dream man, but with my two young cousins from Jamaica, but partners and cousins are on hold for a while until I completely come to terms with my parents being killed. We were very close."

Clarissa's face flushed, seeing the wetness in Sophie's amber eyes. "Oh my God, I knew I shouldn't have pried. I'm so sorry."

"No need to apologise," Sophie assured her, blowing her nose. "Besides, it does me good to talk about it."

Clarissa laughed uneasily. "Well . . ."

Sophie interrupted her. "Here, have a refill."

"No thanks—got to drive home."

"Mind if I do?"

"Of course not."

Sophie re-filled her glass and blinked back tears. Watching her, Clarissa felt her own emotions churning in sympathy.

"It was only last year, the day before Granddad's seventy-second birthday—my dad's dad."

Clarissa nodded her understanding. Sophie took a deep breath and went on, "Dad and Mum were in Antigua meaning to catch the daily flight to Jamaica, but they missed it. Determined not to miss Grandpa's birthday, they chartered a plane. It crashed into the sea somewhere between the two islands. Their bodies were found a week later." Sophie's voice cracked and she turned her head away, trying to hide her tears.

"Oh, that's terrible," Clarissa whispered, blinking back tears of sympathy.

"It is, and I'm not quite over it," Sophie said quietly. "I think there will always be a hole in my heart where they ought to be." She sighed and was silent for a moment. "But life has to go on. I've been back to Jamaica once since their death and I've put a plaque in the little church where they were married. It's the best I could do. Dad's parents look at it every Sunday during the morning service. I know they miss him as much as I do."

"What of your other grand parents?"

"They moved to Spain a few months ago."

"It's all so sad," said Clarissa. "I think you're wonderful the way you cope."

"As I said life goes on. Now, how about a nightcap?"

"Not before I leave, which I must do right now. Ted will be back and wondering where the hell I am."

"Why not ring him and say you're going to stay the night? Then we can finish the bottle or have another one if we fancy it."

Sensing Sophie needed company, Clarissa rang to say she was staying the night.

The bed was vast, all chintz and very feminine. Clarissa might have been tempted to wish her life wasn't quite so untidy: that Ted would remove his muddy boots before walking into their small sitting room; that Charlie didn't leave his hairs on the threadbare sofa; that the chickens didn't shit in the porch. But she was content, no envy, no regrets. She firmly believed that everyone in the world was there for a purpose, and it was her destiny to introduce people to the delights of fresh, home grown produce. She snuggled down under the duvet and chuckled. That was her role in life. She wasn't a Sophie London, or a high-flyer like Belinda Musgrove, or a scatterbrain like Polly, or an organised woman like Emily. She was plain old Clarissa Duncan, grower of wonderfully tasty vegetables, hair always in a mess, clothes well worn and face flushed from the elements. She turned her head towards the curtained window. She knew sleep was going to prove elusive, but dawn would soon be breaking. It had been a long time since she'd hit the wine so hard and fallen into the sack at three a.m.

Along the passage, Sophie lay awake, hurting and tearful, reliving the dreadful pain of losing her parents. Maybe it had been a mistake to confide in Clarissa. It was at times like these that she longed to have a man beside her; not that she'd been inclined to divulge this to Clarissa earlier. Someone who understood her, someone who would take her in his arms and give her the security she craved. Somewhere out in the big wide world there must surely be a man who would love her, whose warm body would ease the pain of her nightmares? For a person who was so strong in her professional life, it was surprising how insecure she could feel in the dead of night. It had always been her weak time. Realising she was not going to get any sleep that night, Sophie reached out and switched on her bedroom light. Samantha stirred and opened one eye as if to say, why are you waking me? Sophie picked her up and drew her to her side, taking comfort from the closeness of another living thing.

Belinda wasn't sleeping well either. She'd been thinking of Polly, and however pleasant that was it disturbed her. She had had a strict Presbyterian upbringing at the hands of intolerant parents who, at the first hint that she might prefer women to men, had threatened to disown her. The experience had left her feeling guilty and despised. As a result, she had been careful to keep her sexual orientation a secret from everyone in the squash club, and in her professional life; she was sure that none of them suspected she was gay. It was simply too great a risk to come out now, especially to Polly who seemed so resolutely heterosexual.

She moved restlessly under her duvet. It was not a good time to conjure up images of Polly. She should have taken a sleeping pill so that she'd be fresh and alert for the courtroom in the morning. Instead she was in danger of being woolly-minded and not able to give her client her full attention. Shit! She threw back the duvet and rolled out of bed. It was too late for a pill, it would have to be several cups of strong black coffee. She threw on her dressing gown and forced Polly out of her mind.

Tomorrow being Friday, Emily had, as usual, had a restless night. It was always a struggle to sleep the night before Jack came home, so the lights at 20 Romsey Road were switched on early. She busied herself loading the washing machine with the sheets from her bed; Jack liked the smell of fresh sheets almost as much as the smell of her. She dropped two pieces of brown bread into the toaster. That's all she would eat until the evening. She called Friday her dieting day, though it only lasted until Jack put a plate of *Tesco Finest* in front of her with his usual shrug of apology. "One day I'll learn to cook," he'd laugh. Emily hoped he never would. She glanced at her watch; time was dragging. Would she never lose the feeling of excitement at the thought of Jack returning? Did she want to? Of course not! That was the last thing she wanted to happen.

Chapter Four

Polly locked the door of the spare bedroom. Phil's violence had taken her by surprise and she didn't want him bursting in and forcing himself upon her. Unlikely mind you, given his inebriated state, but she'd learned from experience that Phil's moods were unpredictable, and his threatening behaviour had moved their creaking relationship onto another plane. He'd well and truly blown it this time. The moaning, the sarcasm, and his indifference to her feelings she could tolerate, but violence was a no-go area. She knew there were women out there who took it on the chin, literally sometimes, then smiled bravely, and tried to get on with their lives, but she was not going to be one of them. She touched her swollen cheek, a memento of Phil's welcome when she'd returned from the squash club. Bastard! Okay, he had been pissed out of his mind, but that didn't give him the right to hit her. And all that nonsense about her shagging men from the squash club. Where on earth had he dug that up from? Polly decided it had just been an excuse to use his fists. He'd taken another swing at her, but this time she'd been ready for him. His lunge had been uncoordinated, and she'd easily avoided his flaying hands, quickly putting the kitchen table between herself and her drunken husband.

"Fuck you," she'd shouted, descending into language Phil could understand. "You're a pathetic specimen of a man. I suppose you think it's macho to beat up your wife. Well, I've news for you, Phil Gordon. I've had you up to here." She put a hand on top of her head. "I'm leaving in the morning, and don't think your bullying tactics will work on me anymore." With that she'd turned and run up the stairs to the spare bedroom, knowing he was too drunk to follow. He'd spend the night snoring on the sofa and in the morning he'd no doubt be banging on the bedroom door, all tearful and saying he hadn't meant to hit her and he loved her. Balls! He hadn't an ounce of love in his hairy, smelly body.

Polly woke to the noise of Phil beating his fists against her bedroom door. "Come out, bitch," he shouted. Oh well, that was a change from the tears.

"Piss off, you drunken excuse of a man," Polly shouted. "I want nothing more to do with you, do you hear, nothing. I'm out of here just as soon as you get away from that door. Oh, that's right you dirty bastard, just puke on the floor!" The noise was all too familiar. She screwed up her face in disgust, leapt out of bed and hurriedly dressed. She ran a comb through her hair, worked her feet into a pair of shoes and reached for the door handle.

Phil was on his knees, bullock naked, staring at a stain on the floor. His body was shaking and when he looked up at Polly his face was ashen white. "Polly," he croaked.

"Who else did you think it would be, Sharon Stone?" She nearly gagged on the smell. Deliberately staring at his genitals, she smiled as he staggered to his feet. His hands moved swiftly to cover them. Well, she thought, that got his hands out of the way. "You look a fool, Phil," she said dismissively, ignoring the rank smell of his vomit. "Now listen up. You made one hell of a big mistake hitting me last night. It was the last straw. You're as ignorant a pig as you were when I first met you. If you think that you can knock me about then you're in for a shock." She moved a little closer to him, stabbing her forefinger in his face. "I've been longing to have the courage to say this for some time. I'm leaving you, for good. Did you catch that you lousy bastard? I'm off out of this farce called marriage. It's finished. I'm sick of the sight of you."

Phil's mouth fell open. He had a thumping headache, he felt sick, but he wasn't having any fucking woman speaking to him like that. "Bitch, you stay with me or else."

"Or else what, Phil? Give me a good beating and expect me to cook you meals, sleep with you, and wash your stinking clothes? No way!"

Phil rocked back on his feet. His addled brain ticked over slowly. Aggression wasn't working, so he'd try another tack. "Doll," he croaked.

"Don't you 'doll' me. No amount of sweet talking or begging is going to get me to change my mind. Let me repeat very slowly what I have just said so that even your empty brain can take my words in. We are finished. I'm leaving you. Have you got that?"

Phil's face reddened. He moved his hands away from his genitals and took a wild swing at Polly. She was too quick for him. She stepped away, kicked at his groin, made contact and watched him sink to the floor groaning.

"Now I'm out of here," she said. She didn't wait for his reaction, didn't bother to collect any clothes. She just turned and ran down the stairs. In the hallway, she grabbed her handbag and ran outside, fumbling for her car keys. She reckoned she only had a few minutes before Phil recovered enough to follow her. She gunned the engine and was just pulling onto the road when in the rear-view mirror she saw Phil run out of the house, waving his arms and still stark naked. A new ploy, Polly thought. He looked an ass, which come to think of it, was what he'd always been. You were blind Polly, so blind, she thought. She felt no pity for him; instead, she stifled a laugh. If he thought his theatricals would stop her driving away, he had another think coming. She was not going to weaken. Half way down the street she took another look in her mirror and saw the young couple from next door bent double with laughter, and Phil standing there, legs apart, wagging his dick at them.

She pulled into the side of the road. Her hands were shaking too violently for her to drive. She needed a few moments to settle her nerves, to convince herself that she'd taken the only option left open to her. She blew out her cheeks. Her resolve had surprised her. Had that really been the Polly that most of her friends called, *dippy;* the little rich girl, with a broad smile and happy disposition? Polly caught her breath. Well, this would be the last time her good nature got her into trouble. She couldn't change her character, but she could become more wary, that should not be difficult. She took a wine gum from an open packet lying on the passenger seat and stuffed it into her mouth. Perhaps she'd never quite grown up. The last twenty-four hours had changed that. She restarted the engine and pulled away, a little mystified by her lack of regret over the collapse of her marriage.

"Polly!" She was the last person Clarissa had expected to find knocking at her back door at eight in the morning.

"Sorry Clarissa, but I needed somewhere to bolt to. I'll go if you're busy."

Clarissa stared at Polly's bruised cheek. "I'm never too busy to help a friend, and you look as if you could do with help. "Phil I presume?"

"How did you guess?"

"Intuition Polly. Now come on in, you look as if you could do with a good cup of tea."

"Yes I could." Polly suddenly aware of how dry her mouth was. She followed Clarissa into the kitchen. It was her first visit to the smallholding and if she hadn't had other matters on her mind she'd have openly laughed at the chaos. There seemed to be boxes laden with vegetables everywhere.

"Sorry about this," Clarissa said, reading Polly's mind and waving a mud-stained hand round the room. "Market day in Winchester tomorrow." Then sweeping up a box of carrots from a chair she patted the seat and said, "There you are, rest your bum on here and I'll make the tea."

Polly dropped gratefully onto the chair. "I'm so sorry, Clarissa, to be bothering you, but I've split from Phil. He got very violent last night and that made up my mind. I can take most things but not violence. He'll probably come looking for me and right this moment I don't feel like facing up to him. I need a little time to get myself in order and decide what to do next. One thing I am absolutely certain of is that our marriage is finished. I've had enough of his drunken protestations of undying love and all that crap." Polly touched her bruised cheek. "And this sort of thing is becoming the norm."

Clarissa thought it wise not to say she'd seen it coming. And who could blame Polly for walking out? If Ted ever hit her, he wouldn't see her for dust. Besides, what she'd seen of Phil made her wonder how a nice girl like Polly had ever got involved with such a cretin. What she needed now was a basket full of TLC. Clarissa plonked a large chipped green mug down on the table. "Milk and sugar are somewhere," she laughed.

"No sugar, thanks Clarissa, just a little milk."

Clarissa handed Polly an exquisite small silver jug, which she eyed with surprise. She'd have expected a carton of organic semi-skimmed, not something that was so delicate. Clarissa read her thoughts. "I got it from my parents."

"Oh . . . I've never heard you talk about your parents."

Clarissa laughed. "No. My parents and I have a very difficult relationship, but that is another story. They have a dairy farm nestling beneath Exmoor. Suffice to say I left home when I was seventeen. I was very lucky—knocked on a few farmers' doors around here and got a job. Then I went to the agricultural college the other side of Winchester and once I'd finished there I walked into Barclays Bank and took out a huge mortgage to buy this little place. Oh Polly, I'm sorry; you didn't come to hear this."

"No, it's fine. Just what I need: something to take Phil off my mind. So how are you doing?"

Clarissa sighed contentedly. "I wouldn't change anything for the world. I know it's not everyone's cup of tea, but I love it here with plants all round me, and Ted lavishing his attention on me all the time. Okay, we live a very simple life, but we pay the bank what we owe them each month and most importantly we are happy."

Polly gave a little shake of her head. "Funnily enough it may surprise you to know that I'm not as unhappy as you might expect. Actually, I feel quite light-headed. I know I should be wracked with remorse, bitterness and all that general crap that normally seems to go with the break up of a partnership, but I'm not. I fully accept this mess of a marriage is of my own making—no-one else to blame. My parents and my friends all said I was a fool to marry Phil. So where I am today is one hundred percent my cock-up. All I can feel is relief—big time. Maybe I will be overcome with remorse later, I don't know, but right now I feel great. No more empty beer bottles cluttering up the floor; no more washing stinking socks. What could be better, even if it does cost me a fortune to get rid of him?"

Clarissa, who was old fashioned enough to think that a partnership should be for life, was lost for a reply.

It was unfortunate that Phil didn't feel the same way as Polly. He felt as if a wall had fallen on him. No more Polly was something he'd never considered. He rang her father. The mother answered.

"Left you has she?" came the question. Phil was fool enough to confess. "Good riddance and don't come bleating to me young man," came back the reply. "I'm surprised it's taken her so long to come to her senses."

"You're an arsehole," Phil shouted down the telephone before slamming it onto the table. No point in ringing any of Polly's friends either, he knew what their replies would be. He moved into the kitchen and hurried to the fridge. A cold Stella would sooth his damaged ego. Sitting on his arse and waiting for Polly to come back didn't seem to be an option. He was pretty certain his meal ticket had meant what she'd said. He'd seen the look in her eyes. He cursed loudly to the empty room; he should never have started hitting her. Big mistake. So what was he to do? For a man of Phil's limited intellect, that was a hard question to answer. Maybe the beer would help; a few pints had always seemed to sort out his problems. He drank greedily, threw the empty bottle onto the floor and moved back to the fridge. It was well stocked with Stella. He'd have a quick drinking session and then put his mind to the task of finding Polly.

An hour later, the beer had done the trick. He belched, feeling thoroughly belligerent. A plan was forming in his mind. Stuff Polly, there was plenty more totty around. The marriage was over, therefore make the best of it. He scratched his head and took another swig from the last bottle of Stella. His face creased into an evil smile. He'd take Polly for every penny he could, but first he'd sit tight in the house, and yes, he'd change the locks. Brilliant idea! Denying her access to all her posh clothes and other personal items would really annoy her. And then when he had the money he'd live a life of luxury without having to beg for every penny from a snotty-nosed woman. He laughed loudly. Polly would end up wishing she'd never set eyes on him. He smiled ruefully. More than likely she was already thinking that. He moved unsteadily towards the telephone. He'd ring his dad, he'd help, and he'd never liked Polly. He would know a good lawyer. Expense wouldn't matter; in the end he'd have plenty of cash to pay the legal bills. He belched again, spat on the floor and reached for the telephone. He'd never loved the woman anyway.

Chapter Five

The five girls were sitting round a table at The Hotel du Vin, a popular watering hole just off Winchester High Street. It was a double celebration: Emily's birthday and Polly's split from *bastard Phil.* They had a table by the window, looking out onto a small garden with a fountain. The early spring sun shimmered on the water. The atmosphere was warm and relaxed. They were *not* holding back on the booze. They'd had champagne in the bar while they ordered lunch, and were now on their third bottle of a very tasty Sancerre. Pudding wine was being discussed. The decibels were rising. The six men at the neighbouring table were amused. They raised their glasses and five pairs of eyes smiled back through a rapidly developing haze of alcohol. Only Sophie did her best to ignore the men, and in, particular, the blatant stare of one of them. "Well shall we make this a regular as I suggested the other day?" Belinda asked as their puddings were put on the table. Say lunch every last Tuesday of the month."

"Lovely idea," enthused Polly.

"Sounds fine," said Emily.

"Great idea," agreed Sophie, looking up. The man was still staring at her. He nodded slowly and raised his glass, then smiled at her. Caught unawares, Sophie couldn't help smiling back. She quickly looked away, but she couldn't concentrate on what her friends were saying because she was fighting the temptation to look back at him.

"Okay, if you all want it, I'll go along with it," said Clarissa, too full of food and the warm glow of wine to care about the cost. When the girls left, Ed excused himself from his friends and took Ben, the restaurant manager by his arm. He was eager for any information he could get about Sophie.

Ben would normally have remained tight lipped, but Ed was a regular client. "I think she's called Sophie, but I have no idea of her surname," he confided. "They're members of the local squash team and I do know they're planning to come here for lunch on the last Tuesday of every month."

Ed sighed, well satisfied, and gave Ben a handsome tip.

So, it was no coincidence that Ed Foster was already sitting on a bar stool when the five girls walked in ten days later. He felt a surge of excitement as he recognised Sophie, the beautiful girl who, in a matter of a few seconds, had captured his interest. He could hardly believe his luck. Would she recognise him and, if so, would she want to talk to him? Cross every finger, Ed, he thought. He pulled his car keys from his trouser pocket and deliberately dropped them on the floor. Five pairs of female eyes turned to stare at him. Sophie's stare lingered just that few seconds longer. She remembers, Ed thought as he picked up his keys and smiled at her. The smile was not returned and Ed was surprised at how disappointed he felt.

It was completely out of character for him to be so forward. A disastrous affair had sapped his confidence with the fairer sex, and he had been reluctant to enter into another meaningful relationship. He'd decided he'd rather be on his own than risk the pain and ignominy of another failed relationship. In a matter of moments, Sophie had crumbled his resolve, but it looked as if she wasn't interested.

Sophie touched Clarissa's arm. "Do you see that man sitting by the bar?" she asked.

Clarissa turned to stare at Ed who quickly turned away. "The good looking one who was staring at you?"

"Yes."

"Looks pretty dishy to me."

Sophie gave a low laugh. "He was smiling at me last week."

"Fancy's you then," said Clarissa.

"Oh I doubt that," said Sophie, nevertheless feeling the familiar buzz she got when a man looked at her with admiration.

"You know he does," replied Clarissa. "Go on, move across and say "hello.""

"No, no, far too pushy! I think he should make the move."

But Ed stayed resolutely on his stool, and when the girls were called to their table Sophie felt a stab of disappointment.

This was no less than Ed was feeling as he cursed his indecisiveness. He had let a good chance go begging. Time to leave he told himself. But he hesitated, then waved at Ben. "Got a table for me?" he asked.

"In the bar."

"That will suite me fine, thanks."

Ed ate his rib eye steak slowly, intermittingly sipping at his glass of house wine. With each sip he became more certain that he was about to make a fool of himself. Here he was, a rational man, biting his nails like a child and hoping that a total stranger was going to be bowled over by his charm. He laughed out loud. What on earth was he doing? He put his knife and fork down and signalled to a pretty young waitress. "Coffee," he mouthed. "Double Espresso."

Sophie picked at her food. The man at the bar intrigued her. Was it a coincidence that he was at the bar, or was it something more? Was it possible that he was interested in her? But how could he have known she would be here today? Sophie was accustomed to men trying to pick her up and had perfected a way of getting rid of them, but she was tempted to give this one a chance; there was something about him that had stirred her interest. She half listened to the other girls' banal gossip, wondering if she was brave enough to make a frontal assault.

"You're not with us are you," said Clarissa, watching Sophie playing with her food.

"What?"

"You're' thinking of that man out there."

The table fell silent. Sophie blushed and Polly asked, "What man? Where, where?" She gazed excitedly round the room.

"Sorry," whispered Clarissa to Sophie.

Sophie surrendered to the inevitable. "A man in the bar. He smiled at me last week, and today he tried to attract my attention by deliberately dropping his keys."

"Oh my God, go get him," squealed Polly, which sent the table into uncontrolled laughter.

Sophie shook her head at Polly. "Not with you anywhere near me darling Polly."

Polly shrugged good-naturedly. "Okay, but, wow, I wouldn't let a chance like this go by."

"Who said I would?" laughed Sophie.

Ed had finished his coffee. He couldn't delay his departure any longer. It was time to go back to work. He felt deflated. He'd been dreaming like a boy with his first crush. He smiled and threw his napkin onto the table. Ah well, he'd get over it. Then, as he fumbled in his jacket pocket for his debit card, he saw the vision of his dreams walking towards him. His first reaction was to make a bolt for it.

"Don't you dare run away from me," laughed Sophie seeing him half rise from the table.

Ed dropped back into his chair. Sophie lowered her elegant frame gently into the chair opposite him. "You a stalker?" she asked with a hesitant laugh.

The directness of her question took Ed by surprise and he sucked in his breath.

"Well?" asked Sophie.

"No, I'm no stalker." Ed gave an embarrassed cough. "But I confess to being here in the hope that I might see you again. Do you remember last week?"

Sophie laughed. "Of course. How could I forget? I liked your smile."

Ed breathed a little easier. "It was instant attraction. Totally weird really and most unlike me. I'm not usually this forward. I'm sorry."

Sophie laughed again. "Don't apologise, I'm flattered. And you have a certain something about you that intrigues me. So how about offering me a glass of wine and we can explore a little more."

"Fine, fine," stammered Ed, unable to believe his luck. "Red or white?"

"White please and a small glass. I've had enough already."

Wine on the table Sophie raised her glass. "And here's to you Mr . . . ?"

"Ed, Ed Foster. And you are?"

"Sophie London. Oh God, don't look now but the girls are just coming out of the restaurant. I will ignore them and hopefully they will get the message."

"Sophie!" Of course it had to be Polly.

Sophie glared at her, Clarissa grabbed her arm, and before she could say another word she was dragged out of the hotel.

"Close," Sophie said. "Polly is a lovely girl, but has no idea when not to butt in. Always causes problems."

Ed laughed. Your friends look a happy bunch. Squash team so I gather."

"Oh, you have been busy Ed."

"Maybe a little noisy I agree."

"So tell me, Ed, what's your line of work, or are you rich enough not to work?"

"I'm a doctor."

"Ah, doctor Foster, and have you been to Gloucester?" She giggled.

"Not since I fell in a puddle." They both laughed.

"Sorry, you must have heard that a thousand times."

"Once or twice."

"So you're a doctor," Sophie said more seriously. "That explains the kindness in your eyes."

"It does?"

"Yes. You all seem to have that kindness, that understanding look in your eyes. It has given me great confidence in your profession."

"I'm flattered. It's not often that I get paid a compliment. Most times my patients just moan at me. Don't get me wrong, I love my work, and let's face it if someone comes to see me they must be nervous about what I'm going to say. That's why it surprises me when they tell me they would much rather come and see me than go to the dentist."

"I agree with them. Dentists terrify me. So what sort of doctor are you, Ed?"

"GP. I practise a few miles from here. And you, what do you do?"

"I make handbags and shoes—very expensive ones. I have a small workshop in London, near Clapham. I sell to the big stores in England and the States."

"I guessed you must be something to do with fashion."

"Why is that?"

"Oh you just look as if you might be a model. Handbags and shoes didn't feature." Ed looked at her handbag. "One of yours?"

Sophie held up her bag. "The very latest model."

Ed wasn't lying when he said, "It's very beautiful. "And are you wearing your own shoes?"

Much to Ed's surprise Sophie took one off and put it down on the table. "Like?"

Ed hadn't spent much time looking at women's shoes. "I'm sure it's in great demand. I like the colour. Apart from that I wouldn't have a clue whether it would be a winner or not."

"It is a winner as you say—a very big one."

Ed felt he could talk to this gorgeous girl for ever, but time was eating away his options. So he dove right in. "Look Sophie, I've got to get back to work. Illnesses wait for no one. But I am going to do something on the spur of the moment—most unlike me. Would you like to have supper with me sometime? I know we hardly know each other so I'd quite understand if you say no."

"I would love to have supper with you," Sophie said, then gave a bubbling laugh. "Don't look so surprised. I mean it. Here." She fumbled in her bag. "Take my card. Ring me when you have time. Mobile is your best hope."

Ed took the card. "You live close to here."

"And you?"

A flat in St Cross. Here's my card."

Sophie took it and stood up. "Nice meeting you Ed, don't forget to ring."

"As if I would," said Ed with a smile as he rose from the table.

Sophie walked the short distance to the car park mystified by the feeling of exhilaration that was coursing through every fibre of her body. There was simply no other way to describe it. She felt as if she was walking on air. She unlocked the car and dropped breathlessly into the seat. About to insert the key into the ignition she saw Ed emerge from the hotel garden. Her hand froze an inch above the ignition and she stared at him as he strode purposefully towards his car. He was probably just short of six foot she decided. He was formally dressed in a dark grey pin-striped suit, a blue shirt, and a rather brash yellow tie. Sophie wondered why she hadn't noticed these things when she'd been in the hotel with him. She decided it was because it was his face she'd been interested in. His gentle mouth, even white teeth, dark hair were all attractive. His large blue eyes made him look a little mysterious and incredibly sexy. All-in-all it was a very neat package and, if she was honest with herself, quite deliciously desirable. He'd thrown her normal self-control into complete confusion in less than hour. Where had the cautious, discerning Sophie London gone? Answer: she couldn't care a monkey's. She sighed as she watched Ed drive off, hoping it wouldn't be long before she heard his voice again.

Forty-eight hours later in the squash club bar Sophie was trying to explain her feelings to Clarissa.

"You're smitten."

"He's certainly worth a second look," said Sophie, determined to sound cautious.

Clarissa burst out laughing. "Well, well, I never thought I'd see you so flustered."

"Oh God, is it that obvious?"

"Yes. And how do you think he feels, this man who has thrown you into confusion?"

"No idea. Do you know I sat by the telephone all last evening hoping that he'd ring? How daft is that?"

"Probably pretty daft," said Clarissa. "It's likely he needs a little time."

Sophie shrugged. "Well, I don't expect I'll hear from him ever again, so I best try and forget him and carry on with life."

Sophie would have been very surprised if she'd been a fly on the wall in Ed's surgery. He was sitting at his desk in his consulting room sipping a well-deserved, heavily sugared cup of coffee after a hard day. When he'd left the restaurant the day before, he'd decided to ring Sophie that night. But, feeling that might seem a bit too pushy, he'd decided to wait. He remembered his father once saying to him, "It's no good fretting over things that a telephone call or a few words can settle." Ed smiled and picked up the black and white photograph of his parents standing proudly together, his mother cradling their newly born son in her arms. He ran a hand over the well-worn frame. He touched it every morning when he came into work and carefully placed it in a desk drawer when he left the surgery at night. He had one more photograph of them, and that was in his flat. A holiday snap of the three of them playing on a beach. Three weeks later they were dead.

"Hello, Hello Sophie it's me."
"Ed!"
"You recognise my voice?"
"How could I forget it?"
"Why, is it funny?"
"No, of course not. Just joking!"
"Oh."
"I thought you weren't going to ring."
"I know, sorry. Work just piled up and then my courage nearly deserted me."
Sophie laughed. "Well now that you've got your courage back are you going to ask me out to supper?"
"How about tonight?"
Sophie hesitated only briefly. "Yes please! Any place in mind?"
"Do you know the Wickham Arms Pub, behind the college?"
"I know where it is, though I've never been inside."
"I could come and pick you up."
"No, I want my own wheels."
"Okay, fair enough. Meet you there at eight tonight."
"I'll be there."
"Please don't stand me up. I don't think I could bear it."
"Likewise."
"See you at eight then."
"See you."

Sophie slowly lowered the 'phone. She'd just agreed to go on her first date since the death of her parents with a total stranger just because she liked his face. She'd have been hard pushed to explain the excitement coursing through her veins. She looked at her watch. Four hours to go before she met Ed. She'd take a long soak in a hot scented bath, wash her hair, plan what to wear and drink lots of cups of tea. She could have murdered a gin and tonic but that might lead to another one and she wanted all her faculties about her. She moved to the bathroom and turned on the taps and started to sing. It had been a long time since she'd felt like singing one of her father's favourite tunes.

Ed made sure he arrived at The Wickham Arms ten minutes before eight. He wanted to enjoy the sight of Sophie walking through the door, and he didn't want to risk being late. He had a hunch she was a punctual girl. He ordered tonic water and perched nervously on a stool at the bar, his eyes fixed on the door. He had never quite felt like this before when taking a girl out to a meal; his hands were twitching, his heart was thumping. This is ridiculous, he thought, she's just another girl. And then he smiled into his drink. Well, that was it, she wasn't just any other girl. She had worked her way into his heart so quickly that it had left him quite breathless. He would never forget the first time she smiled at him across the restaurant. He took a long pull at his tonic and realised his hand was shaking.

Then Sophie walked through the door. She *was* beautiful. It was a word that came easily to mind as he watched her move gracefully through crowded bar, her short-cropped dark hair perfectly framing her face, her expression a little anxious. She wore skin-hugging black jeans which showed off her long legs; a white blouse was tucked into the jeans accentuated her slender waist. She wore a single string of pearls which drew his eye to her elegant neck. Ed felt a charge of something akin to smugness as he saw several male eyes turn to look at her as she glided towards him. Back off you lot, he thought, this girl is mine. He slid off the bar stool and held out a hand.

"You look stunning," he whispered as he kissed her on a cheek.

Sophie touched his hand, and deliberately looked him over. She was not disappointed by what she saw. Fawn trousers well pressed; a tie-less plain blue shirt mostly hidden by a slightly rumpled blue cotton jacket. First impressions were good. "You don't look too bad yourself," she said as he patted the empty bar stool by his side.

Ed felt a little flustered by the compliment and gave her a self-conscious smile. "Thanks. Now, how about a glass of something? Shall we make it champagne? I noticed you and your friends seemed rather keen on it."

Sophie bathed him in a smile. "Yes, I'd like that. I love it."

"You look quite stunning."

"You've just said that."

"I know." Ed waved at the barman who came over. "Two glasses of your house champagne and the menus, please."

"Right away, sir," said the barman, appraising Sophie. She was the best bird he'd seen in the pub for months. "Lucky bastard," he said quietly to Ed.

Ed grinned rather foolishly. "I am."

A few minutes later the barman put two glasses of champagne down on the bar, then made a point of handing the menus to Sophie. As she took them, he blew out his cheeks and said, "You're bloody beautiful if you don't mind me saying."

Sophie flashed him one of her dazzling smiles. "Thanks, and of course I don't mind."

Ed started laughing.

"What's so funny?

"I can see I'll be fighting off the whole pub in a minute."

"No you won't. I can do a withering stare." Sophie raised her glass. "Thanks for asking me, Ed."

"And thanks for coming. What are we going to eat?"

"Why don't we go to our table and order there. It's getting a bit crowded here."

"Good idea. Come on." Ed wrapped an arm round Sophie's waist and guided her through the crowd.

"What are you going to eat?" asked Sophie once they were at their table.

"I think I might have the Caesar salad to start, followed by fillets of wild sea bass, new potatoes and spinach. Then, if I have any room, I will have apple pie and cream. What about you?"

"I'm hopeless at choosing. My father used to say he could fall asleep while I made up my mind. So I'll have the same as you, but probably pass on the apple pie."

"Are you sure?"

"Quite sure thanks, Ed."

"Okay."

"That was delicious," said Sophie a while later. "And a very nice wine too. The Chileans have certainly improved."

"I drink quite a few these days, especially their Sauvignon Blancs. Shall we have another bottle?"

"Very tempting doctor, but I think not. We are both driving home."

"We could always take a taxi," suggested Ed hopefully.

"No! I'm going to be sensible," said Sophie. "And you're not getting me into a taxi tonight, Ed."

"Oh damn," Ed said laughing. "I'll order coffee."

"Very wise," laughed Sophie, sitting back in her chair and staring at Ed.

"What?"

"I'm studying you."

Ed shrugged.

"I want to explore you," said Sophie. "Tell me a little about yourself. What makes you tick, why you wanted to be a doctor and any other morsel of interest that can persuade me to want to see you again."

"Very well, but you might not like all you hear."

"I'm listening."

He told her.

Chapter Six

Crumlin, County Antrim, Northern Ireland

David Foster adjusted his tie and then slipped into his uniform jacket. It was nearly time to kiss Ed off to school. He didn't dare take him, nor would he allow Mary, his wife, to make the short journey. The sergeant who slept the night in the house with them drove Ed to school. It wasn't a perfect arrangement because it left the house unprotected, but it was the best David could do. He never left the house until the sergeant returned. He was normally away no longer than half-an-hour. He ran down stairs to where Mary was buttoning up the buttons on Ed's jacket, before handing him his satchel with his sandwiches safely stashed on top of the boy's exercise books. It upset her not to be able to walk him to school, but then, if you were married to a Royal Ulster Constabulary officer there were certain things you could not do in Northern Ireland. One was risking your son's life just because you wanted to walk him to school.

"Bye scamp," David said, patting the six year old on his head. "Have a good day. See you when I get back this evening. Make sure you stay awake so that I can finish last night's story."

Ed reached up and David took him in his arms. As an only child, Ed was very special to him and the love between the two ran deep. "You bet I'll stay awake, Dad." He wriggled out of his father's arms and dropped lightly onto the floor. He was impatient to be gone—a game of marbles with his best friend awaited him in the school playground. He turned to the sergeant who was standing by the front door. Ed liked being driven to school by a man in uniform carrying a gun. It made him feel special. "Ready then Patrick?"

Patrick smiled and opened the door. "I'm ready. He took Ed's hand, turned to smile at Mary and walked the boy down the drive, his eyes darting in every direction, just checking. Ed waved as he got into the car.

Mary waved back and then turned to her husband. "I wish with all my heart you'd give up this dreadful job, David."

David gave her a weak smile. "It's a bit late for that. Enemies have already been made. Leaving the job would make no difference to the danger we are in. But we are as safe as any one else in Ulster these days, maybe safer. The IRA seems to be going for soft targets."

Mary didn't bother to reply; she knew David was lying. He was a prime target, as were all his compatriots. The IRA had scores to settle, and they didn't give up easily. As each year passed and the Troubles rumbled on, Mary was amazed that they were still alive. Anyway, she told herself nearly every day, she'd known all this when she'd married him. That would have been the time to say, 'Sorry, I can't live with a man in mortal danger.' But she'd been in love. She shook her head and reached for her husband's hand as they walked back into the house.

The two masked men burst in through the door five minutes later. David had forgotten to flick on the security lock. Careless, one of the men thought. David saw them a second before a third man came crashing through the kitchen window and grabbed Mary. In a matter of minutes, David was tied to a chair in the sitting room with a gun pointing at his head and tape wrapped around his mouth. There had been no hope of reaching the panic button or the gun that he kept by his bed. Mary had been stripped of her clothes and was tied naked to another chair, facing him, her mouth, like his, taped. She was deathly white; her husband was grey. Both knew what was about to happen. It was a punishment regularly meted out to protestant policeman, however even-handed they had been to the warring factions.

The men didn't speak.

David did his best to smile with his eyes at Mary.

Mary whimpered.

Using the claw hammer with which the third man had smashed the kitchen window frame, the men systematically broke nearly every bone in her body. They started with her toes, then her ankles, her ribs, her fingers, her nose and finally her jaw. Tears flowed down David's cheeks as he watched his wife beaten to an unrecognisable pulp. When she resembled a broken doll one of the men shot her through the head.

He turned to look at David. If the boy had still been in the house they had decided to kill him and leave the hated RUC officer alive to suffer for the rest of his life. But they'd arrived a few minutes too late; the boy was already on his way to school. They made a swift decision. One of the men spat in David's face *and shot away his knees. The second man shot him in the stomach. The third man finished the job.*

They left the way two of them had come in. The killings had taken six minutes. Another five or seven and the sergeant would be back. No time to stand around and savour their work. They whipped off their masks and walked quietly down the village street to their stolen Saab They smiled at each other, raised their clenched fists in defiance and jumped into the car. They were gone before anyone in the street became aware of what had happened.

Two hours later, Ed and his friend ran out of the school building into the playground; he was eager to press home his advantage in the game of marbles. His eyes were alight with excitement. He couldn't wait to tell his father that he'd triumphed over his adversary. Then he spotted a police car parked by the school gates, and getting out of the back were his uncle and aunt, Sean and Alice. His little brow furrowed; he broke away from his friend and walked slowly towards the gates. He waved and smiled.

Then he saw their tears.

His heart missed a beat. Possessing the uncanny intuition that children seem to have he knew something was wrong.

A few minutes later his life changed for ever.

Chapter Seven

Sophie held her head in her hands. "Oh God, what a way to die. How did you ever recover from such a terrible thing?"

"I was shielded from the gruesome details by my aunt and uncle. They told me my parents had been shot by the IRA. Although I was very young I was aware of the danger my father was in. There was no way he could hide that from me. After all, it is unusual to have a bodyguard whereever you go, and father never had a gun far from his side. The house was like a fortress, but obviously not a very good one. So I accepted their explanation. I think it was lucky I was so young. It's given me time to get over it, and my Aunt and Uncle were wonderful. They took me into their family, two boys and a girl, and treated me as another one of their children. It wasn't until I was eighteen that I found out the gory details. That really hurt me. I was filled with a terrible rage. At first, all I could think of was revenge. I wanted to rip the hearts out of the men who defiled my mother. Sadists, the lot of them. Of course, I would never have found them. I just hoped they died very painful deaths. I used to imagine all sorts of ways I would like them to die. Strange as it may seem, that was enough. Slowly the hate became less intense and the idea of becoming a doctor entered my head. It was the last career I ever thought I would take up. I discovered I wanted to save lives, not destroy them, and my parents would never have wanted me to seek retribution. Oh yes, I still wake up at times in the middle of the night thinking about the gruesome way they died, but it's true what they say: time is a great healer. I don't feel bitter now; it was just the way Ireland worked in those dreadful days of civil war. My parents were unlucky to get caught up in the needless violence."

Do you think of your parents a lot?" asked Sophie.

"Yes, I do. I sometimes wonder what I would be doing now if they had lived. I certainly wouldn't have become a doctor. More likely I would have joined the army. Naturally I would have liked to have spent more of my life with them, and had my father's guidance—he was a very wise and gentle man, inspite of his choice of career. But I had six years with them. Lots of children in Ireland didn't even get that. And my aunt and uncle were lovely people."

"*were* lovely?"

Ed nodded. "My uncle died three years ago from cancer. My aunt died soon afterwards. I think she missed him too much."

"You've had a tough time."

"It happens. Anyway, that's enough about me. What about you? Any parents, other family?"

"I've lost my parents too: in a plane crash a year ago. I was devastated. They meant so much to me.

"How did they meet?"

Sophie smiled. "I have always thought it so romantic. Dad was a barman at a hotel in Jamaica where mum was a regular guest. He was also a gifted pianist and according to mum sang jazz beautifully. He used to sing to her after all the other guests had gone to bed. They fell in love, they married. Very unconventional and quite a gamble as you can imagine. Mixed marriages were few and far between amongst the middle classes of their generation but they overcame any racism and were blissfully happy.

"They crashed over water and their bodies were not found for a week. It was awful. I hung on to the hope that they had survived. But they didn't. As for other members of the family, they are all on Dad's side. His parents live in Jamaica, as do a varied assortment of cousins etc. I don't really know any of them, except of course my grandparents. They are lovely."

"I'm so sorry about your mum and dad, what a terrible way to die."

"And here I am unmarried, doing what I like to do," Sophie added eager to change the subject.

"Does that mean you like being with me?"

"Early days Ed, but yes, I think I do, and we seem to have something in common—you know our parents dying violent deaths." And then on impulse she leant across the table and kissed him. Ed felt the gentleness of her lips. Sophie thought he tasted just great.

They stared at each other across the table, both tempted to suggest they took the evening one step further, but neither wanted to risk spoiling something that had been so perfect. Ed decided that however much he wanted to go to bed with her it would be the wrong move. He chuckled.

"What does that mean?"

"Just something I was thinking."

Sophie laughed. "I bet I know what was going through that head of yours."

"Maybe you do."

"But it would be a bad idea."

"I had already decided that."

They both laughed before Ed said, "will you come out with me again?"

"Of course, and thanks for turning out to be the person I thought you were."

"Which is?" Ed reached for her hand. She did not pull it away.

"A nice man."

"Oh God isn't that rather boring?"

"Let me tell you something," Sophie said, suddenly very serious. "Maybe I'm old fashioned, but a nice man in my book is one who respects a woman, just like you have in the last few minutes. Someone a woman can feel at ease with, not always having to be on her guard for the roving hand under the table or the sexual innuendos. A nice man is someone to be savoured like a good wine, for let me tell you Ed, in my business there are very few of them about these days. When you meet one you know you are the luckiest woman alive. And you are a nice man."

"I don't quite know what to say."

"Don't bother. I like you. Can we take it from there?"

Ed smiled. "Suits me. Same place same time tomorrow?"

"It's a date."

Sophie headed south, driving too fast in the light rain that had started to fall. Her head was still spinning from the pleasure of the evening. She felt good, revitalised and happy. Something she realised she hadn't been for some time. She licked her lips as she drove into her driveway, savouring the moment that Ed had dared kiss her outside the pub. It had not been an urgent kiss, but soft as silk, so, so good.

As she opened her front door, her cat, Samantha, crept out of the dark and purred. Sophie picked her up, but she was in one of her awkward moods and fought to be let go so she smiled and dropped her gently onto the drive. Samantha had always done her own thing—well she was a cat!

Sophie felt as fresh as the air. Ed had been a revellation, so different to many of the men she had met and dated. He seemed caring; he was easy to talk to, not looking for a mercy jump. To sum it up he seemed genuine. He too had suffered a terrible loss. It was a pain they could share and that meant a lot to her. Her instincts were telling her that this man was special. She didn't want to lose him.

She made for her sitting room, threw herself onto one of the sofas and kicked off her shoes. "Daft bitch," she shouted to the room and then burst out laughing. She was like a coiled spring, a teenager bursting with excited energy. She looked at her watch. It was just after midnight. She curled herself into a small ball and started to hum rather tunelessly conjuring up Ed's smile, and sighed. "Oh Ed, Ed, what are you doing to me?"

Ed was feeling a little confused as he walked into his flat and made straight for his bedroom. Surgery started at nine and he had two calls to private patients before that. It would not be a good idea to appear too bleary-eyed in front of his patients. His thoughts were much on the same lines as Sophie's. He was mystified by how she'd touched his heart so quickly. Was this reality? Could you really fall in love so quickly? He'd heard a friend say that he'd fallen in love with his wife in ten minutes. Ed remembered laughing in disbelief at the time. Now he understood. When they'd kissed good night outside the pub, he had dared to think that Sophie was sending out a very positive message. He threw off the last of his clothes and jumped into bed naked, knowing he wouldn't sleep. Too bad if he was bleary-eyed in the morning. In their ignorance his patients would smile at the dark bags under his eyes, and think their doctor had had a heavy evening. It was just that he didn't want to waste the hours that could be spent thinking of Sophie. He stretched out on the soft mattress and started to replay every moment of the evening.

It was two minutes past seven when the phone rang.
"Good morning Ed."
"Hi. Still okay for supper tonight?"
He heard Sophie's laugh. "Wild horses wouldn't stop me."
"Great. Will you allow me to come and pick you up?"
"Why not."
"I'll be with you about seven-thirty."
That's far too long to wait, Sophie thought.

Chapter Eight

Jerry Gordon was a notorious criminal. In his youth, he had belonged to a gang called The Invincibles. The problem was they weren't. One member was a crap driver, who was blind in his left eye; another smoked thirty a day and had coughing attacks at all the wrong moments. Jerry ranked as one of the most incompetent safebreakers the criminal classes had ever known. By the time they were twenty, they were all in the slammer serving from one to eight years. Jerry had been the lucky one and was out after eight months, but the experience had a disastrous effect on his life. He came out to discover that his wife had dumped their son on his sister and had then disappeared, never to be seen again.

Jerry was unable to get a decent job because of his criminal record. His only alternative, as he saw it, was to return to a life of crime. He decided he would just do petty jobs on his own. He didn't need a one-eyed driver or a mate with ashtray lungs to help get him caught. Jerry's one redeeming feature was his love for his son. He took his responsibilities as a single parent seriously. He wanted a better life for Phil: a mechanic or a builder perhaps. Jerry visited Phil at his sister's every weekend and attempted to expound the virtues of going straight and the importance of doing well at school. Sadly, Phil was not a receptive pupil. He was inherently lazy and was encouraged in this trait by his doting aunt, who waited on him hand and foot. He also possessed some of his father's cunning and was into every dodgy practice at his school, helped along by his good looks and an unlikely but powerful ability to turn on the charm at will. The headmaster's prophecy that Phil would soon get into serious trouble soon proved correct. By the time he left school, even Jerry could see that his boy was virtually unemployable.

Then, by some quirky twist of fate, along came Polly. When Phil told Jerry he was marrying Polly, Jerry couldn't believe his luck. Okay, he didn't like the snooty little bitch, but she was rich and in time he'd advise his son to divorce her. It was a stroke of indescribable luck given Phil's low IQ and idle nature.

"Got her in the club have you boy?" Jerry asked quite sure that was the only reason that a rich pretty bird like Polly could ever marry Phil. In fact, they genuinely seemed to love each other, and he had to admit that Phil was a good-looking boy.

"You could have knocked me down with a feather," Jerry said to his sister. Priding himself on being an honest man, he added, "What on earth can the girl see in him?"

When the telephone rang in Jerry's Portsmouth council house and Phil asked for help, Jerry was not surprised. The inevitable separation had just come a little earlier than expected, and that meant two things to Jerry. One, his son was soon to become rich, and secondly he would make sure that Phil treated him right. The thought of getting his hands on some legit money made Jerry break out into a sweat.

"Go for all you can get. Leave the little bitch skint," advised a deliriously happy Jerry. "I happen to know a shrewd lawyer and you're sure to need one; that about to be ex-wife of yours will have some top of the range lawyer looking after her. His name is Roger Matthews, known to all as Polecat on account of his diminutive size, his ferrety eyes and his foul smell. He's as sly as they come, and has won some big cases. He's very popular with footballers. He owes me big time. I will have a word in his ear. This is your chance boy."

Phil ventured a rare smile as he put the telephone down. Feeling life might be on the up he rang a locksmith to change the locks. "Like yesterday, mate. There's a tidy bonus waiting if you can do it. Great. See you in an hour."

"Right you fucking cow, let's see how you like that," he shouted to the empty room as he made for the fridge to celebrate.

Belinda's desk separated her from Polly, which was just as well, given the urges that were coursing through her body. She had a strong desire to pull Polly close. It shocked her how unprofessionally she was acting. She reached for a glass of water and sipped slowly, forcing herself to forget Polly's shapely figure, which was half hidden by the desk. "You were saying Polly?" she managed to croak.

"Phil's changed the locks. I can't get a thing out of the house. Can he do that?"

"He can try anything, and possession is nine tenths of the law. We will have to go to court and get an injunction, unless I can talk to either him or his lawyer and hope they will see the pointlessness of his actions. Do you know who his lawyer might be?"

"No idea. Do you think he'll have one?"

"It's amazing how even the stupidest man becomes quite crafty once he's faced with a divorce that might net him some cash. I would bet you anything that Phil will have a lawyer by now, and within the next few days you will be hearing from him."

"But I've no clothes except what I'm wearing," moaned Polly.

"Have you got none at your parents' house?"

"A few discarded rags and I'm doing my best to stay away from them at the moment. Mum will be in '*I told you so*' mood, and that will get me so angry."

"So where are you staying?" asked Belinda a little breathlessly, fighting back the desire to say, *come and stay with me*.

"I'm staying with Clarissa and Ted. They are so kind."

Belinda swallowed her disappointment. What had 'big-boobed' Clarissa, as she had christened her, got that she hadn't? Reluctantly she presumed it was Clarissa's motherly charm and generous nature, something that Belinda knew she lacked. She leaned across her desk and stared at Polly sitting on the edge of her chair, fingers entwining and face flushed. She forced herself to speak calmly. "Well, I'm sure Clarissa will be a great comfort, but tell you what, right now why don't the two of us go on a shopping spree? Call it a celebration that you've got rid of that arse-hole. I suppose you've got your credit cards?"

"Luckily they were in my bag. Are you sure you can spare the time? I can perfectly well go on my own."

Belinda was prepared to give Polly all the time she wanted. "My day is yours. I'll get my secretary to cancel my other meetings. Come on, let's go and have some fun."

"Okay. Thanks for being so kind. I'm in your hands."

Oh, I wish, I wish, Belinda thought.

Chapter Nine

Belinda was feeling guilty. She knew she shouldn't be thinking that Polly's divorce was the best thing that had happened to her in months, but she couldn't resist it. Could she dare hope that one day Polly would share the same feelings for her? She shook her head angrily, aware that she was behaving unprofessionally. She took Polly firmly by the arm and guided her along the passage to Court Three.

"This will be very short and not cost you a fortune," she assured a nervous Polly. "Because the good news is we will win. I can't understand Phil refusing you access to your home. It's something Polecat would never advise. Heaven knows where your husband dug that piece of dung up from."

"I suspect Phil's been taking advice from his father. I met Roger Matthews, or Polecat as you call him, once at his house. Didn't take to him."

"I'm surprised he's taken the case," Belinda remarked. "He's expensive and he must know his bill might never be paid. Phil only stands to get a fair share of the sale of your house, not a penny more, though sure as hell it's his dream to get a lot more than that. You have no children, have only been married three years and Phil has put no money into the partnership. You have paid for everything, even his Stella. If we have to go to court again, I would guess that the judge would tell him to get on his bike, find work, and be thankful that he's got half the money from the sale of your house."

"You really think that?"

Belinda smiled. "I don't bullshit my clients, Polly."

Phil was staring at Polecat in disbelief. "But Dad said you'd win! Now, at the first hurdle, you're telling me to practically kiss the bitch's arse. What's with you?"

"Well, the arse isn't at all bad," quipped Polecat in a rare moment of humour.

"You're welcome to it," hissed Phil.

Actually, Polly's arse was the last thing concerning Polecat. He was cursing the moment he'd agreed to help Phil, but then, as Phil's father had forcefully told him down the telephone, "You owe me one, Polecat." There was no denying that. He'd won a big divorce case, two years back, because Jerry had done a bit of *correspondence lifting* from the about-to-be ex husband's flat. As Polecat had suspected, it had proved vital in the courtroom battle. Jerry had taken a risk for him and although Polecat had given him a generous payoff, in the afterglow of his success he had also rashly offered his services if ever Jerry ran into trouble. He had never imagined that his careless offer would resort in him sorting out his brain dead son's marital problems. Like all barristers, he liked to win and, as he'd remarked ruefully to his secretary, "I'm on a hiding to nothing with this one."

"Listen Phil, I don't care a stuff what your father advised. How many times do I have to say this to get it into your thick scull? You should walk up to your wife right this minute and apologise for locking her out of *her* house. Smile sweetly and give her the new keys. That way some of her antagonism might wane and, you never know, she could feel a bit more generous towards you when it comes to agreeing a financial settlement. So, don't be so pig headed."

"Pig headed! Hey, the woman walked out on me! Whose side are you on?"

Polecat thought, I can't imagine anything worse than being married to *you*. He said, "I'm on your side of course, but it is my job to advise you if I think you are making a mistake. Let me tell you sonny-boy, you are making one very big mistake."

Phil bridled. "I should sack you Polecat. And don't call me sonny-boy."

"Do as you like," Polecat retorted, tucking his briefcase under his arm, ready to run if Phil held to his threat. "I'll send my bill to your father."

Before Phil's brain clicked into gear, Polly appeared round the corner with Belinda. She forced a smile Phil's way as she walked by.

Polecat nudged Phil. "Am I sacked?"

Phil reluctantly shook his head.

"Well, here's your chance son—sorry—Phil. You have nothing to lose by appearing generous now. Save the aggro for when you're fighting for the money. Give her a key. Any barrister would tell you the same."

Phil rubbed his unshaven chin. "Okay, I'll do as you say. I've nothing to lose this time, but you make bloody sure, Polecat, that you win a big settlement for me. Get my drift?"

Polecat didn't bother to reply. He was wasting time. Any minute now, they would be called into the courtroom. A deal had to be done swiftly. He ran after the two women, moving surprisingly fast, for such a slothful man. "Hey Belinda, could I have a word?"

Belinda stopped and glared at the little man who was oozing false charm. She'd come up against Polecat before. "A devious bastard in the matrimonial division," she'd informed Polly. "A real little worm, but good, very good."

"You want a word, Polecat?" asked Belinda, staring down at the little man.

Polecat shuddered; tall women made him feel insignificant. He cleared his throat and did his best to look unflustered. Roger, my name's Roger, he wanted to shout. He hated the other barristers calling him Polecat, but complaining would be a waste of time, and would only rile Belinda who, when riled, could get very nasty.

"My client is aware that he is at a disadvantage here. I think you and I should have a talk, but I must warn you my client is very hostile."

"You mean you want to talk about a deal and avoid another court hearing, which of course you will lose."

Polecat smiled as best he could. "That's about it."

"The ball's in your court."

"Can I have a private word?"

Belinda looked purposefully at her watch. "We'll have to make it quick. Do you want it to be just the two of us or with our clients?"

Polecat certainly didn't want Phil anywhere near. He'd fly off the handle if he knew they were talking about a deal, not just access to the house. "I suggest alone," he said quietly. "My client has nothing between his ears and thinks he's about to take a ride on a gravy train." He smiled apologetically at Polly. "Sorry my dear."

Belinda put a finger to her mouth and Polly got the message. She ignored Polecat. "You do whatever you think is best," she said to Belinda.

"Okay. You sit tight here, and whatever you do don't talk to Phil."

"No problem there," laughed Polly, watching Phil scurrying like a frightened rabbit towards the gents. "He wouldn't dare speak to me. So what are you going to ask for?"

Belinda pulled her out of Polecat's earshot. "Well, we're only here to get access to your house, but it will do no harm to suggest quietly to Polecat that Phil gets half the money from the sale of the house. Zilch more."

Polly was staggered. "What about maintenance?"

"Dearest Polly, Phil won't get maintenance. Half of the house is all he can hope for."

"Okay then."

Belinda turned to Polecat. "Let's talk."

A few hours later, Belinda and Polly were enjoying a celebration drink and a light fish supper at the Loch Fyne restaurant in Parchment Street, close to the courthouse. Belinda was in a triumphant mood. Winning gave her a real buzz, even more so when it concerned Polecat. She loved beating him; it was always a moment to cherish. He had agreed to her demands without a murmur. "I'm on a loser here," he confessed early on in their discussions, so let's not waste time. I've other more lucrative clients wanting my services."

Polly raised her glass of wine. "How the hell did you do pull that off, Belinda?"

Belinda swallowed an oyster before replying. "I told you it would be a piece of cake. Polecat knows when he's beaten, which is not very often, but he gave in as gracefully as he is capable of."

"Well I think you're great."

Belinda looked across the table at Polly and thought she looked stunning. "Thanks," she managed to say. "I'm glad that's all cleared up. You can have access to your house as of tomorrow. The keys will be in my office by ten. You can collect your possessions and then we can go ahead with putting the house on the market. Phil can stay in the house until it's sold. I could have insisted that he left now and you moved back in, but I thought better of it. No point in aggravating him too much. Phil gets half the sale price and fuck all else."

Polly beamed. "That's what I thought you said, but forgive me for thinking this is a dream."

Belinda laid a hand on Polly's arm. "You're well rid of that man."

"I know."

"Good. So get to my office before ten. We don't want Phil playing any silly tricks. After you've taken what you want, don't go near the house again. I don't want Phil to be able to complain that we are harassing him. We still have the divorce to be ratified. After that you're a free woman. Any idea what you'll do?"

It was something to which Polly had been giving quite a lot of thought. "Going back to live with my parents is not an option. My mother would probably refuse to have me anyway. So, until the house is sold and I've found something else to buy, I'll take up Clarissa's offer and bunk down with her and Ted. After that . . . well, something will doubtless come along. I've always been an optimist. I'll just let life take its course."

Belinda nearly choked on her last oyster.

"Will you come with me?"

Clarissa looked at the table, which was stacked high with vegetables ready to be sorted for the next farmer's market. It would be a good two hours work of washing, boxing and pricing, but she never thought to say 'no.' "If that's what you really want."

Polly gave her a grateful smile. "It is. It really is. I don't think I could face Phil on my own. He's going to be so angry. If his father is there, I'm sure I'll run away. I couldn't face them both on my own." She looked at the chaos on the table. "But you have all this to sort. The market's tomorrow isn't it?"

Clarissa patted Polly's hand. "Doesn't matter. Ted can get his arse off his stool and deal with this lot. So don't you worry."

"You're a brick."

Clarissa drove Polly's car because Polly was in a blue funk—no way could she have driven. Her hands were sweating, her heart in her mouth. She was not looking forward to coming face to face with Phil. He'd be bitter and very angry. He would not have liked losing. His gravy train had run off the rails. She would have to be on her guard or he might get violent. He had nothing to lose. If Clarissa hadn't been sitting beside her she'd have long since turned the car around.

Clarissa couldn't honestly say that she was going to enjoy the next hour or so either. She knew enough about Phil to realise that things could turn nasty, and she was wondering what her role should be if they did. Should she stand between the antagonists and work out a truce, or grab Polly's arm and run. Frankly, if Polly ducked out now she knew she would not stand in her way. Which was a pretty negative attitude, and not what Polly needed. Come on you wimp, Clarissa thought, the girl is depending on your support. She fumbled in her sack-like handbag for a packet of wine gums and offered the packet to Polly, who shook her head. "Might make me sick," she said.

Clarissa pulled out a yellow sweet, threw it out of the window. "Hate those, find me a dark one will you, Polly?"

Polly reached for the packet just as Clarissa past the Horse and Jockey and slowed down. "Do you want me to park a little away from your house?"

"Good idea. I'll walk the short distance to the house. Oh God!" Polly dropped the bag of sweets. "His dad's here."

Clarissa braked.

Polly shouted. "Drive on. No way am I going in there!"

"Yes you are. You can't run away now!" said Clarissa, sounding like a rather severe schoolteacher. "Phil won't dare do anything and if his father threatens trouble, I'll deal with him." It was said bravely.

Clarissa flicked on the indicator, pulled to the side of the road and switched off the engine.

"You're right, I'm being pathetic," said Polly. "But I'm not allowing you to get embroiled in this. You stay in the car, I'll be fine."

Clarissa started to object. "No, I mean it, Clarissa, this is my fight not yours. I need to do this on my own. You stay here with the engine running."

Clarissa didn't bother to argue. "Okay, but I'll loiter about outside. If you want me I'll be there in a flash."

"Thanks." Without another glance at her friend, Polly threw open the door and started to walk the last few yards to her house, a small red-bricked thatched cottage, bought at a time when she'd held such high hopes of civilising Phil. It had been a short dream.

She was a few feet from the front door when it flew open and Phil appeared. He looked dishevelled and, Polly thought, rather evil.

"Come to gloat?"

Polly breathed in deeply. "No Phil, I'm not going to gloat. I just want to collect a few things and then I'll be gone. Will you let me pass so that I can do that?"

"Brought your cavalry I see," sneered Phil, spotting Clarissa who had stationed herself on the pavement.

"It's only Clarissa. I didn't feel like driving. I don't think she poses a threat to you, unlike the man I see lurking behind you. Why does he have to be here?"

Because I wanted him."

"Why? Because he'll hit me harder than you can?"

"I won't hit you, I'll bloody well strangle you," boomed Jerry from behind Phil. "Think you're a clever little bitch, do you, depriving my son of what is rightfully his?"

Jerry was quite obviously drunk and although Polly didn't know him well, she guessed he was quite capable of carrying out his threat. She decided not to provoke him by informing him that nothing was rightfully Phil's.

She stood her ground, buoyed by a surge of courage that surprised her. She was determined to get what she'd come for.

"Threatening me, Mr Gordon, will get you and Phil nowhere. Much better to let me collect my belongings and I'll be gone before you know it. That will make life a lot easier for us all. Now, if you don't mind."

Polly pushed past Phil, sidestepped Jerry, and made for the stairs. Her legs were shaking so badly she had to hold hard onto the stair-rail. She could hear heavy breathing behind her, but managed not to look round. She ran into the bedroom and slammed the door. Damn, she'd forgotten there was no lock. She knew what was going to happen next and Jerry did not disappoint her. The door burst open. "Think you're clever don't you, Miss Smarty-pants?" he growled. "Getting some high and mighty lawyer to steal what is rightfully Phil's. So I suggest that you behave like a sensible woman and get the hell out of here. You take nothing do you hear me? Not one fucking thing."

Polly stared at Jerry. He was unshaven, wore a tight pair of jeans that did nothing for his large belly, and he smelt like a distillery. His eyes were bloodshot and his big hands were clenched tight. He was dangerous. She raised an arm, preparing to defend herself. Suddenly there was a shout from downstairs, then a cry and, wow, there was Clarissa, red-faced and glaring at a very surprised Jerry.

"Your son needs you, Mr Gordon," she said in a steady voice, rubbing a fist on her blouse. A smear of blood appeared. "I think I may have broken his nose—sorry."

Too amazed to realise that he could easily overpower the two women, Jerry bolted from the room and ran down the stairs to find a bemused Phil, sitting on the floor and holding a very bloody towel to his nose.

"The bitch," he cried seeing his father.

Jerry knelt beside him cursing. "Right, you bitches," he yelled.

Clarissa had anticipated his next move. She was already half way down the stairs, pulling Polly behind her. She knew that if Jerry reached the bottom of the stairs before they did, the last thing on his mind would be a possible prison sentence for GBH. Luckily, Jerry was not the quickest of movers, and Phil was still dazed. Clarissa and Polly were out of the front door and running down the street before Jerry had struggled to his feet.

"Come on, let's get out of here," gasped Clarissa throwing herself into the car.

"Oh God," cried Polly, "here comes Phil."

"No time to waste then. He'll be on us in a few seconds," said Clarissa, turning the ignition key as she heard Phil bellowing Polly's name.

The VW came round the corner at 40 mph. The driver, late for his next meeting, hit Phil before he could apply his brakes. Phil bounced off the bonnet, smashed his head on the windscreen and flew over the car. He landed on the pavement in a crumpled, bleeding heap, his bones shattered, his head a messy pulp.

It was the end of Phil, the end of Jerry's dream for *his boy.*

"Oh my God!" screamed Polly throwing herself out of the car before Clarissa had a chance to restrain her. By the time Clarissa had switched off the engine and run back along the street, Polly was pushing her way through the small crowd that had quickly gathered.

"Polly!" Clarissa shouted. Her voice fell on deaf ears. When she finally managed to elbow her way through the growing crowd, Polly was on her knees beside Phil's lifeless body.

She looked up at Clarissa. "He's dead. I killed him."

Clarissa didn't have time to tell her she was talking rubbish for, pushing through the crowd, shouting obscenities at everyone, came Jerry. He hurled himself at Polly. "Bitch, bitch," he screamed. "You've killed him!" With that, he drove a clenched fist hard into her face. She rolled away from Phil, putting her hands over her head. Jerry aimed a kick at her stomach. There was no doubt he'd have done her some serious damage if at that moment the shocked driver of the VW hadn't intervened.

"It was me; it was me who hit him."

Clarissa felt quite sorry for the poor man who was obviously badly shaken, but also relieved that he had intervened. She ran to Polly, cradled her in her arms and glared at Jerry. "Back off you bastard," she shouted.

This is what he did, only because he was face to face with the man who had ended the life of his one and only son. He swung a vicious right hook at the man's jaw; as he fell, Jerry kicked him in the groin. Then they were both rolling on the ground, the man screaming in pain while Jerry did his level best to bite the man's left ear off.

"That's enough of that, sir," said a voice above Clarissa. She looked up to see two police officers dragging Jerry off the driver.

"Bitch!" Jerry shouted as one of the police officers clamped a pair of handcuffs on his wrists. "I'll get you for this one day!"

Chapter Ten

Ed took care dressing. He chose a light blue shirt, bought only the week before, and pulled on a pair of carefully ironed beige cotton trousers. He combed his hair then stood in front of the long mirror on his cupboard door and decided it was the best he could do. He smiled to himself marvelling what Sophie had done to him in so short a space of time. He was not a vain man, his job dictated how he looked most of the time, but once free of the regulation dress of tie, suit and black shoes, he favoured casual shirts, slip on brown shoes and a comfortable pair of old faded cords. Now, every small detail—his clothing, his hair, even the whiteness of his teeth—had taken on enormous importance. What it was to be smitten! He moved into his small, rather minimalist sitting room, thinking how much Sophie would brighten up the room. Her charisma would vibrate from wall to wall, making the rather severe surroundings positively glow. He walked into the kitchen where he kept his car keys. On the walls were four large abstract paintings, which he'd bought in a mad moment of inebriated daring from a street artist in Marrakech. He gave a little shudder as he stared at them. They'd cost him a small fortune to ship back to the UK, but he really would have to get rid of them. They did nothing for him any more, never had, but he enjoyed seeing the shocked look of the few people who came to his flat and asked, "what in the hell are these?" He picked up his keys and made his way out onto the street. He felt a charge of excitement. The journey to the pub was going to drag.

Sophie's excitement was draining away with the bath water, her earlier euphoria being replaced by doubt, the delicious moments of the night before fast disappearing from her memory. Things were perhaps moving too fast. Maybe she should have played a little harder to get, not been so obviously keen to see Ed again. What she was at a loss to explain was *why* she felt this way. Was it something to do with the death of her parents? Perhaps she was not yet ready to start a relationship. Yet, a few hours ago, she had been jumping about with excitement. As she pulled herself out of the bath, she knew she couldn't ignore the feeling of doubt that had begun to nag away at her. She still wanted to see Ed, but not have dinner with him again quite so quickly. Sophie knew that her vibes would be negative and they would pass onto Ed. She was the sort of person who could not hide her true feelings. She sighed as she wrapped a towel round herself. She was going to cancel the evening, well aware that Ed might construe her actions the wrong way, and that would be curtains to any hope of seeing him again. It was a risk she had to take, so better to get it over with. She slipped into her dressing gown and made her way down stairs with a very heavy heart.

She was walking slowly across her sitting room towards the telephone when it rang.

"Sophie, it's Clarissa."

"Hello Clarissa."

"Polly's in hospital."

"Oh my God! What's wrong?"

"It's a long story. Tell you when I see you. Suffice to say our visit to her house was an unmitigated disaster, actually a tragic disaster. Phil's dead and Polly was attacked by his father."

"Jesus!"

"I'm in Winchester hospital with her now."

"I'm on my way."

"No need. Belinda is coming. Just thought you would like to know. Anyway, I know you're going out with Ed tonight. It can wait until tomorrow. Polly will be a few days in hospital."

"Actually, it's the excuse I need."

"Oh."

"Tell you about it later. See you in about half-an-hour."

Sophie lowered the telephone from her ear and looked up at the ceiling. It was divine intervention. The God who she'd worshiped blindly since childhood had come to her rescue. She had briefly blamed Him for her parents' deaths and felt ashamed. This was no doubt a sign that He'd forgiven her for such blasphemous thoughts. She now had the perfect excuse to pull out of the evening. She'd ring Ed and then head for the hospital. She looked at her watch. Shit! Ed might have already left to pick her up.

Try his mobile, try his mobile, she said to herself. She wasn't sure she could look him in the eye.

Ed was half way to her house when his mobile rang. "Sophie, you okay?"

I'm fine," she lied. "But I have a problem. One of the girls I play squash with is in hospital. I must go and see her."

"Hang on a minute, must find somewhere to stop." Ed spotted a lay-by, pulled in and cut the engine. "Do you have to? I was really looking forward to seeing you again."

Sophie felt a little irritated. This man seemed to think their supper date was more important than her going to an injured friend, who might well be seriously hurt. Then she realised she hadn't explained this to him. "Ed listen, I'm terribly sorry, but Polly is a close friend. Her about-to-be ex-husband has been killed and his father has assaulted her. That's all I know, but right now I think she needs me more than you do."

She was right of course, but totally illogically, Ed felt a stab of jealousy. In normal circumstances, he would have been understanding, sympathetic even, and immediately suggested another time to meet. Instead, disappointment overwhelmed him and something snapped inside his head. How could she assume this friend needed her more than he did? I'll ring you tomorrow," he snapped and broke the connection.

Sophie looked at the silent receiver with a sense of shock. She had not expected Ed's reaction. He had acted like a spoilt child, but she hadn't been honest with him either.

Polly lay in the hospital bed, her face swollen, her stomach hurting. She imagined that was how you feel if a bull had charged you. If her body was hurting, it was nothing compared to the emotions that raged in her mind. Phil had been many things she'd despised, but once they had been happy, made love, laughed together, planned together, even talked about having children. Well thank God that wasn't a problem! He hadn't deserved to die in such a cruel way. Stupid, stupid man! Why did he have to run down the middle of the road! Why couldn't he have at least looked where he was going? Now she was left with Jerry Gordon blaming her for his son's death, and an unavoidable feeling that he was right on the button.

"Polly, you poor darling!"

Polly looked up and saw Belinda through her swollen eyes. Her mouth cracked into a smile and she pointed to the white upright chair by her bed.

"Wonderful to see you Belinda" she lisped. "Come and sit here. Clarissa's had to go down to the police station to give a statement."

Belinda felt a jab of satisfaction that she'd arrived when Polly was on her own. It would give her time to put an idea to her. She stared at the bruised face that was bravely trying to look cheerful, put a hand gently on Polly's bare shoulder then bent down and kissed her on a cheek. She drew back reluctantly, imagining the sweetness of the body that lay under the sheets and felt close to doing something very reckless. She drew in her breath and forced all such thoughts out of her mind. It was neither the time nor the place to let her desires show. "You're going to press charges against that shit Gordon I presume?" she asked.

"No, I'm not," Polly replied painfully. "I've already told the police I don't want to take it any further. He didn't know what he was doing. He was devastated by Phil's death. Much as I dislike him, I don't blame him." Seeing the look of incredulity cross Belinda's face, she was quick to add, "It will be bad enough seeing that poor driver prosecuted for dangerous driving. It should be me in the dock. If I hadn't been such a bitch to Phil, he'd still be alive and that poor driver wouldn't be facing charges."

Belinda was stunned. "Jesus girl, you can't blame yourself. The car was being driven too fast, and Phil was in the middle of the road."

"Because of me."

"The sooner that crappy thought disappears the better. Now listen, I've got something to cheer you up. Why don't I take you on holiday once Phil's funeral is over? I'm due one, and you will need one. I have a friend with a villa outside Marbella. It's empty for a fortnight after next week."

"I'm not going to the funeral."

"What?"

"I'm not going to the funeral. It would be wrong. I would only be a disruptive influence. Much better to allow his family to bury him in peace. That wouldn't be possible if I was there."

What family? As far as Belinda knew, Phil only had his father and a few boozed up mates from the Horse and Jockey to mourn his passing. It seemed very unlikely that any of the pub lot would put down their glasses long enough to go to the funeral. She kept her thoughts to herself. "Okay, it's your choice after all, but the sooner you stop blaming yourself the better. It was an accident. So, what do you say to a few days in sunny Spain?"

"It sounds lovely Belinda, but my father has offered to take me away. My mother of course refuses to come, even though Dad says she's suffering a period of remorse over treating me so badly since I married Phil. But that doesn't mean she's ready to spend time with me, thank God."

Belinda was tempted to beg Polly to change her mind, but thought better of it. "I understand," she said reluctantly.

At that moment, Emily exploded into the ward, hair everywhere, blouse hanging out of her skirt, bubbling with nervous energy. She held a dozen pink roses in one hand and the regulation brown bag of grapes in the other. "Oh God, Polly darling. I just heard the news from Jack when I got home this evening. How absolutely ghastly! That's the first time I've ever felt sorry for Phil! You poor, poor girl."

Oops, big mistake. Polly began to cry.

A whole forty-five minutes had passed since Sophie's call and Ed was still sitting in the lay-by. He felt thoroughly depressed. He felt let down, which was stupid given Sophie's reason for pulling out, but there was a disturbing thought nagging away at his brain. It was something about the way she'd made her excuse, and Ed had learnt to detect white lies, he heard them all the time from his patients. *Of course I've been taking the tablets as you told me, doctor* or *I haven't had a drink for months.* And the most common one: *I gave up smoking a year ago.* It was the inflection in the voice and the inability to look him in the eyes that gave the game away. Okay, he hadn't looked into Sophie's eyes, but he'd heard her voice. She'd stood him up, that's what she'd done, and been lucky to have an excuse. He ran his hands through his hair and reviewed his options. He could ring her back, but then he might find out that she was not at the hospital and that would mean only one thing. Better to leave it and hope she'd ring another time. He shouldn't have broken the connection. She'd probably concluded that he didn't want to see her anymore He was an idiot. "Bugger!" he said in a loud voice as he turned the key in the ignition.

He pulled out onto the road and drove in the opposite direction to home. He didn't want to cook himself a meal staring at his dreadful paintings. He didn't want to sit down in front of the television with a glass of wine in his hand. He didn't want to end up drunk, feeling even sorrier for himself than he did already. So, he just drove, keen to put as much distance between Winchester and himself as he could. After driving for an hour along the M3 motorway, he pulled into a service station and took a much needed bathroom break. Returning to his car, he realised that he was desperately tired. There was no way he should be driving. He closed his eyes.

*

He woke to the noise of a lorry's horn just as dawn turned into full morning. A gentle southerly breeze was easing high cirrus clouds across the sky; it was going to be a beautiful day, a day to sing, and a day he should be glad to be alive. Ed blinked in disbelief. He had only meant to nap, not spend the whole night in a car park. Now he was in danger of being late for morning surgery, all because of a girl he'd only taken out once. Cursing loudly, he started the car and pulled out of the car park. With luck he'd be back in time for his first patient, unshaven, but at least behaving like the responsible doctor he took pride in being. He smiled at his reflection in the driving mirror. He looked a wreck, but he was focused. He might well have overreacted to Sophie's call the night before but of one thing he was sure: he would ring her later.

Sophie was playing with some new designs for her handbags. A pile of discarded paper decorated the floor at her feet, while Samantha lay beside her, scratching and purring alternately, which was getting on Sophie's nerves somewhat. Every now and then she stared at the telephone, willing it to ring, which was pretty daft given that it had been her decision to break off her evening with Ed. That had been a very big mistake and she was beginning to think that Ed had given up on her. She ripped up another sheet of paper and decided she needed something to eat. She glanced at her watch—nearly midday—she'd been working since nine.

The telephone rang.

In her excitement to get to the phone, she knocked her glass of water over Samantha who leapt from the sofa with a load meow.

Sophie picked up the receiver. "Ed?"

Silence.

She felt a sharp stab of disappointment. "Oh God, I'm so sorry, it's not Ed is it?"

Still silence.

"Hello, who is it?"

"Guess."

"Oh God, it is you, isn't it Ed?"

"Might be."

"Stop playing games with me. It is you! You've rung me! You've rung me!"

"To apologise."

"For what?"

"For ringing off on you last night."

"I should apologise too."

"For what?"

Sophie laughed. "Oh, this is getting ridiculous. Shall we meet somewhere near here?"

"Sounds the best idea I've heard all day. I've finished morning surgery. Where?"

"How about The Hotel du Vin? I'm quite close."

"What could be better?"

"I'll look a wreck."

"Join the club! I haven't yet been home to shave."

"Where are you?"

"In the surgery."

"Well, I don't care."

"Okay, we'll both look like tramps."

Sophie smiled, thinking her hair was a mess, her face needed makeup, and her jeans were torn. What, she asked herself, was more important: looks or meeting Ed just as soon as she could run out of the house and drive as fast as she dared to the hotel?

She said, "I'll be there within half-an-hour."

"I'll be waiting."

They sat at the bar like two speechless idiots, staring at each other. Sophie was thinking that an unshaven Ed looked drawn, but still so, so desirable. Ed was thinking that in spite of her dishevelled appearance, Sophie was the best thing he'd ever set eyes on. They smiled at each other, fiddled with the tray of nuts and sipped nervously at their glasses of white wine. Neither of them worried about the silence, both content to hold hands and gaze into each other's eyes, thanking their lucky stars that the fledgling relationship had survived its first test. The spell was broken by the barman asking Ed if he wanted a table.

Ed turned to Sophie. "Want to eat?"

"That sounds a good idea."

"I'll have to pass on any more wine," apologised Ed as they settled at their table. I'm on call." He tapped his trouser pocket. "My pager."

"So you might have to go at any minute?"

"It's possible, but let's hope for a quiet afternoon. Anyway, tell me how your friend is.—Polly, isn't it?"

"She's doing fine, poor darling. The about-to-be ex was killed by a car in front of her eyes and then the father assaulted her. All very traumatic. And Ed, I'm really sorry I pulled out at the last minute, but I felt she needed support."

Ed nodded. "Of course, I quite understand. "Daft of me to react the way I did. Do you know I spent the whole night in a motorway car park?"

"Oh Ed!"

"I know, bloody silly, but I didn't want to go back to my boring flat, so I drove. And then I realised I was too tired to drive home. I only meant to have a nap, but I slept 'till morning. Just made surgery, looking a bit rough I must admit."

Sophie couldn't help laughing. "Well that really was stupid."

"It certainly was. I just overreacted. I thought you were making an excuse because you didn't want to see me. I'm sorry. Of course you had to go and see Polly."

Sophie gave him a guilty look. "To tell you the truth Ed, I was going to ring and cancel our date. I thought things were moving a bit too quickly for me. I needed time to catch my breath. Then I got the message about Polly and I used the coward's way out. Sorry."

"I guessed it was something like that."

Sophie threw her head back and laughed. "Are you always so perceptive?"

"I deal with porkies in the surgery every day. You get to know when the exact truth is not been told. It's the inflection of the voice."

"I should have been honest with you."

Ed reached out to touch her hand. "I don't care a damn. So, how do you feel now?"

"About what?"

"Us."

"I would like to go on seeing you."

"I would like that very much too."

"Good that's settled then. Now, how about eating before that bloody pager of yours rings?"

The Laurel Ladies had triumphed again. They were beginning to think they were invincible. Two more matches before the end of the season and already they were only two points away from promotion. Good spirits buzzed like a swarm of bees around the bar as they sipped their drinks, having said a breathless good-bye to the opposing team. Polly's team-mates were delighted to see her back and playing as well as usual. The only outward sign of her ordeal was the yellowing of the skin above her right eye. Emily had played a blinder, forcing all thoughts of Jack and the night to come out of her mind. Clarissa had won a close contest and her face was still flushed from the exertion. Belinda, as expected had trounced her opponent. Sophie had been the only one of the team to lose. Unlike Emily, she had failed to wipe thoughts of Ed from her mind and they had proved too distracting.

Sophie had never believed in the *one true soul mate* philosophy, at least not until she'd met Ed. "He's turned my life upside down," she said to Clarissa as they walked slowly to the car park. "It may sound dreadfully corny, but I don't think I knew what the word *love* meant until I met him. Okay, I know what you are going to say. *You've known him for such a short time—step carefully.* I keep saying that to myself as well, but the answer comes back, so what."

Clarissa laughed. "Actually I wouldn't have said that. I fell in love with Ted in a pub, half pissed on pints of warm beer and I've never lived to regret it. Nor am I a guidance counsellor. I think we are all different. Some of us fall in love slowly, feel our way with care, analyzing every move we make. People like us just go for it, and I've yet to see any statistics that tell me the one is more successful than the other."

"That gives me hope," laughed Sophie as they reached the old Morris. "Is that thing safe to drive?"

"It gets me from A to B and it has an up-to-date MOT, but every journey is an adventure."

"I can imagine, said Sophie smiling as Clarissa forced open the driver's door. "Rather you than me!"

"That's what Ted says." Clarissa threw her squash kit on the back seat and pecked Sophie on the cheek. "I think you could be in love, don't fight it." She settled into the worn seat, checked that the gearbox was in neutral and with a wave of her hand started the engine. For a moment, Sophie thought the old car was going to rebel, but after a few turns of the key it spluttered into life. "Good girl," shouted Clarissa. "Better go before it has second thoughts. See you soon—and Sophie."

"Yes?"

"Don't let Ed go." With that parting remark she eased her way out of the car park, leaving a trail of obnoxious fumes in her wake.

Clarissa sang tunelessly as she nursed the old bucket towards home and Ted who, if true to form, would have made her a pile of her favourite peanut butter sandwiches (death to her weight.). He would disentangle his scruffy body from the embrace of the battered old sofa and plant a wet kiss on her lips, before retiring to the sitting room and turning on the dodgy television excited (well, as excited as Ted could get about anything), that in about half-an-hour's time he'd be romping in bed with an eager Clarissa.

Sophie pulled into her driveway feeling great. Too bad that she'd lost her game, but there was a man out there worth more than just one lost game. She parked the BMW and ran towards the house, scooping up Samantha as she ran. Her hand was shaking as she unlocked the front door. In the hallway, she dropped Samantha, threw her squash kit onto the floor and flew to the telephone. The red light was flashing. He'd rung! Ed had kept his word. She pressed the rewind button. His voice floated across the hallway.

"Hello it's me. We forgot to fix our next date."

Sophie sank to the floor and drew up her knees, swaying backwards and forwards. Jesus, he had such a wonderful voice. She dialled his number, held her breath. "Be there, please be there." She was not disappointed.

"Sorry to ring you so late. I expect you need your sleep."

"Stop apologising, Sophie. I've been waiting for you to ring."

"You have?"

"Promise. So when can I see you?"

"Got to go to London for two days," she said sadly, "but how about next Friday?" She heard Ed sigh. "I know it's too long, but like you I have to work and I've got to finish this bag design or I'll be in all sorts of trouble."

"Okay, next Friday it is. I'll pick you up around seven."

"Wonderful, but don't expect me not to ring in the meantime."

"I would be devastated if you didn't."

Jerry Gordon was nursing a very large grievance. Another day was checking out and, as on most evenings since his son's death, he sat alone in the front room of his Portsmouth council house mourning Phil's tragic demise. It was a death that few cared about, or so it seemed by the poor turnout at Southampton Crematorium. Not even his poxy ex-wife or that bitch Polly had bothered to turn up. What kind of women did that make them? Mind you, he'd have probably smacked Polly one, so on reflection she'd made the right choice. Even so . . . BITCH! Jerry gave a wry smile. No doubt if it had been his coffin about to hit the bonfire, half the Hampshire Police force would have been there to celebrate. He drank greedily from his glass of neat whisky. The room did nothing to lift the air of gloom that hovered over him. It was bereft of furniture except for a small pine table and the armchair he was sitting in, which had once been white, but was now dirty brown. The fag ends scattered over the bare wooden floor bore testimony to the fact that Jerry was a heavy smoker. It had not always been this way. Janice, his wife, had kept the little house immaculate, stoically absorbing the strains of a deeply unhappy marriage, but once she'd wisely deserted the marital nest, Jerry had not bothered with such mundane duties as hoovering. Now, with no carpets left and most of the furniture sold to help feed his inexhaustible desire for whisky and cigarettes, the hoover sat in the corner of the grease-encrusted kitchen, covered in the dirt it should have been picking up.

Jerry scratched irritably at his unshaven chin and cursed his luck. In what he'd thought was going to be his hour of triumph he'd been thwarted, firstly by a cow called Musgrove and then by a careless driver. Did he never have any luck? A cut of his son's alimony was the least he could have expected. With it, he'd planned to retire from petty thieving and live the life of Riley. He'd even been down to his local car dealer and eyed up a nice little second-hand Porsche, daring to dream that he might pull a big bosomed bimbo to keep him entertained, but then some demented judge had been swayed by Musgrove and ignored Phil's valuable contribution to the marriage. He had even suggested he was an idle young man. There wouldn't be a cut of the house now that Phil was dead. End of fantasies. The meal ticket he'd been savouring had well and truly gone up the swanny. It was replaced by an irresistible desire for revenge and Jerry, being a rat, decided that nothing would give him more pleasure than re-arranging Polly's attractive features. Better still, confine her to a wheelchair for the rest of her life. He gulped another mouthful of whisky and began to plan his revenge. The Old Bill would be watching him like a hawk so it would be wise not to do the job himself. That would mean hiring one of his mates, and that would cost, and he never had spare cash. Even for a man with the IQ of an amoeba, and half cut from whisky, it became obvious to Jerry that there was only one answer.

Chapter Eleven

"I think we should buy another dog to keep Charlie company in his old age," said Ted, with more hope than conviction.

Clarissa gave him a very funny look. "No! They shit and pee everywhere and slobber over visitors. Not a good idea when we depend on garden produce for a living. Don't get me wrong you old softy, I love Charlie, but adding to the canine population is not a good idea. It's okay in the right place and here is most certainly not the right place, at least not until Charlie departs this world or we retire—if we can ever retire, which given our meagre income is highly unlikely."

Ted was in a persistent mood. He'd just seen an advert in the local paper, The Hampshire Chronicle, for some eight-week-old black Labrador puppies. "Look at Charlie," he said. "He's lonely."

Clarissa snorted, looking at the old dog curled up by her feet, his eyes closed and his back legs twitching gently as he no doubt dreamed of yet another futile rabbit chase. "If he's lonely he's been that since you got him, so why is it suddenly a problem for him now? He looks happy enough to me."

Opting for persuasion rather than argument, Ted put an affectionate arm round her waist. "He needs a young friend to keep him on his toes. It's bad for him to sleep all the time."

"Ted Harvey," Clarissa growled, swinging her large breasts towards him, "there is no way you are going to get round me. Nothing will change my mind. We are not having another dog."

Ted wasn't quite ready to give up. "You'd love it once we had it here, and think how much Charlie would like a companion."

Clarissa's breasts swung aggressively. "Have you asked him? Anyway, it changes nothing; my answer is still NO!"

Ted opened his mouth for one last despairing try. "A black lab it would be. You love black labs. It wouldn't be a problem."

Clarissa snorted again. "Not a problem! An eight-week-old puppy not a problem? Come on Ted, I wasn't born yesterday."

Ted knew when he was beaten, but then a daring idea struck him. He could simply go out and buy a dog without saying a word to Clarissa. Next week, when Clarissa returned happy from the squash club, he could have the puppy waiting for her. It was a gamble, but hadn't moving in with Clarissa been a gamble? Maybe on reflection that was a bad comparison, but he really did want another dog.

Time was dragging for Sophie. The chatter was all focused on what Polly should do next. Sympathetic advice was being given in abundance and Polly seemed grateful, but Sophie was in no mood to join in the conversation. It was not that she didn't have her own ideas, or that she didn't feel sorry for Polly. It was just that she couldn't stop thinking about Ed. Her appetite was zero, her nerves were frayed, and all she wanted to do was go home, lie in a scented bath, and make herself beautiful for Ed—glorious, wonderful Ed—even though they weren't meeting for another three days.

The end of lunch came as a welcome relief.

Once home she put on a Van Morrison CD, and with the best intentions in the world sat down at her dining room table and shuffled through the papers until she found her drawings of her new handbag. She started to hum quietly to the music and soon her eyes misted over and her concentration faltered. Come on, she thought, this is your bread and butter, this is what gives you the money to live in a house like this. She shook her head to clear her mind. Perhaps the wine at lunch had been a bad idea. She moved to the kitchen and poured herself a glass of water before switching on the kettle. She drank greedily, then made herself a cup of tea and walked back to the dining room, passing the telephone. For a moment she was tempted to pick it up and dial Ed, but thought better of it. It was evening surgery and she knew it was the one time he switched off his mobile. Besides, she really had to get down to work. How could she explain to impatient buyers that she'd been distracted by the attention of a man to die for? She could imagine their faces.

Reluctantly she sat down at the table and stared at her drawings.

Her bath was warm and she sank deep into the frothy water, washing off the grime of London. She was on top of the world. Her bag, the design of which she'd finished in the early hours of the morning, had proved a success. Her reputation was still intact. Close call though! Now a new shoe design had to be worked on. But first, there was an evening with Ed. What more could a girl wish for?

"Talk about being a dark horse. Oh oops, pun not intended," said Jack rather sheepishly. "In the short time I've known Sophie, I would have said she was a real loner, dedicated to her work with no time for men."

"I must admit when I first met her I thought that as well," said Emily. "But this Ed fellow has well and truly turned her head. She can talk about nothing else."

Jack laughed. "Like you do about me."

"You conceited sod."

"Are you telling me there are other men?" It was meant as a joke but suddenly Jack felt incredibly guilty. He reddened and stared at the floor.

"I do believe you're a tiny bit jealous," taunted Emily.

Jack was regretting this conversation, fearful of where it might lead. It had to be cut short. He moved quickly to her side and ran a hand through her hair. It was as soft as when he'd first touched it. "Of course I'm jealous," he mumbled, glad she could not see his eyes. "I wouldn't want any other man running his hands through your hair."

Emily moved to his touch, leaning against his body, feeling his warmth through her clothes. She sighed and turned to face him, her mouth half-open ready for his kiss, but the kiss didn't come. Instead, Jack backed away. She looked at him, puzzled. "Jack?"

"Sorry Em, I'm bushed, dreadful week."

She was about to say, "that has never stopped you before," but thought better of it. They had never argued over something as special as making love. She swallowed her disappointment and said, "You do look tired, darling, but maybe later?"

Jack smiled weakly. "Later, yes later. Let's do it later."

Emily controlled her desire and kissed him lightly on the mouth. "Come on, I'll make you a drink and then you can serve me your best *Tesco special* ever."

Jack did his best to meet her gaze. "I didn't have time to . . . ."

"Oh," was all Emily could gulp.

There was an uneasy silence before Emily said, "Well, we will just have to go out to the pub. I've no food here. But Jack . . ."

"I know, Em, and I'm terribly sorry. It was go to Tesco and miss my train, or forget Tesco and get back to you on time. I guessed the latter was more important."

"I need a little time to think about that," said Emily not attempting to hide her disappointment for the second time that evening.

"It won't happen again, I promise, and the roses are by your bed."

Emily sighed. "Maybe I'll forgive you then, and I know how hard you work. I just hope this isn't a prelude for us taking each other for granted."

"No way, and I'll make up to you tonight," promised a relieved Jack, taking her in his arms and burying his face in her neck. How he loved her smell, her smooth skin, the way she moved. God, he loved her to bits. So how on earth had he stepped off the train one day, having made love to her just a few hours before, and put their whole relationship at risk?

It was just like any other day: a real effort for him to get up enthusiasm for the work that lay ahead. He folded the Times, slipped it under an arm and joined the queue to get off the train. As usual, he suffered the pushing, listened to the moaning and thanked God that he had a beautiful woman at home who would be waiting for him in five days time with her usual open smile and welcoming body. He stepped onto the platform and started the walk to the exit, along with a few thousand other people, all making their way to various parts of London. He passed under the large clock and noted he was running twenty minutes late. He would have to forgo his usual taxi ride, which gave him time to relax and turn his mind to the week ahead, and take the tube instead. He hated the crush, the stampede, the noise and the claustrophobic atmosphere of the London underground, but when needs must . . .

She was sitting a few rows in front of him, facing him, her face ashen, her eyes half closed, her blouse torn. In her shaking hands, she held a magazine that was threatening to drop from them at any moment. Her long dark hair was matted. Even so, it could not hide her beauty. A young man sitting on her left was doing his best to ignore her. On her right, an older man was staring at her in disgust. Everyone around her seemed oblivious to the woman's obvious distress; it was the way things seemed to be these days. Jack was jammed between a woman who smelt as if her body had never been touched by soap and two young girls, each lost in the music coming from their iPods. He stood there, staring at her for several minutes wondering whether he should push his way to her side and ask if she was okay; another part of him warned, "Leave well alone." Then they made eye contact. The shock of seeing the desperation written on her face made Jack's heart jump. He tried what he hoped was a reassuring smile and was rewarded by a weak smile back in return.

He made a decision. At the next stop, he'd get to her side.

Chapter Twelve

Sophie met Ed at her door. For some reason she felt flustered, not like her at all, possibly because she had never before opened her door to a man with whom she was dying to fall into bed with. "Ed," she gasped.

"Who else?"

Sophie laughed. "Sorry, I think it's just because it's been such a long time since I've been in this situation."

"What situation?"

"Oh, just seeing a man I want to be with."

It was Ed's turn to laugh. "Well, that's a good start to the evening anyway."

"And right now I want to tear your clothes off," Sophie wanted to say. Instead, she said, "Want a drink here or shall we go straight to the pub? I presume we are going to the Wickham Arms?"

"The idea of having a drink here is very tempting, but I think we should be going. We are going to the Wickham Arms. Is that okay?"

"Anywhere would be wonderful. By the way, you haven't kissed me yet."

"I was saving that for the car."

"Then let's not waste time."

The Wickham Arms was humming. Ed shouldered his way through the crowd towards the bar, pulling Sophie with him.

"Wow this is full!" Sophie shouted.

"Always is on a Friday evening," Ed shouted back. "Want to go somewhere else?"

"No, I love this sort of place. Makes me fizz."

"And you look fantastic if I may say so."

"You're not too bad yourself," Sophie retorted as they successfully reached the bar.

"What's it to be," Ed asked. "Champagne?"

"I think I'd prefer a white wine tonight. Champagne goes to my head very quickly and I want to be able to savour every moment of this evening."

Ed leant across and kissed her gently on the cheek. "You can have whatever you want, and you smell good."

"Can I help you sir?" interrupted one of the two barmen, appraising the stunning woman standing in front of him.

"How about we order a bottle of Sancerre and then we can take it to our table," suggested Ed.

"Okay, that sounds good."

Ed ordered.

"Getting back to your remark before the barman intervened, I would like to add that you don't smell too bad either. Nice aftershave, Ed."

Ed laughed. "Bought it specially."

Sophie liked his laugh; it was light, unforced, and genuine.

A few minutes later, there were two glasses in front of them and a bottle of Sancerre in an ice bucket. The barman uncorked the bottle, taking his time so that he could stare at the lovely vision standing opposite him. Later, while taking a break from the rush at the bar, he announced to his colleagues, "I've never come across such a strikingly beautiful woman before. Made my heart positively thump she did."

They ordered almost the same as they had eaten the last time, only changing the Caesar salad for smoked salmon. The dining area was as noisy as the bar and they had to strain to hear their words. They laughed and shrugged, and gave up the unequal struggle to have a conversation while they ate, contenting themselves with searching each other's eyes and working out what it was that so attracted them to each other. Sophie was surprised how easy she found it sitting with a man who was still a relative stranger to her and saying little. Ed felt the same. He could stare at Sophie all night. No need for conversation. She was drop dead gorgeous in her plain white dress, and a pearl necklace decorating her long slim neck. He was in love, absolutely no doubt about that, even though he knew nothing of what lay underneath the beauty. That, he thought, was going to be his next step once they were out of this mad house, alone and able to explore each other.

This was more or less in line with Sophie's thinking, although the desire to explore Ed's body was uppermost in her mind. She wasn't yet in love.

How could she be? But she was getting very close. As he ate, she took the opportunity to study him, searching for a chink that might tell her he was a con, but his eyes were honest, his smile gentle, and his attention very, very welcome. She liked the way he moved his hands, his long fingers stroking the table. They would be nice stroking her back she dared to think. She liked the way he was dressed: casual, but smart, clean and crisp. Blue and white, nothing flashy, no tie. She admired his hair, the rather military cut suited him and she knew from running her hands through it that it was soft and clean. In short, everything she saw was a plus, but what lay inside this man who had so brazenly pursued her? She finished her salmon and put a hand across the table. The desire to touch him was irresistible. His fingers moved over the back of her hand, softly, erotically. She needed to see into his soul. If she liked what she saw then maybe, just maybe, she'd allow herself to fall in love.

Two hours later they left the pub. Ed put his arm around her waist and they walked towards his blue Volvo. "And now what?" he asked, opening the passenger door for Sophie.

You take me home and we fall into bed, she thought, but a little voice was saying, 'Don't rush it.' So, reluctantly she said, "You drop me off."

Ed sighed loudly. "Okay."

Sophie smiled in the dark. She'd heard his disappointment. She leant across her seat and drew his face towards her. She kissed him hard on the lips. "That can wait, Ed darling." She kissed him again. "Disappointed?"

"Very, but you're right. Just don't keep me waiting too long."

They both laughed. The understanding had been accepted with good humour. "Next time," she said quietly. "I can't wait too long."

"Is that a promise?"

"A promise, and I never break a promise."

Ed chuckled. "Thank God for that!"

He drove slowly because he didn't want to say good night.

Ted had been sent packing to the old green house at the bottom of the garden. Well, that was how it had started out. Now its dilapidated frame served as a storeroom for old flowerpots, bedding-out boxes, bits of leaky hose and several wooden handled garden tools, long since discarded for the more practical steel handle variety.

"You must clean it out one day," Clarissa had suggested. Ted had nodded and thought it would be a few more years before he got round to that. Now he smiled ruefully in the dark and thought it would have been a damn side more comfortable if he'd motivated himself and done as Clarissa had suggested, but then he hadn't planned to spend a night under its leaking glass roof with mice and the puppy as companions. He stroked the soft black fur of the small creature lying up against his chest, aware that this was her first night away from the warmth of her mother. He doubted that his hairy chest offered such comfort. It was not the first night that Ted had planned for her, but if he was honest with himself, it was the one he'd feared. She would be miserable, but no more than Ted. Clarissa had been furious when she'd come back from the squash club and found him sitting on the sofa cooing to a fat bundle of black fur, with Charlie lying at his feet growling. He'd never seen her so angry, and although his stomach was telling him it was time for supper, he knew he hadn't a hope in hell of getting it. One plus: at least Clarissa hadn't thrown him out altogether. So, there was hope he told himself, as his stomach gave him another sharp reminder that it was not up to being starved, but starved it would remain. He'd blown it for today; all he could hope for was that by tomorrow, Mount Vesuvius would have finished erupting.

"Do you know he had the gall to suggest we called her Clarissa," Clarissa laughed. "I said I'd call it shit-arse."

The table shook with laughter. "And how is your bad boy now?" asked Polly.

"Remorseful is how I think I would put it. I don't think he fancied another night in the old green house."

"So he took the dog back?" asked Belinda.

Clarissa smiled. "He offered, which was all I wanted. So no, the dog is still with us. I've made my point. That's good enough. Ted's welcome to the new woman in his life just as long as he looks after her. You know, feed her, clean up her shit, and wash the carpet when she pees. Well actually, come to think of it, the carpets might look better with a new pattern on them. And I must admit Charlie does seem to have taken on a new lease of life. So Ted's forgiven."

This was greeted by further hilarity, only ending when Belinda chose to change the mood by saying, "I wouldn't have let him off so easily."

That only goes to show how little you know about Clarissa, thought Polly.

"There's always a time to be generous Belinda," advised Clarissa. "A partnership is a compromise. If you can't compromise, you're done for. Anyway, I'm a real softy at heart and although I still think it would have been better to wait until poor old Charlie was in his grave, it won't be long before I love the little mite almost as much as Ted and Charlie."

Belinda did her best to smile.

"And what have you called her?" asked Sophie.

"It's Bella."

"Nice name," said Sophie rising from the table. "Sorry girls to break up the party, but I've got work to do this afternoon, and I need to have a clear head. Finishing touches to my new handbag."

"And no doubt an evening with Ed afterwards," stated Emily.

Sophie smiled—hated the way the girls constantly pried—but had quickly realised that gossip was meat and drink to them. She had to admit that she enjoyed it too at times, but she wanted Ed to be off the menu. Fat chance, she thought, the smile fading into a frown.

"Oops, sorry to be nosey," laughed Emily, spotting Sophie's frown.

Sophie smiled shyly. "Apology taken. Oh dear, that sounded terribly grumpy. Not meant, Emily, I promise. Now I must go. See you all on Thursday at the club."

"Bye Sophie," four voices said in unison.

An hour later, the rest of the girls weaved their way out of the hotel. The usual flow of wine had made them light-headed.

"Sophie's love affair seems to be going well," commented Polly as they walked down the street. "She was positively glowing today."

"I wish people could keep their emotions to themselves," Belinda complained. "Quite frankly it doesn't interest me that Sophie is making a fool of herself with a man she hardly knows."

"Well, who's the arsy one?" teased Emily. "Go and have a good shag, Belinda. Lighten up a bit."

Belinda reddened, feeling anger rise to her throat, but thought better of launching a tirade at Emily. Best to smile. Better for the team to think she was frigid, but one day, she thought, I'll have the guts to come out. She threw a longing smile at Polly, raised a hand and walked away.

"That sounded like a bit of jealousy if you ask me," remarked Emily. "Funny girl that, can't make her out. I think her hormones are up the creek."

"How do you mean?" questioned Polly.

"I think she's a lesbian."

Polly looked stunned. "A lesbian? Surely not! I just think she's lonely. She's certainly good at her job and she's always been very kind to me. Even asked me on holiday when that stink was on over Phil being killed."

"Well, there you go then," said Emily. "Need I say more?"

"Meaning what, Emily?"

"Work it out Polly. Even for you it can't be too difficult a puzzle."

Emily was feeling the familiar butterflies in her stomach. It was always the same whenever she met Jack's parents. It was not like her at all. She prided herself on being able to deal with any situation that came along, but Jack's father had made it clear from a very early stage that he did not like her. Even though, under intense questioning, Jack had said she was imagining it, Emily knew that his father didn't think she was good enough for his son.

Five minutes had passed since they sat down to Sunday lunch; when Jack mentioned the word marriage, Emily's stomach tightened.

"Don't you think you should give it more time?" suggested John trying his best to smile at Emily. "It's not that I don't want you two to get married, I just wonder if it's the right time."

We ought to know each other by now, Emily thought, and waited for Jack to say it. He didn't. To her surprise, he nodded and said, "I understand your concern, father, but we are only considering it. Nothing is final yet."

"Nothing is final yet!" shouted Emily as they drove away from the house having endured a thoroughly awkward lunch. John had eyed Emily as if he knew his son would never tie the knot, while Jack's mother had downed glass after glass of red wine and smirked knowingly at her son. "Nothing is final yet!" Emily repeated. "What the hell were you saying, Jack? I thought we'd agreed last night. I've always thought you are frightened of your father. I'm well aware that he thinks I'm not good enough for you and, and," she paused, shaking with fury, fighting for control, "you've known that all along. You're a turd, Jack"

Jack turned white, not from anger at Emily's outburst, but from guilt. He'd been weak, as he always was when facing his father, but worse than that, he was being deceitful. "I know I'm a turd," he tried to joke.

Emily was not even faintly amused. "Don't you dare make fun of the situation," she shouted. "What the hell were you doing in there?"

And that, thought Jack, was the sixty-four dollar question. He could hardly say that to Emily. He made great play of fiddling with his rear-view mirror, buying time to work out an answer. Finally he said, "I know I was wrong and I'm sorry, but I thought it wasn't the time to put pressure on Father."

"Pressure on your bloody father! How do you think I felt?"

"I know. I know I should have just told him we were getting married and faced the consequences."

"The consequences, Jack! For God's sake, we've been living together, sleeping together, and going everywhere together since we were at uni. Is there something wrong with me? Oh God, Jack, don't tell me *you* don't think I'm good enough for you!"

"No, it's just that . . ."

Emily put a hand on Jack's shoulder. "Why don't you just shut up and drive."

"Do you really think this girl is right for you Jack?" asked John hopefully a few days later. "She's the only girl friend you've ever had, apart from a few schoolboy crushes. Don't you think you should play the field a bit before thinking of settling down?"

Jack stared at his father. He'd pulled himself together in the last forty-eight hours and calmed Emily down with the promise that he'd go and see his father and stand no nonsense. "I will discuss marriage I promise."

"And you'd better mean it," Emily had smiled, feeling a little guilty that she was giving Jack such a hard time, especially as she wasn't totally sold on the marriage bit anyway.

"I think it's a bit late taking me to task, Father," Jack said. "We've already settled down. Why don't you just come straight out with it? You don't like her. What's the matter with her? Not good enough for you?"

John moved uneasily in his chair. True to form, he dodged the issue. "You're wrong; it's not that at all. You're free to marry who you like."

Jack knew that was balls. "But only if you approve of her," he said, feeling the familiar anger growing inside him. Why, just for once, couldn't his father be honest with him? "Don't worry, Father I will marry who I like. I don't need your permission to marry Emily."

"Then you might lose everything."

"Oh come on, Father, don't try that one on me. You know I don't need your money. How many times have I told you that I would never live here? So, go ahead, disinherit me and leave your wealth to one of mother's favourite charities, and see if I care. I'm earning more money than you could ever dream of. Come to think of it, you've never earned money." Jack saw his father redden and braced himself for the onslaught."

"Why you ungrateful, arrogant little twerp! I work all the hours God gives me so that one day you can enjoy this place. This small part of paradise. You may well be cleverer than me. Come to think of it, I bloody well hope so given all that money I spent on your education. One thing is for sure though, you didn't learn any respect for your elders."

Jack shook his head. "You're deluding yourself, Father. You haven't worked a day in your life. This was all Granddad's. With his hard-earned money he bought the farm and this beautiful house, and you and mother have lived the life of the idle rich since his death."

John leapt from his chair. "I've had enough of your insolence for one day. I'm going into the garden to help your mother. Much more pleasant than sitting here with you and being abused. Do what you damn well like, Jack. Marry the little girl, but don't expect your mother and me to grace the wedding."

Jack made to walk out of the room, but then thought better of it and stopped to face his father. "Grace the wedding, Father? What makes you think I'd even ask you?"

He was shaking badly as he left the house. Now what the hell was he going to do?" I wish to God that I'd never got off the tube, he thought.

"Oh Jack, perhaps you shouldn't have been so rude," suggested Emily. "I know you find him difficult, but I'm sure he loves you. It's just the way fathers behave sometimes."

"No, you're wrong. Fathers do not behave like that. He is a one-off. He's living in the nineteenth century. Just look at him, ensconced with mother in that vast house, a cook, a butler and a gardener to pander to their every whim. Mother supports various charities only because she thinks it's the right thing to do and will get her a VIP ticket to heaven, and father fiddles about with his garden and plays the stock market. Then he thinks he can dictate who I see and what I do. You should have heard him when I first told him I was going to work in the City. You'd have thought I was committing a crime."

"Well, I do admit I can't quite make him out," said Emily determined to be kind.

"You're not the only one."

"I don't think I've ever asked you if you love him."

"I try, but it gets more difficult."

"And your mother, how do you feel about her?"

Jack ran a hand across his jaw. "That's a question I've been asking myself for years. In a way, I feel sorry for her, stuck with father. I sometimes think it must seem as if she's in prison, but then I hear her agreeing with father when he's having a go at me and I find myself despising her. I'm sure I loved her once, but now I'd be pushed to say I still do."

"That's so sad, we need our parents," said Emily, thinking of her wonderful relationship with her father. She would hate not to love him. "Dad means everything to me."

"But that's slightly different, isn't it," suggested Jack. "After the death of your mother he needed you."

"I don't think that made any difference. I have always loved and respected him. Yes, he does depend on me more now, of course, especially as my sister and her two children are thousands of miles away in Australia. I'm quite sure she loves Dad as much as I do, but I'm here and she's not. I can't expect her to cart two young children half way round the world whenever Dad needs help or cheering up. Anyway, you know this already Jack. I don't know why I'm telling you again."

"Because you were trying to say how important parents are, and probably dropping a hint that I should make more of an effort with mine."

"I wouldn't presume to tell you anything of the sort. I just think it's sad."

"Why doesn't your father remarry?" asked Jack, keen to get off the subject of his parents.

"He'll never remarry. Mum was everything to him. He once told me that there wasn't a woman living who could replace her. Okay, he has a lot of friends as you know, but I don't think that is enough."

"You're right; it's not quite the same."

"No."

"Then I think it's time we cheered him up."

"Meaning?"

"Let's not talk about it any more. Let's get married. Father can go to hell."

"I said yes, of course," a still slightly stunned Emily told her father. "But I was surprised that I didn't feel more excited. Actually Dad, if I'm being entirely honest, my first thought was why spoil something that is so perfect. I have you in the week and Jack at weekends. If Jack and I stayed as we are, life would just move along peacefully and the fragile relationship Jack has with his parents might stay intact.

Jonathan ruffled his daughter's hair; so like her mother's. He constantly thanked his lucky stars that Emily had so many of her mother's traits. It made his loss just a little more bearable, but he'd never want Emily to feel that he was dependant on her, which is why he'd bought her the house in Winchester. He'd been lucky that Jack was away in London for most of the week because it gave Emily plenty of time to visit, and he didn't feel he was in any way intruding on her relationship with Jack. Marriage would more than likely bring this comfortable arrangement to a halt, but it should not be an obstacle to Emily marrying Jack.

"I'm old fashioned enough, darling, to think that if you want a family—and I'm sure you do—marriage is the answer. This living together thing might be trendy, but children need stability. I think marriage provides that. What was it your mother and I used to say to you?"

"What you do with your life is your own affair," answered Emily.

"And there I go lecturing you on the values of marriage," laughed Jonathan. "I must be getting old."

"Not old, Dad, just caring. I love it."

Jonathan smiled. "So, do what you think is right, Emily. If your mother was alive I know she'd agree with me."

Emily shook her head. "I'm not sure what I think is right at the moment. Marriage will make a huge difference, Dad. I can't tell you how excited I get every Friday night when I come back from the squash club and wonder if Jack will be at home with the packet of *Tesco Finest* in the oven and the roses by our bed. Will he do things like that when we're married?" Or is the freshness getting slightly jaded already, wondered Emily. "Marriage will take away a little bit of that feeling of living on the edge, and I'm sure that is one thing out of many that keeps our relationship so very, very exciting. I just hope tying the knot doesn't ruin all that."

Jonathan took one of Emily's hands in his and smiled. "I think it's time we put the kettle on and discussed this wedding. You've known Jack a very long time. I don't think marriage will spoil anything. He loves you Emily and that should be enough."

And he did love her with all his heart, Jack kept telling himself as he sat on the London bound train the following Monday. And yet . . . How could he let doubts creep in now? He gave a resigned smile, wondering how many other people had been caught in the trap. This was nonsense! Emily was his only love, trusting and always there for him. Why was he even questioning marriage?

The answer to that would be waiting for him when he stepped off the train at Waterloo in half-an-hour's time.

As she had done every Monday for two years, Lucy Hemming was waiting for him by the large clock as he walked into the main concourse of Waterloo Station. She kissed Jack warmly. "A good weekend?" she asked.

Jack hesitated briefly. "Tricky."

Her face showed no emotion. "Does that mean it's the end?"

"Might be."

Lucy was quick to pick up the sadness in his reply. There was no need to ask the reason. She had been preparing herself for this ever since they had met. She was ready for it; she guessed he wasn't. She took a firm grip of Jack's hand as they walked to where she'd parked the Smart car he'd bought her on the day he'd presented her with the keys to a flat in Lambeth. She looked up at him and smiled. There was not a hint of rancour in her voice when she said, "You know what you said to me Jack?"

He nodded and squeezed her hand hard. He looked crestfallen.

"That's good then," she said positively. "I always knew this day would come. I hope you don't need reminding."

"But . . . ."

She touched his lips gently. "It was our agreement. I will be disappointed if you can't stick to it."

"How can you be so nonchalant, Lucy? Don't I mean anything to you?"

"Jack, Jack of course you do, but you mean more to Emily. I have never tried to take her place, nor have I ever wanted to, and you should not have forgotten that."

"I haven't."

"Then let's keep to our agreement."

She got off at Green Park Station, Piccadilly. He pushed his way through the mass of bodies and followed her. In the street she stumbled, and he ran forward grabbing her arm before she could fall. "Are you okay," he asked.

"Yes, yes, thank you." Her voice was shaky as she swept her dark hair off her forehead. She looked up at Jack, fear mirrored in her brown eyes. "Don't worry about me, just go. I'm fine now."

She was plainly not okay. Tears stained her pretty face. "I'm in no hurry," Jack said. "You look as if you need help. Here let me . . ."

She reeled back. "No please, just go!"

Jack shook his head. "I can't leave you like this. Let me see you to a bench in the park at least. Or how about me buying you a coffee?"

For a second Jack thought she was going to try to run, but instead she gave a shrug of her shoulders. "No coffee thanks, I hate coffee. A bench will be fine, but please don't touch me."

Jack nodded and pointed to the park. "Come on then, follow me."

"You will go once we've found a bench?"

"If that's what you want."

"It would be for the best."

They walked slowly. Jack saw she was dragging a leg. He risked looking at her face again and saw her wince. He noticed her left cheek was badly swollen, as if she'd received a heavy blow. Had someone hit her? Was that why she was so nervous? He'd noticed she had no handbag. Not many women moved without a handbag. Of course! She'd been mugged. "Are you hurt? Did the mugger get your handbag?" he asked, spotting a bench and pointing.

"No! I wasn't mugged."

"So what happened to you?"

She stopped, turned to face him. "See this," she said, pulling back the sleeve of her left arm. It was black and blue. "And this." She swept her hair back and exposed a large swelling above her left eye. "And this," she said, gently touching her cheek.

"You fell?"

"Oh yes, stranger, I fell hard."

"I think I should take you to a hospital."

"Oh no, not a hospital, more like a lunatic asylum."

"I don't get it."

She gave a bitter little laugh. "For sticking with my husband, my loving gentle adoring husband, or so he told me on our wedding night."

They reached the bench and she dropped onto it. "The loving, the gentleness, lasted all of two months. Then came the blows."

"Your husband did this!" Jack exclaimed horrified.

"Regularly."

"Dear God!"

"Well God did fuck all about it!"

Jack sat down beside her. "Have you been to the police or one of these places for battered wives?"

"If I had I'd be dead by now."

"Your husband would try to kill you?"

"Without a thought."

"Jesus! Want to tell me about it?"

She stared at him biting at her lip. She was making a decision. "How long have you got?"

"All day," he heard himself say.

"I swore I'd never expose my heart to anyone ever again, and yet you look kind. Most men look kind until they've got what they want. How do I know I can trust you?"

He shook his head slightly. "You don't. It's a gamble you must take. I have no way of convincing you that I'm just worried about you. I don't know how to make you believe me."

She smiled then. "Okay."

"I know we had an agreement," Jack said. "But I'm finding it very hard to think I won't ever see you again."

"Then you should have done as I told you that first day when you came to my rescue. You should have left me on the bench and walked away."

"I'm glad I didn't."

They reached the car. Lucy turned to face Jack, a sad smile crossing her freckled features. It was one of the things Jack found so attractive. "It ends here, Jack. I'm not driving you to the office today, or ever again. It has been wonderful knowing you and you have restored my confidence in the human race. I will always be grateful for the way you stood by me against my husband and for all your financial support, but that's it, Jack, you've done enough. I'm a big girl. I can go out on my own and plan my life again. I don't need you, Jack."

Jack grimaced. "God, that's a bit cruel, Lucy."

"I know, but how else am I going to get it into that thick brain of yours that there is someone out there who needs you more, and was with you long before you played the white knight." She kissed him on a cheek and quickly got into the little car. "Goodbye, Jack, have a good life." She stared ahead hoping that he couldn't see her tears.

Chapter Thirteen

Jerry Gordon rode his motorcycle towards Polly's cottage. He wasn't entirely sober, having downed half a bottle of Jack Daniels to bolster his courage, which probably wasn't very wise given that the bike was un-taxed and uninsured. He knew he was taking a risk, but he was not the sort of man to waste money on such trivialities. He just had to hope that the Filth wouldn't stop him, and spoil his carefully laid plans.

The night chill burnt into his face as he coaxed the old machine for more speed. He wrenched at the throttle, impatient to get to Easton while his anger was up. "C'mon you bastard," he spat, but the bike paid no attention. A half-moon dimly lit the lanes and a thin mist rose from the river Itchen. It was not the perfect night for a half-cut man on a dodgy bike to be out.

He reached Easton without incident just as the church clock struck 10 p.m. and drove into the Horse and Jockey car park. Grief ripped through his chest. His boy would still be working there behind the bar if it hadn't been for that bitch Polly. He lingered at the pub door, fighting the urge to throw another Jack Daniels down his throat. He resisted, and patted the bottle of petrol tucked deep in his overcoat. The golden liquid would taste that much better after he'd wreaked his revenge.

There was no one about as he walked the sixty yards to Polly's house. The lights were on. He imagined her curled up on the sofa watching The News. By tomorrow she could be featuring on it. He crept up the path to the front door and silently lifted the letterbox. By twisting his head, he could see the arm of a cream sofa with a foot resting on it. "Time to say bye-bye," he whispered. Then a thought came to him: he'd like to see Polly's face as the flames crept towards her, like to hear her pleading for her life. He wanted to shout, "This is for Phil," as he hurled the bottle onto the floor and then watch it break; see the lethal liquid moving like a snake towards

Polly. Then he'd throw the match, and boom! He imagined her screams. So, instead of lighting the fuse and dropping the bottle through the letterbox, he rang the doorbell.

"Shit," Polly mumbled. Who could that be at this time of night? She rose reluctantly off the sofa and flicked off the television.

As she walked out into the small hallway, the bell rang again. "Okay, okay, I'm coming," she shouted. She flicked back the security lock, turned the key and started to open the door. The door handle was ripped from her grasp as Jerry threw all his weight against it.

"You!" Polly exclaimed, fear starting to rumble in her stomach.

Jerry closed the door behind him. "Yes me, you little bitch. Didn't expect this did you?"

Polly shook her head, shock rendering her speechless.

Jerry grinned. He was aroused by the fear etched on Polly's face; it was good to feel the power. He belched loudly and shook a clenched fist at Polly. "I told you I'd get you one day."

Polly found her voice. "You're drunk," she said bravely. "Whatever you plan to do, don't do it. You know the police will suspect you. Do you want to go back to prison?"

It was not what Jerry had expected; for a moment he was taken aback by this brave talk. He swallowed, licked his lips and stared at Polly. "That sort of talk will get you nowhere," he finally managed to say. "My life is finished without my son, so I don't care about the Filth. I'm in a prison already."

"So what are you going to do?"

"This," crowed Jerry pulling the bottle out of his coat pocket. "This is petrol. I'm going to throw it at you and watch you burn."

Polly's eyes widened with fear. She was frozen to the spot, her brain said run, but her legs wouldn't respond. "Please," she begged, "don't do that. Let's talk."

"Bugger you, bitch," Jerry shouted. With some force he threw the bottle onto the floor. Just as he'd hoped, it smashed and the petrol crept towards Polly. She watched it mesmerised, fear paralysing her. Jerry let out a triumphant laugh and went to pull out the matches. His hands were shaking so badly that he had difficulty extracting the box from his pocket. He swore. Then the box was in his hand. He smiled and tried to open the box, fumbling, as drink made him clumsy. The matches cascaded to the floor. He fell to his knees and desperately tried to pick up a match and the box. He was crying with frustration.

It took Polly just short of ten seconds to realise this was her chance. In desperation she lunged at Jerry, her feet slipping on the wet floor. She fell on top of him and her momentum catapulted them the short distance to a wall where Jerry's head cracked against the unforgiving brick and plaster. He collapsed in a heap and didn't move.

Oh God, I've killed him, was her first thought as she disentangled herself from his limp body. Her second thought was that it might be a good thing. Terrified he would regain consciousness and come after her, she raced into the sitting room and dialled 999. It was answered on the fourth ring. She swallowed and tried desperately to control her voice. "I'm being attacked. I'm being attacked. Please come quickly." She managed to give her address, the calm voice on the other end of the line easing her panic. "Police will be with you as soon as possible."

"Please hurry, I'm trapped!" Then with her heart in her mouth, she went back into the hall. Jerry had managed to roll onto his back so he wasn't dead, but blood was pouring from a gash on his forehead and he was deathly white. For a second Polly felt a rush of sympathy. The man had lost his son. He lived all on his own. He had a right to blame her for Phil's death. He was a failure, one of life's losers. Then she saw the pool of petrol, the smashed bottle and the spilt matches and she remembered his violence, his evil smiles, and his constant threats towards her. Sympathy was replaced by disgust. Jerry was a man it was very easy to despise. Polly then did something totally out of character: she kicked him hard in the ribs and smiled as he cried out. She was moving her leg back to take another swing when three armed police officers burst through the open front door and she found herself being bundled into the sitting room.

"Looks as if we arrived just in time," said an Inspector sniffing the air. "You better get those clothes off a bit swiftly madam, you're soaked in petrol."

Jerry moaned. The Inspector smiled down at him. "Get yourself out of this one, Jerry Gordon."

Polly sat alone, sipping a glass of water, trying to calm herself down. What would have happened if the police hadn't arrived when they did? She shivered at the thought of what she might have done.

When the police had finally left, the Inspector had tried to reassure her. "We have all the evidence we need Mrs Gordon. I don't think Jerry Gordon will be bothering you again."

It would take more than a few comforting words from an Inspector to convince Polly that Jerry was at last out of her life. Okay, he'd be out of circulation for quite a while, given that he'd probably be facing a charge of attempted murder, but one day he'd walk out of prison and then get on with unfinished business. He might even have friends on the outside that would be happy to smack a woman around.

She thought of ringing Belinda, but quickly discarded the idea. She didn't want sympathy. All she wanted at that moment was for Jerry Gordon to be dead.

"Samantha," Sophie said in a voice that Samantha knew meant she was in trouble. "Stop being a nuisance. Leave Ed alone and get off the sofa." Samantha sat up and stretched lazily, her claws deliberately scratching the sofa fabric, her eyes fixed on Ed's grinning face. "Go on get off you rotten cat." Sophie laughed. Samantha, being a wise cat, knew it was time to withdraw. She dropped silently onto the floor, where she sat on Ed's feet and started to clean herself.

"I think she's summing me up," laughed Ed, content to leave Samantha where she was.

"I think she knows she might have to get used to you."

"That sounds good to me."

"But first, Ed, I have something I want to say to you."

"What, that you love me?"

"Don't presume so much."

Ed laughed. "So, if you don't love me, what is there worth telling me?"

"You conceited bastard. Now I don't think I want to tell you."

Ed did his best to look chastened. "Perhaps I better leave."

"Don't you dare."

"Then tell me."

Sophie jumped out of her chair and threw herself beside Ed. "Hey, don't you remember what I said to you the other night?"

"It's slipped my memory."

She slapped him playfully on a cheek. "You lie."

Ed gently laid a hand on her thigh. "Of course I lie. How could I ever forget?"

"Then come on, we're wasting good time."

"Hussy," laughed Ed as he pulled Sophie off the sofa.

"And it was wonderful," Sophie heard herself telling Clarissa the next evening at the club. She was surprised to hear herself being so frank because she had always recoiled in horror at the thought of discussing her sex life with anyone. "No regrets, just this warm feeling still flowing through me. Lucky our season has ended or I might well collapse on court. My knees still go weak when I think of that gorgeous body next to mine. Fantastic!"

Clarissa beamed at Sophie. "Told you he'd be worth sticking with, didn't I?"

Sophie gave Clarissa a broad smile. "Yes, yes you did, thanks Clarissa. I only hope Ed feels the same."

Ed did. Never had he felt so happy, so relaxed. The world could crash around him and he'd never notice. He sat at his desk in the surgery, his mind a mile away from the problems of his next patient, wishing that the hours would fly past until he was once again in the arms of the woman who had seduced him.

A fatal crash on the M3 half-an-hour before he was due to leave the surgery ruined his plans. An emergency call found him driving to Winchester hospital instead of driving to see Sophie as they had agreed. Half way to the hospital he realised he'd left his mobile on his desk back at the surgery. He swore under his breath, determined he'd call her from the hospital. He never got the chance. It was pandemonium in A & E when he arrived and a telephone call slipped from his mind as he fought to save lives. It was not until after ten that he returned exhausted to the surgery to retrieve his phone. As he feared, it was stuffed with messages from Sophie, the first wondering if he'd forgotten their date. The last registered panic. "Ed darling, where the hell are you?"

Ed gazed at the phone, mortified. How could he have forgotten to ring her? It was unthinkable. He dialled her mobile: no answer. He rang her landline.

"Ed! Oh, thank God you're okay. Stupid me, I was getting really worried about you. Where have you been?"

He told her. "And I left my mobile at the surgery."

"I should have guessed you had been called out to an emergency. You poor darling, and there I was thinking you'd walked out on me. I'm going to have to get used to this."

"And I'm going to have to remember there's someone who cares for me. Can I come over?"

"Of course. Hungry?"

"Starving."

"For what?"

"Why on earth didn't you ring me," scolded Belinda, guessing she'd missed a chance to hold Polly in her arms.

"I wanted to be on my own, to get my head together. To work out why a man could hate me enough to try and kill me."

"What makes anyone want to kill someone? But look on the bright side, just thank your lucky stars Jerry isn't one of the world's brightest sparks." Polly giggled. "Otherwise," continued Belinda, "you might have been a piece of burnt toast this morning."

"Don't remind me." Polly shivered at the thought. "I was scared witless. He was out of his mind and he'd been drinking."

"That's probably why he dropped the matches," suggested Belinda. "Now you've no need to worry about him any longer. He'll be facing a very long stretch inside one of Her Majesty's prisons."

"I know, but one day he'll come out and I don't think Jerry is the sort of person to forget. He'll come looking for me, if his tentacles haven't already reached out from the prison walls."

"I don't think that will happen. He hasn't the money to get an outside job fixed up and it will be years before he comes out. He might be old and bitter, but I can't see him having the will to come after you."

"You may be right," said Polly, "but I'll be looking over my shoulder for a long time to come."

"You must try not to dwell on it or you will become a nervous wreck. My advice is to forget him. I'm confident we've heard the last of Gordon."

"I'll try, but I don't think that's going to be easy."

Belinda gazed at the unhappy girl sitting opposite her and was filled with a desire to leap across her desk and gather her in her arms. She was falling in love. Maybe some people would be disgusted, but she didn't care. God had made her who she was and, being a fatalist, she knew there was damn all she could do about it. So, the question was how could she tell Polly without frightening her away? Maybe now was as good a time as any, when Polly was obviously in need of a little TLC. She rose slowly from her chair, her legs feeling weak, and crossed over to Polly, reached out to touch her and lost her nerve.

Clarissa was sitting on her patio enjoying a well-earned cup of tea. The summer sun was bathing the garden in a golden glow. It was the time of year she loved. The garden was showing the benefits of her hard work and, so far, the season had been pretty good. She laughed as she watched Bella doing her best to get Charlie to play. She was tugging vigorously at the old dog's ears. "Stop it pup," she laughed, taking a friendly swipe at the puppy. "He's old." Bella looked at Clarissa with her large mischievous eyes and continued to pull at one of Charlie's ears.

"Go on get off him," said Ted joining Clarissa on the patio. "The old fella needs a rest." Bella released the ear and jumped onto Clarissa's lap.

"Oh, you can't get round me like that," laughed Clarissa pushing Bella off her knee and smiling up at Ted. "Painting going well?"

Ted grunted, removing his stained cap from his head and dropping a paintbrush onto the table.

"That means you're stuck."

"Just a little. Bloody light's all wrong."

"A new landscape in the making?"

"That's the idea, but I seem to be lacking any inspiration."

"How many times have I told you that you must persevere? You're talented Ted, but painting is rather like writing a book, lonely, sometimes extremely hard work, and you have to possess the drive to finish the subject, and then you can sit back and be proud of what you've achieved."

Ted smiled wistfully. "I just wish I could paint something that I was proud of."

"You have. Those discarded canvasses in the attic are good. The trouble is you don't believe in yourself."

Ted shrugged his wide shoulders. "All I need is someone apart from you to tell me that, but no one has, so maybe I have good reason not to believe in myself."

"Oh Ted, that's downright stupid talk. How about the pictures you've sold? The buyers love them. Look at that couple who bought one every Christmas for five years, until you told them you'd run out of ideas. Sometimes you drive me to distraction. How on earth you survived before you met me I really don't know."

"I muddled along," Ted replied, slightly irritated by Clarissa's assumption that he'd been incapable of looking after himself.

"Well, I've got some news for you that will knock you sideways."

Ted grunted. "Nothing will cheer me up today."

"Why you miserable git," laughed Clarissa. "Here we are, sitting out on a lovely sunny day, our two dogs romping on the grass, and all you can do is moan—and I know how you will react to my piece of news."

"Then why bother to tell me?" His irritation was still stirring.

Ignoring him, Clarissa continued undaunted. "Last week I met a lady in the squash club who runs a picture gallery in Winchester. During our conversation I just happened to mention you were a painter, and a good one."

Ted snorted.

"Shut up Ted. As I was saying, I told this woman that you painted in watercolours, mostly landscapes, but a few portraits. I also said you were over-critical about your work and lacked confidence."

"Thanks a lot."

Clarissa ignored him again. "She asked me if you exhibited anywhere and I said only when I pushed you, but you had sold several pictures over the years to private clients. I told her it was lucky I worked as well!"

Another snort came from the other side of the table.

"I told her I ran a small market garden and that we weren't married."

"Did you tell her how many times we have sex in a week?" snapped Ted.

"Of course not! Now, where was I? Oh yes. The outcome of our conversation was that she is prepared to take a look at some of your paintings. I'd already told her there are at least a dozen gathering dust in our attic. Well, I knew I would never get you to the gallery so, the other day when you were in Bath trying to sell one of your paintings, I whipped a couple out of the attic and went along to the gallery."

"Why, you sneaky bat."

"I know, but here is the best thing. She and her partner really like them. No, don't look at me like that, they were wildly enthusiastic."

"Who are these con artists?"

"Sometimes you make me so angry, Ted. The woman I met at the club is called Jo Hawksworth. Her business partner is Amanda Flindt. They want to meet you with the idea of giving you an exhibition of your own. They like to support local talent."

"Local talent! You think I'm local talent? I really do wish you hadn't done this."

"I knew that would be your reaction, but let me tell you something, I'm going to get you into that gallery somehow."

"Never."

"Okay, then I'll send you back to sleep in the greenhouse until you change your mind. I'm serious about this, Ted, very serious, so you might as well give in now."

Ted sat back in his chair and looked up at the sun. He had no doubt that Clarissa would carry out her threat to banish him to the bloody greenhouse yet again, and probably deny him food as well. It was not a pleasant thought, and did he want to fight her that much? Maybe he shouldn't turn down this chance. He stroked his chin and fixed her with a stare. "It's blackmail."

"Call it what you like, but I have your best interests at heart. What harm will it do, just to take a few of your paintings to be looked at? Come on, I've done all the hard work."

"That you have."

"So?"

Ted rose slowly from his chair, stretched and walked to Clarissa's side. He put her head in his large paint-stained hands and kissed the top of her head. "Okay," he said gathering Clarissa in his arms and carrying her back into the house. "But you owe me one."

Clarissa made no attempt to wriggle out of his grip; she just let out a whoop of joy and held onto him tightly as he heaved her up the stairs. She was only too happy to pay a forfeit, especially the one Ted had in mind.

Chapter Fourteen

The sun beat down on the Winchester law courts from a cloudless sky. It was in stark contrast to the dark cloud that hovered over Polly. It was the second day of Jerry Gordon's trial, and within the next hour or two, she'd be facing him in the witness box. The first day had produced an unexpected surprise: Gordon had pleaded not guilty to attempted murder.

His barrister, a young man working for legal aid had been flabbergasted. "Better to plead guilty," he'd advised his client. "All the evidence is stacked against you. Might make a difference to your sentence."

Jerry was having none of that. He was resigned to going to prison for a long stretch so his last pleasure for some time would be to see Polly squirm in the witness box as he stared at her, his eyes radiating his hate. He would smile at her and shake his head and she would know this was not the end. The revenge festering in his heart would never die.

Polly had had a sleepless night. She had been so sure he'd plead guilty, despite Belinda's warning that Gordon was not the sort of man to give in easily. She squeezed her father's hand as they walked into the law courts and threw Belinda a weak smile. Already she could imagine Jerry leering at her from the dock. "Well here goes," she said weakly. "Wish me luck."

The prosecution barrister opened his case by calling the Inspector who had been first on the scene. His report was precise and left very little doubt of Jerry's intentions. The defence declined to cross-examine. Then Polly was walking slowly, with head bowed, towards the witness box, feeling Jerry's eyes burning into her back. The prosecution and defence barristers realised they would be dealing with a very nervous witness, but Polly surprised them both by giving her story in a clear and competent way.

To the prosecution barrister's last question, she answered in a strong voice, "Yes, I have no doubt that Mr Gordon came with the sole intention to burn me to death. The only thing that saved me was that he dropped the match box." Then she added looking directly at Jerry, "If you knew him, that's what you'd expect." There was a ripple of laughter round the courtroom. Jerry spat onto the floor.

To the much more aggressive questioning from the defence, she stood her ground. "He came for one purpose only, and that was to kill me," was her firm answer. Most people sitting in the courtroom agreed.

It took the jury two hours to come up with a unanimous verdict. "Guilty of attempted murder your honour," said the jury foreman. Jerry was sent to prison for life.

Polly had looked into his eyes as she'd stood in the witness box and had experienced a second of all-consuming fear, just as Jerry had hoped. She felt a terrible certainty that she had not heard the last of her ex father-in-law.

Jerry asked to see the governor. "To ask for early release eh, Matches? Bit soon for that," taunted the Screw.

Jerry's fist tightened. The Screw was not slow to spot the movement. "Go carefully, Gordon or you'll never get out of here."

Jerry forced himself to relax, trying to deck a six-foot-five Screw was not on his agenda.

"Perhaps you'd better tell me why you want to see the Governor before I bore him with some sob story."

"It's no sob story, and I'm not going to complain about my sentence. It's personal. Now just do me a favour and ask him."

"And what do I get in return," asked the Screw. "It'll cost you."

Go fuck yourself, thought Jerry. He said, "If that's what you want, you're on. Say a pony."

The Screw laughed. Since Gordon had arrived, he'd not lived up to his reputation as a man you crossed at your own risk. Far from it, he was pathetic. "I'll take that," he said, "and see what I can do."

"Thanks," said Jerry, surprised with the alacrity of the acceptance. Where the hell was he going to get the money? It was a problem he'd deal with later. He didn't dwell too long on the consequences of not paying up.

Two days later Jerry got his wish.

*

"Perhaps I should tell you the date that Jack and I have fixed to get married," Emily announced a few seconds after they had sat down at their regular table.

"When?" asked four excited voices in unison.

"The last Saturday in July, so make sure you're all doing nothing."

"Good luck to you and Jack," said Belinda glancing over at Polly.

Glasses were raised, Emily's dress discussed, honeymoon destinations suggested.

Emily held up a hand. "Okay girls thanks for the advice, but the dress is chosen and we are honeymooning in Venice. Only for a week. Jack can't be away from his job too long."

"What about bridesmaids?" Sophie asked.

"I hope you will all agree."

"What agree to be a bridesmaid?" laughed Clarissa, hoping that Emily was joking.

"That's right, Clarissa, I want you all to be bridesmaids."

"Oh my God!" exclaimed Clarissa. "I will have to get my hair done. What was that salon you told us about earlier Emily?"

There was more laughter, more wine and the time flew by.

Belinda stared at Polly.

Clarissa noticed and smiled.

The next morning, Polly woke with only the slightest headache knocking at the back of her brain. Another boring day beckoned unless her father cared to take her out to lunch. She glanced at her watch. She'd ring him once she knew her mother had gone to the golf club. It would be a chance to talk things over with him, matters that she would never dare mention to her mother, but her father would listen even if he didn't understand or approve. She desperately needed to talk to someone.

Ed woke with the sun in his eyes. One thing he'd already learnt about Sophie was that she hated having the bedroom curtains drawn. He smiled and disentangled himself from her limbs that were snaked around his body. She smelt warm and infinitely desirable, but work beckoned. He'd moved in with Sophie a week before. Sophie had been adamant. "It's daft moving into your cramped apartment when I have all this room, and then there's Samantha."

That had swung it. He put his flat on the market. It was, he thought, very courageous, cutting off the chance of retreat if anything went wrong. He was a little sad as well; it was the first property he'd ever owned. So far they'd adjusted well. It had been a week he would never forget. Deep incurable love had grown like a cancer inside him, and the pain was excruciating.

"Do you have feelings?" Sophie asked from the bed, watching his gloriously firm buttocks as he walked across the room.

Ed turned and gave her a quizzical look. "How do you mean?"

"You know, feelings. Feeling that things are okay, that the right decisions have been made, feelings for the person you live with."

"Are you asking me if I have feelings for you?"

"In a way I suppose I am."

"I would have thought that was obvious. Have you any doubts?"

"No," said Sophie thoughtfully. "I have no doubts. I love you."

Ed smiled down at her. The warm feeling inside his stomach was something to be savoured. The desire to launch himself onto the bed had to be fought—he had surgery in an hour. "Damn," he said loudly as he made for the bathroom.

Sophie smiled into her pillow, longing for him to come back to bed, but she knew he would never be late for his morning surgery. "See you tonight," she said sleepily, breathing in his smell, which lingered on the pillowcase.

"Will you be late back from London?" he asked over his shoulder.

"Doubt it. It's lunch, then a meeting. Should be able to catch a train back around five. How about you?"

"Usual time I expect."

"I'll have supper on the go."

Ed showered, dressed and went down to the kitchen. He hadn't quite got used to its size; it was half as big as his flat. He made toast, boiled an egg and made himself a cup of instant coffee. He ate quickly, not bothering to sit down. Finished, he raced up the stairs and as silently as possible walked into their bedroom. Sophie's regular breathing told him she was asleep. He stood at the end of the bed and stared down at the face that had so captivated him. Each time she smiled at him he felt as if the sunshine had fallen on him. He let out a contented sigh and left the room.

Sophie woke as she heard the front door close. She stretched contentedly. She felt really good; she was even looking forward to showing off her new shoe design. Eat your heart out Lulu Guinness. There was a new zest to her step; a feeling of well-being that she thought she'd lost forever. She had never imagined she could love someone so intensely in so short a time. He had literally bounced into her life, quite brazenly chasing her. Now that she knew him better his behaviour was even more of a surprise. Darling Ed, straightforward honest Ed. Honest as the day he was born, loving, attentive and able to bounce her out of the odd moment of misery when she thought of her parents. She dwelled on their lovemaking, which was still new and utterly entrancing. Love and sex rid the soul of cynicism and selfishness. All she hoped for was that it would last forever.

She threw back the bedclothes and let out a whoop of joy. Tonight she'd broach the subject of going to Jamaica.

Belinda was standing on the platform waiting for the London train when she saw Sophie. She was struck by how radiant she looked. It was beyond Belinda's comprehension that a man could do this to a woman. She smoothed down her dark blue skirt, brushed the shoulders of her white blouse—her battle dress as she called it—and waved at Sophie. Sophie waved back and walked towards her.

"Hi Belinda."

"Hello Sophie. Got work in London?"

"Yes, taking up my new shoe design for some Americans to see. And you?"

"Court appearance this afternoon. Divorce case. Lunch with my client first."

"You going to win?"

"Don't I always?"

"Yes, I believe you do." Sophie said with some admiration, but also feeling sorry for the bloke who was going to come face to face with Belinda later in the day. She hoped he'd have a strong drink before going into court; by all accounts the poor man would need it; Sophie knew Belinda took no prisoners.

"How's Ed?" asked Belinda.

"Just great. No, that's an understatement, he's bloody great."

Belinda was about to voice her opinion that men always seemed perfect to start with and it was later, when they had their feet firmly under the table, that their personalities changed, but she didn't get the chance. The tannoy announced the arrival of the 10.05 for Waterloo. "See you Thursday," she shouted above the hubbub.

"Yes, see you, Belinda," Sophie shouted back as she made for the first class part of the train. It was with a feeling of relief that she realised Belinda would not be in the same carriage.

Belinda always travelled second class. She could see no point in wasting her hard-earned money on a slightly larger seat. Besides, there was an even chance that at this time of the morning, wherever she sat, some lecherous man would be trying to look up her skirt. She found a seat with surprising ease and her thoughts immediately turned to Polly. It was troubling her that Polly had made no contact since the lunch. Did that mean she wouldn't be at the club on Thursday? She was letting Polly get to her, disturbing her well organised life. She looked out of the window, smiling ruefully. Why was she so surprised? Her sexuality had always bothered her. Truth be told she would love to be heterosexual. She had tried, really worked on it for a while, but in the end she had succumbed to the wiles of another woman. Now here was Polly, gorgeous seductive Polly, who had really raised her heartbeat. The feeling, as always, was disturbing, but so fucking exciting. She shook her head angrily and opened her brief case pulling out the case file. She had a job to do. Nothing must get in the way. She'd make sure she sucked every last drop of blood from the man in court today.

Jo Hawksworth watched Clarissa and Ted walk through the door of the gallery with some trepidation. Maybe she'd been a trifle over-enthusiastic at the squash club, but then two glasses of wine had often been her undoing. Now she was about to face another consequence of not being able to keep her mouth shut. For a split second she thought of diving into the back room and sending Amanda out with instructions to say she was away for the day, but that would be cowardly and she really had liked Clarissa. So, she put on her best shop-like smile and advanced with hand out stretched.

"Clarissa, how nice to see you again. And this must be Ted."

Ted did his best to scowl and failed miserably. He had not expected such an attractive woman.

"Yes, this is Ted," Clarissa laughed. "And these are two of his paintings. It took a spot of blackmail to get him here."

Jo chuckled and sent a radiant smile Ted's way. "Well, I'm glad you came, Ted. Now, let's have a look at these paintings of yours."

If Ted hadn't been transfixed by the swell of Jo's bosoms overflowing from her blouse, he'd have grabbed the paintings from Clarissa and run from the gallery.

Clarissa felt Ted tense and firmly put her free hand on his arm. He wasn't ducking out now. She handed over the brown packet and held her breath. She wanted this so much for Ted, and she liked Jo's open face, her dimples seemingly sparkling in the sun that was shining through the window. Not that a smile, or attractive dimples made any difference when business was on the line, but it certainly made Clarissa feel that at least Ted would be let down lightly when the rejection came. She thought that if she believed in God it would be a good time to look to the heavens and ask for His help. As she didn't believe any such baloney, she let go of Ted's arm and crossed her fingers behind her back.

Jo pulled back the sleeves of her green cashmere jersey, which Clarissa thought clashed with her yellow skirt and white shoes. But then, Clarissa was no connoisseur of fashion herself. "Let's have a look then," Jo said, pulling the two pictures out of their wrapping. She moved to a table and propped them up on stands. Then she took a few steps back and stared, one hand rubbing her chin.

Clarissa held her breath. Ted coughed nervously.

"I've seen worse," Jo said thoughtfully. "Actually, much worse. In fact, these are quite good. Do you mind if I get my partner in to take a look?"

"Feel free," gasped Clarissa daring to hope.

"Is it worth her while?" asked Ted.

"Of course it is," Jo answered fixing Ted with a *you really are a miserable sod* look. "Amanda," she shouted. "Can you come and look at these paintings?"

Amanda Flint came bustling into the room. She was petite and in her mid-forties, Clarissa guessed, and comfortably dressed in a long brown skirt and matching blouse. Paint covered her hands and a paintbrush rested behind her left ear. She was rather drab, Clarissa thought, but then, remembering Ted's scruffy ways, perhaps that was the way all artists dressed. "Yes Jo?" Amanda asked.

"Amanda, can I introduce you to Clarissa Duncan and her partner, Ted. I had a talk with her at the squash club the other night and suggested she and Ted paid us a visit. What do you think of these?"

Amanda took her time appraising the paintings; she had learnt it was a mistake to be too eager. Finally, she said carefully, "Not bad. Which of you painted them?"

"I did," apologised Ted. This earned him a painful kick on the shins from Clarissa.

"Did you now, Ted, if I may be so familiar?"

"Call me what you like," said Ted. "I doubt if we'll see each other again."

"Oh, you really are a dreadful pessimist," laughed Jo. Turning to Amanda, she asked, "Well?"

"I like them; yes I do, very much. You have talent Ted."

"You're kidding me," gasped Ted.

"I never do that," retorted Amanda. "This sky on the moor painting is exciting, and the trees on the other landscape seem almost real. How long have you been painting?"

"Many years now."

"How many a year?"

"Maybe seven, most of which have been crap."

"Clarissa kicked him again."

"Let me assure you these are not crap," said Amanda. Jo nodded her head in agreement.

"So where do I go from here?" asked Ted, rubbing his sore shin, but brightening up considerably.

"Well, first of all we've got to persuade you that you have great talent, get you over your shyness. I think the best way to do that is to discuss an exhibition or, if that is too big a step, we'd very much like to buy these two off you and decide on any more that you have stashed away."

"He has dozens," interjected Clarissa, looking at Ted.

"An exhibition!" gasped Ted. "I couldn't possibly agree to that. I would just be making a fool of myself. Come on ladies, these two paintings can't be worth more than £25 unframed."

"Is that what you've been selling them for?" asked Jo.

"Sometimes less."

"Well, this will surprise you then." Both women stood for a moment looking at the pictures one more time. "We'd have to frame them," said Amanda. "Then I would guess we would sell them within a month. I would pay you a £100 each. How about you Jo?"

"Yes, I think that's about right, maybe a little on the generous side for a first timer, but we'd look at it as an investment."

Ted felt his knees go weak.

"And" added Jo moving close to Ted and displaying more of her ample bosom, "I think it would be safe to say that if your other paintings are as good as these we could pay you the same price. Go away and think about it. My choice would be to have a small exhibition. There would be lots of interest. I wouldn't be suggesting it if I wasn't sure. Give us a ring in a few days." She lent forward and gave Ted a peck on a cheek.

Ted reddened. All he could do was nod.

"In a few days," confirmed Clarissa.

As expected, Sophie arrived home before Ed. That was good. She'd rustle up his favourite meal, a chicken casserole. That would keep both her lodgers, as she called them, happy. Samantha would get the left over pieces of chicken and Ed would rub his stomach and say he wondered how he'd ever survived without Sophie's cooking. Life was so, so good. She needed a bath before getting to work in the kitchen. London made her feel dirty, but she loved it—the bustle and the noise always managed to excite her. Not to mention the adrenalin rush as she'd sat the other side of a table and heard the complimentary remarks about her new shoe design wash over her. She ran up the stairs and threw off her clothes. Samantha, lying at the end of the bed, purred and did her usual flip onto her back. "No tummy rub tonight, I'm in a hurry," said Sophie, blowing Samantha a kiss. Samantha gave Sophie one of her hard-done by looks and jumped off the bed.

By the time Ed walked through the door Sophie was bathed, scented, and dressed in jeans and a light blue T-shirt. She closed the oven door on the casserole. He came up behind her and wrapped her in his arms, kissing the nape of her neck. "You smell good."

Sophie turned round and smiled. "It's new. I bought it today. Like it?"

"I'll say."

"Which is more than I can say for you," she said wrinkling her nose. "You smell like a hospital."

"That's where I've been. One of my old patients was admitted with a bad heart attack this afternoon. I've been visiting him. Doubt if he'll survive the night."

Sophie knew by now how much Ed hated seeing a patient die. She would never be able to understand how emotional he got. It made her realise that doctoring would not have been his first choice if his parents had lived. She'd always thought doctors had a sort of indifferent mechanism to death, but not Ed. He would do his best to be his usual cheerful self tonight, but his mind would be elsewhere. He was gentle and caring and suffered with his patients; probably even felt their pain. She'd never try to change him, because it was part of the Ed she loved. "I'm so sorry, darling. Was he young?"

"Eighty-five."

Sophie ran her hands down his cheeks. "We all have to die sometime you know Ed, and it seems to me he's had a pretty good innings."

"I know. But . . ."

"You're a loving man," said Sophie completing the sentence her way.

When Polly walked into the Café de Paris, a small chic restaurant on Winchester's Jewry Street, she was half-an-hour later than she should have been. The restaurant was noisy and she was feeling distinctly uneasy, not at all sure in what direction her hormones were taking her. She had been careful to dress in a way that Belinda could not construe as being flighty. She was deliberately late, rather hoping that Belinda would give up waiting for her. That was not to be; there she was, sitting at the back of the restaurant nursing a glass of wine. The only outward sign of concern was the frown on her face. Polly moved hesitantly towards her, unsure what the next hour would bring.

Belinda made no effort to stand, just waved at the chair opposite her. Polly sat. "I'm sorry I'm late, Belinda; bloody car parks are jammed full. I expect you thought I'd forgotten or something."

Belinda gazed with longing at Polly. "No, no I had every confidence in you," she croaked.

"That's good then," laughed Polly. "Not many people have confidence in me. Anyway, here I am. So what are we going to gossip about?"

Where the hell is this taking us, thought Belinda. She was a mish-mash of emotions. She was in no mood to discuss Polly's tardiness or the state of the city's bloody car parks. She wanted to voice her feelings. "I haven't asked you out to supper to gossip, Polly."

"Then what?"

Belinda leant across the table and reached for one of Polly's hands. "I love you."

Polly rocked back in her chair and pulled her hand away. "You what?"

"I love you."

Polly's first inclination was to burst out laughing. She stared at the large picture behind Belinda. It was of two young people kissing in Paris. Had Belinda chosen this table to make a point? Paris and kissing added up to love. No, that was bizarre. Yet what could be more bizarre than a woman asking her out to supper and, before they could even order their meal, proclaiming undying love! This was not what she'd expected. What had she expected? She knew that Belinda had strong feelings for her. But love! So she swallowed the laughter and said, "Jesus Belinda, isn't that a bit strong?"

"Don't tell me you haven't noticed?"

"I . . . I had an inkling you liked me."

"Liked you! Come on Polly, you must have known it was more than that."

Polly was still very close to treating the whole scene as a joke; it was too weird to be anything else. Yet, simmering close to the surface was a strange feeling of exhilaration. She bit back the dismissive reply that was her instinctive response and, instead, said, "I've never been in this sort of situation before, you know, being propositioned by a woman. It's a little hard to get my head around. And you certainly don't mince your words, Belinda." Suddenly aware of the other woman's vulnerability, she softened it with a gentle smile.

"What's the point," Belinda replied, feeling a little apprehensive. Had she moved too fast?

Polly shrugged. "At least you're honest. No point in beating round the bush I suppose." She suppressed a laugh at her unintended pun.

"Glad you see it like that. Drink?"

"I'm gasping."

Belinda filled Polly's glass from the bottle she'd ordered earlier.

Chardonnay. Not Polly's favourite wine, but she badly needed a drink.

"So you're not going to run for it, tell me I'm a dirty lezzy, or whack me with that rather large hand bag you're carrying?"

Polly carefully crossed her legs under the table and forced herself to take a long slow drink. She needed time to get her head together. Eventually she said, "No, I'm not going to do any of those things, but I can't say I love you, Belinda. I'm not saying it's sick, but, wow, it does seem weird. Sorry."

"You needn't be. But I had hoped." Belinda grimaced. Why was it she always made a fool of herself in situations like this?

Polly fiddled with the menu a waiter had given her. "I'm just stunned at how forthright you have been. Is this how a lesbian behaves, so brazenly? No courtship, no subtlety. It was so unexpected. As you have been so blunt, maybe I should be as well. I admit I have been having strange feelings about you: some exciting, all very disturbing. Right this moment I can't explain any of it, but I do know this scene does not come naturally to me. I have always thought of myself as one hundred percent heterosexual. It's a bit scary."

"When you think of me?"

"Yes, and being so brazenly propositioned doesn't make things any easier." She paused and watched the disappointment cross Belinda's face. "Tell me honestly, Belinda did you expect to sleep with me tonight?"

For the first time in her life, Belinda felt herself blush. She fiddled with her napkin unable to meet Polly's stare. "I was hoping," she said quietly, looking at the tablecloth.

"Oh my God! Oh my God!" exclaimed Polly. "You can put that idea right out of your head. If you only got me here in the hope of dragging me off to your bed, I think I'll skip supper. Listen, I mean no offence, Belinda, but I really can't take this heavy stuff."

Belinda blew out her cheeks. "I'm sorry. I went over the top, but please remember what I said. I was not lying. I have deep feelings for you, Polly. Are you sure you won't stay and eat with me; the food is delicious."

"I think I'd better not."

"Okay. Still friends?"

Polly rose from the table. "Of course, always friends. See you tomorrow night at the club."

Belinda watched her walk away, her emotions playing hell with her stomach. For someone who carefully researched every word she uttered in court, it was amazing how careless with words she could be in her private life.

Polly walked into her house and hurried towards the kitchen. She was gagging for a chicken sandwich and a very strong mug of sweet coffee. Once the sandwich was made and the coffee in the mug she moved to the sitting room and threw herself on the sofa. That had been quite an experience! The burning question was how should she deal with it. There was no doubt she felt something, but Belinda's rather crude advance had completely thrown her. How could Belinda have imagined that she could sleep with her just like that? Couldn't she have been a little more subtle! She thought knicker-ripping was a male prerogative! She took a long pull of her coffee. She had to do something about this situation. Doing nothing was what she'd done for most of her life and look where it had got her. Alone and confused—surprise, surprise. This time it was no good putting her head in the sand. Belinda wouldn't go away. Did she even want her to? That, she decided was the sixty-four dollar question.

She crammed her mouth with chicken and bread. Eating had always livened up her brain cells. All her privileged life she had been like a dog running after a bone. It had got her nowhere. Not quite true; she had caught Phil.

"You'll never have a career," her mother had enjoyed telling her. Well she liked to think that marrying Phil had been some sort of career, but not many people saw it that way, more like a charity. So where did that leave her? Lost. She was stuck in a house that wouldn't sell; she dreaded having another relationship with a man; she worried every day that Jerry Gordon would somehow get to her, and getting a job did not appeal. Just bloody great! She drained her mug and finished her sandwich. Maybe cuddling up to Belinda would solve all her problems, or would it just bring on new ones? Think before you jump this time, she thought. Okay here goes. She liked Belinda very much, so no problem on that count. Could she sleep with her? Could she love her? Unlikely, but she would almost certainly feel safe under her protection. That would mean a lot to her. Belinda was strong and successful and she admired that. Polly shook her head and was tempted to do what she always did when faced with a difficult problem: move it onto the back burner and conveniently forget all about it. Not this time.

Chapter Fifteen

"How about coming to Jamaica with me?" suggested Sophie.

"I can't imagine there's anything I'd like to do more," answered Ed. "Just one tiny problem; I doubt if I'd get any leave."

"I don't mean right now, but say in a week," Sophie laughed.

"You're serious."

"Never more so."

"I might be able to swing it in a fortnight. That would give the practice time to find a locum."

"Use compassionate grounds."

"I don't think wanting to go away with my girl friend would come under that heading."

"But to see her ageing grandparents might. Worth a try."

Ed smiled. "Okay I'll have a go tomorrow, but I can't promise, so don't dash off and buy the tickets."

Sophie pushed Samantha off Ed's lap. "That cat is in danger of usurping my place," she joked.

"Getting close," laughed Ed, winking at Samantha as she stalked out of the room.

"Well watch it, I don't like competition."

"I'm all yours."

"That's what I like to hear."

"I just want to make you happy."

John O'Rourke had started his practice, three miles out of Winchester, twenty-five years ago with three doctors and one receptionist. Now there were ten doctors and a team of nurses, receptionists and pharmacists occupying a large modern building, and administering to nearly four thousand patients.

Sometimes the sheer size of the operation left him reeling and thoughts of retirement were niggling away, which is why he'd interviewed Ed. He'd immediately liked the young man and thought he had the potential to make the sort of GP he'd want in the practice. He'd offered him a post, in spite of suspecting that he might not yet be ready to settle into a country practice. He'd had a small bet with his wife that this idealistic young man would turn down his offer. No one had been more delighted than O'Rourke when Ed had proved him wrong.

Now he sat behind his desk, fiddling with a paperweight, as Ed asked if he could have time off to go to Jamaica with his new girl friend. "Very irregular," he growled at Ed, "Damned inconvenient. Do you really have to go?"

Ed decided to be honest. "No, I can always say I can't go, but it would mean a lot to her if I could go with her. She lost her parents last year in a plane crash and this would be her first visit to her father's parents since the crash. I think it will be an emotional time for her. I would like to be there."

O'Rourke said nothing, just stared at Ed and drummed his fingers on his desk. Ed feared all was lost, but when O'Rourke eventually spoke, it was with a smile and a shrug. "I'm persuaded, Ed. This girl of yours sounds just what you need and of course you must go with her. I look forward to meeting her. So, I can offer you a month's sabbatical. That should do shouldn't it?"

"Yes, yes, more than enough," said Ed excitedly.

"Good, that's settled then. One more thing before you go Ed. I happen to have a high regard for you, or you would not be getting this favour off me. I think you are making a good GP. I like your approach to your patients and I admire your dedication, something sometimes lacking in young men these days. It is hard to find men of your calibre, so when you return, which you will won't you?"

"I promise."

"We would like to offer you a partnership. What do you say?"

"How did you pull that one off?" asked an amazed Sophie that evening.

"I have absolutely no idea," said Ed, deciding it would be injudicious to tell her that he'd played a little on the death of her parents. "O'Rourke is a man of few words and is not known for being generous. I must have got him on a good day. By the way he wants to meet you."

Sophie could hardly contain her excitement. "I think I'd like to meet him too. Fix a day and time, probably before we leave. He sounds a generous man, and of course wise as well."

"What do you mean by wise?" Ed asked.

"He's offered you a partnership hasn't he? Obviously, like me, he thinks you'll make a great doctor."

To say the letter came as a surprise to Belinda was an understatement, and it left her with quite a problem. Did she tell Polly or did she deal with this on her own? She had to look at her options circumspectly, and not allow her emotions to take charge. She read the letter three more times before coming to a decision. She picked up the telephone and rang the prison. The answers the Governor gave to her questions made up her mind. Gordon was up to something. He was not the sort of man to apologise, whatever sob story he had spun. It was a ruse to try to get his sentence shortened or, more than likely, to try to put the frighteners on Polly. Rightly or wrongly, Belinda decided to deal with him on her own. For the second time that day, she rang the prison.

Clarissa was sitting on her garden seat, a glass of very cheap, almost undrinkable white plonk in her hand. She was looking across the table at a beaming Ted, who was on his second whisky. They seldom drank in the daytime because it made them both feel sleepy and they seldom had time for a bit of shut-eye during the day. Today was different. Things like this didn't happen every day and the plants could take a back seat for once. Ted had at last been recognised!

"Good on you!" Clarissa said loudly, reaching out to touch Ted's hand. "I'm thrilled for you, darling."

Ted looked at Clarissa over the rim of his glass. "Still can't believe it. I keep thinking I'll wake up any minute and find myself digging another row of potatoes."

Clarissa chortled. "Don't go getting any ideas. You will still have to dig potatoes. This is not an excuse to put down your spade forever. Your paintings aren't going to keep us you know."

Ted squeezed Clarissa's hand. "I know, love, I know, but just let me live in a dream world for today."

Clarissa looked lovingly at his flushed face. The years seemed to have dropped off him. She realised how much it meant for him to have his talent at last recognised; a talent he'd constantly denied. It was everything she'd always wanted for him: a career. No longer would he walk around the smallholding thinking he was always in her shadow. His confidence needed a boost and he'd got it. "You can dream all day," she said with a smile. "You deserve it."

Sophie was browsing the web for airline deals. The offers were so numerous that she felt quite bewildered. Ed had suggested she might find it easier to go to a travel agent, but she'd been determined to find a good deal. Now her enthusiasm was waning. Perhaps Ed had been right. She sat back in the chair and stared at the screen. Her mobile rang. Shit! She ignored it and turned back to the screen. A few minutes later it rang again. "Shut up you bloody thing," she shouted reaching for a glass of water by her side. She drank and waited. Silence; good the message obviously had got through. Okay, one last attempt to find a deal. After that she'd take Ed's advice. The telephone rang again. "Oh damn," she cried and picked up the mobile. "Hello!"

"Oh, feeling grumpy are we?" a familiar voice enquired.

"Ed! Sorry. I was busy on the internet and thought you were bound to be one of those bloody people trying to sell me something, or telling me I've won a bus trip for two driving through Croatia."

"Sorry to disappoint you. I'm ringing to say you've won two tickets to Jamaica."

"What are you talking about?"

"I've got the tickets. Business class as befits your status. We leave next week."

"But I thought . . ."

"I thought it would be easier if I did it. I know what an expert you are on the web."

"You're not too hot either," Sophie countered.

"Correct, but there's this great secretary in the practice."

"You cheating toad!" She heard Ed laugh. God, how she loved that laugh. "But thanks, I was just about to put my shoe though the bloody computer. Only problem would have been if I'd already booked."

"Well you haven't so no point in worrying about it."

"Oh you are so damn pragmatic."

"Must go. Love you. See you this evening."

"Love you too, and that all sounds great. See you."

Emily was sitting in the garden with her father. It was at times like these that she loved just being by his side, watching the sheep in the paddock at the bottom of the garden and the swallows elegantly swooping over the pond. A comfortable silence enveloped them. No doubt her father was thinking of her mother as he often did, but it no longer bothered her. She knew he still missed her terribly and no doubt sometimes wished it was her sitting beside him, rather than his daughter. The hurt she had experienced when told this by the well-meaning friend had evaporated. Besides, she was happy and all she wanted to do was pass some of her happiness onto her father. What better way than to discuss her wedding plans? She looked at her watch and broke the silence. "Dad, the caterer and Jack will be here any minute."

Jonathan jumped, mentally pulling himself back into the present day. "Of course, we'd better go inside." He reached for Emily's hand and gave it a squeeze as he rose from the garden chair. "Let's go and have some fun with your future husband."

Happiness was the last thing on Jack's mind. Lucy filled the space. Their parting had been much more painful than he'd ever imagined. What else could he have reasonably expected? He'd been deluding himself by thinking that he could walk away from her without feeling any emotion. She'd warned him many times, but he'd chosen to ignore her. Now he was paying the price—a very painful price. The feeling of guilt that stubbornly refused to go away did not help it. It was no good trying to kid himself that he had nothing to feel guilty about. He had blatantly deceived Emily. It might not have been quite so bad if he hadn't slept with Lucy, but he had. The first time was brought about by too much alcohol. It had broken the agreement between them and was, initially, deeply regretted by both of them. It had, inevitably, led to more sex. Jack sighed. What was done was done, and he'd have to live with it. Now Lucy had proved that she was much stronger than he was, able to walk away as she had always said she would, providing he still loved Emily. He did, by God he did. He'd told himself this every day since he'd kissed Lucy good-bye, but the truth was he loved Lucy as well. He was in a no-win situation. Of course, he wasn't entirely to blame. Lucy could have walked away at any time and disappeared back into the heaving mass that was London. Perhaps he should feel that she'd treated him badly, had taken his generosity, played with his emotions. No doubt that would assuage his conscience, but it just didn't wash. He'd enjoyed the relationship; now he was miserable and heading for a marriage that he wasn't sure he wanted. At least his parents would be pleased if he voiced his doubts. Deep down in his heart, Jack had always feared he was a coward. He wasn't brave enough to see the pain on Emily's face as he confessed his duplicity. Nor did he want to see the look of *I told you so* on his father's face. So, he would say nothing and hope that, once married, he'd find it easier to forget Lucy's freckled face and go back to loving Emily the way he had done for so many years. He was disgusted with himself. He looked at his watch. Damn, he was going to be late for the meeting with the caterer. Better get his skates on.

Lucy felt so alone. It was proving harder than she had thought it would be to wipe Jack out of her mind. She had been deluding herself, telling herself that she felt nothing for him except gratitude. Jack was Jack, infinitely desirable, clever, good company and very handsome. How she'd managed to get into such a mess amazed her. It was no good saying he'd insisted on going on seeing her; it had been a two-way thing. After all, she could have walked away, should have walked away. She thought of him holding Emily in his arms, whispering sweet nothings in her ears, and for the first time in her life she experienced jealousy. She wiped a tear from her face and looked round the little flat. There was only one thing to do: draw a line on two years of happiness, years that she knew she didn't deserve, and write to Jack to tell him she was leaving the flat and had no more use for the car. They were his to sell, or whatever. She reckoned it was the only way she could forget him. She found some writing paper in a desk drawer and started to compose the most difficult letter she was ever likely to write.

Chapter Sixteen

Belinda walked through the gates of Belmarsh prison, feeling good. Jerry Gordon was in for a big shock and that pleased her greatly. She couldn't wait to see the smile wiped off his fucking ugly mug.

A warden led her into the visiting room. "There he is, madam," he said, pointing at Gordon. "Take care. He's easily upset."

She didn't bother to tell him she'd already been on the receiving end of his temper, or that there was a pretty good chance he'd explode within the next half-hour.

Jerry looked up as she sat down, facing him across the wooden table. His face went through several emotions before it settled on shocked surprise. "You!" He managed to croak.

Belinda gave him an acid smile. "Right on the button, Gordon. Did you honestly think I would allow Polly to come and see a low-life like you?"

Jerry's face reddened, but somehow he managed to keep his temper in check. "I told the Governor I wanted to apologise to her face. I've changed Miss fucking Musgrove. I told the Governor that I wanted Polly to know that. I wanted to tell her I no longer blamed her for my son's death and that I was sorry for trying to set her on fire."

"That sounds pathetic, Gordon. Let me tell you what you really wanted to do. You wanted to shout at her, threaten her, and tell her you had boys on the outside who would finish the job you made such a hash of. You didn't want to apologise, you know you won't get your sentence reduced just by uttering a few rehearsed words. You tried to pull the wool over the Governor's eyes you pathetic little man, but he's not a Governor for nothing. He saw right through you, so he wrote to me, not to Polly. She has no idea I'm here and never will. I'm here to watch you squirm because I'm a sadistic bastard rather like you. So go and crawl back to your cell where you belong. You must be in your element here." Belinda looked round the room at all the shifty faces and repeated, "Yes, you must be in your element."

Jerry's desire to stop her taunting him by decking her proved too much for his brittle temper. No amount of prison counselling could ever eradicate this fault-line in his make-up, and the bitch was getting to him fucking big time. She was enjoying every moment. He leant across the table and spat in Belinda's face, his fists clenched.

Belinda was wiping the saliva from her face when Jerry erupted. With a roar he leapt out of his chair, sending it crashing to the floor. For a man not known for his agility, he leapt onto the table before a warden could stop him.

"I want you dead, bitch," he screamed, successfully bringing the whole room to a stunned silence. "Do you hear that, eh? I want you and that fucking little whore dead! I'll get you both I promise."

All hell broke loose. The other prisoners started banging their tables with their fists and thumping the floor with their feet. Some tables were overturned and fights broke out with the screws. In the melee, one warden grabbed Jerry's feet and hauled him off the table before he could swing a punch at Belinda.   •

"Alright Gordon, that's it," shouted the warden, putting a tight lock around Jerry's neck. "It's the cooler for you and then up in front of the Governor tomorrow. I always suspected you were faking this remorse bit."

Red-faced and half-strangled, Jerry couldn't reply. The warden turned to Belinda. "Sorry love, best to get out of here quick with all the other visitors. I think we're going to have a bloody riot. All because of you, you tosser," he shouted at Jerry, tightening his hold on his neck."

Belinda was already on the move with the other visitors. The majority were talking excitedly to each other, but a few who thought she'd messed up their visiting time, jostled her, mumbling obscenities under their breath. She didn't care. She was feeling thoroughly pleased with herself. She doubted that Jerry would ever try to get in touch with Polly again, and as for his threats, well, they were a load of hot air. He didn't have the kudos or the money to pose a threat from inside the prison.

The West Indies flight from Heathrow landed smoothly at Montego Bay. It was a hot cloudless morning, though scattered thunderstorms were expected later in the day. The last time Sophie had felt so excited was when Ed had moved in with her. She looked out of the window as the plane taxied down the runway towards the terminal building. It had been a long time since her last visit. She felt Ed's warm breath on her neck and she turned to smile at him. Even after a night on a plane, he looked as if he'd just slipped into fresh clothes. "How on earth do you manage to look like that?" she asked.

"Like what?"

"So tidy and clean."

"I just went and freshened up."

"And changed your shirt and trousers," Sophie accused him. "You've made me feel dirty. I need a good wash and a fresh set of clothes right down to my skin, but I was in such a hurry it slipped my mind. And before you launch off into one your encouraging lies I know I look a mess."

Ed chuckled, and ran a hand down Sophie's bare arm. "You should learn to plan ahead."

"Okay big head, you're a wise boy, but you were hassling me."

Ed laughed. "Well, I actually I think your dishevelled look suits you fine. A wild dusky lady has always turned me on."

Sophie slapped his face gently. "Ed, I love you."

"Well, that's lucky then, isn't it?"

"Ha! I'll have more to say about that later. Ah, we've stopped. We've arrived Ed, we've actually arrived!"

Ed went along with her excitement, releasing his seat belt and leaning over to give her a kiss. "I know how much this trip means to you, darling Sophie, and I'm excited as well. I can't wait to meet your grandparents and your two cousins."

"Really?"

"Absolutely."

"Ed, you're a star. Where on earth did you come from?"

"Haven't I told you? I came out of a Christmas cracker."

She slapped him playfully again. "Well, the cracker must have been a very expensive one!"

The drive to Ocho Rios was bumpy and hot. There was no such thing as air conditioning in the cab driven by Stirling Dover, a tall young man with a wide multi-coloured woollen hat worn over his dread-locks. He gave a smile as he explained, "No point in having all this here modern technology when we've got windows and lots and lots of fresh air man."

Sophie grimaced at Stirling's back and winked at Ed. With the dust and heat rushing in through the windows, any thought of the delights of air conditioning was best forgotten. Not that air conditioning was uppermost in their minds for long. Stirling didn't know the meaning of the word *slow*. From the moment they hit the highway it was hang on and pray.

They made it, skidding around the last corner onto a long drive leading to the hotel entrance. When they screeched to a stop, Stirling looked with satisfaction at his watch. "Record time," he announced with pride. "Daddy always says I'm wasting my time being a taxi man."

"I can see his point," Ed answered good-humouredly. "Follow Formula One do you Stirling?"

Stirling beamed. "You a racing fan, man?"

"I watch it a bit."

"Daddy and I never miss a race. No taxi driving on formula one days. But daddy doesn't think the modern driver is a patch on Stirling Moss."

"Hence the name Stirling," Sophie whispered to Ed.

Ed laughed, and then patted Stirling on the shoulder. "Thanks for the drive."

"Enjoyed it did you?" Stirling asked.

"Let's say it was exciting," replied Ed. "Your car corners well."

"Like a Ferrari," came back the reply.

"Like a Ferrari, as you say," said Sophie, exiting the cab with haste.

Ed paid Stirling and gave him a generous tip. Any man who could drive all the way from the airport to the hotel without touching his brakes deserved a reward.

"See you around, man. Here's my card. Just get the hotel desk to ring me if you want to go anywhere."

Ed made a mental note never to ask for Stirling.

Jamaica Inn was five star luxury. Two eccentric Americans—father and son, had once owned it. Both were now dead, but the memory of them lingered on with a few of the older staff, who delighted in telling newcomers of how things used to be "*in the good times*" as they put it. Dinner jackets were de-rigueur for dinner, which was served on the terrace exactly at eight every evening, and woe betide anyone who was late. The sea could be heard lapping lazily on the sandy beaches of the bay below. Every table had a candle and a red rose placed on a white linen tablecloth, and the glasses glistened in the candle light. Over the pudding, a pianist always played jazz; the two Americans who had come from New Orleans to Jamaica permitted nothing else. The food was superb and the wines good, but horrendously expensive. The rum punches, which were cheaper, more alcoholic, and tantalisingly delicious, were most people's choice. The service was cheerful but unobtrusive and every evening father and son had walked round the tables making sure their guests were relaxed and happy. After a meal, lasting never less than an hour-and-a-half, but never permitted to drag out for much longer, the guests moved to the bar, which was open to the cooling night air. There the men drank their brandies and puffed on cigars, while the women sipped liqueur of their choice. Guests could dance to the piano, sing a favourite song—if the pianist knew the tune—and go to bed knowing they had enjoyed the best hospitality on the island. It was a place to recharge exhausted batteries, to honeymoon, to maybe rekindle a love that was dying, or cement a romantic liaison and, as Sophie's mother had discovered, it was easy to fall in love with a handsome smiling barman who could sing.

Five years ago a well known chain had bought the hotel. Although the standard was still high, open necked shirts, trousers of every colour, had replaced the dinner jackets and sometimes, even trainers were spotted on men's feet. Most of the women still liked to dress for the occasion and there were not many evenings when several well-known designer brands weren't on show. The plunge pool had been enlarged, something that the Americans had steadfastly refused to do, even though they had many requests from their older clientele. "You've got the whole ocean to swim in," was always their reply. The croquet lawn had been dug up and a hard tennis court had been laid in its place; the old wooden bar on the beach had been pulled down, a larger one replacing it. There was no doubt that the old-fashioned unique hotel had changed, but the two Americans would probably have smiled and said "that's progress" without actually agreeing it was for the best.

Ed sat in a large wicker chair on the balcony of their bedroom. The sea was only a few feet away and the manager told him that it was quite safe to dive into the water from the balcony. "The fish are not quite what they used to be," he explained. "Too many boats, too many tourists, and the coral has been damaged." He shrugged and smiled an apology. "But we need the tourists so what can we do?"

Ed nodded understandingly. "The world is getting too small, but the view cannot be spoilt."

"Indeed not, sir," the manager said looking out on the azure blue sea as he handed Ed the bedroom key. "Enjoy your stay."

"So this is where your mother met your father," said Ed, once he and Sophie were on their own. "Very easy to fall in love in a place like this I would think."

Sophie walked onto the balcony wrapped in one of the hotel's white bathrobes and moved to stand behind Ed. She began to gently rub his neck. "Its heaven isn't it? I wonder if they still have a pianist and a singing barman."

Ed leant into her hands and laughed. "Well, just don't you forget it's me you love."

Sophie kneaded his neck a little harder. "Just as long as you come up to scratch there is no danger."

Ed whirled round and pulled her onto his lap. She was naked under the robe. She hadn't showered yet and she smelt slightly of sweat. Ed buried his head between her breasts and started to lick the dried sweat from her body. She moaned. "Ed, no, I stink. Let me have a shower first."

"You're out of luck, lady. I like the smell."

They slept fitfully, their bodies entwined, the gentle whirring of the air conditioning the only sound in the room. When they woke it was evening. They stood on the balcony, holding hands, watching the sun sink below the horizon and happy not to talk. The sound of the sea was hypnotizing. How long they stood there they were not sure, nor did they care, but they grew hungry.

Ed glanced at his watch and the spell was broken. "God, I'm starving," he said.

"Me too," confirmed Sophie. "And this time I'm going to have that shower. After that, let's eat."

"Suits me," said Ed. "I'll join you in the shower."

"Oh no you won't! I want to have dinner!"

"Spoilt sport," Ed teased.

A little over an hour later they walked into the bar. The clientele were mostly the same age as Ed and Sophie. The bar buzzed with animated conversation. The atmosphere was relaxed and happy. The fashionable time to visit the Caribbean had passed; the rich and famous had departed to spend their money elsewhere. In England there was Ascot and Wimbledon. On the Mediterranean there were warm seas and luxury yachts. In America the social season was in full swing. The Caribbean was at the mercy of a wilder bunch of tourists, a lot younger and hell bent on enjoying themselves. It didn't matter to them that it was hot and humid, or the beginning of the hurricane season, or that it rained most days. It was low season and the hotel prices were affordable, even in a place like Jamaica Inn. The beaches were still enticing and the kudos of having a holiday on one of the islands outweighed the disadvantages.

Ed politely edged his way through the throng of chattering people to the bar and ordered two rum punches from a smiling barman. He tried to imagine Fleming London standing there beaming at his clientele and Sophie's mother just beginning to feel the first stirrings of desire. He gave his room number and made his way back to where Sophie was standing, her back to the terrace. He stopped for a moment to enjoy her, silhouetted against the darkening sky. In her simple white dress she looked stunning; not for the first time, Ed felt his heart turn a summersault. No doubt if he was writing a book, his readers would by now be sick to death of his constant references to Sophie's beauty, but he wasn't writing a book and he wouldn't have cared a stuff what his readers thought. He had no one to bore except himself and he wished with all his heart he'd never get bored of Sophie. She was a dream come true and he would never do anything to put their relationship in jeopardy.

Which was more or less what Sophie was thinking as she watched Ed weaving his way through the packed bar with two rum punches held firmly in his hands. She was also glad that she'd taken the gamble to come to the hotel where her father and mother had fallen in love. It could so easily have been a retrograde step, stirring up memories best forgotten. Ed had tactfully voiced his doubts, but Ed being Ed had left it up to her to make the final decision. In the short time that she'd been in the hotel, she knew she'd made the right choice. There were no ghosts, just a warm glow of satisfaction that she was in the place where her mother and father had stepped across all the social barriers and fallen in love. How happy her parents would be that she'd met a man like Ed. "One in a million" she knew her father would have said.

"Hey, I'm here," laughed Ed holding out a glass. "Where were you?"

Sophie said, "Miles away. Boy that looks good." She took a sip. "Um, it certainly is."

"Let's drink this and then eat," suggested Ed. "Too many of these on an empty stomach would not be a good idea."

"Okay."

"So, are we off to see your grandparents tomorrow?" asked Ed.

"Not tomorrow, Ed. I wanted to spend a day relaxing with you here. When I wrote to Grandma, I told her we'd be with her after we'd had a day to relax. Do you realise we have hardly had a whole day together since we met. I suggest we change that."

"I think that's one of the best suggestions you've ever made. But are you sure?"

"Darling Ed, we've got two weeks here. One day without seeing Grandpa and Grandma will hurt none of us, and we will be rested."

Ed finished his drink, already feeling its affect. Food was a must. "You ready to eat?"

"Ready to go," laughed Sophie taking Ed's hand. "And you want to know something?"

"Tell me."

"It's been all of eight hours since I told you I loved you."

The next day dawned overcast and very humid. Low cloud hung over the mountains behind Ocho Rios, but that couldn't dampen the excitement Sophie felt as they left the hotel. Ed sat back in the coolness of the air-conditioned cab and thought of Stirling torturing his next lot of victims with tales of Stirling Moss, and how good it was for them to breathe in the beautiful clean Jamaican air.

"You thinking what I'm thinking," he asked Sophie as she sat down next to him.

She chuckled. "Stirling Dover?"

"On the nose!"

"Wouldn't want to be in the back of his cab today," said Sophie, stretching her legs out in front of her.

They heard their driver, Randall, give a low laugh. "You drove with Dover?"

"Yes, from the airport," answered Sophie.

Randall half-turned in his seat. "That boy is a law unto himself man. That father of his should take him in hand and make him get a decent car. We've told him this a thousand times when he's moaning about getting no business, but you can't make a tree see sense. There are many young-uns out there, all the same. Think they can do the job on the cheap."

Ed and Sophie laughed, thankful that at least one driver on the island kept up with modern technology.

The drive up into the Dry Harbour Mountains to the outskirts of Christiana was uneventful, except for several Stirling Dovers who seemed hell bent on killing themselves by careering past Randall on hair-pin bends. This reckless action was met by a long blast on his horn and a mumbled expletive followed by a return horn blast and a V sign from the passing car.

By the time they arrived at Sophie's grandparents' house the cloud had broken and the sun was glistening on the tin roof. Sophie just hoped they had received her letter, or their arrival was going to cause mayhem.

She need not have worried, for as they pulled to a stop the car was surrounded by a horde of laughing children, chickens scurrying under their feet and adults waving happily. As Sophie had suspected, Grandma had made sure all her friends and several dubious cousins had come to greet her. Most came from Christiana or the more distant Mandeville by car or bus.

Ed looked at the children tapping on the windows of the car and couldn't help comparing their smiling faces and wide bright eyes so full of life with the children he'd met in Darfur on his year helping the Red Cross. Most of them had been listless, their eyes dull, their bodies emaciated from lack of food and a proper diet. Those that survived starvation, aids, or the bullets of the marauding soldiers could only hope to live into their mid-thirties. For a moment, Ed remembered the desperate looks of the mothers as their children died, and felt ashamed that he hadn't found the stomach to stay longer. His thoughts were jerked back to the present as the door flew open and he and Sophie were greeted with a cacophony of sound. Dozens of voices were raised in welcome and eager hands tried to pull him out of the car. Their joy was contagious, and his moment of guilt swiftly passed.

Sophie moved to his side and shooed the children away. "Later children, later, we've got to see Grandma and Grandpa first, otherwise you know what will happen." The children laughed and backed away, kicking playfully at the chickens.

"Quickly Ed, on to the terrace before we get squashed," she laughed. He grabbed her hand and together they forced their way through the excited crowd. "Its obvious Grandma issued one of her '*don't you dare not be here*' edicts," she shouted above the noise of the children. "No-one would ever dare disobey her!"

Then they went up the wooden steps onto the terrace to meet the two people that Sophie had spoken about so much. The children held back; they knew the terrace was out of bounds. Ed didn't quite know what to expect. What he saw was a little lady sitting in a rocking chair, a smile spreading across her face revealing toothless gums. Her face was all wrinkles and her hair thinning. Next to her, in another rocking chair, sat a wizened old man smoking a clay pipe; he seemed even smaller if that was possible. Both looked extremely fragile, as if a puff of wind would blow them away. Yet Ed saw a sparkle in Grandma's eyes and sensed that within her wiry, slightly dilapidated frame there still lurked great energy. He wasn't sure time had been so kind to Grandpa.

Sophie's Grandmother slowly eased herself out of the rocking chair. Ed swore he could hear her bones creaking, but she was firm on her feet as she walked towards Sophie, her vein covered arms outstretched. "Ah, my happy little girl, thank you for coming to see your old grandparents again."

Sophie bent down and kissed her on the cheek. Ed reckoned she was a little less than five foot. "Grandma," Sophie said, "I told you I'd be back, and you haven't aged a bit."

"Maybe not too much on the outside, but it's in here Sophie love," Grandma said, touching her chest. "I'm not as strong as I used to be. The heart beats a little slower, and the mind is not so sharp."

Sophie smiled, remembering her mother saying she'd as good a brain as anyone who had had a fortune spent on their education. "I know she can't read or write, but tell her something and she'll never forget. I once brought her a backgammon set and within a week she was beating me."

"Well, you sure look good to me Grandma," said Sophie. "And how about you, Grandpa? I see you still love that filthy pipe." Unlike his wife, Grandpa made no attempt to get out of his chair and Ed guessed he seldom left it, just perhaps to fall into it in the morning and struggle out of it when it was time for bed. On the other hand he might never move thought Ed as he saw the pot under the chair.

Grandpa smiled, exposing a set of teeth almost black from the stain of nicotine. "I'm as good as I could expect, Sophie." His voice was weak, but melodious and Ed imagined him and Fleming once singing blues together. "Life is catching up with me," the old man continued, "but no more of this nonsense. You didn't come all this way to listen to me moaning. Come over here and let's see how you're looking. My eyesight's not quite what it used to be."

Sophie moved over to his chair and dropped to her knees. "So Grandpa what do you think?"

"You look on top of the world." He screwed his eyes up and looked towards Ed. "Is this bloom I see something to do with that man beside you?"

Sophie laughed and took Ed's hand. "Listen you two," she said to her grandparents. "This is Ed, the most wonderful man on this earth, except of course for you two."

All four of them laughed and then Grandma said, "Come here young man, let me take a closer look at you."

Ed obliged. Already he was a little in awe of Grandma. There was a stoical look about her. No doubt brought on, he thought, by years of poverty, the fight to bring up a large brood of demanding children and changes that did not always bring happiness. Through it all, Ed surmised, she'd stood there like a rock, immovable, determined, always with a smile on her face, accepting that God had dealt the cards and there was nothing she could do about it. There was no way, even if he lived to be a hundred that he could ever hope to gain such an indomitable spirit. He took her outstretched hand. It was a small, calloused hand, the veins almost breaking through the translucent skin. "Grandma, if I may call you that."

The little figure laughed. "Of course you call me Grandma, all the family do. The others call me Ma. I can't remember what I was christened."

"Flora," Sophie reminded her.

Grandma laughed. "Well, there you go then, lucky I forgot it! Now young man, what are your intentions with me granddaughter?"

Taken by surprise at the directness of the question, Ed glanced at Sophie.

"Well Ed, what are your intentions?" she teased.

"To make you happy," Ed stuttered.

"Good enough," Grandma replied. "I can see you are an honest boy." She turned to Sophie. "So don't let him go. No more of your hang-ups that you tell me about."

"All gone," Sophie assured her.

"Good. Now you and I are going to join the rest of the women and make a big feast to celebrate your arrival. Daisy and Millicent will be here soon."

"How about Goldie?"

Grandma scowled. "I never see my daughter these days. Too busy with that layabout she's living with. He's no good, Sophie. Besides, she's nervous of seeing you."

"Now why is that?" asked Sophie.

Grandma shrugged. "Maybe I should have said nothing, but as you know that's not in my genes.

The girls want to tell you something. Their mother is too much of a coward to be around, but better they tell you themselves. Now come on, let's leave the two men to talk and we can get on with the cooking." She made her way down the steps waving at the children as she went. "Away from here you horrors, leave the men alone. Follow me!"

They followed along with several dozen scrawny chickens and Ed couldn't help wondering if some of them wouldn't soon be in the pot for the lunch. Sophie looked questionably at Ed. "You going to be okay?" she asked quietly.

"I'll be fine."

"See you later then," she said over her shoulder, as she followed Grandma down the steps.

Ed was left standing on the terrace, a little apprehensive at the thought of spending time with the old man in the chair. His concern was unfounded. Once he'd pulled a chair up beside Grandpa and opened the two bottles of Stripe beer that had been on a table close to Grandpa, the old man launched into his life's history. Ed found it riveting and also sad. No man should have to put up with such indignities during his young life, but Grandpa never once complained, never blaming anyone, not even the plantation owners who, Ed decided, must have been bastards. He told his story as if his life of toil was the most natural thing in the world, which he probably genuinely thought it was, cut off from the world as he'd been all his life.

Lunch came as a welcome relief to Ed, not because Grandpa had run out of conversation, but because once the beer was finished, Grandpa had enticed him onto the rum and Ed was feeling distinctly woozy. Apart from a slight glaze over his eyes, Grandpa seemed unaffected.

"Lunch is ready," called Sophie from the bottom step of the terrace, laughing as she watched an unsteady Ed feeling his way down. "Grandpa's rum?" she asked.

"Beer first and then rum. You could have warned me. Another glass and I think I'd have passed out."

"I wanted it to be a surprise," laughed Sophie. "And let me guess, Grandpa is unaffected."

"Seems that way. Is he coming to lunch?"

"No, he'll sleep now. I'll bring him some soup later."

"Does he ever move from that chair?"

Sophie shook her head. "When it rains, Grandma helps him inside. Otherwise he pisses and shits in the pot and grandma feeds him and changes his clothes once a week. He'll die in that chair."

Ed looked up to the terrace and saw the old man's head had already dropped. "How old are they?" he asked.

"Neither of them knows. I don't think their births were ever registered. Grandma admits to being over seventy, which I reckon is not far off the mark given how old my father would be. As for Grandpa, your guess is as good as mine. I don't think he's much older than Grandma; he's just rotting faster."

"He's a tough old bugger though, given his life."

"They don't breed them so tough these days," Sophie said in admiration. "Anyway, a feast has been prepared so we mustn't keep the ladies waiting. Afterwards I would like to visit Mum and Dad's graves."

"Of course. We can do it now if you like."

"No, later, when we have more time and the children have dispersed. If we go now you can bet your bottom dollar it will only be a short time before they join us, and I want to be alone."

"I understand, so let's go and stuff ourselves."

Sophie had been right on the button. Lunch was indeed a feast, laid out on three tables covered with brightly coloured red paper tablecloths. Wooden benches lined the tables. Banana trees provided the shade. Only Grandma's closest friends had seats, the rest would have to eat standing with the children. Grandma directed Sophie to the head of one table, Ed to another, and then she sat down at the third. She'd done her bit she said, now it was up to the younger women.

Ed was looking at the dishes piled high with food, most of which he had never seen before, when a pretty girl sat down on his left. "Hi, Mr Ed, I'm Dahlia. My mum and dad have known Ma for ages."

"Hello Dahlia."

Dahlia gave a toothy grin. "Want some help with all this?" She waved a hand at the tables.

"That might not be such a bad idea."

"Okay, let's get started." Dahlia said with enthusiasm. "Now, over there on that far table are the patties, Jamaican callaloo—all vegetables, ackee and saltfish—the Jamaican national dish, and corn bread. On the next table is jerk chicken, steamed cabbage, boiled dumplings, codfish balls and bulla, my favourite. Then on our table here we have sweet cassava pudding, cornmeal pudding, yellow yam rissoles, and stripe beer, which may well be the only thing you recognise." Her braless bosoms shook with laughter. "So there you go, Mr Ed, just tell Dahlia here what you fancy and I'll bring it all to you."

"Okay" said Ed. "How about you choosing for me?"

"If that's what you want, Mr Ed, then Dahlia will do it."

Five minutes later, Ed had two plates heaped with food put in front of him and a bottle of Stripe beer.

"Wow," he gasped. "Am I expected to eat all this?" The whole table broke into laughter. "You eat it all, Mr Ed," they shouted, "or we will be mightily offended!"

Ed ate. Dozens of eyes fixed on him. Every now and then someone asked, "That good?"

"Delicious," he replied.

When his plates were empty, Grandma asked, "You like our food Ed?"

"Best I've eaten in years."

Everyone started clapping and Sophie came over and hugged him. "They love you Ed."

Ed burped and rubbed his stomach. "Got any Rennies?"

Ed and Sophie made their excuses and left the lunch, promising to be back in time to see Daisy and Millicent, who were scheduled to arrive about three in the afternoon.

Now they were standing quietly by her parents' graves. Their names and the dates they had died were carved on wooden headstones. The small cemetery was beautifully maintained, putting some of the English ones to shame.

"Who maintains their graves?" asked Ed.

"Grandma, every week."

"She loved your father."

"He was her favourite and she was so proud of him. Like me she will always miss him."

"And when she's gone?"

Sophie smiled. "There will always be someone. That is the way here; it is an exceptional place."

Ed nodded. "It certainly is. I'm so glad we came."

"Are you really, Ed?"

"Cross my heart."

"You have no idea how happy that makes me feel. I know I don't come here very often, but it will always be a special place. This is where I feel Dad's spirit. Sometimes, when I've been on my own, right on this spot where we are standing now, I imagine I can hear him singing his jazz, but today it is different: before he was haunting me; now I just feel good that he had a wonderful life with me and Mum. Can you understand what I'm saying?"

Ed thought it was a little muddled, as it always was when Sophie was talking about her father, but he had no intention of saying so. Sophie could express her feelings anyway she liked and he'd go along with that. He said, "You make perfect sense, Sophie. I think it's wonderful."

"Do you have good memories of your parents?" Sophie dared to ask.

"A few."

Sophie saw the usual sadness come into his eyes and regretted bringing up the subject. "Sorry Ed."

"Don't be."

She reached for his hand and gently pulled him away. "Come on, we've been here long enough and Grandma will be fretting. Soon, Daisy and Millicent will be on the scene. I wonder what they will have to say."

The girls arrived a few minutes after Ed and Sophie got back. A large open, beaten-up Ford Mustang of indefinable age, came to a halt in a cloud of dust outside the house, sending chickens flying in all directions. Two men with dread-locks, who Ed thought looked too young to drive, sat in the front; two girls leapt agilely from the back, not bothering to open the doors.

"Aunty Sophie!" they exclaimed in unison, proceeding to land lipstick-laden kisses on her cheeks.

Ed stared in amazement. He wasn't sure what he'd expected, but he was certainly surprised by these two pretty girls, covered in bling and with more metal punched through their faces than a grenade victim. Mini skirts and T-shirts left little to the imagination. Their hair was black and close cropped something in the style of Sophie's.

"Jesus!" Sophie couldn't help exclaiming. "You two have changed since I last saw you."

Ed thought they could have passed as two whores from the streets of Kingston. Why he thought that when he'd never seen the whores of Kingston, he wasn't too sure.

"We've got boy friends now," said Millicent proudly, as if that explained everything.

Sophie turned to look at the two young men getting out of the car.

"Randy's mine," said Millicent with a sigh.

"And Clint's mine, "Daisy said, smiling at one of the young men.

"Which is which?" asked Sophie.

Millicent called to Randy. He hurried over, a gangly tall youth with a wide friendly smile on his face. He wore tight fitting black jeans and a faded T-shirt with 'Reggie Blast' emblazoned on the back.

"This is Randy. Randy, meet my aunty Sophie."

Randy politely took Sophie's hand. "Pleased to meet you Aunty Sophie; I've heard a lot about you."

"And this is Clint," said Daisy, hugging what might have been Randy's twin to her cleavage. He did not have the same cheerful smile and looked around him in a detached manner before rather reluctantly shaking Sophie's hand.

"Hi lady" he mumbled staring at the ground.

Doesn't want to be here, thought Ed.

"Okay you two girls," Grandma ordered, "it's time you talked to your Aunt. Go on you boys, get a drink and any food there is left. This is serious business."

What they had to say came as a surprise to Sophie. The two girls had fallen madly, desperately in love. Randy and Clint were the bees-knees, and hopefully Aunty Sophie understood they would much rather stay in Jamaica than come to England. "We plan to get married next year and hope you will come over," said Millicent.

"Bloody fools," mumbled Grandma.

Sophie looked at Ed and shrugged. She couldn't help feeling a sense of relief. To have the girls living with her would have been fine when she was on her own, but with Ed around, things had changed. Anyway, it was obvious that the two girls had no intention of leaving without Randy and Clint. "Well, I can't argue against love," smiled Sophie."

"Bloody fools," Grandma repeated.

The two girls laughed uneasily and said, "We're very sorry, Aunty. Please don't think we are ungrateful. It's just—well it's just we've had a change of mind."

Sophie graced them with a benevolent smile. "Don't worry girls, I understand." She didn't add that Grandma was probably right. What was the point of trying to make two headstrong girls see sense?

"Thanks Aunty Sophie," Millicent said, as they turned away to join Randy and Clint who were stuffing themselves with what was left on the tables and already on their second Stripe each.

Grandma glared at them.

Sophie put an arm around her and said, "I know you wanted them to come back with me, but if they love these two men it's better they stay here. It is their home after all."

"Bloody fools," Grandma muttered again.

An hour later, Randall arrived to collect Ed and Sophie. The lunch party, including Millicent and Daisy, had dispersed madly and blowing kisses. Sophie smiled, knowing what they were thinking: *Job done! Now back to some fun. Not that they didn't love Grandma or Aunty Sophie, but they were so old. Yawn, yawn.*

Sophie settled Grandma down in her chair on the terrace and cleared up around Grandpa who smiled and reached for his pipe. "Okay you two," Sophie said, "we will be back the day after tomorrow, but no feast this time you hear."

Grandma gave her a weary smile. "I promise. Now go carefully with this girl," she said to Ed. "She's all I've got except for that old dilapidated thing in that chair over there."

They all laughed, even Grandpa, although he hadn't a clue what had caused such hilarity. Sophie kissed them both and then took Ed's hand.

Half way back down the mountains, Sophie turned to Ed. "I'm relieved really about the girls. It was different when I was on my own, but now I have you to think about. Moreover, did you see them! Jesus Ed, they looked like a pair of tarts. I think I might have had great difficulty in controlling them."

Ed gave a low laugh. "I think they would have kept our hands full!"

"I doubt if those boys will stay with them," said Sophie. "They're just out for a good time if you ask me. There are thousands like them on the island. Those girls are in for a shock, which is why I wanted them back home with me. All I can hope is that they don't drift into trouble. Kingston is a dangerous place. On average there are nine killings a day. You need to be streetwise to survive. I think their mother may have been too lax in the way she's brought them up."

"It's not your problem any more," said Ed by way of encouragement.

"I know, but they are family."

Ed nodded. He knew it would be useless to say there was very little Sophie could do from half way round the world.

On the days when they weren't up in the Dry Harbour Mountains, they lay by the hotel swimming pool, swam in the gloriously warm sea, snorkelled from their bedroom balcony, or took drives with Randall around the island. They went to Dunn River Falls and stood under the waterfall. They drove along the coast to lunch at St Anne's bay. They visited Port Antonio and drove back through the Blue Mountains. They took a boat out so that they could see Goldeneye. It was while they were rocking gently to the swell that Sophie told Ed that Goldeneye was where her father had probably been conceived.

"How do you know that?" he asked intrigued.

"Mum told me. Apparently, when Ian Fleming was away Grandma would drop in every now and then and clean the house. Sometimes Grandpa would go with her. Grandma proudly boasts that one day they made love on Ian Fleming's bed and bingo, two weeks short of nine months later, out pops Dad!"

"Did your mother believe that?"

"She went along with it. Grandma was always teasing Dad about it. If you asked Grandma today, she'd tap her nose and tell you to mind your own business. So true or false? I will never know, but hearing about those two when they were younger, I'd be prepared to put my money on it being fact."

On their second last day, when Randall met them at the hotel portico to take them into Kingston, he was not his usual smiling self.

"Something wrong?" Sophie asked.

"Yes, Mrs Ed," he said, as he'd started calling her. "Very bad business last night. Stirling, he kill himself. Drove over a cliff right into the sea."

"Oh no!" exclaimed Sophie. "Anyone else involved?"

"No, just Stirling. He was dicing with death every day, Mrs Ed and sooner or later your number comes up. No doubt he's up there somewhere, begging God to give him a Ferrari! Randall pointed to the sky and gave a little laugh. "Maybe roads better up there and not so twisted."

"Maybe," Sophie said. "What a waste of a young life! Listen Randall, if you'd rather not take us today please feel free to say so. We'll be very happy here."

Randall took Sophie's hand. "I much appreciate that, Mrs Ed. I would very much like to go and see Stirling's family."

"Go on then," Sophie said. "See you tomorrow morning."

Randall winked at Sophie. "See you tomorrow, Mrs Ed. Wouldn't miss it for the world."

"What was that wink for?" asked Ed later, as they lay by the pool each sipping their first rum punch of the day.

"What wink," asked Sophie.

"You know perfectly well that Randall winked at you."

"Must just be his way of saying thank you," said Sophie.

Ed shrugged and smiled into his glass. "You haven't been hatching something have you? Come to think of it, Grandma looked mighty pleased yesterday and even Grandpa took that filthy pipe out of his mouth and smiled."

"Okay I have a secret."

"Ha, ha I was right!"

"But I'm not telling, so shut up."

Ed jumped off his sun bed and started tickling her.

"Ed, please stop that," she gasped leaping onto the sand. "Ouch, that's hot!"

Ed chased after her and pulled her down onto the sand. "Come on, tell me your secret. Do you remember saying we should never have any secrets from each other?"

"I lied, and get off. Get off, my bum's burning!"

Ed released her. "So you're not going to tell me?"

"No I'm not."

"Then I'll sulk all day."

"Good. At least that will mean you won't keep pestering me for sex."

They both laughed.

"Race you to our bedroom," said Ed jumping up and starting to run.

They arrived at their bedroom door panting, hot and sticky. They didn't bother to shower.

"Ed?"

"Yes, said Ed sleepily.

"I hope tomorrow is going to be a special day."

Ed disentangled himself from Sophie and propped himself up on an elbow.

"Tell me about it."

"Sorry, as I said, my lips are sealed. Just remember it's going to be special and very exciting."

"Well, how can I get excited about something you obstinately refuse to tell me about? Give me a clue."

Sophie laughed and sat up in bed. You're beautiful thought Ed, as she smiled and ran her hand over his chest. For at least the thousandth time he wondered if he'd ever get bored of looking at her naked. Come to think of it, she wasn't bad fully clothed either.

"Okay, a tiny clue. I'm taking you somewhere."

"So we're not going to your grandparents?"

"That's right."

"That means we won't see them again before we leave."

"We will, and that's the clue."

"You mean they are coming somewhere with us," Ed guessed.

"That's right."

"Not much of a clue."

"Just think what might get Grandpa out of that chair."

Ed shook his head. "Beats me."

"In that case you'll just have to wait until tomorrow. Ed no, please!"

They were up early. Sophie fussed around in the bathroom and then carefully put on a little make-up. She dressed in a long light white skirt and matching blouse. She wore a single string of pearls round her neck and the emerald that Ed had given when he'd moved into her house. "A sort of engagement present," he'd said.

"Why are you dressing like that?" Ed asked.

"Because I feel like it."

"Very poor answer."

"The best you're going to get. And I want you in a shirt and trousers."

"And if I refuse?"

Sophie laughed. "Then I will just have to force you."

"I'd win."

Sophie shrugged. "Maybe, but you're not going to ruin my day are you?"

"Not when you ask me like that."

"Great. Now come on Ed, Randall will be waiting."

"What no breakfast?"

"We can stop somewhere en route."

Ed blew out his cheeks. He could almost taste his first cup of coffee. "This has got to be good."

Sophie gave him a hug. "Oh it will be, Ed, I promise you that."

Randall was standing by his car as they came out of the hotel, a broad smile on his face. The sadness in his eyes from the day before had vanished. He was wearing a threadbare blue suit, which had seen better days, but it was a change from his usual sweat-stained shirt. "You're in on this aren't you," Ed accused him, pointing first at the suit and then at the car, which had been cleaned, exposing ever more rust than usual.

Randall smiled at Sophie. "Mr Ed not know?"

"Not yet."

Randall seemed to find the whole thing very amusing. "Well, you're in for a big shock man!"

Ed shrugged. "I just hope it's something I'm going to like."

Sophie pushed him into the back of the car. "If you don't I'm in serious trouble."

When they were only a few miles from Christiana, Sophie tapped Randall on the shoulder. "Pull in when you see a suitable place."

"Okay Mrs Ed," he replied, fighting back the laughter that was threatening to explode. A few moments later, he found what Ed presumed he would call a lay-by. Ed thought it was more like a rubbish tip.

"Did you remember the coffee," Sophie asked.

Randall held up a thermos. "And the plastic cups," he said proudly.

They exited the car and the damp heat hit them. "Wow!" said Ed, "thank God for your air-conditioning, Randall."

This made them all think of Stirling and they stood in silence for a brief moment as Randall poured the coffee into the plastic cups. Once the cups were full, Randall tactfully moved back to the car, even though he knew what was to come.

Sophie took a deep breath; sent up a silent prayer to God as she took Ed's hand. It was no good beating about the bush so she looked into his eyes and asked, "Marry me Ed."

Ed took a step back.

"Not too far," Sophie cried, "or you'll fall into the sea and it's a long way down."

"Say that again," Ed said, fighting to steady his voice.

"Will you marry me? Like right now?"

"Now!"

"Well not right this minute, but in about an hour."

"You're playing games with me."

"I wouldn't joke about something so important."

"So this is your secret."

Sophie nodded, her stomach clenching with nerves. She'd been so sure. Had she been wrong? Wasn't Ed ready for such a deep commitment?

"You want to marry me in an hour," Ed exclaimed.

"That's what I'm asking."

"Oh God, Sophie. I have a funny feeling in my stomach."

Sophie laughed nervously. "Me too."

Ed grinned sheepishly. "And I think I know where. The little church?"

"You've got it in one. Please say yes; for God sake Ed, please say yes!"

"Oh Sophie, Sophie you're quite a girl!"

"But are you going to say YES?"

Ed's eyes widened in astonishment. "You want to marry me, here? Now? This is a bit sudden."

Sophie's heart plummeted. "Oh God," she exclaimed, "I've blown it!"

Ed reached for her hand. "I think I need a little time to think about this. Are you sure this is the right time? Are you sure we're ready for this momentous change in our lives? Sophie, darling, I don't think I can move quite as fast as you want me to." He saw the tears well up in Sophie's eyes.

"I was so sure," she mumbled. "So very, very sure you'd say yes."

Chapter Seventeen

Jerry Gordon was in deep, deep shit. He'd welched on his deal with the warden; the bribe could not be paid. Worse, he'd thoroughly upset Slasher Williams, so called because of the number of throats he'd slit before being apprehended by the Filth. Jerry had to admit he'd brought this all on himself, but he was obsessed. Polly was playing on his mind day and night. When he'd gone to the Governor with his sob story about wanting to see Polly to apologise for all the grief he'd given her, he'd been confident enough to approach Slasher, one of the most feared men in the prison, and foolishly asked him for a knife. Hatred had built up inside Jerry to the point when he felt his head was going to burst, causing him to lose his grip on reality. To an irrational brain, it had all seemed so simple. All he had to do was get Polly opposite him at a table then plunge the knife into her heart. It would be so quick, all over before the wardens knew what was happening. Jerry didn't care a fucking toss that he'd be tried for murder. He didn't care that he'd spend most of the rest of his life banged up. All he wanted was to see Polly dead, but then Miss fucking Belinda Musgrove had turned up and he had been, to say the least, a little fucking thrown! The knife had remained in his trouser pocket.

Now all he could do was await his fate. You didn't owe money to a bent screw, and you most certainly didn't have a knife hidden in your socks, which, when discovered, dropped Slasher well and truly in the shit, without suffering the consequences. Jerry's knew that his time on earth was getting shorter by the day.

For a week since the incident, Jerry had been waiting, sweating over the visit he knew would inevitably arrive. Already his stomach had turned to liquid; he could hold little food down and his cell constantly stank of shit.

The screw took every opportunity to whisper, "When Slasher gets out of the cooler, Matches, your life will end." Jerry didn't need the fucking man to tell him that.

The cell door flew open just as Jerry thought he'd got through another day. Two of Slasher's bullies stood in the doorway grinning. There was no sign of the warden.

"It's to the showers for you, Matches," one of them said.

Jerry was too terrified to speak. Urine ran down his trouser leg.

"Tut tut," said the same man. "Forgotten your nappy today, eh Matches?" They walked towards him and picked him up bodily. "You fucking stink man," one of them said.

Slasher was waiting in the showers. "Matches, so good to see you," he said, holding his hands behind his back. "Let's get the party started, shall we?"

Jerry knew it was pointless begging. He knew the score. If he'd had something to offer the sadistic bastard, like drugs, or a stash of money hidden on the outside, he might have just got away with a beating, but Jerry's cupboard was empty. He stared wide-eyed at the sharpened wooden stake that had appeared from behind the big man's back. Jerry opened his mouth but no sound came out. His knees turned to water and he sank to the floor blubbering.

"Strip the fucker," Slasher commanded.

Jerry's clothes were ripped off his body. He looked a broken pathetic little man.

"Bend him over," Slasher said with relish.

Jerry screamed then. Braver men had done the same thing when they realised what was about to happen.

Slasher had used this method before, when he was particularly pissed off with someone who had dared to try muscling in on his patch. He considered throat slitting too humane for these scumbags. Jerry's head was forced between his legs, the stench of his shit filling the shower room. The pain as the stake was roughly jammed up his anus, splitting the flesh, was excruciating His screams must have been heard, but no one came to his rescue. Besides, it would have been too late. Jerry felt the warmth of his blood flow down his legs as the stake reached his bowels. For a second it felt comforting, took away the pain. And then he died.

It had taken five brutal minutes to end his miserable life.

"You asked him to marry you! On a mountain road, drinking coffee from a plastic cup!" Clarissa was astonished by Sophie's bravery. "That's what I did," said Sophie.

"And how did he take your sneaky bit of planning?"

"It was terrible," Sophie confessed, remembering Ed's rejection. "He asked for more time, and there I was, so confident he'd say 'yes.'

Clarissa glanced at the ring. "So what happened?"

Sophie laughed. "The bastard was having me on, wasn't he! Made me cry, made me sweat, made me think I'd gone too far and lost him. For what seemed an age he just stared at me, and then his face broke into one of his delectable smiles and he said, "I'm kidding, Sophie. Of course I'll marry you."

"That was cruel."

"I admit I wanted to hit him, but at the same time I wanted to throw myself in his arms and kiss his grinning face."

"And what did you do?"

"I did both."

"And his reaction?" asked Clarissa.

"He never stopped laughing all the way to the church. I can't tell you how happy I was. What I did was a bit underhanded I admit. He called me a devious woman, but he's still telling me how he loved every moment of our rather whacky wedding. Grandpa was sitting in the front pew farting loudly, Grandma was bashing him with her handbag and Millicent and Daisy, dressed like two Kingston hookers, were my bridesmaids. Then there were the children that Grandma had gathered together to sing the hymns that *she'd* chosen. Yes, whacky is the right word, Clarissa, but Ed and I loved every moment of it. It really was a day to remember. The only sad note was the fact that it was probably the last time I'll see Grandpa. He's in terrible shape. At least he'll die knowing his granddaughter is happy. Now, tell me what's been going on since I've been away?"

Clarissa told her.

"Well, I'm thrilled to hear things are going well for Emily. I've always thought Jack was special. I can't wait for the wedding, and it's good to hear that rotten man Gordon is out of the way. How did he die?"

"No idea," said Clarissa, but Belinda says he upset the wrong people."

"I don't think we want to know then," grimaced Sophie. "Much better to think of the wedding."

It was the last Tuesday in June.

Chapter Eighteen

It started at eight fifty a.m. on Thursday 7ᵗʰ July.

The bombs rocked London and changed the lives of hundreds of people. Three explosions were on tube trains on the London underground system. One between Aldgate East and Liverpool Street, another between Russell Square and King's Cross, and finally one at Edgware Road Station. Then, at nine-forty-seven, the fourth explosion destroyed a bus in Tavistock Square.

London shuddered with horror. The long expected terrorist attack had come. Fifty-two people died and seven hundred were injured.

Emily watched the scenes on her television with disbelief that anything so horrific could take place in London. The suicide bombers were British Muslims. How, she wondered, did that add up to the saying from the Prophet Mohammed that *'one of the worst sins a person can commit is to murder a human being'*.

She was scared. Jack travelled to work on the tube. She tried to reach him on his mobile, but got his voice mail. Reluctantly she rang his parents. Jack's father answered her question with a brief, "No, we haven't heard a thing. I will let you know if we do." The phone went dead before she could say any more. She tried Jack's mobile; again she got his voice mail. She told herself that was nothing to panic about, given the chaos that was unfolding on her television screen. He'd know she was worried and contact her as soon as he could.

At midday she called his father again. She got the same response, but thought she detected concern. By seven that night the call from Jack still hadn't come. She was now terrified he'd been caught up in the bombings. At worst he was dead; at best he was lying in some hospital horribly wounded and unable to speak. She couldn't bear her own company for another moment. She rang her father. "I need you Dad."

Jonathan, who'd been following the disaster all day on the television, felt his heart turn a somersault. "Not heard from Jack, darling?"

"Not a word from him all day. I'm pretty sure he's been caught up in the bombings. I don't think I can take this not knowing much longer."

"Have you rung his parents?"

"Twice, but you know what his father's like. All I can hope for is that he'll ring if he gets any news."

"Of course he will, and I'll be right over," Jonathan promised.

They sat staring at the 'phone. Jonathan made several calls to hospitals and police stations, but such was the chaos that he couldn't get any news. He then rang Jack's father, just to make sure he hadn't heard anything. He knew Emily would be low on his list of people to ring.

"It doesn't look good," he told Jonathan, his voice full of anxiety. "I've rung every hospital in London. They can't tell me anything."

Jonathan confirmed he'd done the same.

"I promise I'll ring if I hear anything," said Jack's father, and then asked, "Your daughter okay?"

Jonathan bridled, wanting to tell the arrogant man that his daughter's name was Emily, but it was not the right time to pick petty arguments. "As good as you can expect, given the dreadful circumstances. We look forward to hearing from you if you have any news," he said curtly, and cut the call.

Throughout the night they drank copious amounts of sweet tea. Emily listened for Jack's key turning in the lock. The hours dragged.

By eleven a.m. the next day, Emily knew that Jack wouldn't be coming home. Ever. No more *Tesco Finest*; no more pink roses by her bed; no more touching of his naked body. His body parts were mixed with other people's flesh. She vomited. She wanted to die.

The tears flowed the whole of the first day. Sometimes quietly despairing, sometimes terrible, tearing sobs. Her father sat by her side, his head bowed, knowing there was nothing he could do to relieve her pain. He rang Jack's father and was told they were going up to London, in the hope of getting some information about their son.

On the second day, Emily began to scream. Jonathan held her in his arms, rocking her back and forth.

On the third day, Jack's father phoned. His news came as no shock to Jonathan. Jack was dead. When he told Emily her head dropped forward into her hands. He watched her shudder and then heard the sound of a helpless moan from behind her hands. She began to cry again, her shoulders shaking violently. Feeling helpless, Jonathan reached over and touched the back of her neck.

On the fourth day she at last fell silent, worn out and drained of every last bit of emotion. Her face was so swollen that Jonathan could hardly see her eyes. She smiled at him, touched his face, mouthed *thank you* and went to her bedroom. She drew the curtains to cut out the light. She did not come out again for three days, except to go to the bathroom. Her father took her food and water, but made no attempt to force her out of her room. He judged it better to let her grief run its course.

In the hours on her own, Emily learnt what people meant when they said their heart had been broken. She felt as if part of her had been hacked to pieces, that her life was ebbing away. How was she ever going to pick up her life again? On the fourth day, when her father walked into her room with her meagre breakfast she was dressed and waiting for him. "I want to go out," she said, taking his arm. He nodded and guided her down the stairs. Outside she breathed in deeply and stared up at the sky. Somewhere up there was Jack. She wiped away a tear and smiled weakly at her father. "This is hard, Dad," she said.

Jonathan nodded. He knew how she was suffering. He'd been there.

He drove her to Winchester Cathedral because that is where she and Jack had worshipped from time to time.

"This place is awe inspiring," Jack had said the first time he'd taken her there to worship, staring up at the ceiling high above them. She couldn't quite see that, but she'd loved the music, the singing and just being there with Jack.

She told her father she wanted to pray alone, so he left her there, waiting patiently for her at the back of the Cathedral. She sat in the same row of chairs where she and Jack had sat on their first visit: six from the back, on the left. It was a long way from the altar, but the row was never full, so she and Jack could sit together and thank God for their love. Jack would sing lustily, she would mouth words, knowing that she sang dreadfully out of tune. She closed her eyes and summoned up an image of Jack. She smiled towards the altar, dropped her head and prayed. She prayed that Jack hadn't suffered; she thanked God for putting him on earth even though his time had been cruelly cut short. She begged God to look after him until she joined him. Finally, she asked God to give her the strength to get through the coming days and months. The pain of separation was excruciating, but with His help she was determined to claw her way back up the precipice and live a life again. She was sure it was what Jack would wish.

Lucy Hemming closed the door of the flat. Picking up her battered plastic suitcase, which held her worldly goods, she headed for the lift. She'd finished with crying, but hadn't finished with mourning Jack's death. It made no difference to her that she had already cast him aside. In fact, that made it worse, because the look on his face as she closed her car door on him kept floating in front of her eyes. Her mind, mercifully numb at first, had come round, confronting her with what she had done. She was devastated by his death, not least because the guilt she'd been harbouring was now bursting out. She'd stolen time with Jack, which he should have been spending with Emily. She knew she could never be quite the same person again, because the guilt would never completely go away. Whatever she did, wherever she went, however her life panned out, that guilt would nag away at her. She walked out of the lift and headed for the street. She had one very urgent task to perform.

She had to retrieve the letter.

After that she'd head for her parents' home in Cardiff and try to pick up the pieces of her shattered life. She hailed a taxi. "Cheyne Walk please."

Only when she got to the house did she remember that she'd posted the key to Jack. How could she have forgotten? A terrible feeling of inevitability swept over her. She dropped down on to the steps leading to the front door and thought how much better her life would have been if she had not left home for a nursing job in London. It had all seemed so exciting at the time; a new life had beckoned. She hadn't planned on falling for a man who had turned out to be a violent monster. She'd suffered abuse for three years, unable to work up the courage to leave him, because she was sure he'd track her down and kill her. Finally, after a particularly horrific beating, she had ended up on the tube, at her wit's end, lost and terrified, wondering what to do.

Jack had rescued her, as she liked to call it. At first, he'd only been her protector, seeing off her husband, giving her back her self-esteem and wiping the fear from her mind. That was how she'd intended their relationship to remain. How many times had she told herself the relationship was wrong, going nowhere, and how many times had she decided to tell Jack she would not see him again and yet, there she'd been, every Monday morning, for the best part of two years, waiting for him at Waterloo Station for her weekly fix. She could find no justification in her actions. She'd cheated on another woman, slept with Emily's future husband, and grown to love him. When she'd at last slammed the door in Jack's face, it had been far too late. By then she stood condemned as a wrecker, and Jack as a cheating bastard, having his cake and eating it. From the moment she'd driven away from the station, her face wet with tears, she knew the only thing she could do was sever the link completely, and that was why she'd penned the letter. Only fate had intervened. Now, more than likely, someone who was not meant to read the letter was going to unlock the door to Jack's house, find it lying on the hall carpet and learn that Jack was a two-timing bastard.

That person was likely to be Emily.

Lucy felt her life was about to implode. She picked up her suitcase, her eyes misting over with tears. She'd never intended to hurt Emily, but probably in the near future, she was going to hurt her so badly that her life would never be the same again. She walked slowly and very deliberately towards Chelsea Bridge. She stopped half way along the bridge and stared down at the water. She opened her suitcase, withdrew a photo of her parents and held it to her chest.

A strange feeling of peace caressed her

Chapter Nineteen

Clarissa heard the shrill ringing of the phone from the lettuce patch. She decided to ignore it. She was in no mood to talk to anyone. Emily's distress had upset her more than she could ever have imagined. It was not her way to feel morbid, but she had to admit that Jack's death had affected her, made her realise how tentative a hold one had on life. Emily had bravely said, "It's God's will," and for the first time in her life, Clarissa had wished she believed in that mysterious person who was supposedly mapping out everyone's destiny. At a time like this to have such faith must be so very comforting. She shrugged and smiled at a lettuce, feeling that perhaps she'd missed out on something.

"Clarissa!" Ted's voice came from the house. "It's your mother. Urgent, very urgent she says."

Mother was the last person she wanted to talk to today. "Oh damn. Tell her I'll ring her back."

Ted hurried out of the house holding the 'phone. "You must speak to her. Your father's ill."

Reluctantly she took the receiver. "Hello Mother. What's wrong with Dad? Has he overdone the booze again?"

Molly Duncan heard the annoyance in her daughter's voice. "Your father's had a stroke."

"How bad?"

"Very. He's in Taunton Hospital. I think you should come."

"Now? Why on earth should I?"

"Because he's probably going to die."

Clarissa wanted to say *Good riddance*, but she could hear the distress in her mother's voice. However much she despised her father, in his own selfish way she supposed he'd been a good husband. Just a pity he'd done his best to ruin his daughter's life.

"It's a very busy time here, Mother. I've got produce coming out of my ears and markets to go to. Couldn't you just ring me when he dies? He doesn't want to see me."

"You can be so cruel."

"So what was Father?"

Clarissa heard her mother choke. "Okay, okay, I'm sorry, Mother. This is not the time to discuss Father's behaviour. I'll get Ted organised this end and I'll leave here tomorrow. How's that?"

"If that's the best you can do."

"It is, and more than Father deserves."

"He may be dead by tomorrow."

"Well I won't miss him."

Clarissa heard her mother burst into tears and then the line went dead. Her father brought the worst out of her. She shook her head and walked towards the house. Perhaps she'd better behave like a loving daughter and take herself and the Morris down to Somerset today. "Ted!" she shouted. "We have a crisis!"

By road it took most people about two hours to get from Winchester to Taunton, but the Morris did not like to be pushed. Its maximum speed was fifty, and that was on level ground. The trip would take a good three hours, providing the Morris didn't decide it needed a pit stop. Clarissa knew she should go by train, but then she'd be trapped, at the mercy of her mother. Not a good idea. So, however hazardous the drive might be, her freedom to decide when she left Somerset outweighed all other possible dangers.

The July morning was warm and sunny. Clarissa could have done with some rain. Her plants were looking thirsty; the potatoes especially needed a good soak, and the Morris didn't overheat in cool weather.

"Now listen up, Picasso," she said to Ted as she threw her battered small brown over-night bag into the Morris. "Painting must take second fiddle until I return. Remember we have three markets this week, but you can always call up help. The names are on the pad by the phone, and don't spend hours dreaming about Jo Hawskworth's attributes. There's work to be done."

Ted smiled and patted Clarissa's bottom playfully. "Don't worry, darling girl, I won't let you down, and if I have time to dream it will, as usual, be of you my little butterfly."

"You smooth flatterer," Clarissa laughed. "I know you won't let me down, and don't worry, I'll be back as quick as I can. Bye Bella, bye Charlie, keep an eye on Picasso for me." She forced her door closed and turned the ignition key. The Morris's engine gave a groan, spluttered and then fired. "Come on my love, we've got a few miles to go," Clarissa shouted above the noise of the complaining engine.

Ted waved. Bella barked and Charlie sneezed as the full blast of the exhaust caught him in the face.

The Morris chugged steadily along. Clarissa had years of practice coaxing the best out of the old lady, but it resented being hurried, and having made the decision that she should go to Taunton Clarissa was in a hurry. What was the point in arriving only to find the old bastard had popped his clogs while she'd been on the road?

She looked at her watch. She'd been driving for little short of two hours and she was only on the Wincanton by-pass. At least another hour to go. She tried putting her foot down a little harder on the accelerator only to hear the engine miss. She quickly eased the pressure of her foot and sighed. No good arguing with the cantankerous piece of metal under the bonnet; it was the boss. She reached over for the bottle of water on the passenger seat and took a long pull of the now tepid liquid. The sun was warm through the windscreen and she felt a little drowsy, even though the windows were open and a breeze ruffled her hair, but she was reluctant to stop. The Morris had been known not to start again until it had had a few hours rest. She glanced at the petrol indicator and reckoned she'd make Taunton, but falling asleep was becoming a real threat, as it always did on long journeys. Probably because, as Ted had told her many times, "This bloody car is a death trap. Can't you smell the fumes?" She made a mental note to take the car to the garage—sometime. To think of her father was not an option; to relive the hours she'd spent with Emily after Jack's tragic death was definitely a no-goer. What lay ahead was depressing enough. She resorted to singing, very loudly, and thumping the steering wheel in time with the tune. It worked. More than likely because her singing was so dreadful that no one, not even the singer, could fall asleep with such a noise echoing round the car.

Almost exactly an hour after looking at her watch on the Wincanton by-pass, she pulled into the car park of Taunton Hospital. She squeezed into a vacant space and patted the steering wheel. "Well done my beauty," Clarissa said, before opening the door and dragging her aching body out of the little car. She sniffed. The engine smelt hot. Nothing new, but always a worry. Perhaps it was time to take Ted's advice and retire the old thing. She'd give it some thought when she got home, which would be as quickly as she could tactfully disentangle herself from her mother.

She took a deep breath. "Now listen up, Clarissa," she said to herself, "don't say something you might regret, remember to give Mother a kiss. Right here we go." She hitched up her skirt, ran a hand through her hair and walked towards the hospital entrance.

As soon as she was through the doors she spotted her mother. Something was very wrong. She had a strong urge to turn and run, but her chance was gone even before she could give it serious thought. Her mother had spotted her.

"Clarissa!" she shouted waving her arms wildly in the air.

I can see you, I can see you, Clarissa thought, feeling the familiar jab of irritation at seeing her mother, and then Molly was standing in front of her, tears pouring down her face, her body shaking.

Oh my God, Clarissa thought.

"He's dead! You're too bloody late! He died an hour ago. Why can't you have a decent car?" Molly shouted.

Why was it her mother always managed to make her feel guilty? She took her in her arms and whispered, "I'm sorry."

"He wanted to see you. It was one of the last things he said."

"I'm sorry."

Molly pulled herself away from Clarissa's embrace. Her brown eyes were flashing. "Is that all you can say?"

Clarissa fought to keep her temper. "What else can I say? I did my best. And might I be permitted to point out that even if I'd had a faster car I probably wouldn't have got here in time."

Molly shrugged. She always did when she was losing an argument. "Well that's as maybe."

"Could I see him?" Clarissa asked.

"You want to see your father?"

"That's what I said."

"I can't think why. You never wanted to see him when he was alive."

"That's not true. I loved him for many years, but as you well know his whole character changed for the worst. At least now he's dead he can't mess up my life anymore."

Molly burst into tears. "How on earth could I have given birth to such a cruel person?"

Clarissa thought her mother was like a stuck record. It left her cold. "You didn't. Father made me this way over several years. You knew what was going on and you never once tried to stop him, did you? Anyway, do we have to rake up old sores in this very public place? Take me to see father and then I'll be gone. You can make the funeral arrangements and Ted and I will come down for that."

"There's no need. I can manage on my own."

"Suit yourself," Clarissa bit back. "You know my feelings about funerals. Now come on."

Colin Duncan was lying in the bed where he'd given up on life a little over an hour ago. Clarissa stared at his expressionless face. In death, she thought he looked like the gentle man he'd once been. The lecherous blue eyes that had followed her every move were sightless. Once, a long time ago, he'd been kind to her, loving her, playing games with her when she asked, and teaching her how to ride. "You can't be a child of Exmoor and not ride," he'd told her. And she'd returned his love in spades, shared his enthusiasm for the farm, smelt the seasons changing and thought Exmoor was the most beautiful place she'd ever set eyes on.

Then the farm started to lose money. Her father started drinking. The bank was uneasy and creditors were banging at the Duncans' door. Some land had to be sold and Colin's pride took a tumble. His character completely changed after that and suddenly Clarissa became the child he'd never wanted. "A chattel of no use," he told her. He retreated into the whisky bottle, and one evening after a particularly heavy session when Molly was out at a meeting he tried to sexually assault Clarissa. She'd managed to get away from him that time, but that was only his first attempt. He grew more cunning, sneaking into her bedroom and locking the door behind him. Sometimes he'd rape her, other times he'd just beat her, taking his anger at his failure out on her. Clarissa tried to take shelter anywhere on the farm where she thought he wouldn't find her, but he was very persistent at hunting her down. Confused and desperate that this once kind man could treat her in such a cruel way, she'd turned to her mother for help. None had been forthcoming—she was in denial. Slowly love turned to hate, and that hurt Clarissa almost more than the attacks. This was a monster, not the father she'd once known. The whisky had destroyed him. He was deranged. A week after her seventeenth birthday, Clarissa decided she had to leave home. It was a terrifying prospect, but she'd never lacked courage. With the help of a friend's mother she'd found work on a farm in Hampshire before going to Agricultural college. Then, taking the biggest gamble of her whole life, she'd borrowed money to buy a smallholding at the tender age of twenty. She always said that she'd been lucky. No thanks to her lecherous father. Unexpectedly, as she looked at the drained face, the unseeing eyes, she felt unbearable sadness. She'd loved him so much once. It was in her heart to love him again in spite of everything that had passed between them. If she'd believed in all the claptrap nonsense about religion she would have prayed then that he'd died loving her. Instead she touched his ice-cold hand and smiled. "Remember the good times Dad, wherever you are. I will."

She turned away, surprised to feel a tear trickle down a cheek. She wiped it away quickly. She didn't want her mother to see. She'd only make some cutting remark. Once out in the passage her mother grabbed her arm. Clarissa sensed her panic. "There are huge debts to be paid. The farm is mortgaged up to the hilt. I don't know how I'm going to survive," she moaned.

Clarissa's first inclination was to say, "Too bad mother, that's your problem," but then she looked at the pathetic figure and felt pity. "Can't you sell the farm and buy a small house. Surely there would be some money left? You can't spend the rest of your life struggling with debts and working all hours."

Molly gave a bitter smile. "If I sell, I will have nothing. I have to stay; it's the only way."

"I'm sorry."

"Why do you keep saying that?"

"It's the best I can do."

"Then watch your poor mother struggle."

"I'm sorry," Clarissa repeated, "but there is nothing I can do." She saw the despair in her mother's eyes and put a hand gently on her shoulder. "I'll talk to Ted and try to get to the funeral. I'm sure there must be a solution," she mumbled.

Relief crossed her mother's face, or was it cunning? Had Molly just played on Clarissa's fragile state of mind? It would be just like her. "I must go," Clarissa said quickly.

Molly said nothing.

Ted held Clarissa close. It wasn't often she needed comforting, but this was one of those times. She sat with half-closed eyes on the sofa in their sitting room still deeply affected by the events of the last two days, enjoying the feeling of security that Ted gave her. She had arrived home deeply depressed and feeling guilty about doubting her mother's dire situation. Now she was exhausted, mentally and physically.

"Perhaps," Ted dared to suggest, "I should talk to your mother and see if we can help her. I know you have your doubts, but maybe she's in real financial trouble. Maybe we can meet with the creditors and talk to the bank. It might save you a lot of stress."

Clarissa smiled. "Maybe I'm wrong to doubt her, but I suppose I'll soon find out the truth if we help her. Anything you can do would be wonderful."

"Whatever you want Clarissa."

She kissed his stubbly chin, enjoying his familiar earthly smell. She'd only been away forty-eight hours and she'd missed him after the first two. Reluctantly she pushed herself away from Ted. "That's enough time thinking about my mother and feeling sorry for myself," she said standing up and stretching. "Dogs to be fed, and there's a vegetable patch out there that needs seeing to and boxes to be filled for tomorrow's market. Come on, no time to waste."

Ted reached for her hand and walked with her out into the garden, the dogs bounding optimistically in front of them. A light rain was falling. The distant downs were clad in mist. Clarissa loved this summer rain, which felt so gentle and warm on her face.

They decided to go together, united in grief. Belinda drove her 4 x 4. Polly, looking pale, sat beside her praying for Emily. Clarissa and Sophie sat in the back. They spoke little, each wrapped up in their own private thoughts. In spite of the sadness of the day, Clarissa could not stop thinking about the financial mess her father had left behind. One word with the bank had proved that her mother was not exaggerating her plight. Sophie was wondering how she'd feel if this was Ed's funeral. Belinda was wondering if Emily could ever recover. "How about turning the radio on," suggested Sophie. "Might lighten up the mood a bit." Belinda turned it on and found some music. It did nothing for the atmosphere in the car.

The church was packed; white lilies seemed to fill every space. The scent was overpowering; Clarissa wrinkled her nose. The coffin holding what remained of Jack was already in front of the altar. There were two wreaths on the lid. One, of pink roses, was from Emily and had been picked and made up by Clarissa the day before. The other was a mixture of summer flowers from Jack's parents.

The girls slid into a back pew. Three knelt and prayed. Clarissa, feeling uneasy, as she always did when she was in a church, fidgeted with the handkerchief she'd brought along to wipe the tears from her face. Although she thought the whole rigmarole of handing over a body to the care of God was a bit of a farce, she knew she'd cry buckets. Emily was sitting with her father three rows back from the steps up to the choir stalls. She was wearing a large grey hat almost hiding her face, a dark blue trouser suit with a pink rose pinned to her left breast. Although Clarissa couldn't see her face, she knew it would be etched with grief and stained with tears. "This is going to be the worst day of my life," she'd cried to Clarissa the day before. "And Jack's father doesn't make it any easier. Do you know what he told me yesterday?"

"No."

"That I wasn't to sit with the family in the church. How can he be so cruel when he knows how much Jack and I were in love? Has the man no heart?"

Clarissa glared at John Talbot's back and imagined the pleasure she'd get by thrusting a knife in the bastard's back. Oops, irreverent thought.

Clarissa found the funeral utterly depressing and meaningless. What on earth made all those people gather in an ornate building and wish poor Jack a better life above? How could that be? Well, it was their God's fault anyway wasn't it? If most of the world threw religion into the dustbin, wouldn't it be a more peaceful place? No terrorists blowing themselves up for a start. No doubt she was guilty of blasphemy, but so what? Was *their* God going to hear her and strike her down? Well come on God let's see what you're made of! Oh yes, of course you forgive everyone. Okay the hymns were fine, the music lovely, and one reading struck a cord, especially the last line, which went '*love and go on.*' That was what she hoped Emily could do. John Talbot's address was all about his wonderful son. Not one word of his relationship with Emily; it was as if Emily had never existed. She'd cried as Emily gave her a weak smile as she walked down the aisle behind the coffin, and again when the coffin had been lowered into the ground, but she heaved a sigh of relief as she walked away from the churchyard. She'd had a bellyful of John Talbot.

Now they were standing in a marquee on the lawn of the Talbot's fine Queen Ann house, surrounded by manicured lawns, and with highland cattle grazing in the park beyond the garden. The view across the Meon Valley was stunning. It was clearly the home of a very wealthy man and like so many mega-rich men he was obviously a mega-shit as well, thought Clarissa. How could he treat Emily the way he had, when he knew how much she and Jack had loved each other? The answer Clarissa knew lay in the British curse called *class*. John Talbot saw himself as upper class; he saw Emily as common. He was old money from the tip of his Gucci shoes to his Trumpers of Curzon Street haircut. He'd inherited a tidy pile from his father and never worked for a day in his life. On the other hand, Jonathan Roper had come from a humble middle class family, and by graft and sheer determination had risen to being one of the most influential men in the private equity business. He was also a thoroughly decent man, ready to admit that he'd been in the right place at the right time, and always willing to help the less fortunate. Clarissa suspected John Talbot envied him his hard won success. It was as simple as that: envy and class, two pernicious emotions. How pathetic could that be? John Talbot was the sort of man who wanted to arrange his son's marriage so that he could keep control of him not risk common blood entering the veins of his family. What a turd! On any other day, Clarissa would have been tempted to give him a piece of her mind.

She was standing with the other girls watching this piece of shit and his over-made-up wife oozing charm to the mourners. They had all moved swiftly to Emily's side, so avoiding any handshakes.

"If I'd had to shake that man's hand," Belinda confided to Sophie, "I think I'd have tried to break his fingers." She grabbed a glass of champagne from a passing waitress and knocked it down in one. "Let's drink as much of this as we can," she laughed, "without hitting the canvas floor of the tent and passing out of course."

"That's exactly how I feel," said Emily a little sadly." She gave her friends a wan smile.

"You okay?" asked Sophie.

"Not really. I know I'm not wanted here and that hurts terribly."

"I think you're being very brave," said Polly.

"I'm crying inside," gulped Emily. "Why can't he just forget his antipathy towards me for a few hours? I have a right to be here. Jack would want me to be here, and his father need never see me again after today. He was against us getting married from the start, and if that wasn't enough he's driving a knife into my heart. Oh my God, I didn't think a man could be so cruel."

Emily's father joined them, his face lined with concern. He was troubled by Emily's mood swings.

Sophie put a hand on his arm. "We're here for Emily; we love her; we loved Jack. We know what they say about time being a great healer, but it's how long that time stretches into the future that no one can foresee. So, until that time comes we will do every thing we can to see her through the bad times."

Jonathan said, "Thank you Sophie. I think I'll need help, don't you?"

"I think we need each other."

"Here comes the waitress again, girls," said Polly. "Let's get stuck in."

Sophie took two glasses from the tray and handed one to Jonathan. "To happier times," she said and raised her glass.

"To happier times," Emily intervened. "And to darling Jack."

Two hour later, stuffed with canapés and more than enough champagne, the girls wove their unsteady way back to the car. "I'm over the limit," slurred Belinda.

"We all are," said Polly stating the obvious. "So what do we do?"

Belinda looked round the acres of grass. "Nice big field. No animals that I can see. We can kip here. In a few hours we'll be fine. No one will notice us."

That was where she was completely wrong.

A violent banging on one of the car windows woke Clarissa from her alcohol-induced sleep. She had no idea where she was. She shook her head and said "Wow!" as the headache hit her. The next thing she knew the door she was resting her head against flew open and she toppled out onto the grass, her legs in the air and her skirt up to her waist. John Talbot had a good view of her blue knickers.

"What the hell are you doing?" he shouted at Clarissa as she frantically tried to make herself decent and work out where she was. "This is private property not a camp sight for riff-raff."

Clarissa did her best to get off the grass with as much dignity as she could muster, which was not much given her crumpled clothes, her wild hair and lack of shoes. "Excuse me," she said squinting at the man standing with his hands on his hips and steam rising from his head. "Who the hell are you?"

"John Talbot, that's who I am young lady."

"Oh my God! Oh my God," gulped Clarissa recognising him.

Talbot looked down his rather large nose at Clarissa. "I want you all off my land NOW! So wake up your friends and get your arses out of here."

"Who's that waking us up?" came a gravely voice from the front as Belinda opened her door and tried to focus on the man who had so rudely interrupted her sleep.

Clarissa whirled round. "It's Jack's father. I think he's a bit miffed that we chose his field to sleep in."

Belinda was surprised how quickly she got her marbles back in to order. She was used to dealing with belligerent barristers and Talbot didn't intimidate her one bit. She started by giving him the menacing smile that had put the fear of God into men with a lot more bottle than Talbot. He had unwittingly picked a formidable opponent. She eased her way out of the car, brushed down her knee-length brown skirt, and moved to within a foot of his face. Then she jabbed him in the chest. He took an involuntary step backwards. "So you're the wanker who has treated Emily like a pariah. I've been longing to meet you," a second's pause "Talbot," she spat. "Do you think because you own all this," Belinda waved a hand dismissively, "that it gives you the right to muck about with other people's lives, to almost destroy a girl who has loved your son ever since university? You must be heartless." Then Belinda finished with a flourish. "People like you Talbot are scum. Got me?"

Talbot held his ground. He was well known for his belligerence and no hung-over trollop was going to knock him off his stride. Placing both his hands against Belinda's chest, he shoved her backwards. Belinda staggered and Talbot laughed. "Now get my message girl, out of here in the next five minutes or things will get nasty."

Managing to regain her balance Belinda gave him what she hoped was a derisive smile. "Alright, we're on our way, but let me say one thing. You don't hold a candle to the likes of Jonathan Roper. He's a proper man, so piss off back to your posh house and frigid wife." With as much dignity as she could muster, given that she had lost her shoes, her skirt was crumpled and her hair a mess, she turned back towards the car where three pairs of eyes were doing their best not to show their amusement.

Talbot went puce, but held his tongue. He snorted loudly and turned away. Belinda watched him until he disappeared behind a yew hedge. "I feel sick," said Clarissa.

"Not surprising," said Belinda, "there's a nasty smell around here."

Emily watched the removal men putting the boxes into their van. The little house in Romsey Road had yet to be sold, but she couldn't spend one more day inside it, surrounded by all the memories. She was taking nothing with her to her father's: no furniture; no pictures; no photographs; just a few clothes and the odd personal item, but nothing that could remind her of Jack. Every item going into the van was to be given to a hospice outside

Winchester. All Jack's possessions were going to be burnt along with anything that she and Jack had bought together. When she felt a little stronger, she'd go to the house in Cheyne Walk and go through the same process. If Jack's death had done nothing else, it had reminded her that her father was special.

Then there were her friends. They had been there for her: constantly by her side; pumping courage into her veins; trying to make her laugh. Despite all that, a huge cloud of doubt still hovered over her. Could she make a new life without Jack? Wonderful handsome, witty, loving Jack, who had made her unbelievably happy and who she missed every second of the day? Could anyone ever light the same fire or play the same chords? Did she want anyone else to do that? She shivered as she stared round the empty sitting room where she and Jack had laughed, made love, drunk a little too much wine at times, and planned their wedding. The answer was quite simple: it was not how she'd planned her life.

Chapter Twenty

Lucy swayed. Staring at the dark forbidding water was making her feel dizzy. She stepped back from the guardrails. She'd been so certain what she wanted to do. If she pitched forward she could let the cold envelop her, until she could hold her breath no longer and only see darkness. Peace would soon follow. She imagined Jack waiting there in the watery darkness ready to rescue her yet again.

The sound of a car horn jolted her back from her reverie. Jack was dead and Emily was about to find out, in the cruellest way, that she had not been the only woman in Jack's life. It suddenly dawned on Lucy that it was Emily who now needed rescuing, and she was the only person who had any chance of doing that. The flat that Jack had given her was only a short distance from the Cheyne Walk house. She'd make sure she passed by the house every day. She was sure Emily would come at some time.

Emily had thought long and hard about going to London on her own. In the end she'd decided it was for the best. She'd leaned on her father's shoulder enough just recently, and besides, she wanted to prove to herself that she could deal with Jack's legacy without too much pain. Seeing the removal men and the estate agent would be a severe test. It had taken her several weeks to get to this point, and it was taking all her resolve to board the train to Waterloo. As she settled into a seat she thought of her father, sitting in his car, willing himself to drive away from the station, but reluctant to do so until he heard the train leave, safe in the knowledge that she was on-board. She fumbled in her handbag—a present from Sophie—and pulled out a packet of wine gums. Chewing seemed to relax her. She screwed up her eyes, as she'd done every day since Jack's death, imagining him beside her. She was sure he'd agree it was best to sell the London house. After all, she'd spent little time in it and apart from a few items that she and Jack had bought together there wasn't anything of sentimental value in the house. She'd been surprised that he'd left it to her in his will, much to the fury of his mother and father. There had been several threatening letters demanding that she give the house back to the family. Well, maybe she should, but Jack had left it to her and that was the end of it as far as she was concerned. Emily smiled as she thought of Belinda's reply to *that* demand. So fuck you Talbot.

She stared up at the carriage ceiling. A light was flickering; it looked as if it might peter out at any moment. It was rather like Jack's presence: slowly becoming more distant. She didn't want to let him go. If she closed her eyes she could still see every line in his face, and the tiny grey hairs creeping in over his ears. She could feel him close to her. She put a hand on her shoulder expecting to find his there to touch. It wasn't there. She let out a long sigh. Even in her imagination she couldn't hang on to him.

The hour and five minutes to Waterloo seemed to flash by. Emily soon found herself walking along the platform, conjuring up memories of her and Jack walking fast, hoping to reach the taxi queue before it grew too long. She imagined she could see him walking in front of her, every now and then looking over his shoulder and laughingly telling her to get her skates on. This time she dragged her feet; she was in no hurry to reach Cheyne Walk.

As so often happens just when you want time to drag the opposite occurs. A line of empty taxis was waiting. Reluctantly she told a driver her destination. Twenty minutes later she was pulling the house keys out of her bag. She planned to spend the day sorting through Jack's personal things and deciding what to do with everything else. It was a depressing thought, but it had to be done. With luck she'd be finished in time to catch a train back to Winchester, and then on to Ted's big night at the gallery. For some time she'd been pondering whether she was up to going. Clarissa had persuaded her it was time to try to start enjoying herself again, telling her, "It's what Jack would have wanted."

That had swung it, and it would cheer her up after what she knew was going to be a very traumatic day. As she turned the key to open the door, she had no idea how traumatic.

The hall smelt a little damp. Jack had suspected dry rot and had intended to get a builder to have a look. She moved quickly into the small sitting room and looked with horror at all the mail piled on one of the tables. Jack's cleaner had carefully sorted them into letters, magazines and junk. Emily made a mental note to give her a ring and ask her what she owed her and tell her that she would no longer need her as the house was going to be sold. She decided to attack the letters first; one envelope in particular caught her eye. The writing was so neat, and the pen that had been used was red. Curious, she slit the envelope open with her nail.

A cry of despair broke from her mouth as she read the contents.

By the time Ted and Clarissa sat down for breakfast, it was already showing signs of being another wet late August day. What did Ted care? This was the beginning of a dream. Today was going to be the culmination of all his hard work and Clarissa's belief in him. If it hadn't been for her, he knew he'd still be painting landscapes for his own enjoyment, not for people to come to a gallery and actually buy. He felt sick! Scared shitless. How long to go? Ten hours, hours that would crawl by. He smiled across the table at Clarissa who was calmly sipping her tea. "It's no good I can't eat," he apologised, pushing his plate of bacon and eggs away. "My stomach is churning something awful."

"Well you'd better eat something before tonight or else the first drink will go straight to that head of yours, and I don't want you falling into Jo Hawksworth's bosoms."

"I wish," he said with a little more enthusiasm than he'd intended.

Clarissa threw him a look. "You randy old bastard! Mine not good enough for you anymore?" she quipped, kicking him playfully under the table.

"More than good enough," Ted replied quickly. Though he had to admit that Jo Hawksworth was a very comely woman; once or twice in the gallery he had playfully tweaked her bottom. On several occasions when they were alone, Jo had intimated that she'd like to go further. As Ted kept telling himself, he was after all only a virile man and easily flattered. So far he'd rejected her advances with polite rebuttals, fearful that she might decide his paintings were no longer wanted. "I have a good woman," he'd said. "A little flirting is one thing; an affair would be explosive."

"Right then, Picasso, I've got work to do," Clarissa informed him. "Wow, I'm bloody stiff!"

"It's all that prancing about that you do in the club."

Clarissa bridled. "I'll have you know it's a bit more than prancing. Last night I ran myself ragged trying to beat a cocky twenty year old."

"So I presume you lost."

"You cheeky so-and-so. I'll have you know I won."

Ted clapped his hands and stood up. "Good for you. Want any help this morning?"

"Apart from some weeding, which you're very welcome to do, there's nothing urgent. No market until Monday. Once I've dealt with the dogs and weeded the rose bed, I'll have time to take a breather this morning and be fit and healthy for your triumph tonight. I can't wait to see the gallery packed with people all looking at your paintings."

"And actually buying them," added Ted.

"Oh God, Ted, I'm so proud of you. It's unbelievably wonderful."

"Come here," Ted said.

Clarissa moved into his arms. "Tell you what," she said, "why don't we give the weeding a miss? It can wait for another day. Why don't we go upstairs and plan what we are going to wear tonight; that should pass the time, eh?"

"But we've only got one . . . Oh, I get you. You're thinking of something else aren't you?"

"You dumb suddenly?"

Ted chuckled. "Are you up to it? Not too tired? Not too stiff?"

"Try me," Clarissa said, a big smile creasing her face as she ran out of the kitchen and up the stairs.

Ted was quick to run after her, thinking what a bloody fool he was fantasising over Jo's breasts.

Sophie was getting restless. Her business partner had been yakking on for what seemed hours about how talented Sophie was. Waste of time, thought Sophie, digging her elbow into her partner's side, you've already got them hooked. Just zip that mouth of yours and let's get the deal signed. The elbow did the trick. An apologetic smile crossed her partner's face. Sophie glanced at her watch. The train she'd planned to catch was just about to leave Waterloo; she was in danger of being late for Ted's grand opening. She looked around the table. Could she make her excuses? No! She could not afford to take her eye off the ball in what was a very cut-throat business. One day your designs could be the talk of every buyer in Europe and the States and the next you were history. There were plenty of designers out there who were only too willing to walk all over her and take her place. She did her best to smile sweetly at the small balding buyer from Debenhams and thought how much she was missing Ed. She resented the time she was away from him. She'd have to text him and tell him she'd meet him at the gallery.

Polly had taken up Belinda's suggestion that they might have an early supper at the Hotel du Vin before going to the gallery. It had been some time since they had been alone together, and Polly, to her surprise, was missing Belinda's attention. Belinda felt the same about Polly, but she was in control of her feelings, even though the sight of this stunning girl sitting next to her had surely raised her blood pressure. "Going to be an interesting evening later, I think," she said, fighting the urge to say, "God you look fantastic."

Clarissa was praying that the Morris wouldn't have one of its moods and let them down. It didn't sound too good and she could see that Ted was getting fidgety. "We'll make the gallery on time," she said with more confidence than she felt.

Ted grunted. "I wish you'd agreed to take my van. We can't afford to be late." The Morris coughed. Ted wiped the sweat off his brow. Clarissa whispered encouraging words to the recalcitrant car. "Bugger," said Ted.

"Oh, stop fussing," said Clarissa.

The Morris coughed again, and Ted shook his head.

Half an hour later they made the car park.

"Never again," said Ted. "This heap of junk has just signed its death warrant."

Clarissa said nothing.

Amanda Flint met them at the door of the gallery. "Thought you were going to be late," she scolded.

"So did I," said Ted throwing a smile Jo's way. "It's Clarissa's bloody Morris. It's clapped out, but for some reason she won't part with it."

"It's what you call financial restrictions darling Ted," Clarissa replied with a wink at Amanda.

"Well, you're here now darlings so no matter," said Jo, stepping in front of Amanda and landing a kiss on Ted's cheek before giving Clarissa a light peck. "We're ready for the rush."

Ted looked appalled. "How many are you expecting this evening?"

Jo smiled at his obvious panic. She put a hand lightly on his arm—God how she'd like to bed this man. He was *so* earthy! She swiftly took her hand away. "It's all by invitation tonight. I would expect about eighty."

"That many!" exclaimed a shocked Ted. "You told me about two dozen the other day."

"We got carried away," laughed Amanda. "But don't worry, they won't all be here at one time and it's good Ted, real good to have so many people eager to come. You're going to surprise them." She waved her hand round the room. "Just look at your paintings, don't they look great. You should be so proud."

Ted moved into the middle of the room and let his eyes roam from picture to picture. He'd spent years honing his art, hour upon hour perfecting each painting, feeling frustrated at times, regularly losing his cool when his brush just wouldn't do what he wanted. He'd never had much ambition. As long as he enjoyed creating something on paper he was happy. If someone had told him that one day he'd be exhibiting in a gallery in Winchester he'd have laughed in their face. And yet, here he was looking at his work and thinking that it was not bad, not bad at all. He was not a conceited man, but looking at his paintings made him feel proud. He moved back to Clarissa and took her hand, the love shining out of his eyes. "I . . . I don't know what to say."

"You don't need to say a word," said Clarissa with a swift smile. "I always knew I'd married a talented and wonderful man. You deserve your success." With that she pulled him to her ample bosom and landed a wet kiss smack on his lips.

Eat your heart out Jo Hawksworth, she thought.

The gallery was a jumble of raised voices, the crowd spilling out onto the street. Couples were moving round the floor, wine clasped in their hands, glasses being constantly topped up by Jo while Amanda passed round the nibbles. Journalists from local papers were snapping away furiously with their cameras and a television crew from South Today was interviewing Ted for an evening spot after the national news. He was red in the face, overawed by all the attention, but enjoying his bit of fame.

Polly downed yet another glass of red wine. She was doing her best to look interested and she had to admit that she actually quite liked one or two of Ted's landscapes. Belinda was earnestly studying each painting; she felt she had a good eye for art. Polly was impressed. "Why don't you go and chat up Ed while I have a word with someone about buying one of these," Belinda suggested. "I think they are really very good."

Ed was chatting to Jo Hawksworth as if he'd known her all his life. Polly knew he was like a magnate to people because of his easy going manner and willingness to talk or listen. Ed was quite simply a great guy. A man in a million. She might even like men again if she could find another Ed, but knowing her fiendish luck, she'd never recognise one even if he was dumped right under her nose with a sign on his chest saying: *Hello lady I'm your great guy.*

"Hi Ed, said Polly, looking round the room, "no Sophie tonight?"

"Nice to see you Polly," Ed replied, bending down to give her a light peck on the cheek, surprised that Belinda wasn't one step behind her. He'd heard the gossip. "She's been delayed in London—should be here soon. Oh, look who's just walked through the door. Let's go and say hello."

By the time they'd pushed through the crowd, Emily's father had been joined by Clarissa who was introducing him to Jo and Amanda. "Hello Ed," Jonathan said. "Emily got here alright?"

Ed threw a questioning look at Clarissa.

"I don't think she's here yet," she replied.

"I assumed she was," said a concerned Jonathan. "She was going to London to sort out the Cheyne Walk house, and planned to meet me here."

"Probably missed the train, like Sophie. No doubt they'll be here later," suggested Ed.

Jonathan nodded, "Yes, probably. Quite a crowd your husband has attracted," he said turning to Clarissa.

"These two are responsible for that," said Clarissa smiling at Jo and Amanda.

"And where is the great artist?" Jonathan asked.

"Somewhere in the middle of the scrum, lapping up all the attention," laughed Clarissa. "Come on let's go and find him."

"You need a drink," added Jo. "White or red?"

"Not for me," answered Jonathan. "I've got to drive. Now who's going to show me these paintings?"

Clarissa took him firmly by the arm. "Me, but first I will introduce you to the brilliant artist."

"That sounds a good idea," Jonathan replied, casting a concerned eye towards the gallery entrance, only to see Sophie walk through the door alone. For a second he felt a stab of panic. No, he was being silly. Emily would be along any minute.

The gallery was beginning to empty and Ed was holding Sophie's hand. "I thought you weren't going to make it. Missed you like hell. Here, let me grab you a drink if there's any left. I think Polly's drunk most of it!"

"Boy do I need a drink."

"I can imagine. Bad day?"

"Unbelievably terrible, but a good result. They liked my shoes and even flirted with the idea of taking my new range of handbags, but it took hours. That partner of mine could talk the hind legs off a bloody donkey."

Ed kissed her lightly on a cheek. "Well you're here now and I bet you wowed all the buyers. I think you do a great job."

Sophie returned his kiss. "Oh, I just do something I love. It's no big deal."

Ed moved his arm to her shoulder. He knew how hot the competition was and how hard Sophie worked to keep one step in front of her competitors. Then he spotted Jo. He reached out and touched her arm. "Jo—I hope you don't mind me calling you that—I'd like to introduce my wife."

Jo stopped and looked at Sophie. "Wow, Clarissa said you were beautiful! Hello Sophie, good to meet you. Take your husband and have a look around before we close the doors. Plenty of paintings left if you fancy landscapes." Then she was gone, weaving her way through the dwindling crowd. She was feeling a little worse for wear.

Sophie laughed. "I think she's had a bit too much of her wine. Now let's go and see what Picasso, as Clarissa calls him, has painted."

By ten p.m. the gallery was empty and Ted was swaying like a branch in a breeze. Totally smashed, Jo was collecting glasses and singing to herself. Amanda was sitting on a stool by a desk, trying to focus on working out how much money had been taken, while Clarissa was curled up on a beaten-up old armchair sound asleep.

"A very successful evening," said Amanda with satisfaction. "Twelve pictures bought."

"That good?" slurred Ted.

"Absolutely brilliant," said Jo. "I never thought we'd sell that many in the whole week. It means we've only got eleven more to sell. If we go on like this we'll have to put you on overtime, Ted."

Ted raised a hand with difficulty. "No way. I'm not going to become a machine churning out inferior paintings just to satisfy our greed. Ten a year is the most I will do."

"Twelve" chivvied Amanda. "We'll guarantee to buy them all off you. I quite agree with what you've just said. Mass produce and you will lose your appeal."

Clarissa started to snore.

Jo laughed.

"Time for home," said Ted.

"Not in your state," said Amanda, "and Clarissa is certainly beyond driving a car. We can all sleep here. There are two sofas in the back room, and we brought sleeping bags because we thought we might drink just a tiny bit too much!"

Ted started to object.

"No!" said Jo. "You both stay here. I'm not allowing you out of this shop in your state, so make the best of what we can offer you."

"Yes madam," teased Ted. He looked across at Clarissa snoring contentedly. "I think we can leave her there. No point in spoiling her dreams."

Clarissa woke the next morning with a headache threatening to rip her scull from her brain. Every limb seemed reluctant to move and she was bursting for a pee. She forced her eyes open and stared round the gallery. Bloody hell, she thought, we didn't go home. The poor dogs. I didn't realise I was that pissed. She heard a familiar grunt from the back room. Ted was waking up, probably suffering like her. She managed a smile—difficult with her tongue stuck to the roof of her mouth—and prised herself out of the chair, her bladder complaining.

Emily read the letter again. Each written word was like small daggers being driven into her heart. She stood in the middle of the room gasping for breath. How could this be? How could Jack have managed to keep this woman a secret from her? They had been close, very close, by the tone of the letter: a flat, a car, probably money as well. Had they made love on *their bed?* Her darling Jack, the man she'd been mourning, the man she'd almost taken her life over, was turning out to be no better than any other man: a cheating adulterous liar. She stared round the room in disbelief, feeling so bloody stupid. How could she have been so blind? Devastation threatened to unhinge her mind, but even in this state she knew that at sometime there would come anger, anger so strong that it would eclipse any love she'd ever felt for Jack. How could he have robbed her of that love?

"Damn you Jack," she cried. She threw herself across the room and picked up a Halcyon Day ceramic box inscribed *You mean the world to me.* She remembered the moment Jack had given it to her. She hurled it against a wall and watched it smash into dozens of small pieces. It was beyond repair. Just like their relationship would have been.

Lucy took her now familiar route via Cheyne Walk to the tube. Every day for several weeks now she'd passed the house at least twice a day, her heart in her mouth. She looked up at the windows, the curtains usually drawn. Today the downstairs ones were drawn back. She saw a figure at one of the windows. Could it be Emily? She stopped and stared at the window.

It had to be either the cleaner or Emily. She saw a young face. It was Emily! This was the moment she'd been dreading and yet, in a perverse sort of way, longing for. Purging her soul she called it. She was under no illusions. This was going to be hell, the worst day of her life, but it had to be done. She wasn't sure what it was going to achieve. Was she seeking forgiveness, or was she hoping that she could ease Emily's pain? Probably a little of both, and she had a horrible feeling she wouldn't secure either. She wished she could be anywhere else on earth.

Emily heard the doorbell ring. Her face was puffed-up by crying, a small pool of vomit was slowly seeping into the carpet. She was a mess. The house she'd loved, now felt like a prison. Everything she touched was tainted. She would take nothing from it. The bell rang again. "Go away!" she screamed. The bell rang again, longer this time, as if the person on the other side didn't mean to go away. She dragged herself out of the chair, jammed her feet into her shoes, and listlessly made for the door.

She stared at the young woman who stood on the doorstep.

"Emily?"

"Yes, what do you want?" Emily spat.

Lucy's first reaction on seeing the state of Emily was to turn and run away faster than she'd ever run before.

Then Emily said very quietly. "You're not the estate agent?"

"No."

"Or the removal man?"

"No. I'm . . ."

"You're Lucy! It's you, it's you isn't it? You're the writer of the letter?"

Lucy's chance had gone.

Lucy could feel Emily's hostility. Unable to look her in the face, she mumbled, "Yes, I'm Lucy. Lucy Hemming."

For what seemed an age, the two women stood staring at each other, neither sure how the other was going to react. In the end Lucy stammered, "Can I come in?"

Emily was caught between two stools. She wanted to shout, "Fuck off," yet her curiosity was nagging away at her. Lucy spoke again before she could make up her mind.

"Please Emily, I need to explain."

"Explain what?" screamed Emily. "Explain how you came to sleep with Jack?" She was aware that several passers by were staring at her. She ran a hand through her dank hair and shook her head. "I don't know, I really don't know. Everything is such a mess. Why did you have to write that letter, why did you come here?"

"I need to talk to you. If Jack hadn't died, you would never have read the letter. Now I need to explain my relationship with him."

"As if you were brother and sister?" Emily said bitterly.

Lucy judged it better to say nothing. She took a step towards Emily. Emily reeled back. "Don't."

Lucy stopped. Emily moved back into the house, and for a moment, Lucy thought that Emily was going to slam the door on her. She started to turn away.

"Come in," said Emily.

Lucy stopped, turned and followed her into the sitting room, reflecting that she probably knew it better than Emily.

"Sit there," Emily ordered, pointing to a chair by the window without making eye contact with Lucy.

Lucy sat.

"I'm not going to offer you a drink," said Emily, dropping into the chair opposite Lucy. "I just want you to explain this letter without a load of lies, and then I want you to go, and I never want to see you again."

"I think it might be best if I started at the beginning."

Emily did her best to stop the tears that were threatening to burst out again. Why she wanted to hear all the sordid details of the affair she had no idea, but she nodded. "Okay."

In as calm a voice as she could muster, Lucy began.

Emily crossed her legs and stared at the pretty freckled face, the trim figure, the delicate hands now entwining with nerves, the short mousy hair, the crumpled grey skirt and the blue blouse that had seen better days. She looked as if she needed a good wash, but strip away her dishevelled appearance and there would be a very attractive woman sitting opposite her. She felt a stab of jealousy. If Lucy was telling the truth, Jack had only been in one of his white-knight moods, but she found that hard to believe.

"Why the car, the flat?" she asked as Lucy paused for breath. "Isn't that what men buy for their mistresses?"

Lucy chose her words carefully. "I was never his mistress. It was always only a friendship." She saw Emily shake her head. "He had a heart of gold. Like I said, he saw I was in trouble and came to my rescue. Simple as that."

Emily's eyes widened in disbelief. "Are you telling me you never slept with him?"

"We kissed, that was all."

"You expect me to believe that?"

"You can believe what you want. I can't alter that, but I came here to tell the truth. I know I should have thanked him for his help on that first day and sent him on his way, but I was terrified for my life and Jack seemed the sort of man I could trust. I certainly should have refused his gifts."

"I thought *I* could trust him," Emily said bitterly.

"You could."

"Oh come on! I'm prepared to believe that Jack had no other intention but to help you at first, but the car, the flat . . . it stinks of a lurid affair." Emily was getting angry now. "All the time I was in Hampshire, he was here, in the house I thought was our love nest, fucking you. For the last two years, all those roses by our bed on a Friday night were not for love, but to assuage his guilt—the bastard!"

"You must believe me. It wasn't like that," said Lucy desperately. "It was never more than a platonic relationship. I never slept with him. I admit we were fond of each other, but it was never my intention to come between you and Jack. He loved you Emily, he really did. I meant nothing to him."

"Then why the letter? Why say you're returning what he gave you because that would be the final break in the relationship? Why say you hoped he understood, and apologise for allowing him to think that he could go on seeing you after we were married. How could you say that unless there was more to the relationship than you're prepared to admit?" Emily fought back the tears. "Why did you bother to come here? Did you hope to get hold of the letter before I did? Grab it and think of yet another lie? What excuse were you going to make? I'll tell you something, I wish you'd never come near me. I wish you'd dropped down some fucking big hole and disappeared. I wouldn't be looking at you now, imagining all the things you and Jack got up to in this house."

Lucy felt a lump in her throat, deciding it would be disastrous to mention she'd already been to the house to try to retrieve the letter. She said, "I think I know how you feel, and maybe coming here was a mistake, but I wanted to tell you how guilty I feel about the time I spent with Jack when he should have been with you. I wanted to convince you that I meant nothing to him compared to you. Only Jack was supposed to read the letter and if he'd lived no-one would have ever known about us."

"That wouldn't have happened," accused Emily, "because your sordid little affair would have continued to go on behind my back even after we were married!"

"No, I would never have done that."

"Jack would have tried to persuade you. You've just admitted that, and you would have weakened. He was an attractive man, very persuasive. You have destroyed any respect I had for the man I loved with all my heart. Are you satisfied?"

"I didn't love him."

Emily threw her a stare of sheer disgust. "You didn't sleep with him, you didn't love him! You liar; you liar. Of course you loved him, and I'm sure you slept with him. How could you hold off a man you saw regularly for almost two years?"

Lucy looked down at her hands. Stood up slowly. "I'm sorry," she said sadly as she made for the door.

"Sorry," screamed Emily. "Is that all you can say - sorry. You have lied through your teeth and destroyed something special."

Lucy said nothing.

"Get out!"

Lucy turned and walked out of the room, quickening her step once she reached the hall. She never looked back; she couldn't bear to see Emily's face anymore. She couldn't get out of the house fast enough. She opened the front door and stepped onto the pavement, gulping in the fresh air. What had she done? She'd lied; she'd destroyed all the memories of Jack that Emily cherished. It was probably the one thing that had kept her going these last few weeks. Now despair would be flooding her senses, all the memories shattered. Lucy thought she knew exactly how she'd feel if the roles were reversed. Her visit had been a disaster. In the end, her emotions had got the better of her. All her attempts to explain were nothing but dust, because, at the end, she'd been unable to deny Emily's accusations. It would have been better if she'd jumped into the Thames.

She turned left and headed for her flat. Somehow she hurt all over, physically, as well as emotionally. Her skin was tender, her eyes burned and she felt utterly exhausted. She couldn't imagine ever feeling properly happy again. There was only one decent thing she could do: go home, and never ever return to London, and try somehow to rebuild her life.

Jonathan dialled Emily's mobile number. He'd been dialling every half-hour since he'd left the gallery and now it was eight in the morning. There was still no answer. He tried the landline with the same result. It was fourteen hours since she should have shown at the gallery. Where was the girl? Panic was now threatening to consume him. Keep calm, he kept telling himself, panicking will get you nowhere. He was seriously thinking of ringing the police. He knew Emily's state of mind was still very fragile and he feared going to the house on her own had proved too much for her. What had she done? Had she gone to a friend or stayed the night in the house? Perhaps the removal men had taken longer than expected, and were coming back today. All perfectly logical explanations except for one thing: Emily would have rung him. He sat down at the kitchen table and put his head in his hands. He should never have let her go on her own. He would go to London. He prayed he was not too late. Oh God, don't think like that, he admonished himself.

When the house telephone rang, Jonathan jumped up and grabbed the receiver with shaking hands. He was convinced it would be the police saying his daughter was dead.

"Hello."

"Dad, it's me. I need your help."

"Where are you darling?" Jonathan asked, fighting to keep his voice calm.

"At the house."

"What's wrong? I was worried. Why haven't you phoned me?"

"Please, Dad, no questions, just get here as quickly as you can."

For the second time in a matter of weeks, Jonathan found himself rushing to his distressed daughter's side.

They were sitting round the kitchen table. Jonathan had found some instant coffee and sugar in one of the cupboards. They had decided to pass on the milk. It would have meant finding a shop. Emily was holding both his hands across the table and staring at him with wide, desperate eyes. "I'm sorry I didn't ring, Dad."

"I understand," he said patting one of Emily's hands. "What a nightmare. You already had more than enough on your plate."

"She didn't have to come here, Dad."

"No, she didn't, but I think it was for the best. Oh, I know you don't see it that way right now, but once your anger has died down you will be glad that you saw her. At least you can put a face to the name, and she has tried to put her side of the story. Isn't that better than just reading the letter and imagining what she was like? Whether you believe her or not is another matter, and no doubt it will play on your mind for some time."

"I've already made up my mind; I don't believe her," Emily said wearily. "I have no doubt she loved Jack, and that she slept with him in spite of her denial. She was very convincing, but how can you love a man for two years and not sleep with him? If what she said was true, it must have been a very strange relationship, too strange for me to believe. I was obviously lacking something. God only knows what. I thought we were the perfect package. Now I discover, in the cruellest way possible, from a letter, that Jack was just your average man trying to get his leg over another woman."

"You mustn't think like that."

"How can I help it? Do you know, Dad, I'm so angry with him, I almost hate him for what he's done to me. I don't blame Lucy. She was having a real bad time when Jack flew to her rescue. I think he took advantage of her when she was under threat from her violent husband. I think he honestly wanted to draw a line under their relationship, painful as it would be, hence her intention to return the things Jack had given her, like the car."

"He gave her a car?"

"And a flat, and no doubt money."

Jonathan was stunned.

Emily gave him a sad smile. "So you see why I don't believe her. I know she loved him and I'm sure Jack loved her. There is no good me trying to think otherwise. I can't even spit in his face and walk away from him, making him feel like the bastard he was. I'm glad he's dead."

"Oh my darling, you don't really mean that."

Emily shook her head. "It's wrong, Dad, I know, but my whole life has been destroyed: my happiness, my dreams, my hopes for our children, our love maturing like a good wine as we grow older, our grandchildren. All gone."

Jonathan was lost for words. It was no good saying that if Jack had lived she would never have found out about his liaison with Lucy Hemming, because that would be pure conjecture. From what Emily had told him it might have all turned very nasty.

Emily read his thoughts. "And don't tell me that if Jack had lived I would never have found out about Lucy, because I know I would. And do you know why?"

Jonathan shook his head.

"Because Jack had made up his mind not to marry me."

"You can't know that."

"I do Dad. I'm certain. There were no pink roses by my bed the last two Fridays before he died."

Chapter Twenty-One

The doorbell interrupted Belinda's thoughts. She looked at her watch; it was a bit early for the postman. She shrugged, and moved out of the kitchen towards the door. As soon as she opened it, a fist slammed into her face, splitting her lip. She reeled backwards, blood trickling down her chin. Desperately, she tried to close the door against the large man in a Balaclava, who was forcing his way into her home, but he was too strong and swatted her away as if she was a fly. He hit her again, this time in the stomach. She was still doubled up in pain when the next blow caught her on the chin and sent her crashing back against the wall. She sank to the floor, whimpering. A boot thumped into her ribs. The man bent down and grabbed her by the hair, half-pulling her off the floor and shaking her, like he would a small dog.

"Let this be a lesson to you, lady. Even in death, Jerry Gordon has friends. You're the lucky one. Polecat is on his way to hell and little Polly will be next."

Belinda sank into unconsciousness.

A voice came from above her. Belinda groaned and stirred. The voice came again. A face appeared in front of her eyes. She stirred but made no attempt to get off the floor. The pain was excruciating. She felt a hand touch her face. In her confused state she thought she was about to be attacked again. "No!" she screamed.

"Belinda, Belinda, it's me!"

Belinda forced her eyes open. "Clarissa," she managed to say, through her swollen lips.

Clarissa stared at Belinda's bloodied face in amazement. "What, what has happened?"

Belinda touched her side and winced as the pain shot through her. She shook her head and tried to focus. Clarissa swam in front of her eyes. She swallowed the bile that was threatening to choke her and managed to push herself into a sitting position on the floor. "Christ that hurts. I think my ribs are broken."

"You look in a pretty bad way," said an alarmed Clarissa. "Don't try and move. I'm going to call an ambulance." Questions could wait. Belinda smiled weakly and sank back onto the floor.

Ambulance called, Clarissa dropped onto her knees beside Belinda. "Where's the pain?"

"My face and ribs. He drove a fist into my face and kicked me with his fucking great boot." Belinda spat out a mouthful of blood.

"Someone *did* this?" asked Clarissa breathlessly.

"A sodding large man." Belinda tried to smile. "And not a very friendly one." She screwed up her damaged face. "What brought you here, Clarissa?"

"I was on my way to the club, thought I'd drop by to see how you were after last night. I've come from seeing Polly, who is a little worse for wear, so I thought I'd check on you."

"Polly, my God Polly!" gasped Belinda. "Christ Clarissa, we need to do something!" She struggled to get up, but the pain from her ribs took her breath away. "Oh shit!"

It dawned on Clarissa that something very serious was up; Belinda was not one to panic. "Belinda, what exactly is going on?"

"Gordon's returned from the dead. One of his thugs did this to me. He told me he'd killed Polecat and Polly was going to be his next target. I don't think he was bluffing."

Polly looked at her father in amazement. "You're going to leave mother!" she gasped. "Why?"

"I can't take it any longer: her constant nagging, her total disregard for my feelings, and now this refusal to see you. I have no reason to keep this farce of a marriage going. She's a cruel self-centred woman, Polly."

"My God, Dad, I didn't know you had it in you!"

"Nor did I."

"So, what are you going to do?"

David gave a sheepish smile. "Firstly ask if I can move in with you."

Polly jumped up and gave here father a kiss. "You've come up trumps at last, Dad! And of course you can come and stay for as long as you like—at least until I sell the house."

"Well if that happens . . . ."

Polly's mobile rang. It was Clarissa. "Hang on Dad, I must take this."

Belinda beaten up! Clarissa wouldn't say any more than that, but she'd made it pretty clear that Polly should get to Belinda's house as quickly as possible. Polly had heard the urgency in her voice and quickly handed her house keys to her father. Sorry Dad, Belinda's hurt. Must go! See you later."

Polly drove as fast as she dared. She risked a dangerous overtaking manoeuvre and was rewarded with an angry blast from the other driver's horn. She took a left past the prison, then another left and skidded to a halt outside Belinda's house. Clarissa, who had been watching from a window, opened the door before Polly was half way up the drive.

"Wow that was an exciting drive," gasped Polly. "What's the urgency?"

"I think you better let Belinda tell you that," said Clarissa. "She's in her bedroom. Just got back from the hospital. She's looking a bit worse for wear."

Polly took the steps two at a time and burst into the bedroom. She stared in horror at Belinda's damaged face and the strapping round her chest. Without a second's thought she rushed to the bedside and kissed her

"Ow!" Belinda exclaimed. "Careful!"

Polly felt her heart turn over. She really cared for this woman. It came as quite a surprise. "What happened to you?" She asked gently, settling down on the edge of the bed and reaching for one of Belinda's hands.

If she hadn't been in such pain Belinda would have taken Polly in her arms then, but even if one was in love there were some things one couldn't do when you had three broken ribs and split lips! She made do with a weak smile. "It's not as bad as it looks," she said painfully. "A very nasty man came visiting and it's bad, bad news I'm afraid. We are facing a very serious situation."

Polly's eyes widened. "I hope it's not what I think it is," she said, feeling the first tentacles of fear.

"Jerry Gordon," said Belinda by way of explanation.

Polly looked horrified. "But he's dead," she said, feeling stupid the moment the words had come out of her mouth.

"But some thug of a friend isn't. And he's already killed Polecat."

Polly's hand flew to her mouth. "Oh my God! And now he's done this to you. That means . . . ."

Belinda knew there was no point in mincing her words. "You're his next target."

"What are we going to do?"

Belinda grimaced. Talking was very painful. "This man, whoever he is, must be looking to commit suicide. The police have already been alerted. If I was him I'd make myself scarce while I had a chance of getting away, but he's obviously hell-bent on getting to you. He'll be sneaking around waiting for a good time to attack you. You are in great danger, Polly. This man is dangerous and out of control. Although the police have promised to watch over you, they cannot be with you every minute of the day and night. I suggest you move to Clarissa's; he won't know where she lives. You certainly can't stay here."

Polly thought for a moment. "Well, I'm certainly not going to risk putting Clarissa and Ted in danger. Yes, I'm scared, but I've got Dad at home now—he's walked out on mother—so I'll take my chances there. Besides, the police are sure to catch him soon."

"You can't bank on it," warned Belinda.

"I really don't mind you and your father coming to stay with me," interrupted Clarissa.

"No! I'm not doing that, but thanks Clarissa. I must trust in the police, and I don't expect I will have long to wait before this man makes a move."

That was where Polly was wrong. Jack O'Brian was in no hurry at all. He wanted her to sweat. He was used to doing nothing but stare at four walls for months on end. Waiting for the right time to strike would give him something to concentrate on; he had nothing else to do except claim the dole. He'd been out of the nick for six months and had kept his nose clean, so he doubted that the Filth were too interested him. They didn't know that he and Jerry had been close. Getting even for Jerry had meant calling in a favour from his old partner, Willy McBride, who lived at the top end of Winchester. Willy had once grassed on him to save his own skin and was none too happy to find his ex-partner standing on his doorstep, but he had no choice but to let him in. Willy owed Jack big time.

At the age of fifteen, Jack had committed his first burglary with Jerry, but soon he grew bored of Jerry's petty thieving. At sixteen he was in a young offenders' unit for aggravated burglary. At nineteen he was in prison for GBH. And so it had gone on all his life—in and out of prison—a habitual criminal. Prison was his home; he only felt comfortable when he was locked up. So robbery, a contract beating, and murder were all the same to him. He'd been glad to find Jerry in the same prison and he'd been quick to rekindle their old relationship. He owed him for starting him on his road to crime. Jerry had confided in him, the bitterness oozing out of every pore. Jack had made him a solemn promise: when he got out of the nick he'd deal with those who had crossed his friend. Now that Jerry was dead, revenge had taken on added importance. He hadn't intended to kill Polecat, but the little man's neck had proved to be rather fragile. Tough, but who was he to care? A life meant nothing to him, but it meant that the police would be taking a special interest in Polecat's death and his unwise threat to Musgrove about Polly meant that she'd be closely guarded, but he'd get her in the end. It was his proud boast that his targets never got away from him. He would just have to tread carefully, watch and wait and choose his moment.

He sat in his stolen blue Ford Mondeo, watching Polly's house, thinking it was time he dumped it and nicked another one. He'd keep one eye on her and one on the Filth. He was surprised they weren't already parked outside her door. He guessed it wouldn't be long. Then he saw a middle aged man walk up to the house, pull out a key and open the door. Fuck, this was something he hadn't reckoned on. Polly had a lodger, or maybe a lover. That could be a slight problem; he'd planned to have a bit of fun with Polly. He shrugged and gunned the engine. Time to go back to Willy and think strategy.

Polly played her heart out. The team owed it to Belinda. They'd discussed cancelling, but Belinda had begged them to play. "I know a good replacement, nothing to worry about. Besides, it will do us all good to do something other than think of poor Polecat and the danger Polly faces."

Polly didn't think it would be too easy to forget Polecat, or that some man was out there waiting to beat her up or even worse, but she'd agreed it would do her good to play, and she felt safe with the team and the squad car in the car park.

Emily had decided to play as well—a first step to trying to get her life back together. She'd decided to say nothing about Lucy to her friends, or to Jack's parents who would probably have gloated and reminded her that they had always known that she was not the girl for *their* Jack. Her father was the only one who shared her secret. Her heart was broken; she was certain it would never completely mend. Obviously she'd failed to make Jack happy and Lucy had filled the void. She'd thought she'd known all of Jack's needs. She'd been wrong, and so had sacrificed his love, but that didn't mean he wasn't a turd. He should have told her what was wrong and they could have worked on it together, that's what couples did. You bastard, she thought.

As she walked off court, she smiled an apology at Sophie and Clarissa who hadn't yet played. "Sorry I lost," she said.

"You'll be fine next time," said Clarissa.

"Hope so," Emily said, as she slowly made her way to the showers, wondering if she'd ever be fine again.

Sophie's eyes followed Emily as she walked away. "Do you know," she said to Clarissa. "Sometimes life can be very cruel."

Chapter Twenty-Two

Sophie was on a high. Her latest handbag design had been well received and her interview with Harpers Bazaar had gone far better than she'd expected. She'd been surprisingly nervous. Her first interview! It meant she was well and truly accepted as one of the top shoe and bag designers of her generation. She knew her shoes would never quite touch the popularity of Jimmy Choo or Lulu Guinness, but her latest sales figures confirmed she wasn't lagging far behind. Where she did have an advantage over those two was in her versatility. Her bags were running Anya Hindmarch close. All-in-all life was great. She knew that at some time in the future her popularity would begin to fade—there was little loyalty amongst the buying public—but for the time being she was determined to enjoy her success. She boarded the evening train to Winchester light of heart. Soon she'd be back with Ed.

The lights were on in the house as she swung the BMW into the drive. Excitement made her shiver. It meant Ed was back. She loved coming home last. There was something so comforting to see darling smiling Ed standing in the kitchen holding out a cool gin and tonic. Samantha made her usual appearance out of the bushes as Sophie stepped out of the car and she swept the cat into her arms. "Let's go and see that wonderful man," she whispered, burying her head in Samantha's fur.

When she walked in, she could hear the radio playing in the kitchen. Dropping Samantha gently onto the floor she hurried towards the noise. And there he was, just as she thought he'd be, standing in his blue suit, his tie loosened, holding a cold gin and tonic and a beaming smile on his face. "Welcome home darling!"

Sophie let out a low moan of pleasure, grabbed the glass and kissed him full on the lips. "No wine yet?" she laughed.

"I always wait until you're home. Lone drinking, as I tell some of my patients, is the first step to alcoholism."

"What rubbish," she said.

"No it's true," Ed said moving to the fridge and pulling out an open bottle of white wine. He poured a glass. "To us," he said.

"To us, you wonderful man." She took a sip of her drink. "Mm gorgeous. Any mail today?"

"Two letters. One from Jamaica. They're both on the work top over there."

"Jamaica! Ah, that's Millicent's writing." Sophie moved over to the worktop and opened the letter. Seconds later her hand flew to her mouth. "Oh Ed, Grandpa's died!" She burst into tears.

Ed ran towards her and took her in his arms. "Oh Sophie, I'm so terribly sorry. When did this happen?"

"A couple of weeks ago."

"So long ago? Why didn't she ring?"

"She couldn't, Ed. She doesn't have our number."

"Didn't your grandmother have it?"

"No point was there? She can't read and no telephone."

"But you'd have liked to have been there."

"Of course, but I have always known that would be impossible."

"We must go out there immediately."

Sophie wiped away the tears and looked at Ed with renewed love. "You know Ed you really are something special. I wasn't even going to suggest it, but as you've brought it up."

"I'd like us to go," said Ed.

"Do you think you can get away from the practice?"

"I think so. When is the funeral likely to be?"

"Oh, they will already have had that."

"Yes I suppose so. Is there any way we can get in touch with Grandma?"

"I could ring Jamaica Inn and ask them to send Randall up to her with a message."

"Good idea. Okay, you do that. Tomorrow I'll see when we can get tickets."

Damn, she was going to cry in front of Ed again.

Jack O'Brian moved into the bushes. He could see the taillights of the police car outside Polly's house. It would be impossible to get to her tonight.

No doubt she felt safe protected by the police and her lodger/lover. He smiled. Luckily she didn't know about his reputation. He glanced at his watch as hunger pangs worked on his stomach. He might as well go back to Willy's for a beer and a take-away. He stepped out into the road and walked back towards the VW parked opposite the Horse and Jockey.

It was raining heavily when they arrived in Montego Bay. Randall was waiting for them outside the airport and greeted them with his beaming smile. "Mrs Ed, good to see you. And you Mr Ed," he said taking Ed's hand. "Sorry about your Grandpa, Mrs Ed. The hotel gave me your message and I went up and told your grandma that you were coming."

"You're a kind man. How is she?" asked Ed.

"Sad man, very sad, but she said she'd been expecting it for some time. She cried a little when she heard you were coming."

"Poor Grandma," said Sophie. "I think we should go there right now. Can you spare the day Randall?"

"No problem Mrs Ed. The island very quiet right now."

Sophie and Ed did not go to the hotel that night. They decided to sleep on the floor of the shack and ask Randall to come back late evening the next day.

"What's late evening?" he asked.

"Can you make it around nine?"

"Sure can, see you then."

Grandpa had been buried next to Sophie's parents. Grandma told Sophie that the little church had been packed and there had been a lot of crying. A character had died; a man who, to old and young, had seemed indestructible. "He played a part in so many lives in different ways," Grandma explained.

"There will be no-one to replace him," added Sophie. "God just doesn't make people like Grandpa any more." She squeezed Grandma's hand and smiled at her. "You okay?"

"I've done my crying, child," she said. "No amount of tears will bring him back. Besides, he'll be happier in God's home. Life was becoming a struggle."

Sophie gave her a big hug. As grandma said, there was no point in crying, but another link between her and her parents had been severed. The relationship between Fleming London and his parents had been as close as her relationship with her own parents. When they died, she had transferred some of that love to her grandparents as a way of keeping their spirit alive. Any break in the chain, however inevitable, caused her terrible distress.

She broke loose from her embrace and gave Grandma what she hoped was an understanding smile and squeezed her hand. For both of them, another chapter of their lives had come to a close.

Two days later, she and Ed paid what was to be their last visit to grandma. She was busy packing up grandpa's small collection of clothes. They would only fill one small battered suitcase. It seemed incredible to Ed that someone could have lived for so long, surviving on three shirts, four trousers, four pairs of shoes and various socks and underwear. No ties, no coats. Yet the man had probably been more content than millions of people who lacked for nothing. Ed felt profoundly humble.

"What are you going to do now?" asked Sophie, knowing the answer before Grandma spoke.

"Stay here child until I die, and that won't be long. I have plenty to do."

Ed wondered what on earth she found to do, but then decided sitting in her chair watching the chickens and the children at play amounted to 'plenty to do.' How wonderful that in the twilight of her life everything could be so simple.

"You won't come back with us?" suggested Sophie.

Grandma's wrinkled face broke into a smile. "I wondered when you'd ask that and I can see you know the answer already. It's a lovely thought, but no, this is my home. Everything around me is familiar, and an old lady likes that. It gives me confidence. Besides, I have my chickens to feed, and what would the children do without Ma's stories of years past. I want to die close to where I was born. I would hate all that cold and rain; it would put a quick end to me and, God willing, he doesn't want me just yet. He's got to get Grandpa settled in first."

Sophie bowed to the inevitable. "I understand, but I'll miss you."

"I know child, I know. Just make sure you come back to bury me."

"Oh Grandma!"

Sophie and Ed never saw Grandma alive again, and nor did they get to her funeral. While they were flying back to England, Grandma struggled out of her chair to go to bed, tripped over a chicken on the terrace and tumbled down the steps, breaking her neck as she hit the ground. Sophie didn't hear a thing until two weeks later when she got a postcard from Randall. By that time, Grandma had joined Grandpa at God's home.

"I'm so glad that I had the chance to witness the magic that was Grandma and Grandpa," Sophie said, fighting the pain of tears behind her eyes. "The wonderful memories will always be deeply ingrained. I can see them now, sitting on that rickety old terrace, laughing at the simplest things. It was the way they looked at each other, holding hands as if they could never let go. And now they will be back together."

Chapter Twenty-Three

Belinda was surprised by how long the healing process was taking. Her ribs were frustratingly slow to mend.

"If you'd rest at home instead of going to the office every day, the ribs would heal quicker," advised her doctor.

Belinda's anger was a palpable thing. A man had beaten her up and threatened Polly, and he was still on the loose. She had no time to waste sitting around at home.

"No progress yet," the Inspector was forced to admit. "He seems to have disappeared into thin air."

"Well, that might well be, Inspector," Belinda admitted over the phone, tapping her desk with frustration. "But my hunch is that it must be one of Gordon's cronies. Have you checked to see who has left prison in the last few months?"

"Not yet."

Don't lose your temper, Belinda thought, wishing to tell the Inspector in no uncertain terms that he should have done that three weeks ago. She took a deep breath, and with as much calm as she could muster suggested, "I think perhaps you should do that, don't you? Then you could run his face in the papers. He must be sleeping and eating somewhere; he can't exist on air,"

She heard a grunt.

"Was that you agreeing?"

"I'll get my men onto it right away."

"Good." Belinda put the phone down slowly then, slamming her fists down on the desk, she glanced across at Polly who was making the first cup of coffee of the morning. "At times I'm staggered by the incompetence of some police officers."

Polly nodded. She had faith in the police, and to be told by Belinda that some were not up to the mark sent shivers of apprehension down her spine. "Two sugars isn't it?"

"Please."

Polly was the upside to Belinda's injuries. She dropped by the office every morning to see if she was okay. The more Polly fussed over her, the more she enjoyed it. When she'd finally forced herself to tell Polly it wasn't necessary for her to give up every moment to her welfare, Polly had assured her it was what she wanted to do, and that gave Belinda hope.

Polly put the cup down on the desk and asked, "What about the lunch at the end of the week? Are you going ahead with it given Emily's situation and the death of Sophie's grandma?"

Belinda paused for thought. "Why not? They both played squash the other night, and I'm okay if I'm careful. Give them a ring; see what they say. If both would rather not come, I think it would be better to cancel. I wouldn't like to go ahead without us all being present."

"I agree," said Polly picking up the phone.

Jack O'Brian walked past Belinda's ground floor office and glanced in through the window. He smiled when he saw Polly. She looked good; he was looking forward to playing with her. Police security was being wound down, but the man was still at the house every evening. He was spoiling his plans. Maybe he'd have to take the man out. It made no difference to him. When he was sentenced—for he had little doubt he would be caught—he was already looking at life behind bars. I'll just wait a little longer he thought, as he reluctantly moved on.

Clarissa was standing at the bar of the Hotel du Vin ordering another round of drinks when the restaurant manager approached her. "Telephone call for you, madam. Your husband says it's urgent."

"Look after the drinks will you, Emily," said Clarissa. "I'll be back in a mo. I expect it's only Ted in a panic about something trivial."

It wasn't trivial. After a hasty apology, because he knew Clarissa hated being disturbed at one of her stupid lunches, he said, "It's your mother, Clarissa. I've just had a call from Taunton Hospital. She's had an accident and she's in a bad way. They think you should get down there as quickly as possible, and they want you to ring right away."

Clarissa rang the hospital. A short explanation was all she needed. "I'm on my way," she said. She hurried back into the bar. The look on her face telling the party that there was something very wrong. "Sorry," she apologised. "My mother's had a bad accident, must go."

Sophie put a comforting hand on her shoulder. "Want me to drive you?"

It was tempting. The old Morris might well object to another trip to Somerset, but Clarissa quickly discarded the offer. She might have to stay for several days. "Thanks," she said gratefully, "but I'm best to go on my own. Now, you all go on and enjoy yourselves. I'll be in touch as soon as I get back."

Lunch was very quiet. Belinda decided she'd made a mistake. There was too much on all their minds.

Clarissa pushed the Morris as never before, certain that it would break down before it made home, but like so many times in the past it confounded her.

Ted was standing at the garden gate when she pulled up. He put an arm round her shoulder and asked, "It sounded bad. What did they say?"

"That the silly old fool was knocked down by the bull. Well, they didn't use the words silly old fool of course. She's badly crushed; not much hope. What was she thinking Ted? She knows damn well that bull is dangerous. Anyway, what's done is done, so no good cursing her for being so bloody foolish. After all what's changed? I better get on my way."

"We can take the van. We have no markets this week and at least we'll get there."

"You can't come. There are the dogs and the holding to look after, not to mention your paintings. Have you forgotten you promised the gallery another two by the end of the month? No, Ted better you stay here. God knows how long I'll be away."

Ted struggled to hide his relief. "Will you be okay?"

Clarissa smiled. "When have I never been alright? This is wasting time and I need to get there as quickly as possible. I'll run in and pack a bag, and ring you when I get to the hospital and let you know how bad she is."

Her mother had died of her injuries half-an-hour before Clarissa arrived breathlessly at the hospital. She was too late again.

"There was nothing we could do," a sympathetic young doctor advised her. "Nearly every bone in her body was broken and she'd lost a lot of blood. Add the shock factor to a woman of her age and really she stood little chance. I'm so sorry."

Clarissa reflected that it must have been decreed from some unseen source that she should arrive too late at her parent's deaths. If she'd believed in God, she'd have been tempted to think it was some sort of retribution meted down from on high because she'd walked away from home and hadn't really cared much for either of them since. Of course, that was a load of tosh. The reason was much more mundane than any edict from above: she and Ted had two clapped out cars and lived a long way away.

"Can I see her?"

"Of course, but I must warn you her face is a bit of a mess. We have tidied it up as best we can in the short time available."

Clarissa smiled at the doctor. "It takes a lot to throw us farmers you know, doctor, I expect I can cope."

She hadn't reckoned on the destruction that the bull had administered in its rage. Her mother would have been unrecognisable if the doctor hadn't assured her that it was her lying on the mortuary slab. After the bile had settled in her throat, Clarissa realised that if she'd been a little more concerned for her mother's wellbeing after her father's death this accident might never have happened.

Molly had been loading the cattle for market when the bull had attacked her. Clarissa knew she would have been on her own; she had got rid of the last member of staff when Clarissa's father had died. "No point in running up more debts for you to pay off," she'd informed Clarissa over the phone, in one of her 'I'm hard done by' tones. After that, she had proceeded to refuse all of Clarissa's frequently repeated offers of help. Clarissa knew she should have persisted; no matter what had passed between them in the past, there was no excuse for neglecting an ageing parent. Now mother lay dead, literally mangled to death. To add to her mounting guilt, Clarissa realised that she couldn't feel any sadness at her mother's death. She turned away abruptly. "Thank you doctor, I've seen enough. Can you tell me what I do now?"

The telephone rang just before ten in the evening. Polly got there before her father, which was lucky as it was her mother, all steamed up and obviously tanked-up.

"Mother, hello." Polly made no effort to hide her annoyance at being disturbed so late by the one person she least wanted to speak to.

"I want to speak to your father," Sarah slurred.

That was the last thing Polly was going to allow. "Sorry Mother, he's in bed."

"Then wake the bastard!"

"No."

"What did you say?" Sally exploded.

"I said that he was in bed. Anyway, he doesn't want to speak to you." Then, feeling thoroughly bitchy, she added, "At last he's seen the light. He won't be coming back."

There was a cry of despair down the line. "He can't."

"Well he has."

The telephone almost shook in Polly's hand. "What have I done to deserve this?" Sally screamed.

"Are you even dimmer than I thought, Mother?" Polly enjoyed asking. "Look at yourself and then answer your own question. It's staring you in the face. You're a living nightmare." She heard a sharp intake of breath. "And Father has just woken up to it. Good on him I say. Now off you go, Mother. Swill down another bottle of gin and ring around your friends, and you'll feel better. Oh sorry, I forgot, you haven't got any friends left, so you probably won't feel better. Don't expect me to shed tears. You blew it with me when you gloated over Phil's death, but I held in there, hoping that under your unforgiving exterior there might beat a kind heart, but no. When I needed you again the other day, what did you do? You refused to see me. So tough, Mother. It's my turn to behave like a bitch, and shall I tell you something? I'm going to really enjoy it. Good night Mother." She slammed the telephone down and turned to smile at her father. "Next stop court, Dad," Polly said with some pleasure. "Ready for it?"

"Never more so," David replied, wondering how much it was going to cost him.

Chapter Twenty-Four

Ted was sitting in the sitting room's only armchair, reading a paper. A paper! Clarissa couldn't remember the last time she'd seen him with a paper in his hands. "You're reading," she said intrigued.

"That I am," came back the reply, "and very interesting it is too."

"Must be. I didn't think you ever read a paper. What's interesting enough to make you break a habit of a lifetime, or is it a secret?"

Ted held the paper out to her. "Not at all."

"The Western Gazette. What made you order that?"

"Take it," said Ted. "Read this."

Clarissa took the paper from him. It was open on the property. She threw a questioning look at Ted. "This one?" she asked, jabbing a finger at the ringed advertisement.

"That's the one. Makes interesting reading."

And so it did. Clarissa blew out her cheeks. "Are you serious Ted?"

"I might be. What do you say?"

Clarissa scanned the advert again. *Picture Gallery for sale in the picturesque town of Dulverton, Somerset, nestling under Exmoor. Two bedroom flat above. Private sale. Bargain price. Owner emigrating to New Zealand.*

"Might be the answer to our dreams," said Ted.

Clarissa laughed. "I've never had dreams about living down there, so don't try that one on me."

Ted was persistent. "It makes sense. I get a gallery to exhibit my paintings as and when I like, we can let out the upstairs flat, and we can keep your parents' farm. Acre upon acre for you to do what you like with, not just a small patch of ground where you are limited to what you can grow. We could easily afford the gallery with the proceeds from this place and have enough to pay off your father's creditors. We're sitting on a little gold mine here. Don't turn it down flat Clarissa my love. Just give it some thought."

This is exactly what Ted had been doing for some time. For all of their life together he'd been happy to play second fiddle to Clarissa. He had been content with that, having no ambition to be anything else, but that had all changed when Clarissa had gone to the Winchester gallery. Suddenly his life had taken on a new meaning. He had a goal to aim for; a role in life. His purpose was to paint pictures that people actually got pleasure from viewing. He was no longer the man who walked a few feet behind his partner. He was up there with her now. It was a position Ted had never imagined he'd be in.

There had been another position on offer as well, one that Ted had accepted gladly, but unwisely. Two days after the exhibition, Jo had made her move.

As soon as Clarissa disappeared down the drive en route for Somerset, Ted wasted no time in nursing the Morris into Winchester. His heart was beating fast. He parked in the multi-story, close to the gallery. Giving him her come-on wink, Jo had told him that she was often alone in the gallery in the afternoons between three and five when Amanda went to pick up her grandson from school. The lure of her mesmerising breasts had been too much to resist.

On the street, close to the gallery, he was paralysed by fright.

"Hey mate, you don't own this fucking pavement," an angry voice shouted behind him.

Ted jumped, apologised, and moved over. He knew exactly what would happen if he found Jo alone in the gallery, but that was why he'd come to Winchester. He was being the biggest fool of all time, threatening to ruin a relationship that had stood the test of time and given him years of pleasure. Why on earth was he risking all that for, at the most, an hour of illicit pleasure? He started to walk again, slowly at first and then quicker. The devil was in him, and nothing was going to stop him. He began to salivate thinking about what awaited him in the back room. A good deal more than just a look at some new paintings, he thought. "Oh Jesus," he moaned as the gallery came into sight.

That was his main reason for wanting to move away. His weakness appalled him. It would have been easy to say, "Thanks Jo, that was great, but a one off. You understand don't you?" But it was just as easy to welcome her advances. The odd feel of her delectable breasts and tweak of her bottom had become something far more serious. He'd gone way beyond what he'd planned, and even though he suspected Jo was far too nice a person to want to ruin his relationship with Clarissa, he also knew she was as weak as him. It was a recipe for eventual disaster. So he was desperate for a chance to put that all behind him and live with the one person he really loved.

"Let' do it," said Clarissa two days later, as she packed a box of runner beans. "You're right, it makes a lot of sense"

Ted, who had just come back from delivering two paintings to the gallery and had endured a somewhat frenzied half-hour with Jo, heaved a sigh of relief. "You sure about this?"

"Absolutely. Of course I'll miss some things, especially the team, but I work my arse off here for very little and I wouldn't need to do that any longer. Anyway, a change is as good as a rest. In addition, my darling Ted, it will get you away from that sex-crazed Jo Hawksworth; I don't know how much longer you can hold out. There is a limit to a man's resistance."

Ted quickly looked the other way, praying that Clarissa hadn't seen him redden. "You've noticed?" he asked weakly, disgusted by his husky voice.

Clarissa was not slow to pick up on it. For the first time since they had met Jo, she wondered if Ted was doing more than tweaking her bottom. Clarissa was a realist. If Ted was indulging in a bit of sex-on-the-side she would of course be furious, but did she really want to know? They weren't married, and most men got the itch at sometime in their life. She swiftly decided not to dig any deeper. If a crisis occurred that would be the time to vent her not inconsiderable wrath. Giving him a playful dig in the ribs she said, "Darling Ted, of course I've noticed. How could I not when she is slobbering all over you? I admire you for having the self-control to keep that extraordinarily rampant pego in your pants. No doubt it was also because you love me."

Ted was disgusted with himself. How could he have got himself into such a position that he was having to lie to the woman he loved? He did his best to make his voice sound convincing. "Of course I love you and there was never any question of me taking anything further than a little light flirting. You do believe me don't you?"

Clarissa smiled. Ted's last sentence rang alarm bells, but she said, "I do," adding in a low voice, "Because I want to."

Ted turned away, unable to look her in the face.

"You're leaving us," cried Polly. "I'll miss you terribly. "Devon seems such a long way away." Even though she now had Belinda to turn to for help, that didn't soften the blow. It meant the end of the Laurel Ladies team. She would never forget how the friendship they had offered her had increased her shaky confidence. Okay, there were plenty of likely replacements at the club, but it would not be the same.

"Somerset actually," laughed Clarissa.

"Oh well, wherever," Polly laughed back. "But it's still a long way away."

"And it won't be for a while," continued Clarissa. "We haven't been to see the gallery yet and it may have already been sold. Besides, I might change my mind."

"Well we've had a good run as a team," said Belinda leaning back on her sofa to ease what was still a nagging pain in her ribs. "And nothing in this life goes on forever."

"Nothing," said Emily sadly, and then forced herself to smile. She was tired of people being extra nice to her. It wasn't that she didn't appreciate their concern; it was just that she was longing to be treated as a normal person again, not as a person to be pitied.

"Let's drink to us," proposed Sophie. "The best team in the South of England. Thanks for asking us over tonight, Belinda."

There was a tear in Clarissa's eye as she raised her glass.

"Sit down Ed, please," asked Sophie, the next morning.

Ed dropped onto a sofa. "What's so important that won't wait until tonight? I've got a surgery to get to."

"I think you might like to hear this before you go. It could be of some importance."

"Okay, five minutes."

"It won't take that long," Sophie assured him.

"Well, go on then, I'm all ears."

"I'm pregnant."

Ed leapt up from the sofa and hugged Sophie.

"Careful, you might squash him or her," she laughed.

Ed put a hand on her stomach. "It's in there!"

"Where else, you chump?"

"Oh my God, that is so wonderful. You clever girl!"

"It takes two."

"Maybe, but now it's all up to you—until it is born of course!"

"What do you want Ed, boy or girl."

Ed rubbed his chin. "I don't care. Whatever comes out of that tummy will be precious to me. But if it's a girl it will dazzle men like you always have, and if a boy it will be . . . ."

Sophie cut him short, putting a finger against his lips. "If it's a boy it will grow to be as kind and loving as you." She took her finger away and replaced it with her mouth, her tongue gently teasing Ed's teeth. When she drew away they were both breathless, and Sophie saw the look she'd got so used to in Ed's eye. She put a hand on his chest. "Brace yourself, another piece of news coming up."

"There's more?"

"If you have time."

Ed pretended to consult his watch, all thought of getting to the surgery on time abandoned. "There's time."

"Grandpa made a sort of will."

"Sort of will?"

"It might not pass in a court of law, but I don't think anyone will challenge it. There wasn't much to leave."

"Go on."

"I've had a letter from a solicitor, if you can call him that, telling me that Grandpa left me the shack and a small piece of land."

"Oh Sophie, that is so wonderful. I know how much you love that place. We must make sure we go there every now and then. Problem will be who can we get to look after it?"

"As you say Ed, it presents a problem. So best to sell it or give it to one of the nieces."

Ed smiled. He'd just had a mad idea. "Come to think of it, why don't we move out there?"

"To a tin shack? When I'm having a baby?"

"We don't need to rush. I think my idea sounds great. We can make it really nice in time."

"You are joking?"

"Nope. Never been more serious," replied Ed, warming further to the idea. "I will be welcomed as a doctor and you can design from anywhere in the world. Besides, you will soon be a mum and that will take up a lot of your time. You don't need to work so hard, Sophie. You're already a wealthy and successful woman."

"And success breeds a desire for more success," voiced Sophie. "It's probably an ego thing, but you're right, Ed darling, maybe it's time to become a mother and housewife, but please don't suffocate me. I need to be my own woman."

Ed smiled. "I know that, and anyway we don't need to make any decisions right this minute."

The possibility of being forced to live in a tin shack, or something like it, wasn't far off Sally Gascoigne's mind as she stamped her high-heeled shoes on the last unbroken photograph of David. "Divorce! You sod," she yelled, as she bent down and retrieved the photo from the broken frame and tore it into little pieces.

Her last vestige of self-control had deserted her the night before when several strong martinis had emboldened her to ring Polly. That had been a big, big mistake. "Bastard," she'd shouted as she began to trash the house, cutting up David's shirts, tossing his expensive shoes into the fire and smashing every photo of him that she could find. She never wanted to see his smirking face again. She was certainly not going to admit that she missed him like hell already. Her whole life was about to come crashing down around her. No longer could she pose as the happily married woman when, all around her, other peoples' marriages were falling apart. Her social status would soon be in tatters. Well, if David really wanted to ruin her life and make her the laughing stock of her friends she'd at least suck his wallet dry. It would be no tin shack for her.

Suddenly exhausted and shivering, Sally realised she was standing naked in the mess of her rage. She went to the bathroom and for a few minutes slumped under a hot shower. She needed to think. There was no time for self-pity. She needed to be positive, to plan her attack. The first thing she would do was turn her back on her daughter for good. Despite what Polly had said the night before, she, not Polly, would be the one to cut the umbilical cord. She gave an evil smile. Discarding that comforting thought, she forced herself to think of her next move. A good lawyer was needed and she knew the very person to ask for help.

By the time she exited the shower, her skin tingling from the hot water, she felt considerably better. She dressed and moved to the telephone.

Rita Hawkins was flushing the toilet when she heard the phone ring. She was surprised. Her friends knew never to ring her before midday. They risked a tirade of abuse as Rita sweated and farted the excess alcohol from the night before out of her system. She toyed with letting the bloody thing ring, but then changed her mind; it would only ring again. Besides, it might be an invitation to a party, and Rita loved a party, especially the boozy kind.

She'd been Sally's bridge partner for several years. "Gawd knows why," she'd confided to another friend. "I'm divorced from a violent husband. I'm practically an alcoholic, and smoke like a train! I'm as common as muck and probably a bit too loud for most people's taste. I don't drive a Mercedes coupe or have a villa in the Algarve. I'm not rich by most of her friend's standards and I'm a lousy bridge player. Strewth knows why she's taken me under her wing. I don't care. She is useful to me. She's the biggest snob I've ever met and "*I know all the right people dear."* Very useful for intros to parties and for my little business. And I'm learning to speak proper," she finished with a wink.

In fact, there was a lot more substance to Rita then Sally gave her credit for. She was tough, had brought up two children on her own, and successfully bled her complaining ex dry, though she squandered the pittance she'd dragged from him on booze and horses. She'd had several affairs with married men since her divorce, but walked away from them as soon as they mentioned three things: divorce and marriage, and their children." She'd come to Winchester from Reading when her two children went to university, mainly because her last affair had brought the wrath of God down on her head. "Time to get out, Mum," advised her son, who was used to his mother's indiscretions. She'd seen a shop advertised in Winchester and moved her small interior decorating business south. Since she'd been befriended by Sally, her business was positively booming.

She was two years younger than Sally, with dark green eyes and tightly permed black hair. She stood at five foot two and wore size eight clothes. "When you're small you simply *must* keep your body in shape, darling," she'd told Sally, casting a critical eye over Sally's bulges the third time they met. She'd never been one to mince her words, however new the acquaintance was.

The criticism had bitten deep into Sally's pride. She was four inches taller and wore size fourteen.

"Should be a twelve," Rita told her.

Sally had immediately gone on a diet.

But, when the mood took her, Rita could display a surprising amount of loyalty, and right this moment, loyalty was something Sally craved.

"Blimey Sal, what's happened here?" Rita asked, slipping easily back into her northern brogue as she stood in the drawing room and gazed opened mouthed at the smashed furniture, the ripped curtains and the broken china. "You been raided?"

Sally shook her head. "Nothing like that. I simply went berserk."

"Wow! What brought this on?"

Sally held up a piece of the torn photo. "This bastard," she spat, jabbing her finger at the photo. "The swine has left me."

Now that was no surprise to Rita, though she would never say that to Sally's face. Loyal as she was prepared to be to Sally, she had wondered how any man could live with her. She suspected there was not much excitement generated in the bedroom and, seeing David's eyes running over her trim figure at times, Rita suspected he was up for a bit of fun. Her first thought was good on you David, but she raised her hands in pretend horror and said, "The bastard! Men just don't know when they are lucky."

"And what makes it worse he's going to live with Polly."

"Your lezzy daughter?"

"That's about it."

"I don't blame you for being hurt and angry, but to do this," Rita waved a hand round the room. "What else have you wrecked?"

Sally began to snivel.

Please, please don't do that, thought Rita, but Sally was well away, snivelling for Britain.

"Every room," croaked Sally. "I've wrecked every room."

"Then we better start clearing up, and you must come and stay with me. You can't live alone in this chaos."

The snivelling stopped. "Do you mean that?"

Not really thought Rita, but I have a kind heart. "Of course. You're welcome in my house for as long as it takes you to sort out that low-life bastard. And I know just the woman to do that."

Belinda sat behind her desk trying to remain calm under Sally's hostile stare. When Rita Hawkins had rung and called in a favour, it had titillated Belinda's curiosity. Now, face to face with a woman who so obviously detested her, given her relationship with Polly, she was having doubts. The more Sally opened her mouth, the more Belinda realised she had made a big mistake. Sally was of the same opinion. If she hadn't felt so desperate, she would never have allowed Rita to drag her along to see Belinda fucking Musgrove. Now she was making no attempt to hide her disgust, and Rita was clearly embarrassed. In fact, Rita was wishing she could be anywhere else but sitting beside her spitting friend.

She was rescued by Belinda who, professional to the last, smiled at Sally and said, "Look, Mrs Gascoigne, I'm very grateful to you for asking me to represent you, but I'm the wrong person for you. It would cause great pain to your daughter, and I really don't want to . . ."

Sally cut her short. "Ms Musgrove, or perhaps you prefer to be called Mr."

Rita winced. Belinda's expression did not change,

Sally warmed to her task. "I'm only here because my friend said you were the best divorce lawyer this side of the Atlantic. I have no reason to argue with her assessment, but if I decide I want you to represent me, please don't think I will ever feel anything but disgust for you. Frankly you make me sick."

Oh, you ungrateful cow, thought Rita.

Belinda started to rise from her chair, but Rita was on her feet first. Grabbing Sally by the arm, she hissed, "Out of here now, Sally. I can't believe you're saying these things! Don't expect my support any longer. I brought you here because I felt sorry for you and thought you needed help, and what have you done? Thrown shit at Belinda, and thoroughly embarrassed me."

Belinda lowered herself back into her chair and allowed herself a satisfied grin. "Thank you Rita, I think you've said it all." She turned to Sally and favoured her with a long, cold stare before saying, "Mrs Gascoigne, if you got down on your knees right now and begged me to represent you, I would be very tempted to kick you in the teeth. Your daughter is a lovely person. She doesn't deserve to have a mother like you." As her anger threatened to boil over, she added, "What's more your daughter wants nothing more to do with you." Whoops, she shouldn't have said that! Very unethical.

A strange sort of gurgling sound came out of Sally's mouth. She banged her hands on the desk, her mouth opened like a fish out of water, and for a few seconds she was struck speechless. Finally, she managed to string some words together. "Okay, *Ms* Musgrove, so you don't want to act for me. Great, because I've decided I don't want you anywhere near me. Somehow you have contrived to seduce my beloved Polly."

Rita snorted.

"You are responsible for tearing my family apart."

Another, louder snort from a now enraged Rita.

"But I'm glad I came here because I can tell you to your face that you're a marauding lesbian; a man in a woman's clothes; an utterly foul and dishonest person. I would rather lose everything than have you as my divorce lawyer. Come on Rita, let's get out of here before I puke all over Ms Musgrove's no doubt expensive carpet."

Rita was already on her way.

Outside on the pavement Rita was visibly furious. She stopped and turned to face Sally. "I meant what I said in there. Don't blame me if things go belly-up for you. I was only trying to help."

"Help me? By making me see that . . . that . . . pervert?" Sally spluttered.

"Right! That does it! I'm out of here. I am finished with you." Rita stared with satisfaction at the shock registering on Sally's face. "Get another bridge partner, go and find a fucking lawyer for yourself. Clear up the mess in your house on your own. You're not coming back with me. I completely understand why your husband left you. Enjoy the rest of your lonely life." Rita turned away and stalked off.

The expletives that followed her down the street would have given good cause for Sally to be served with an ASBO.

Polly was sitting in the chair that her mother had vacated a week earlier. "I've come to ask you a very special favour." she told Belinda. "I know you have never touched a male client in a divorce case, but I wondered if you would represent Dad. I know I shouldn't be asking you this, but Dad needs good advice and a hot-shot lawyer."

Belinda did her best not to leap up and shout, "Yes!" Instead she took a deep breath, quickly deciding it was better not to mention the unpleasant scene with Polly's mother and said, "Well . . ." she smiled at Polly. "For you I just might change. Give me a few days to think about it."

Forty-eight hours later, she rang Polly and gave her the good news.

"Great," exclaimed Polly. "When can I bring Dad along?"

"This morning, in about an hour any good to you?"

"No problem. I have a viewing of the house due any minute, but that shouldn't take long. Thanks Belinda, see you then."

On the way to Belinda's office, Polly felt decidedly uneasy. It was one thing to admit to her father that she might have feelings for a woman, quite another to take him along to meet her, but the pros outweighed the cons. Belinda was, without a doubt, one of the best performers in a divorce court and sure as hell that was what Dad needed. She had no doubt that her mother would not be slow in hiring a pretty formidable opponent. She looked across at her father who was nervously running his hands up and down the steering wheel.

"You'll like her Dad, you really will," she said resting a hand lightly on his knee. "She's not the wicked predator that mother has made her out to be. Okay she's tough, but she has a very warm and welcoming nature under her slightly frightening façade."

David allowed himself a smile. Who was he to argue!

As they approached the small car park at the back of Belinda's office, David was aware of a tall man standing on the other side of the road. For some reason his senses clicked into alert mode. He was aware that Polly was probably still in danger, and since the police surveillance had been reduced, he'd become very vigilant. His eyes were constantly searching for anything that seemed out of place. The man was staring in their direction. He slowed and lowered his window to get a better look, but a second later he was opposite the car park entrance and had to give the left turn his full attention. By the time he'd parked, exited the car, and walked back to the street, the man was gone. He shrugged. It was probably just a pedestrian, but he made a mental note to inform the police about it later in the day.

"Something wrong, Dad?" questioned Polly.

David walked back into the car park. "Just thought I saw a friend. I was wrong."

"I'm getting careless," murmured Jack O'Brian, moving swiftly on.

Chapter Twenty-Five

Jimmy Spencer was Jack Talbot's best friend. They had been as close as two people could be since the age of nine, when they were dumped at prep school by their parents. They gallantly fought homesickness, comforting each other in the dormitory at nights so that in the morning they weren't called cry babies or sissies. By the time they went to Eton, they were agreed that if they ever had children there was no way they would subject them to such torture. However, they acknowledged that they were stuck in a system that their parents thought was best for building character and would equip them to deal with a tough adult world. So, they dug deep into their survival kit and got on with life.

At Eton, they both excelled at sport, playing cricket and boxing for the school. Maybe their academic prowess was a little below their parents expectations, but they had little cause for complaint when the boys were accepted by Edinburgh university. As far as they were concerned, all the planning and expense had proved worthwhile. If they had put that view to their sons, they would have got a more negative response.

At Edinburgh, the friends went their different ways. Jack chose to be a hard-working student with a burning desire to enter the City and make fistfuls of money. Jimmy, on the other hand, started down a road to disaster. He became obsessed by dark temptations that were constantly in his face. It was not long before he was seduced by a slim auburn-haired druggy named Chloe. She had wide, green come-to-bed eyes, and in spite of both Jack and Emily warning him, Jimmy was unable to resist the allure of her body. His life rapidly went down hill, but what did he care, this was really living!

Jimmy sat in his parents' kitchen, waiting for Emily's knock on the front door. He sipped nervously at his second cup of coffee thinking his and Jack's roles had been reversed. He could now understand how hopeless Jack must have felt when he tried to rescue him from his debauched life with Chloe. At times Jack had almost burst with frustration at his unwillingness to see reason. Then, two years ago, when Jack had first told him about Lucy, he had promised his support and loyalty, but first he had done his best to warn Jack.

"Walk away from her now Jack," he advised. Jack had agreed, and then done exactly the opposite.

What the outcome would have been had Jack lived was anyone's guess, though it would not possibly have been as devastating as what had happened to him and Chloe.

Chloe had died in childbirth. Their poor disabled boy had followed her to the grave a year later. The two terrible blows had almost destroyed him. If it hadn't been for his parents he would never have recovered from his downward spiral. He was clear of drugs now, and he had various jobs, such as helping his parents in their ceramics shop or even working as a labourer mending potholes in the roads. It was a far cry from the hub of the financial system he'd once hoped he'd be part of, but it kept him solvent until the time when his parents retired and the shop passed to him.

He thought back to his years of deprivation, which had not only undermined all his parents' investment in his future, but also threatened him with an early grave. It had been a wild, debauched adventure of which he was not proud. Mindless of the future, he had lived on a cocktail of sex and drugs, happy to wander around in a drug-induced state with Chloe never far from his side.

Then, in his second year, the bombshell had dropped.

"She's got herself pregnant," Jimmy said in shocked surprise as they sat on Jack's bed in their digs.

Jack felt like asking who the father was; there must be dozens of likely contenders, but he held his tongue. Jimmy was in shock and felt guilty. Enlightenment could come later. "So what are you going to do, you chump?" Jack asked.

"Stand by her, of course."

"Jesus Jimmy, do you know what that could mean?"

Jimmy nodded. "Yes, chances are I will be thrown out of uni and any idea of a worthwhile career will go up in smoke, but I'm as much to blame as her, so I must accept my responsibilities. And I love her."

Jack thought it was time for some sense to be knocked into his friend's addled brain. "Listen up, Jimmy. You can't throw your life away on that worthless girl."

"Don't you dare call her that!"

Jack threw his arms up in despair. "Okay, okay, but consider this. You're well on your way to being a regular user. Chloe is already there. I don't think I need tell you that her parents won't want to know about a baby. I know you will say that doesn't matter because your parents will support you both. I'm sure they will, but do you want to dump that responsibility onto them? Because sure as hell you and Chloe are going to be incapable of looking after a baby. Look at the both of you; you hardly know the time of day! I don't like to say this, Jimmy, but do the sensible thing and make her have an abortion. The chances are the baby will be addicted anyway. Then walk away from her for Christ's sake. You don't even know you're the father."

Jimmy's face reddened with fury and his fists tightened. "You bastard," he shouted, pushing his face close enough to Jack for him to smell his rancid breath. How dare you suggest that Chloe has been with anyone else!"

"I know of at least three people," Jack retorted, bracing himself for a fist in his face. The blow never came. Instead, Jimmy smashed his fist into the wall shouting, "You're a filthy liar, a filthy fucking liar and I was fool enough to think you were my friend."

"I am, and that's why I'm telling you this."

"Go to hell, Jack. I'm going to marry her. I'm the only one in her life, so shut that fucking mouth of yours."

Jimmy smiled ruefully as he took another sip of his coffee. Jack's unforgivable behaviour was about to rebound on him. How was he going to defend his actions to Emily? How was he going to explain why he hadn't told her about Lucy? Whichever way he looked at it, he'd done her a terrible miss-service. The best he could do was to be honest, and hope that she could forgive him, but he didn't think there was much chance of that.

The ringing of the doorbell made him jump; coffee spilled onto his shirt. There was no time to put a fresh one on. Anyway, a small stain was probably going to be the last thing on Emily's mind. He rose from his chair, took a deep breath, and steeled himself for what he suspected was going to be a very uneasy meeting.

He opened the door and forced a smile. He'd last seen her red-eyed and pale at Jack's funeral. Since then he'd been close to picking up the telephone and ringing her, but each time he had decided that she'd ring him when she was ready. Foolishly, he'd thought that *the Lucy problem* as he called it, had finally gone away with Jack's death. When Emily's father had called, telling him about Lucy's letter and her confrontation with Emily, he had realised that he owed Emily an explanation.

"Hello Emily, good to see you," was all he could think of saying, before swiftly moving towards her and wrapping his arms round her. He felt her stiffen. "Sorry," he mumbled, quickly stepping back.

She looked at him, so obviously nervous, and was glad. At least he was suffering. "Are you really pleased to see me, Jimmy?" Her voice was hostile. "Are you not scared of being called a traitor?"

"Emily, please don't say that. I'm no traitor, just a friend put in an impossible situation. Come on in and have a cup of coffee, and I will try to explain. We can talk freely. Mum and Dad have gone out."

It had taken all her courage to come and see Jimmy, and for a second she felt like turning around and bolting back to her car, but her father's advice prevailed. "Go and see him, darling. He's always been a good friend to you and Jack, and I'm sure whatever he did, he did it with you in mind. I know Jack had no secrets from him and he must have known about Lucy, but I'm sure he wouldn't have condoned it. It may have been a mistake not telling you, but try to see it his way. Jack put him in a no-win situation."

"Okay, a quick cup and then I'll be gone," she replied tersely. She walked ahead of Jimmy into the house and made for the kitchen, memories of happier times immediately flooding back, times when laughter had seldom been far away. Emily gritted her teeth and dropped into the familiar chair where so many times she'd sat next to Jack for breakfast.

For a split second as he walked into the kitchen, Jimmy imagined he saw Emily, looking as beautiful as usual, her sunny disposition shining through, holding Jack's hand under the table. He blinked and the mirage disappeared. "Milk with your coffee if I remember rightly," he croaked, as he put the mug down and pulled up a chair.

She nodded.

Coffee on the table, Jimmy took a deep breath. "Look Emily, I'm not going to lie to you. I hope you know me well enough to accept that I would never do that."

Emily fought back the tears. "But you have already lied. You have been utterly deceitful, Jimmy. Tell me, how many times have we met since Jack confessed to you about Lucy?"

"Emily," he said lamely.

"You haven't anything to say have you, Jimmy? Don't make matters worse by trying to deny that right from the start, Jack took you into his confidence. I know he kept no secrets from you. What you did was inexcusable."

Jimmy found his voice. "I know. At first I just hoped Lucy bloody Hemming would just go away—that it was nothing . . ."

"Huh!" It was a nasty, sneering sound.

"I need you to know that, at first, that was Jack's intention. He never meant it to come to anything, never meant to get involved. But, as you know from talking to Lucy, two years down the line that was not how it worked out."

"And at that point you should have told me," said Emily, pointing an accusing finger at him. "You owed me as one of your closest friends."

Jimmy blew out his cheeks. "I'm not going to make excuses, but I found myself in an intolerable position. Whatever I did, I was going to hurt one of you, maybe risk losing both of you as friends. Believe it or not, I did think that Jack would give up Lucy when you got married. It was always his plan."

"His plan! His bloody plan! His and Lucy's bloody plan! I don't care a fuck about any bloody plan. Give her up just before our wedding! He should never have been with her in the first place!" Emily paused to get her breath.

"Jesus, this is tough Emily."

"Too right it is!"

Jimmy decided to try again. "Please Emily, listen to me."

"Go on then, dig a deeper hole for yourself."

"At the beginning, when Jack told me how he'd met Lucy and gone to her help, I thought he was just doing the white knight stuff he was rather good at, but he let his emotions go too far. He felt sorry for her, tried to protect her against her husband. Somehow, pity turned to affection. I know as well as anyone that once you go down that slippery route it is hard to pull up. Maybe that was the time I should have told you, and perhaps the whole sordid episode would not have got out of control, but I was always clinging to the hope that Jack would see sense. Lucy was not trying to take him from you; far from it, she always felt that you came first in Jack's eyes."

"Good for her," snapped Emily. "It didn't stop her sleeping with him."

"I don't think she did that."

"Oh God, Jimmy, don't try that one. Of course she did. She couldn't deny it. Ug, it makes me want to puke. I made love to him on Friday evenings when he came home, probably only a few hours after he'd been shagging her."

Jimmy looked away. "I didn't know that. I do know that Lucy was ready to wash her hands of him; it was Jack who persisted. He told me once that the terror of you finding out made his adrenaline run high; that the come down was fearful. I think she became his personal addiction. He confessed that he felt he couldn't go ahead with your marriage while he was so obsessed. I tried to talk sense into him, I promise, but he was very persistent. I'm truly sorry, Emily. I tried to persuade him he was making a terrible mistake."

For the first time since she'd walked into the house, Emily managed a smile of sorts. "Thank you, Jimmy, for being so honest. I know it can't have been easy. It's hard to betray a friend, but telling me . . . Would that have been betrayal? I don't think so. What I do know is that Jack has not turned out to be the man I thought he was. He was a cheat. He deceived me. I will never be able to forgive him. You at least did the honourable thing with Chloe and married her. I think Jack would have dumped her."

"And he would have been right," interjected Jimmy.

"Maybe, but that doesn't mean he was right to plan to dump me. Unlike Chloe, I have done nothing wrong, unless loving a man with all your heart is a sin. Do you know something, Jimmy?"

"What?"

"I told Dad I was glad Jack was dead. Now I'm telling you."

"That's a terrible thing to say, but I understand."

"Do you, Jimmy? I wonder if you really do."

Emily stood up and walked away from the table, making for the door. Jimmy thought she was leaving, but suddenly she whirled round to face him, tears pouring down her cheeks. "Oh Jimmy, Jimmy I can't leave like this. It's all wrong. I realise now, even more than when Jack was alive, that I need you as a friend. I came here to break off our friendship, to tell you I never wanted to see you again, but I don't really want to do that. It was wrong of me to blame you for hiding his sordid little relationship from me, because if I had been sworn to secrecy by a close friend I would have done the same as you. We've known each other a long time, you, me and Jack. I can't walk away from you just because Jack turned out to be a rat." She sighed and wiped away the tears. Jimmy watched, barely daring to hope. "I think we are the same, Jimmy. We have both been through hell and back and when you fall, the only thing to do is get back up again. You've done it, now I must." She smiled wanly at him. "Can we still be friends, Jimmy?"

Jimmy felt relief flood over him. She had good cause to be angry with him, but he didn't want to lose Emily as a friend; his feelings for her had not diminished over the years. Friendships did sometimes reach choppy waters and come out the other side with the bond stronger than ever. He hoped this might prove to be the case with them. So much of their lives had been entwined, the good and the bad. It would be a dreadful thing to turn away from that friendship, that special relationship. He found the words to answer her question the easiest he'd ever spoken. "Of course we can remain friends, if you want it. I'm sorry that Jack has put such a strain on our relationship. I know we can never forget what he has done to us both, but I'm sure as, time moves on, we can come to terms with Jack's cruelty. It'll be easier for both of us if we can do that together."

Emily raced over to him and threw her arms around him, tears twinkling in her eyes. "Jimmy, lovely kind Jimmy, you're a real brick!"

Embarrassed, Jimmy laughed. "Oh, I don't know about that!"

Emily kissed him lightly on the cheek. "This is the point at which I start my life again," she assured him. "With you and Dad beside me I think I may . . . ."

Jimmy put a finger on her mouth. "None of this maybe stuff. Be positive, that's the way to go"

Emily wondered why on earth she'd nearly thrown Jimmy in the dustbin. Her change of heart had been swift and had taken her by surprise. She'd been so close to walking out of the door without a backward glance. What had changed her mind was that she was damned if in death Jack should split up a treasured friendship. Hadn't he done enough damage already? She held Jimmy tight for several moments before reluctantly moving away. His warmth had spread over her whole body, easing the tension that had built up. It surprised her. "I must go," she said, a little flustered. "I told my dad I'd be back for a late lunch."

Jimmy made an instant decision. "Ring him, tell him you're staying here to see my parents. The four of us can have lunch in the pub. Better still, get him to come over."

"I'd like that very much. Yes very, very much. I'll give him a ring. Thanks Jimmy . . . you know what I mean."

Jimmy smiled. "I know what you mean."

"You always were good at mind reading," laughed Emily.

Emily could not believe how a few hours could change her so much. She seemed to have shed a great lump of her bitterness. There was still resentment simmering under the surface, and she knew the tears would still roll at times, but lunch had worked wonders. No longer did she feel so vulnerable. She had experienced true honest friendship from Charlie and Madge, Jimmy's parents, and realised that her father was not the only one who cared for her. Jimmy's parents had been their usual jovial selves, there was nothing contrived, they were just the way they always were. It was the tonic she needed. It was nothing short of a miracle, but then she'd always believed that God moved in mysterious ways. She'd gone to Jimmy dispirited, lost and angry. She'd left determined that in death Jack would play as small a part in her life as she could possibly manage. In the presence of four good friends she knew that her struggle to start her life again was going to be accelerated. She would not allow a rat to destroy her.

In front of her she saw her father's brake lights flick on and was surprised that they were nearly home. She'd been driving in a dream, so many thoughts hammering at her brain. As she pulled into the drive she remembered Jimmy's last few words, said a little hesitantly, which had made her laugh.

"Listen Emily, I'm in London the week after next. I gather from your father you'll both be there too."

"Yes, we're taking in a couple of concerts at the Albert Hall."

"So why don't you let me take you both out to dinner one night?"

She'd said, "Yes, that would be lovely," and she'd meant it.

As Emily drew to a halt outside the house she was smiling.

Chapter Twenty-Six

Clarissa really didn't care for the new van at all. It was a white Ford, four years old and, if you could believe the man who had sold it to Ted, with low mileage. Clarissa wasn't sure that Ted hadn't been had for a mug. She'd whispered her opinion and had been rewarded with a *this is man's business* stare. She'd shrugged and murmured, "Well don't blame me when the thing falls apart," and walked away.

Now, on her first solo outing in the van, she was sure her intuition had been right. The engine sounded rough for a twenty thousand mile car; more like a hundred thousand she thought, as she struggled up a hill on the A272 out of Winchester, pumping the accelerator vigorously. Not that she knew a damn thing about cars, but she knew a dodgy dealer when she saw one. This one had been far too brash for her liking, but maybe she would never be satisfied with any motor again. She was in mourning for the loss of her beloved Morris. It might have been showing its age, a little cantankerous every now and then, but it had never failed to get her to her destination in the end. Sadly, she'd had to accept its days were over when the engine fell out with a clatter on the way to Winchester, but as she struggled with the gears of the Ford she wasn't sure they hadn't traded in one crock for another.

At the top of the hill, still four miles short of home, the engine coughed, coughed again, and Clarissa knew she was in a spot of bother. Not wanting to be stuck on one of the most dangerous roads in Hampshire, she nursed the van into the car park on Cheesefoot Head. There were three cars parked there. Two were empty, their occupants no doubt walking the South Down Way. The third, a silver Honda saloon, had two women, past middle age by the look of them, leaning against its bonnet. They wore woollen bobble hats and had cord trousers tucked into thick brown socks. Boots covered their feet and over their shoulders they hefted rucksacks. Jeannie and Hetty

Jones had just finished their walk and they were enjoying a well-earned mug
of sweet tea when they saw Clarissa's steaming van expire.

"You fool, Ted," Clarissa said as she exited the van, surveying the steam
rising from the bonnet. "Shit!" she shouted before becoming aware of two
pairs of eyes staring at her. "Sorry, didn't mean you to hear that," she said,
smiling at the two women.

"Not to worry, dear," said Jeannie. "We've heard far worse. Looks as if
you might have a wee bit of trouble there."

"You could say that," Clarissa replied.

"Have you got a mobile to phone for help?" asked Jeannie.

"Yes, I'm fine thanks." Clarissa pulled her mobile out of the van. "Oh
damn!"

"Flat battery?" asked Hetty knowingly.

Clarissa smiled. "Afraid so."

"You'd better use ours then," suggested Hetty."

"That would be wonderful. I'm sorry to be a bore."

"Not at all, my dear," said Jeannie, as Hetty bent into their car to retrieve
her phone. "Here you are, and by some fluke it's charged. By the way I'm
Hetty and my sister is Jeannie."

"Clarissa Duncan," said Clarissa accepting the mobile. "Very kind of
you." She dialled Ted. He answered after the fourth ring. The conversation
was brief, toned down for the sake of the listening couple.

"Darling Ted," she said, a determined smile on her face. "That buy of
yours has given up the ghost in Cheesefoot Head car park. Can you come
and help?"

What she really meant was, Ted get your arse up here pronto. That
fucking wreck you bought last week has died on me. Told you it was a useless
piece of junk, but you wouldn't listen would you? Well, let me tell you, Ted
Harvey, it's a piece of rubbish!

Ted put the telephone down a little mystified. The tremor in her voice
had warned him she was angry and yet her request had been very polite,
not Clarissa's usual style when she was blaming him for something. Then
it dawned on him. In the car park she'd more than likely be surrounded by
people, hence the polite request. So watch out when she gets you alone, he
thought.

Clarissa handed back the mobile. "Thanks a lot. Saved me a long
walk."

"That's alright, and might I suggest you charge that phone of yours.
They are a wonderful invention."

"I will," said Clarissa, deciding not to divulge her opinion of mobile phones.

"We're off then. Hope you don't have to wait too long."

"I won't, provided my partner can find his car keys."

"Ah well, that's men for you," laughed Hetty.

Clarissa laughed back and waved them goodbye. She noticed the other two cars were still empty so she had the car park to herself. She looked at her watch: nearly five p.m. Still a few more hours of autumn daylight left. She guessed it would take Ted about half-an-hour to get to her, maybe a little longer by the time he'd put the dogs in the kennel and found his car keys, which as she'd told the two ladies, was always a problem. She went to the van and pulled out her field glasses. Carrying them with her was a habit she'd picked up from her father. "It's good to take a pair with you when driving—you never know what's over the hedgerows," he'd said. He'd been right. She'd watched deer grazing on Exmoor, even seen a stag covering a hind. Watched pigeon flighting into fields of flat corn, their wings set as they planned their landing. She'd spotted fox cubs playing and . . . she smiled . . . the odd courting couple oblivious to her prying eyes. Going to sit on the grass verge, she put the glasses to her eyes and followed the line of the Downs wending their way towards Winchester, surrounded on all sides by grassland and stubble where the corn had been harvested. She spotted a couple of riders cantering, and four walkers maybe coming back to their cars. She watched two buzzards floating in the light breeze, no doubt looking for a meal, she spotted two hares standing on their back legs boxing as if they hadn't a care in the world. She listened to the constant hum of traffic on the A272 and marvelled how nature and the modern hectic world seemed to be able to co-exist. It dawned on her that like so many other people she took the survival of nature for granted. In fact, she should be sitting here thanking her lucky stars that it was so resilient, and that it still provided enjoyment to so many people like herself, trying to escape their hectic lives. It had survived heat waves, droughts, two world wars and the intrusive march of urbanisation and now, if the scientists could be believed, its next battle would be against global warming.

She lowered the glasses and sighed. She and Ted were facing a new challenge, moving away from a cosy environment to pastures new. She had always hated change and going to Somerset was not only a change but also a challenge in so many ways. Sometimes at night she would break out into a sweat dreading living again in her childhood home with all its terrible memories of rape and abuse. She kept telling herself that with

Ted by her side all would be well; she'd be far too busy to let the horrors of the past invade her thoughts. She'd fought tougher battles in her life. Sometimes she found herself wishing that she'd never gone to the gallery with Ted's pictures, but that was unfair on Ted. He so deserved his success. He'd blossomed under the guidance of Jo and Amanda, even if there had been a little more than artistic guidance from Jo. And she *was* jealous. Keeping her mouth shut was proving difficult, but she didn't want to force the issue. Better not to know the full facts. The move would solve the problem. Despite her simmering anger, she still loved the rascal, but her absent minded friend and lover had moved on; success had changed him. Although he was in many ways still the Ted she'd fallen in love with, his endearing innocence had gone, and she missed that. However, she still had the man she loved, unlike poor Emily. Nor was she the intended victim of a revengeful man, or haunted by her sexuality like Belinda. She really shouldn't be moaning. She was lucky, yes lucky and she must keep telling herself that every hour of every day. She lay flat on her back, folding her hands behind her head and closed her eyes.

Ted arrived with engine revving violently, face dripping with sweat and a hangdog look on his face. As he turned off the engine and exited the car, an apology was already on his lips. "I'm so sorry, yes very sorry Clarissa darling. I'll get onto the man tomorrow."

"I don't want an apology you old goat," she said, flinging herself into his arms. "I don't care if you do buy shitty awful vans or are being chased by an over sexed woman. I just want you to say you love me."

"I love you," he said. "I really love you."

That was all Clarissa wanted to hear.

Clarissa leant on the railings of the balcony overlooking the squash court, watching Belinda destroying yet another opponent. It was her first match since the attack. She had lost none of her competitive edge. Clarissa never got bored of watching her play. Her power was awe-inspiring and she had a touch that Clarissa knew she could never match. It was going to be a sad day when the present Laurel Ladies squash team broke up. She and Ted would soon be moving to Somerset, and Sophie and Ed were seriously considering living in Jamaica. Who could predict in what direction the other three girls might go? Their lives had changed so much in the last fifteen months. She would miss them all. Each one in some way had contributed to broadening her life. They had embraced her as a friend even though she had absolutely nothing in common with any of them. Her body bulged in the wrong places; her clothes were a mess; she eschewed makeup, and didn't eat meat. Nor did she believe in the Almighty. They were rich, some spoilt, all beautiful, and seemed to have the world at their feet, but none of these attributes had protected them against tragedy or change. It seemed that she had become the agony aunt of the team, giving sympathy when necessary and always ready to listen. It had been quite a revelation.

Belinda gave a shout of triumph as she won her match and Clarissa smiled. Belinda's joy was one of the things she'd miss. Along with the calls for help and advice, the banter over a drink at the club bar after a match and getting rat-arsed once a month at the Hotel du Vin. She waved a clenched fist at Belinda and hurried towards the stairs. She was next on court.

"Murder her," whispered Belinda as they passed in the corridor.

The next day Belinda was smiling reassuringly at Polly and her father across her desk. "David, your wife's solicitor rang me earlier to tell me who was representing her if we need to go to court, which with my albeit brief meeting with your wife, I would guess will happen." She gave David a reassuring smile. "However, I can confidently tell you that you have little to fear. I know this man from old. We have been adversaries several times and I think he will encourage her to be greedy. Of course, your wife has a right to a substantial sum, as I'm sure you are aware. But the judge will take into account the fact that she has never contributed to the household, and that Polly does not live at home anymore So, I have asked this barrister to send me your wife's demands. Then we can look them over and decide what to do. How does that suit you?"

"I don't think I've the stomach for a fight," David confessed. "I would rather pay up and be done with it."

Belinda leant across her desk. "Why not, David?"

David shrugged. "Whatever you say, a man never wins."

"I understand, but let me assure you a woman doesn't always win. If your wife's demands are unreasonable, I will tear them to pieces. I'm quite good at that."

"Does that make any difference?"

Belinda had to concede it didn't always. "Look, judges notoriously favour the woman in a divorce case. However, if their demeanour is aggressive, and I suspect your wife will find it difficult not to become aggressive, most judges take exception to that. Especially if it is a male judge."

"I still would rather settle out of court."

Belinda sighed. "Okay, we may still be able to do that. I suggest that we look at your wife's demands and then make a decision. There's no need to decide right away."

David slapped his thighs. "Sounds good to me. When shall we meet again?"

"Why don't we go and have some lunch now," suggested Belinda. "The documents should be on my desk when we get back."

"Oh God! As soon as that?"

"It's better to know quickly."

"Yes, I suppose so," said David reluctantly.

"Lunch then?" asked Belinda.

"Good idea," said David, none too enthusiastically, but thinking it was another good chance to get to know Belinda better. He had a feeling he would be seeing quite a lot of her in the future. To his surprise that didn't worry him. He was beginning to quite like his daughter's friend.

Jack O'Brian was once again loitering outside Belinda's office, risking another look through the window at Polly. She was juicy; she quite turned him on. The thought of ripping off her clothes made him salivate. He'd enjoy raping her. Jerry would be proud of him. He quickly forced such carnal thoughts out of his mind and moved on. It was nearly time for him to make a move. He ran his hands through long brown hair that hid eyes that were deep set and dangerous. He was growing restless and Willy was complaining that he was getting too expensive, which he wouldn't be doing if he knew what lay in store. No one informed on Jack O'Brian and got away with it. Anyway, his holiday, as he called it, was beginning to drag. He was missing his cell, the daily routine and the dangers that hovered beneath the surface of the prison. He would no longer wait for the man in Polly's house to move on. He was certain it was her father, and if he got in the way he'd worked out a rather enjoyable plan for him.

The demand was on the table when they returned from lunch where they had drunk water, mindful of the fact that there was business to deal with back at Belinda's office. There would be plenty of time to celebrate or drown their sorrows later.

When Belinda read the document she knew immediately that there would be no celebration. Sally's demands were outrageous and yet Belinda felt David was going to capitulate. Pity—she would have loved to face Mrs Gascoigne again.

David saw the look on her face. "Bad news?"

"Exorbitant."

"Can I see?"

Belinda handed over the piece of thick paper.

David ignored the covering letter and moved to the relevant contents. "Wow, read this Polly."

Polly read the document once, then again. "That's a bit greedy isn't it, Dad?"

"Greedy!" interjected Belinda. "It's robbery."

For a second there was silence in the office. Then David put the document back on Belinda's desk and smiled apologetically. "I'll pay it," he said.

Belinda grabbed the piece of paper and waved it at him. "You'll pay this?"

David nodded. "Yes. I want rid of Sally as quickly as possible. If I fight it, we could be at each other's throats for years, and I can afford this. I'll pay."

There was nothing more for Belinda to add.

"He wants to do what?" asked Sally Gascoigne in disbelief.

"He's agreed to your demands," said the solicitor, almost as surprised as his client.

Sally wrinkled her nose. "There must be a catch. My husband hates giving money away, certainly to me the tight fisted bastard." She was also disappointed. She had hoped her demands, which she'd been sure David would refuse, might lead to reconciliation, although as she admitted to herself, that was probably only to save face with her friends, not because she was missing David. Now she was well and truly fucked as her ex-friend Rita would say.

The solicitor did his best to smile. "He wants you to agree to a divorce, if you call that a catch."

Sally hesitated for a moment. It seemed so mercenary to take the money and say goodbye, but the money was tempting, very tempting, and the bonus was she'd never have to speak to Polly again. Sally had never been one for emotion. Material things were far more important, and as for her friends, well she'd tell them that David was a cheating bastard and had been for several years. So, money it would be. She'd have a much better life without David. She might even find another man, another rich man; there were plenty of suckers about and she wasn't bad looking. She asked, "I don't suppose there's any chance of bleeding him a bit more?"

"I would think not a hope in hell—he has met all your demands. My advice, Mrs Gascoigne, is to agree as quickly as you can before Ms Musgrove changes his mind."

Sally looked suitably horrified. "God, has he instructed that bitch? She'd like to see me in a tent, begging on the streets."

Best place for you, thought the solicitor, who was beginning to wish he'd never taken on this avaricious woman. It was at times like these that he wished he'd chosen another profession. "I don't think she's like that."

"Ha! I'd never trust a dyke," spat Sally.

Ignoring her outburst he asked, "Well?"

Sally threw her hands in the air. "Alright, I accept." Then, deciding it might be a good idea to look heart broken at the break up of her marriage, she burst into tears.

Polly was feeling uneasy. There were two things playing on her mind. One was her father. It was all very well breaking up with her mother, but where did that leave him? She knew him well enough to know that he liked having money to splash around, and why not? He'd worked hard for most of his life, and sold his business at the right time. Now he would certainly have to watch the purse strings, something he'd never been very good at. On top of that, he was on his own. Knowing him the way she did, she knew he'd need company. He was bunking down in her little cottage, which might be sold any day, and then what? Buy a house and move in together? Polly wasn't sure she was keen on that scenario, but she couldn't desert him in his hour of need. She felt sure that when the excitement of getting rid of her mother had died down, her father would be wallowing around in shallow water like a whale. Her second, and far more threatening concern was the man who had killed Polecat and beaten up Belinda. It was the uncertainty of not knowing if the danger was over. The police surveillance had been reduced and that made her very nervous. Belinda had warned her that she should be on her guard. She looked nervously out of her sitting room window and wondered if the man was lurking outside. It was not a pleasant thought.

As David drove into Polly's drive, he felt surprisingly low. There had been no elation as he had thought there would be, just a feeling that twenty-six years of his life had been wasted. Now he was facing a life alone, except of course for Polly, but that was where his worries truly lay. It was nice to think he could spend the rest of his life with Polly; it would give him a chance to make up for his failings when she'd been a child; but Polly had her own life to lead. Would she want her father constantly getting in her way? Sadly he knew the answer already.

Jo took Ted's news philosophically. She'd never harboured any idea of dragging him away from Clarissa. It had just been a little naughty adventure for her, but she had to admit it had been rather underhand, given that Clarissa had introduced her to Ted, and so improved the gallery's cash flow quite considerably. However, it had happened, so there was no point in having regrets. No harm had been done, thank the Lord. She kissed Ted warmly on the cheek. "Ah well, most good things come to an end. It was probably time to call a halt anyway; these things can get out of hand."

Relieved that Jo was obviously not going to make a big emotional fuss, Ted gave her one of the smiles that had so captivated her when he'd first walked into the gallery. A shy, almost innocent man, she'd thought then. How he'd changed, but she was not vain enough to think it was her body that had changed him. She knew it was the success of his paintings, and he owed that to Clarissa.

"Well, Amanda and I wish you all the luck in the world, and mark my words, we'll be down there to see you very soon. Can you make me one promise?"

"What's that?"

"Let us have a painting every now and then, please."

"Of course I will. Thanks Jo, you know, for everything. I wouldn't have missed it for the world." That, thought Ted, is the biggest understatement I have ever made.

"Nor I," Jo replied, flicking away a tear. She couldn't remember the last time she'd cried.

Chapter Twenty-Seven

Dulverton nestled in a natural bowl in the landscape, surrounded by deciduous woodland and small fields. Approaching it from Taunton, you would cross a three-arched bridge over the river Barle into the town. It had once been a thriving market town; the sheep coming off the moor and the livestock from the lower ground filling the square on market days. In those days it had been known as the county town of Exmoor. Now the market had gone and the town's livelihood depended a great deal on tourism. Small businesses lined either side of the twisty main street with a bank and pharmacy splitting the main shopping area from residential houses, the car park and the Lion Hotel. The picture gallery was squashed between a butcher and a fishing tackle shop. Ted and Clarissa were staying two nights at the Lion because Clarissa was not yet ready to spend nights in a house with so many frightening and unhappy memories.

"I can hardly believe we've done this," said Clarissa as they walked out of the estate agents and made their way back to their car. "Our offer accepted, providing we can get a bridging loan from the bank. It scares me."

Ted put an arm round her waist and stopped on the pavement. It scares me too," he said looking at Clarissa's dishevelled appearance. She'd spent most of the morning running her fingers through her long hair and sweating profusely as they had discussed details about the purchase. God knows how many cups of coffee she had drunk. "You okay?" he asked.

Clarissa smiled. "Oh, I think so; it's just . . . ."

"I understand, and if you'd rather we didn't . . . ."

Clarissa cut him off in mid sentence, because she knew what the next few words were going to be and she'd be tempted to say, "Yes, I'm getting very cold feet and perhaps we should call the whole thing off." Instead she said, "Don't give me the opportunity to change my mind, Ted. We're moving and that's an end to it. It's a chance of a lifetime, and any doubts that I have just prove what a silly woman I am." Then she said what she'd been telling herself for the last two nights. "Everything will be okay, it really will be."

"Well, if you're absolutely sure."

"I am. Now let's make tracks for home."

As they moved into the car park, Ted said, "I think I'm being a little selfish."

"No you are not! You are the most unselfish man I know, and why shouldn't you want to have your own gallery. Don't fuss about me."

Ted chuckled. "Okay, let's get things sorted out. Once your cottage is sold we can move here and start the job of clearing your parents' debts and making a go of the farm and the new gallery. Do you know something Clarissa?"

"What?"

"I'm excited love, really excited."

Clarissa thought her feelings bordered on the apprehensive. Feeling quite emotional she said, "I love you. You're really something, Ted. I knew it the moment I saw you passing my stall in Winchester, hunched against the wind. A man with a big heart I've always said. "I hope I can soon be as excited as you."

Ted reached out and she moved into his arms. "You're the best," he said vehemently, knowing how close he'd been to messing with their lives.

Emily looked out of her hotel window overlooking Hyde Park and felt the stirrings of excitement in her stomach. She hadn't experienced anything like it since Jack had died. In an hour she'd be lunching with her father and Jimmy. She smiled as she took one last look at herself in the mirror and then made her way down to the hotel lobby. Her father was sitting reading the paper. "I'm not late am I," she asked a little breathless.

"No, no, you've plenty of time."

"Why the 'you'?"

"Because I can't come to lunch. Got a sudden call to a meeting that I can't turn down."

"I thought your meetings were over."

"Most of them are."

"You're telling a porky, Dad."

"No."

Emily smiled. "You cunning old rogue, you can't fool me."

Jonathan laughed. "Would I lie to you?"

"Sometimes."

Jonathan raised his hands in surrender. "I just think it might be nice if you went on your own."

Emily's brow furrowed. "I'm not sure I'm quite ready for that, but then maybe . . . Do you know, Dad, this may sound a terrible thing to say, but if Lucy hadn't existed I would never have stopped mourning Jack. I could never have gone out with another man. I would have just withered up until I died from a broken heart. It's perverse, but Lucy did me a favour. She opened my eyes to what a shit Jack really was. So yes, you go to your meeting and I'll have lunch with Jimmy. Thanks Dad. And by the way, who's your lunch date?"

"Myself. And I'll be fine."

They both laughed and she kissed him hard. "You're the best, Dad."

He touched her gently on an arm. "You look lovely, darling. It's good to see the sparkle coming back into your eyes. Now you go off and enjoy yourself."

Emily's stomach churned. She hadn't felt so light headed for a long time.

"We've got the bridging loan," exclaimed Clarissa as she ran down the garden to Ted. "It's all systems go!" She rubbed Bella's nose as the dog nudged her leg. "Yes darling, a new home for you and Charlie, and lots of rabbits for you two to chase." She watched Charlie lumbering across the lawn. "Well for you to chase, Bella," she corrected.

Ted leapt up from his chair, knocking over the easel as he did so. "Bugger, the paint wasn't dry! Got the bridging loan, eh," he said, as he bent down to pick up the ruined picture. "Well done my beauty! Well bloody done. So what's next?"

"We put this on the market and wait."

Ted blew out his cheeks. "How long do you think that will be?"

"How long is a piece of string? In this market it should sell quite quickly and you know the farmer next door has had his eyes on this place for years. The house would be ideal for his son. You have no need to worry, Mr Picasso, we will soon be in Somerset."

Sally Gascoigne was sitting alone in her bedroom. She was thinking of going over to Rita's to try to make her peace. It would be difficult because she'd be forced to apologise and Sally couldn't remember the last time she'd done that, but when needs must . . . Besides, she missed her ex-friend. The phone was an unwelcome interruption to her thoughts.

"Mother, it's me your daughter."

Sally didn't bother to disguise her irritation. "Hello Polly, what can I do for you? I'm in a rush. So much to do now that your father has left me."

Polly smiled. Her mother would never change, always the theatrical queen. Perhaps this was a bad idea, but she decided to persevere. "I just rang to say that I'm very sorry about you and Dad. If I can be of any help to you, let me know." She heard the snort down the line.

"Sorry! Oh I bet you are." Sally's voice was shaking with bitterness. "You nasty little girl. When have you ever been of any help to me? You've been nothing but a problem from the moment you came out of my womb. Come to think of it, you were a problem inside my womb, always moving, giving me terrible pain. God, I could have done without you. Now you want to help me! That's rich, Polly. You have always sided with your father. I suppose he approves of you cavorting with a lesbian. No, thank you very much, I don't want your help!"

Sally swore loudly but the phone had gone dead.

Polly gently lowered the phone. I've tried, she thought sadly as she walked over to where David was sitting. "You were right, Dad, she didn't want to know."

David shook his head. "I hate to say this, Polly, but your mother is not worth your trouble. Forget her, move on."

Polly felt like crying, but managed to stay dry eyed. Her father was right; her mother was not worth her tears. "But she's my mother, Dad," was all she could say.

A few minutes before one o'clock, Jimmy was standing on the pavement outside Zafferano's, a fashionable Italian restaurant off Sloane Street, which in normal circumstances he'd find far too expensive. His fingers were firmly crossed. Would she come? He was beginning to think that her father's suggestion might be one move too soon. Taxis passed him, some slowed down and others drew up to the kerb and disgorged their fares; none of them was Emily. At ten past one, Jimmy feared the worst. He couldn't believe how disappointed he felt. Head down, he turned to walk away and almost knocked Emily off her feet. "It's you!"

Emily laughed. "I was when I last looked. Sorry I'm late, Jimmy. I decided to walk and it took a little longer than I'd expected. Did you think I wasn't coming?"

"I was beginning to wonder."

"Oh Jimmy."

"I know. I shouldn't have doubted you, very stupid of me. All that matters is that you're here now."

The pleasure in his voice washed any last doubts from Emily's mind. "Well here I am, so let's go and eat. Wow, this place looks a bit pricey."

"Only the best for you, Emily."

She laughed and slipped her arm into his; it felt right. "I don't want you going bust because of me."

"I can't think of a nicer fate."

Emily blew out her cheeks and smiled. "Still the same old flatterer, eh Jimmy?"

The restaurant was a bustle of excitement that matched Emily's. Fashionably dressed women flashed smiles and jewelled hands as they lunched across white clothed tables, designer carrier bags at their feet. Couples deep in romantic conversations held hands under the tables.

Silver cutlery clattered and wine glasses chinked like celebratory bells as successful businessmen clinched final deals. Emily was impressed; she could sense the affluence. Jimmy had really gone overboard for her. A suave waiter guided them to the window table that Jimmy had reserved. "Senorita," he lilted, as he seated Emily at the table and handed her the menu. She suppressed a "WOW" when she saw the prices. She wondered what surprise the wine list had for Jimmy. "Hey, you sure this is okay? Why don't we share the bill?"

Jimmy raised his hands in mock horror, even though he was thinking he might have been a bit too ambitious. "No, that's very kind, but this is my treat." Then, with one of his engaging smiles he added, "I come here often."

They laughed in unison and any tension that might have been hovering between them vanished. Emily decided she was going to enjoy the next two hours.

"Okay," Jimmy asked, "what do you fancy?"

"It all looks delicious. Tell you what, why don't you order for me—makes life much easier, and I'm not very clued up on this sort of Italian food. Take-aways are more my line."

"You sure?"

"Absolutely."

Jimmy waved to a waiter who came over to take their order. "How about thin slices of rare smoked beef with a salad? My one and only affluent friend says it's to die for."

"Sound fine."

"Then for a main course I suggest the crab and lobster ravioli—again recommended."

"Anything you say."

"And a Sicilian white wine?"

"Sounds great."

"Water?" asked the waiter.

"Tap please," said Jimmy, thinking he would make a contribution to saving the ozone layer.

The waiter gone they fell silent, Emily remembering the last time she'd been alone with Jimmy in his home, convinced she'd walk away and never see him again. If she was honest, she had to admit it felt very strange not having Jack sitting beside her, but Jack was not going to ruin this lunch. Jack was in the past: a dead rat. Almost immediately, she felt guilty at such a terrible thought. She reached out, took a piece of bread from a basket on the table, and smiled at Jimmy. "Are we going to be okay?"

"Too right we are," Jimmy replied. "I know what you were thinking just now."

"You do?"

"Yep, and he's best forgotten."

Emily spread butter on her bread and nodded. "I never thought I'd hear you say that, and I certainly never thought I could think the same, but you're right. So, okay, that's out of the way, thank God. Now tell me, Jimmy, what's your latest joke?"

"Heard the latest Paddy one?"

"No."

So he told her. As usual for a Paddy joke, it was long and utterly stupid, and Jimmy was the world's worst joke teller, but Emily clapped at the end. "Better than usual," she laughed. "Oh, this looks good!" she exclaimed as their first course was put in front of them. She took a bite. "Delicious!"

"My friend is never wrong where food is concerned; he's a greedy bastard."

"Must be loaded if he can eat in this sort of place."

"He is, but very generous with it."

"The wine is nice too. In fact, everything is fine, Jimmy, absolutely fine," she said, meaning every word.

They raved about their crab. Jimmy ordered a half-bottle of the same wine, and time slipped by. Neither of them was in any hurry to break up such an enjoyable lunch. They dwelt over their double espressos, and talked until they were the last ones left in the restaurant and the waiter was hovering with the bill.

"Do you think he's trying to tell us something?" laughed Jimmy.

"Could be."

Jimmy pulled out his card and paid.

"Emily," he said, as she prepared to pick up her handbag and make a move.

"What Jimmy?"

"Would you ever consider doing this again?"

Emily beamed. "I thought you'd never ask."

Walking back to the hotel, Emily reflected that Jimmy really was rather good looking. Perhaps not as dashing as Jack, but she had always liked his eyes and his rather wild hair. In fact, she'd liked a lot about him. She wondered why he'd never had a girl friend after Chloe. Okay, he was disorganised, normally broke, and carried quite a bit of baggage—he talked a lot about his baby son, wondering how he might have grown up if he'd lived—not everyone's choice of conversation. Maybe that would turn off a new girl friend big time. She found herself thanking her lucky stars that Jimmy didn't have a girl friend, and that meant she was ready to move on.

She walked into the hotel singing, saw her father in the lobby and ran towards him. Then her mobile rang. Coming to an abrupt halt she said, "Be with you in a minute, Dad."

It was Jimmy. "Emily, had an idea. How about lunch before you and your father go home tomorrow?"

Emily smiled at the phone. "I have a better idea, Jimmy how about supper tonight on me? No, don't start to argue. Good. I'll leave you to find somewhere. Pick me up at around seven. Bye Jimmy."

"A good lunch then," stated Jonathan.

"It was a very good lunch, Dad, and you probably got the gist of that conversation. Do you mind being on your own tonight?"

"Darling," said Jonathan, "I can't tell you how much pleasure it gives me to see you happy again. Of course, I don't mind my own company. I've got used to it, and it's not so bad."

"Oh Dad, I'm sorry. I sometimes forget how much you miss Mum."

Jonathan pulled her into his arms. "Your life, darling, is far more important than mine. You have it all in front of you; three quarters of mine has gone. Don't fret about me, Emily, I'm doing fine."

"I know Dad, and thanks. I will never stop loving you."

"Go out and enjoy yourself, darling. You deserve it."

Emily threw him a slow smile. "Look Dad, Jack dying threatened to break my heart. If he'd lived, he would almost certainly have done so. I have always liked Jimmy and the good thing is he is very different from Jack, but I have learnt my lesson, and very painfully. If I ever have another close relationship, it will have to be with someone I can trust. Right now, I don't know whether I've the stomach for such a gamble. I'm a long way from putting any money on it. So don't read too much into my friendship with Jimmy."

Jonathan nodded. "I understand how you feel, but tread carefully with Jimmy. I don't think he's a very confident person, and I know he cares for you."

Four hours later while she was waiting for Jimmy in the hotel lobby, her father's words were still ringing in her ears.

Chapter Twenty-Eight

Emily took the route to Abinger Hammer that she had travelled many times. The village nestled under the downs in one of the most beautiful valleys in Surrey, but she was unaware of the beauty. Her mind was on other things, big decisions that had to be made. Her relationship with Jimmy was at a crossroads. It was pull back or move on to something more intimate. Although part of her kept saying she was not yet ready to commit to another man, another part was tugging her in the opposite direction. By the end of the weekend she would have to make up her mind, because Jimmy had written in his almost illegible scrawl asking her to stay.

"And perhaps we could discuss the possibility of you coming to France for a few days with friends. Of course separate bedrooms, Emily, so absolutely no pressure," he had written.

She loved it. How wonderfully old fashioned of Jimmy to write rather than ring or email. His promise of separate bedrooms just showed how honourable a man he was and was really quite quaint for the twenty-first century. It would be difficult to refuse, especially surrounded by the warm and welcoming atmosphere of his parent's cottage.

She passed the village sign and drove under the large nineteenth century clock that jutted out above the main street. She passed the ceramic shop bought by Jimmy's father after he had retired from being a commercial airline pilot. Emily couldn't help smiling as she remembered how glamorous she had thought his job must be when he'd told her he flew Concorde. She slowed to let two mallard cross onto the village green, no doubt heading for the Tillingbourne river. Then she was drawing up beside the cottage and her heart turned a somersault. Before she could get out of her car, Jimmy was running down the drive towards her.

"Emily, lovely to see you."

"And you, Jimmy," she replied, experiencing a flutter in her stomach as she got out of the car.

"Luggage?"

"Suitcase in the boot." She tossed him the keys.

Suitcase in one hand he held out the other to Emily. She took it, turned and kissed him. "I'm glad I came," she said.

"Seems a long time since we had dinner in London. Did I say something wrong?"

"No, you were lovely, but I needed time to think, to evaluate the way I wanted my life to go. You know how difficult it is to forget someone you've loved, however foolish. I just had to be sure I was moving in the right direction, mull over all the crap us girls worry about."

"Am I part of the crap?"

"In a way I suppose you are!"

"Thanks!"

"Oh Jimmy, I'm sorry, that sounded awful. I didn't mean it like that. I think what I was trying to say was that us girls worry about relationships, love and commitment a little more than men do. I called it crap for loss of a better word."

Jimmy threw one of his beaming smiles at her. "No offence, Emily. I know what you're trying to tell me and let me say I have no intention of spoiling our friendship. It was nearly lost once, I'm not taking that gamble again. Before we go into the cottage and the chance is lost, let me tell you that you look absolutely stunningly beautiful."

Emily looked into his eyes. God they looked so sexy. "Thank you, Jimmy. You don't look too bad yourself."

The weekend had been bliss, utter bliss. The French jaunt had only been mentioned once and no pressure had been put on her to make a decision. Now she was packing her suitcase ready to return home, reflecting that she hadn't been so happy or relaxed for a long time. Jimmy had been the perfect gentleman, so attentive and yet never making any move that she could interpret as a sexual advance. Even his kisses were only on her cheek. She laughed as she realised she'd have given anything for a soft lingering kiss on her mouth, but the move was up to Jimmy. She didn't want to give him the impression that she was ready for anything else but friendship. God, that's a bit old-maidish, she thought, and threw her last piece of clothing into the suitcase. Downstairs she could hear Madge Spencer in the kitchen, singing an old Barry Manilow song in her melodious voice. No doubt she was cleaning up the remnants of yet another delicious lunch. Emily wished she could cook like her. In fact, she wished she could be like Madge: so gentle, so unflappable, and there to give advice if asked, most times with a smile on her round rosy face. Emily thought that in a way she was just like her father. That made her think she wanted to talk to Madge before she left the cottage. Praying that no one else was in the kitchen she zipped up her suitcase and, as quietly as possible, went down the stairs. She was in luck, only Madge was in the kitchen.

She heard Emily's footsteps and turned with a smile, hitching up her long grey skirt over her wide girth. "Emily dear, ready to go?"

"Think so."

"Have you enjoyed the weekend?"

"It's been great, really good fun. I can't thank you enough for asking me."

"It wasn't me, it was Jimmy. But of course you are always welcome here."

Emily nodded her thanks, not quite sure how to put the question that was on the tip of her tongue. Finally she plucked up the courage to ask, "Jimmy really wants me to go to France with him, doesn't he Madge?"

Madge put down the dishcloth she was holding and looked at the girl she admired and loved. Emily's question required more of an answer than a simple confirmation, because it raised several other issues that Madge felt needed airing. She cleared her throat. "Darling Emily, can I just say something before giving you my answer?"

"Of course." Emily dropped into one of the kitchen chairs.

"A few months after I'd first met Charlie we fell in love. I will never forget him taking my hand and asking me to marry him. Since then I have felt warm and safe and absolutely happy. The years have passed, but our love is still steely and strong. It is just as sweet and just as joyous. I wake up every morning thanking the Lord that Charlie asked me to marry him. I acknowledge we are very lucky. You, my darling girl, have already experienced much unhappiness, just as Jimmy has. I think it is very tempting for both of you to fall into each other's arms. I have never stood in Jimmy's way. I welcomed Chloe into this house in spite of all my misgivings; I looked after that poor little baby as if it was my own, but I don't ever want to see Jimmy hurt again. So, what I'm trying to say is yes, Jimmy wants you to go to France very badly, but I beg you to walk away afterwards if you see no future in your relationship. I don't think I could ever forgive you if you caused him pain. Jimmy likes you very much, Emily, maybe *like* is becoming the wrong word. I trust you to remember that and do the right thing. Now my darling, I've said enough, get on your way home to that lovely father of yours and give a little thought to what I've just said."

Emily rose slowly from the chair and walked over to Madge. "I promise you," she said in a quiet voice, "I will never give you cause to stop loving me."

In her car, having said her goodbyes to Jimmy and Charlie, Emily thought about what Madge had said. Once through the village she drew into a lay-bye and texted Jimmy. "Love 2 come to France—will b in touch."

Chapter Twenty-Nine

The Inspector shuffled his feet uneasily under Belinda's unforgiving stare. "I have some news at last," he said.

"About time," snapped Belinda. "How difficult is it to track down a friend of Jerry Gordon's who was released in the last few months? I can't believe Gordon had that many friends."

"Ah well, you see that was the problem," the Inspector explained. "He didn't." The prison authorities came up against a brick wall. Of course they received no cooperation from the in-mates. And if they were unable to put a face to the man who might have killed Polecat and assaulted you there was very little they could do."

"So what's changed," asked Belinda.

"A stroke of luck," smiled the Inspector, congratulating himself that at last he was about to counter Belinda's scepticism. "A letter addressed to a habitual criminal by the name of Jack O'Brian, or the Big Man as he was known inside, was opened after his release so that it could be returned to the sender. The letter referred to O'Brian's partnership with Gordon many years ago. Two and two was put together and suspicion dawned that he might be our man."

"And if he's our man, where is he?"

"Either he's a long way away by now, or he's still waiting for the right moment to attack your friend. Given his record, I believe he is still around. He's been in and out of prison for the last twenty years. He looks upon it as home, which means he won't have gone far because he doesn't care a damn if he's caught, and he has a reputation for keeping his word. If he gave his word to Gordon that he'd carry out the attacks, he's still somewhere close. I'm going to ask to have his picture put in every national paper and hope that might draw him out."

"Or attack Polly," Belinda suggested.

"That is a risk, Ms Musgrove, but we will put a twenty-four hour surveillance back on her. "I don't think she will be in much danger."

"Spoken like a true policeman, Inspector. You have more confidence than I do, but I think you have no option. Poor Polly can't go on thinking that this man is behind every street corner. Let's see what your plan coughs up. Thank you, Inspector, for telling me this. I suppose it's better late than never."

The Inspector left Belinda's office hoping he would never come face to face with her in a court of law.

Sophie pushed Samantha off the sofa. "Get off you soppy girl," she laughed. She'd had enough of Samantha's advances, which normally she liked, but she had other things on her mind and scratching a cat's tummy was not one of them. Top of the list was the arrival of her first baby, then moving to Jamaica, followed closely by the worry of trying to find out how Ed really felt about giving up his job and moving to a remote part of the island. She decided to broach the subject again as soon as he came home from the surgery. They needed a serious discussion before the final decision was made.

"Fuck me" Clarissa shouted as she put down the telephone. "We've had an offer!"

"How much," asked Ted looking up from brushing Charlie, who seemed to be moulting more than ever.

"It's his age," Clarissa said, needing a little time to catch her breath.

"Okay it's his age; now come on, how much?"

"Seven hundred and fifty thousand smackeroons!"

"Jesus!"

"Nothing to do with Him," laughed Clarissa. "This is not make-believe, this is reality."

"How on earth do they come to that figure?"

"Ten thousand per acre, and six hundred and fifty thousand for the house and outbuildings."

"But the house is falling down."

"Makes no difference these days apparently. The agent says it's a very desirable property. Nice village near Winchester. That's all you need. If it had development potential we would be looking at double that."

Ted blew out his cheeks, once again thinking what a lucky bastard he'd been. He'd sailed pretty close to the wind he had by God. "Well I'll be! I never thought I'd be living with a woman who had money and a farm!"

"And you'd better watch it, Ted Harvey, because now I'm quite a catch."

Ted laughed. "Well, whoever came along would have to get to you over my dead body and that would mean they'd never get near you because they'd be doing time for murder."

Clarissa chuckled. "Sometimes you say the most wonderful things. Perhaps most people would wonder what the hell you're banging on about, but I know you're saying you love me. So do we accept or try and go for a bit more?"

Ted rubbed his chin. "It's a lot of money and having paid two hundred thousand for the gallery in Dulverton we will be left with a tidy sum. Enough to modernise the house on Exmoor, pay off your father's debts and have a little left to top up the measly amount we put into savings after I sold my bungalow. It will be waiting for us when you get too arthritic to work the farm and my fingers will no longer hold a paintbrush. Greed has been a lot of peoples' undoing, so I say we accept."

"That's what we'll do then," said Clarissa. "And if I shed a tear, don't go telling me we will not sign the contract. My mind is made up; it's just that for a while I'll miss this old place."

Ed had been definite; he wanted to go. His enthusiasm could not possibly have been made up. "After the baby," he'd said, a little surprised to find that Sophie had any doubts. "But if you prefer we could give it a try for a month or two. You don't need to sell this house, so we are in no way burning our boats."

"But you'd lose your job and you've just been made a partner."

"No worry. I'd have no trouble getting a job. There is a shortage of doctors. I suspect my fellow partners might not be too pleased, but that's tough. They don't dictate to us about our lives and I have a desire to do something a little different, like opening a medical centre."

"That sounds interesting. When did you come up with that idea?"

"I've been doing some investigation and mulling it over for some time now."

Now he was back at work and wouldn't be home until at least nine and by then she'd be missing him. She marvelled at their chemistry, which just seemed to get better and better. She began dreaming about their life in Jamaica. This idea of a medical centre seemed a good one, and obviously Ed had been doing some research. He liked a challenge and he was a good ideas man. Sophie knew he would love to try to get the idea off the ground. Sophie lovingly stroked her growing belly. She was looking forward to being a housewife and mother after the rat race of the fashion world. She decided she would keep designing, but on a smaller scale. Her work was still well sought after and she knew she would be inspired by Jamaican colour and culture. She would keep it going as long as possible until her star had waned, as it certainly would. She mixed herself a gin-and-tonic, telling herself that this one had to be the last until she gave birth.

Emily was standing in the Spencer's small ceramic shop, watching Madge and Jimmy talking to customers. Charlie, who seldom came to the front of the shop, was busy with the accounts in the little office at the back. Emily's eyes focused on Jimmy. He was talking animatedly to his customer about a small porcelain figure that the woman was holding, assuring her it was a genuine eighteenth century piece and worth every penny of its cost. Jimmy returned Emily's smile. She thought she would never get bored of his smile, it was so warm and kind. To say France had been a success would have been the understatement of the year she thought. It had been three days of heaven. They had laughed with Jimmy's friends, sat in restaurants holding hands, walked round the picturesque port of Honfleur, gazing into each other's eyes and finally, on the last night, tumbled into bed together. Emily sighed. She had never thought she could enjoy making love again. Of one thing she was absolutely certain: she was never going to hurt Jimmy. On impulse she crossed the floor of the shop and touched Jimmy's arm. "I love you," she whispered. The customer smiled and Jimmy reddened, but Emily didn't care. She made a vow there and then that she would tell Jimmy she loved him wherever and whoever was there. Recovering from his embarrassment, Jimmy winked at her. She turned away, happy and content, knowing that God was smiling on her again.

Sophie wiped the sweat off her forehead with her towel before shaking her opponent's hand. "Good game. Nice to finish with a match like that."
"And with a win. You played your socks off," said her opponent graciously.
Sophie smiled. "Thanks, it will seem really funny not playing any more."
"Baby due soon?"
"In five months. Twins in fact, big surprise, just learnt today, so time to stop." Boy, how she'd miss it; not only the games, but socialising with the girls too. Come to think of it, she might never play again once they went to Jamaica. She walked off the court towards the showers feeling excited, but also a little sad. A part of her life was ending.

*

After the opposing team had left, it was suggested that the Laurel Ladies reconvene in the club bar. Belinda had ordered champagne and as Sophie walked in Belinda handed her a glass. "Here's to our star player."

"Well I don't think that's quite right," corrected Sophie, just remembering to refuse the glass and ask for a tonic water. "I think we are all pretty much equal. Here's to the Laurel Ladies. We may be about to break-up, but my bet is that no other team will ever beat our record of . . . how many wins is it Belinda?"

"Off the top of my head I'm not too sure," Belinda replied. "I think two losses since we started playing as a team. A record that will be hard to beat. What a pity it all has to end."

"That's life," interjected Clarissa, "but I'll miss it."

"We all will," added Emily.

Belinda ordered another bottle of champagne. "So let's all get smashed," she suggested. There were no objectors, even though Sophie knew it would be tonic water for her. They raised their glasses to each other for the last time and Sophie could swear she saw tears in Belinda's eyes. Well, she has a heart after all, she thought.

An hour later, they decided to go; it was time to wend a weary and slightly hazy way home.

"Don't forget our last lunch next Thursday," said Belinda. "See you all there I hope."

Four heads nodded in the affirmative.

Thursday's dawn saw the sun slowly rise above the downs overlooking Winchester; a white mist hung over the river Itchen. It was a quiet peaceful morning, one that got the joggers out early and the paperboys whistling to the tunes on their iPods. As was his custom, O'Brian closed the door on Willy's house and sauntered down past Winchester prison, ignoring its welcoming gates with some difficulty. He was making towards WH Smith newsagents in the high street. He bought at least four papers every morning, which might have puzzled some people if they had known he couldn't read, but he liked looking at the pictures. Maybe he'd learn to read once he was back in the nick for a long stretch—it would pass the time.

Today he found himself staring at his own image.

Momentarily shaken by the sight of his unshaven face scowling from every paper on the stand, he made a hasty retreat from the shop. He automatically shielded his face with a hand and stared at the pavement.

The Filth were onto him at last. Shit! Not daring to go back into the newsagent's he retraced his steps to Willy's, his brain working overtime. It was time for a change of plan. There would be no time to play with the girl's undoubted smooth skin; no time to watch the man tied to the bed screaming for him to stop torturing his daughter. Time was no longer on his side. He had to make a move today. He rubbed his unshaven chin and gave his options some thought. It never entered his head to abort—that was not his way. By the time he reached Willy's house he knew what he was going to do. He smiled, and opened the door. Willy was cooking breakfast, ham and eggs, just how O'Brian liked them. He cracked his finger joints as Willy put the plate down in front of him. He had some unfinished business to attend to before he left. He felt no compassion as he eyed Willy's neck.

Emily left her father's house half-an-hour before she was due to meet the girls for lunch. As it was a beautiful morning, she decided to walk across the water meadows, skirting the playing fields of Winchester College and then head up from the bottom of Southgate Street to the hotel.

Polly was meeting Belinda in her office at twelve-thirty. "We can walk to the hotel together. Pity to drive on such a lovely day," Belinda told Polly.

"Okay, I'll get Dad to drop me off with you. See you later"

Like the others, Sophie had decided to walk. It was good for her and she was getting a bit idle as the weight in her tummy increased.

"Have a good lunch," Ed said as he left for work. "And don't forget your no alcohol promise; we don't want the twins born alcoholics."

Sophie had playfully slapped his face and then planted a wet kiss firmly on his mouth. She'd smiled into his eyes and pushed him out of the front door. "See you later, doctor," she'd laughed. Now she was breaking open a carton of cat food for Samantha, which reminded her that soon she'd have to find a new home for her. She stroked the soft fur, kissed Samantha's small fluffy head and made for the door. She was looking forward to the lunch.

Ted drove Clarissa. He parked in the St George's Street car park as they'd agreed. He was going to the gallery with a picture he'd painted for Jo and Amanda; it showed their small shop nestling under the spires of the cathedral. He was rather proud of it. Clarissa was going to Waterstone's to buy a couple of books she wanted and would then visit the estate agents before going on to lunch. "See you back here about three," she said as they exited the car. "You will be okay won't you Ted."

Ted knew what she meant and gave her a broad smile. "Of course I will," he said, tucking the watercolour under an arm, before kissing Clarissa. "How many times do I have to tell you I love you?"

"You can never tell me enough," Clarissa replied.

O'Brian stood on the opposite side of the street to Belinda's office. He felt very exposed, but he had no option if he wanted to reach Polly. He saw Belinda arrive and go into the building. He was confident that if Polly followed her usual routine she would soon follow. The risk was that now his face was splashed all over the papers, the police might advise her to remain in her house until his inevitable capture. If that was the case, he would have to get to her house. There was no more time left for waiting. It was today or never; if he failed he'd fester in the nick, plagued by the knowledge that he'd failed his friend. So he waited. He'd always been good at waiting. He fixed his eyes on the office opposite praying to the Devil to deliver the girl to him. An hour later, he was getting distinctly nervous and was glancing at his watch every few minutes. Another half hour went by; he was sweating. Then a car drew up beside the office and Polly got out. He nearly wet himself with relief. His excitement was short lived; pulling up next to the office building was a squad car. It was going to be difficult to get into the office unobserved, but surprise might give him enough time to reach Polly and pull the trigger. He was just psyching himself up to make his move when Polly and Belinda came out of the building and walked up the street together, talking animatedly. The squad car followed behind. He fingered the Beretta in his left trouser pocket. The adrenalin flowed. Wherever they stopped, he'd shoot her. It would be his last chance.

Slightly breathless, Sophie stopped on the steps of the hotel as she saw Clarissa and Emily approaching. She waved and waited for them. A minute later, the three of them spotted Belinda and Polly walking towards them. "Let's go in and get the champagne ordered," suggested Emily.

"Why don't you two go and do that. I'll wait for the other two here," suggested Sophie, who felt she needed a little longer to catch her breath. "Don't forget, only tonic for me."

"Okay," said Emily, climbing up the steps to the hotel. "See you in a minute."

O'Brian walked on the opposite pavement, level with Polly and Belinda, keeping a careful eye on the patrol car that was moving slowly up the street about thirty feet behind them. Traffic was building up. O'Brian reckoned he could get a shot in, before the police realised he was there. He slipped off the safety catch and took a deep breath, and then the two women stopped by the steps to a hotel where another woman was smiling, clearly waiting for them. It dawned on him that they were going in. Perfect! He would get a clear shot as Polly went through the hotel door. The police car pulled into what he assumed was the hotel car park, leaving Polly exposed. "Big mistake Filth," he mumbled under his breath as he gripped the Beretta and crossed the road. He could have shot Polly then, but O'Brian had a failing: he liked his victims to see his face. As Polly stopped on the top step he shouted, "Polly!"

Polly turned. O'Brian raised the Beretta. Belinda saw the pistol in his hand.

"NO!" Belinda's scream was clearly heard above the street noise. She threw herself down the steps and crashed into O'Brian. Taken by surprise he toppled backwards onto the pavement with Belinda on top of him. The Beretta fired. Belinda groaned. Her mouth fell open and her lifeblood started to ooze from her. With a cry of rage, O'Brian roughly pushed her off and raised the Beretta to get a shot at Polly, who was standing frozen to the spot on the steps, her mouth open in terror. He pulled the trigger just as the two police officers ran into the street.

Pandemonium broke out. The police officers, oblivious to the danger they were in, rushed at O'Brian. He sidestepped them with ease. "Too late, Filth," he jeered, throwing the Beretta at them, before raising his arms above his head. "My job's done."

The noise in the street was deafening. Pedestrians were screaming in panic, some with children were endeavouring to cover their eyes and get them away from the scene as quickly as possible. Those with more ghoulish tendencies tried to get closer to the scene. Already there was a traffic jam. Horns were blaring and voices were raised in panic.

Sophie let out a cry of anguish and stared at the scene in shock. She dropped down onto the pavement and as much as she wanted to rush and help her two stricken friends, her legs would not move. She seemed to be floating in the clouds, as if it was all a dream from which she would soon wake up, drenched in sweat, but relieved it was only a nightmare.

Clarissa, who had heard the two shots, ran out of the hotel. What she saw took her breath away and stopped her in her tracks. She had an intense desire to cry, but controlled herself; crying would get her nowhere. Sophie was on her knees on the pavement sobbing uncontrollably; Belinda and Polly were laying half on the pavement and half in the road, their blood pooling together in the gutter. Clarissa's immediate fear was that they were dead. Quickly getting control of her inertia and reckoning there was little she could do for her two injured friends who were being tended by police officers, she ran to Sophie's side "Sophie!" she cried, putting her arms around Sophie's shoulders. "It's me!"

Sophie looked up, her face wet with tears. She saw the two bodies and realised it was no dream. "Dear God, Clarissa, what has happened here? What a mess! They're dead. I know they must be dead. Look at all the blood!"

Clarissa fought back the bile that was gathering in her throat, forcing herself not to look at Belinda or Polly. "We can't be sure," was all she could think of saying as she firmly took hold of Sophie and pulled her towards the hotel. "Listen, I can hear the ambulance siren. It won't be long now before they are in good hands."

"Move away please ladies," ordered an ashen-faced young constable, his voice unsteady. He'd never seen blood flowing down a street before. "We must clear the area."

"Come on, Sophie," Clarissa said severely. "Let's get you back into the hotel. We'll find out soon enough how they are."

Sophie allowed herself to be guided back up the steps leading to the hotel, noticing that dozens of police officers had arrived on the scene and were pushing the most ghoulish of the onlookers off the road so that the ambulance could get through. She saw O'Brian standing hand cuffed by the squad car. His lips curled as he saw her; the evil in his eyes was something that would haunt her for a long time. She took one last look at the two inert bodies—there seemed to be blood everywhere—and then stepped back into the hotel. Inside, amongst a crush of bodies all talking at once either to each other or on their mobiles, Emily was crouching in a corner swaying from side to side. Clarissa let go of Sophie. "Stay here," she said urgently and ran towards Emily. "Emily!"

"I must be cursed," Emily cried. "How many more people that I love are going to die?"

Clarissa pulled Emily to her feet. "Listen to me, Emily. This has nothing to do with you. Nothing you could have done would have prevented this." Then she said, "Belinda and Polly will be fine," desperately praying that would not turn out to be a lie. Right now, it was more important to get Emily away from the crush and try to console her. She looked round for Sophie, hoping she hadn't rushed out into the street again, and saw her in the middle of the crowd. She waved urgently. Sophie came over. "Give me a hand will you," said Clarissa. "We must get Emily away from here." Looking around frantically, Clarissa quickly realised there was only one-way to go: out the back of the hotel and into the small garden. She and Sophie almost had to carry the shivering Emily outside. The garden was as crowded as the foyer, but at least there was fresh air. They managed to find room on a bench and lowered Emily onto it, before Clarissa reached for her mobile. She dialled Ted's number, praying that he'd turned his contraption on.

He answered after the third ring. "What's happening? What's happening?" he asked, his voice full of apprehension. "Can't get sense out of anyone here. People seem confused. Some say there's been a shooting."

Speaking as calmly as she could, Clarissa explained what had happened and what she wanted him to do. "Go home if you can. You will never get to the hotel. I will stay with Sophie and Emily until we can leave. That might be some time. The police will almost certainly want statements from us. I will keep you informed, and don't worry, Ted, I'm fine. It's all just a fucking awful mess." Then she turned to Sophie and said reluctantly, "I think all we can do is wait."

Sophie nodded, desperately trying to regain control of her shattered nerves. "I agree. I'll ring Ed. At least he might be able to find out about Belinda and Polly. They are bound to be taken to the hospital." She fumbled in her bag for her mobile and dialled Ed.

He was quick to answer. Already he'd heard there had been a shooting in the city, but was not sure where. "Thank God you're okay. I was worried stiff. Rumours are flying about here."

"Where are you," asked Sophie.

"At the hospital visiting a patient."

Sophie took a deep breath, trying to control her voice. "Stay there Ed, please. Belinda and Polly have been shot. No idea how bad either of them is, but I saw lots of blood. Oh God, Ed, it's terrible."

"Calm down if you can Sophie, it would help if you told me what happened."

In an unsteady voice she told him as best she could, when all she wanted to do was burst into tears. When she'd finished he said, "Okay, I'll stay here until they arrive. Keep in touch. I expect you'll be there for some time."

"Almost certainly. I was witness to the shooting. Once the chaos outside the hotel has been sorted, the police will want to interview me."

Ed thought for a moment. "Listen to me. Whatever happens you stay where you are. I will find out about Belinda and Polly and then make my way to the hotel. I don't want you walking home on your own."

"Okay," she said with relief. She put the mobile back into her bag and turned to Clarissa. "Thank God. Ed's at the hospital. He's going to find out how Belinda and Polly are and then come here."

"Good," Clarissa said. "And now I'm going in search of some tea."

*

"Not the lunch we were expecting," said a quiet voice from the bench.

Sophie gave Emily a sad smile then sat beside her, taking her cold hand in hers and preparing for a long wait.

The police closed all the Winchester motorway slip roads. No vehicle could get in or out of the town. Within half-an-hour, the city was gridlocked. Drivers banged their steering wheels in frustration. The ambulance carrying Polly and Belinda lost vital minutes fighting its way through the log jammed street leading to the hospital. The paramedics looked at each other with increasing alarm, knowing that time was running out.

Chapter Thirty

Eighteen months later.

Polly reached out to switch off the alarm clock. It was just past six in the morning. She stretched and fingered the scar on her right side where the bullet had entered. The damage had been repaired, but the mental scar, like the physical one, would always be with her. She eased herself out of bed, carefully slid her feet into her slippers and began to prepare for another day. First, down to the kitchen to put the kettle on, then a quick wash of her face in the sink, fill the bowl that was sitting on the work-top with warm water, and put a clean flannel (always a clean one at the beginning of the day) into the bowl. Wait patiently for the kettle to boil and then put one mint tea bag into a mug, stir for about thirty seconds and then remove it, add two sugars, and she was ready to go and wake Belinda.

It had been the same routine ever since Belinda had come back from Stoke Mandeville Hospital seven months earlier, and Polly had moved into her house. Belinda was paralysed from the waist down, but Polly thanked God every day that at least she was alive because she didn't think she'd ever stop blaming herself for what had happened. It had been a close run thing. At first, Belinda had no desire to live the life of a paraplegic and had begged the doctors to end her life.

"How can I live with only half my body working? What will I do now that I can't walk, swim or play squash?" She tearfully asked Polly. "I'll be forced into spectatorship, always sitting on the sidelines, feeling out of everything. How am I going to cope with my work, the loss of boozy nights out with my friends? Relying on them and being permanently grateful, always different from the rest. How am I going to live with myself, imperfect and maimed? How, Polly? How!"

Polly found she had few answers, but although assurances were totally inadequate that was the only encouragement she could give.

Gradually, with Polly's gentle counselling and constant companionship, Belinda became resigned to spending the rest of her life dependant on others and in a wheel chair. "After all," she kept telling herself, "I'm lucky to be alive." She still had bad days when she had to pour tranquillisers down her throat to stop herself reaching for a knife, but Polly was always there, handing out armfuls of love, but cajoling when necessary.

When Polly had announced to her father that she was going to dedicate the rest of her life to caring for Belinda it would have been easy for him to take a negative stand, but he'd smiled and said, "I hope you know what you're doing, Polly. You are about to make a great sacrifice."

Polly's mind was made up. "At last I can do something useful. I've found my niche. Belinda saved my life, Dad. I owe it to her. I also love her." There wasn't anything more for David to say.

Now her resolve was going to be tested to the full. Getting Belinda to Heathrow was not going to be easy. There were so many things an invalid needed for such a long and arduous journey. For the next few hours, until Emily and Jimmy arrived to take them to the airport, she was going to have to keep convincing Belinda that a holiday was just what she needed.

Emily dug Jimmy in the ribs. "What?" he groaned, refusing to look at the clock by the bed.

"Time to open the shop, you lazy sod. If you remember you told your parents last night you'd do the first two hours."

"Oh God, it seems as if I've only just got to sleep."

"That is not my problem, now get up. We leave later today. We've Polly and Belinda to collect and I have a thousand and one things to do. Oh yes, and it's your turn to do the breakfast."

With another loud groan, Jimmy fell out of bed. "Bloody bully," he teased.

Emily didn't follow him downstairs immediately. She wanted a few moments to reflect, to marvel how she'd survived all the disasters that had taken such a heavy toll of her emotions. If it hadn't been for her father and Jimmy, she would surely have been a nut case. She would never forget the tragedies, but now she was able to confine them to the recesses of her mind and get on with her life with wonderful, kind, supportive Jimmy.

She would never forget Madge's words when she'd told her that she and Jimmy had decided to live together and that marriage might come later.

"You love him so much and he loves you as I'm sure you know. Love is a wonderful thing, Emily. People say faith can move mountains, but I think love can too."

There was no doubt in Emily's mind that Madge was bang on. Emily stretched and jumped out of bed. She was excited about going to Jamaica and was looking forward to seeing Sophie and Ed again, and of course the twins.

Clarissa finished the milking just after seven, a little later than usual, as she had to say goodbye to each of her girls, as she called the cows. She would miss their early morning smell and the welcoming mooing that greeted her as she herded the first of the cows into the milking parlour, but a trip to Jamaica was too good to miss. It would be the first time since she and Ted had moved into the farm six months earlier that she would miss the morning milking. She was worried that the relief milker she'd employed would not give her girls the same love that she bestowed on each of them. At first she'd thought Ted would refuse to come—she knew of his fear of flying—and then she wouldn't have had to worry about a thing, but, much to her surprise and delight, Ted had told her he was coming. "Jamaica is full of colour. I'll take my paints, and create a masterpiece," he'd said.

Today was the day. Only a few hours until they left for Heathrow airport and she was beginning to panic. There had been so much to arrange. The relief milker and his wife were moving into the farmhouse, the wife promising she would look after Bella (the move had proved too much for Charlie) as if she was her own. What could possibly go wrong? Everything seemed to be in place, but she was still like someone walking on hot coals. She took one last look at the cows contentedly munching their morning feed of silage and started to walk the short distance to the farmhouse, where she hoped Ted was making the coffee. She thought of all the people who would give their right arm to be leaving their desk-bound jobs for a week in Jamaica, and here she was reluctant to go. Count your lucky stars, she thought, that you are not one of those millions of people breathing pollution, fighting the morning rush hour to get to work, and coming home to a house so close to another one that they could hear the neighbour farting.

The air was heavy with humidity; the sun was just appearing above the mountains. The shack, as Sophie still liked to call it, was already warm. Installing air-conditioning was the next thing on her list. She heard the twins getting restless and knew she'd have no more sleep that day. She rolled over in the bed and found Ed had gone. She smiled. She'd been in such a deep sleep that she hadn't heard him get up. By now he'd be on his way to Mandeville to work on his project. His new medical centre was coming on well. Sophie reckoned he'd never been happier. He clearly had no regrets at leaving the relative cosiness of a rural practice in England. She wiped the perspiration off her forehead and switched on the overhead fans. They had moved in a year ago when the twins were two months old and since then the shack had changed dramatically. The tin roof had been replaced with wood; the terrace had a new floor and the extension was finished. It was still not quite 17 Chilbolton Avenue, but she wouldn't swap it for anything.

She started to dress in a loose skirt, bikini top and sandals, her working clothes as she called them. She smiled as she thought of all her designer clothes gathering dust in the cupboards. She heard another whimper from one of the twins, probably Jake. He always seemed to be the most fractious. Eliza was by far the most content. "I'm coming babies," she called out as she slipped into her sandals and moved into the small ante-room that Ed had converted from Grandma's bathroom—well the room had had an old tin bathtub in the middle, but it was common knowledge that the old lady had never stepped into it. Sophie bent down to pick up Jake; he was warm. She wondered if he was getting a fever. She'd consult the duty doctor, as she called Ed, when he came home. She gently lowered Jake into the playpen and turned her attention to Eliza, who was lying peacefully in her cot gurgling as she played with her tiny toes. She always seemed to be smiling. Sophie reckoned she could leave her where she was while she cleaned up Jake.

An hour later, the twins were in their high chairs creating a mess with their food. Sophie was doing her best to eat a piece of toast and drink her first, much needed cup of tea of the day. Her eyes moved to the calendar hanging on the wall above the stove, reminding her that in three days time, six more people, one of whom was an invalid, would be living in the shack. Today the workmen were coming to fix a ramp onto the terrace, and a handrail in the bathroom. Ed was going to bring back a special bed. She gave a contented sigh. All would be finished in time. There was room for everyone. It was wonderful that they were coming. She'd had a small bet with herself that Polly would never persuade Belinda, but she was glad she'd lost the bet. She stood up to wipe the twin's faces. It would be fun to see her friends again. She would make quite sure that no one mentioned any of the momentous incidents that had changed all their lives since their first meeting in the squash club.

She and Ed were determined that that only laughter would fill the hours.

The End

About The Author.

Michael Pakenham is part of a prolific literary Irish family. Born in Belfast his family moved to America after his father was killed at Dunkirk. Returning to England after the Second World War the family moved to Hampshire, never to return to Ireland. Michael has lived there ever since, first farming and then in 1990 he started writing. This is his fifth book.

Lightning Source UK Ltd.
Milton Keynes UK
UKOW04f1941121213

222930UK00001B/4/P